CW01508405

Praise for *Ruthless Women*

'All rise for the new Queen of the bonkbuster ... Glamorous women, hunky men, mendacious producers, insecure actors and people stabbing each other in the front, back and side.' **The Times**

'Revenge, treachery and lust… shockingly good.' **Sun**

'Jackie Collins for a new generation.' **Heat**

'Glitz, glamour and ambition – it's all there! A truly addictive page-turner. Melanie Blake's *Ruthless Women* is the binge read we all need right now.' **Woman & Home**

'A page-turning bonkbuster so gloriously sexy, funny and gripping, it's sending the showbiz elite WILD!' **New**

'Buckle up you're in for a raunchy ride! So addictive we couldn't put it down – it's a real roller coaster of a ride.' **Sunday Mirror**

'Revenge, betrayal, murder and some of the hottest scenes you'll ever read… *Ruthless Women* has got it all.' **Sunday Express**

'A twist so shocking, you'll be talking about it for years ... This is the book of 2021.' **Daily Mirror**

'Does for TV what *The Devil Wears Prada* did for fashion; shows the rotten truth hidden behind the golden facade. The must-read novel of the year; unmissable.' **OK!**

'The bonkbuster is back with a bang! *Ruthless Women* is the read of 2021.' **Woman's Own**

'Think *Sex and the City* 20 years on, injected with a career-hungry cast. Suspense soaked in glamour. Beautifully written, a nod to the old genre of career women having it all, revved up for 2021 with romps, rivals and ruthless ambition to die for.' *My Weekly*

Praise for *Guilty Women*

'You'll laugh, cry, be shocked and left wanting more… *Guilty Women* is an unmissable read. Pure escapism. 5 stars!' *Ok!*

'Revenge, murder, sex and greed… *Guilty Women* has it all. Blake's latest novel proves she's here to stay as the new queen of the blockbuster novel. Jackie Collins would have loved it.' *Bella*

'Not for the faint hearted! An unputdownable, revenge and lust filled romp of a read that you won't want to end!' *Heat*

'The perfect killer thriller with sexy scenes that'll keep you reading late into the night.' *Notebook*

'If you only read one book this year, then *Guilty Women* won't disappoint. It will leave you breathless.' *Daily Express*

'*Guilty Women*'s stamped its razor sharp, blood-stained stiletto heel firmly in the lead to be 2022's book of the year.' *Daily Mirror*

VENGEFUL
WOMEN

Also by Melanie Blake

The Thunder Girls
Ruthless Women
Guilty Women

MELANIE BLAKE

VENGEFUL WOMEN

PIRANHA
PUBLISHING

First published in the UK in 2025 by Piranha Publishing.

Copyright © Melanie Blake, 2025

9 7 5 3 1 2 4 6 8

A catalogue record for this book is available from the British Library.

ISBN (HB) 9781738562244:
ISBN (E): 9781738562237

Typesetting: Ruth Rudd

Printed and bound in Great Britain by Clays,
Popson Street, Bungay,
NR35 1ED

Piranha Publishing
21 Culverlands Close,
Stanmore, Middlesex,
HA7 3AG

This book is dedicated to YOU, my readers,
who led me on a journey I could
never have dreamed of.

Meet the players

The Living

Amanda King – Early fifties, kind-hearted, truly decent woman, a real rarity in show business. She was the executive producer of global smash hit drama *Falcon Bay*. Talented, caring and a devoted mother with a good heart, she is now in prison, awaiting trial for perversion of the course of justice in the case of the manslaughter of Madeline Kane. She longs to see her child again and reunite with her partner, production accountant Dan, with whom she is finally happy after years in a loveless marriage with her estranged husband Jake Monroe.

Jake Monroe – Former Head of Drama and showrunner of *Falcon Bay*, he was ousted by his wife Amanda and her all-female associates at CITV, the production company which makes the long-running soap. In revenge, he helped send them to prison and then regained control of the island, transforming it into a theme park complete with robot versions of the *Falcon Bay* stars. Well preserved mid-sixties, but whilst attractive on the outside, he's ugly on the inside.

Catherine Belle – *Falcon Bay*'s leading actress. Early seventies and fabulous with it. She won every award all over the globe for her portrayal of lovable 'Lucy Dean' – *Falcon Bay*'s famous beach bar owner. She is currently in prison, awaiting trial for the involuntary manslaughter of Madeline Kane.

Sheena McQueen – Fifty-something strong alpha female. Agent to Catherine Belle and CEO of the McQueen Agency. The toughest agent who has every network by the balls. Once a child star on a globally syndicated drama called *Second Chances*, she was a victim of dead sexual predator, Ed Nichols. She's sexy, ballsy and most importantly she takes no shit from anyone. Now in prison, awaiting trial for conspiracy to cover up manslaughter, she's determined to find a way to get her and the girls acquitted…

Helen Gold – Head of Casting on *Falcon Bay* and has been at the network since day one. A determined, sensual woman in her early sixties who has always had a thing for younger men, but recently started a long-term relationship with an age-appropriate police officer, Matt. Terrible timing, since she's now in prison, awaiting trial for conspiracy to cover up manslaughter.

Farrah Adams – Late forties. Former child actress turned writer and only female director on *Falcon Bay*, she is close friends with Helen, Sheena, Catherine and Amanda. After an ill-judged one-night-stand with her hated enemy Jake

Monroe, she fell pregnant and had a baby boy. Now she is in prison, awaiting trial with the other women, and unable to see her beloved son.

Candy Dace – Australian, mid-twenties, ruthlessly ambitious Head of PR living on the island of St Augustine's. She will do whatever it takes to climb the career ladder, in six-inch heels.

Lauren Jones – Norland Nanny, mid-twenties, employed by Jake Monroe to look after his two young children.

Tabitha Tate – Previously a reporter on tabloid newspaper the *Herald*, she is the author of the runaway bestseller *The Curse of Falcon Bay* about actress Honey Hunter's dramatic stint in rehab. After a disastrous public appearance, she got cancelled on social media and is now back at the bottom of the journalism ladder, working at a low-end newspaper in LA. Sassy, determined and dangerously ambitious.

Mickey Taylor – Owner of Fonda Books, home of the tell-all celebrity biography. Dripping in money and lacking in taste, subtlety is not Mickey's thing and he can spot a battered celebrity with a juicy tale to tell a mile off. Publisher and agent of the infamous but reclusive Honey Hunter.

Dustin Morgan – The geeky ex-producer of *Falcon Bay*, sacked by Jake Monroe soon after the infamous shark attack on a live Christmas episode of the show.

The Missing

Chad Kane – Forty-something widower of Madeline Kane. Six foot five with shoulders like a tank. Ruggedly gorgeous and deeply likeable son of an extreme Southern Baptist evangelical preacher from the Deep South. Avenged his adored wife's death by broadcasting a secret recording of Sheena and Catherine's 'confession' to a global audience of millions, then disappeared.

Honey Hunter – Oscar-winning actress who was due to take a leading role in *Falcon Bay* during its Christmas Day live episode. She disappeared out of the public eye on the eve of her big comeback, and ended up in a rehab centre where she suffered appalling abuse at the hands of a sadistic doctor, Andrew Durand. Since she escaped his clutches, she has not been seen in public.

The Dead

Madeline Kane – Former owner of CITV, stunningly beautiful and married to billionaire Chad Kane. She died on screen in a tragic accident involving a live shark, during the broadcast of a now infamous live episode of *Falcon Bay*.

Ross Owen – Ruthless showbiz hack and editor of tabloid newspaper the *Herald*. Toxic blogger and would-be author, he was a true low-life. He was found dead at the bottom of a cliff one night. There was alcohol in his blood and his death was ruled as 'accidental', but some have their suspicions...

PART 1

CHAPTER 1

Jake

Jake Monroe breathed in deeply, his blue eyes sweeping the shoreline. No, sweeping *his* shoreline: it was 6 a.m. and no one was around except for him and the waves. So, for his daily morning jog, a swim in the Cove's perfect water, and – he smirked – a quick 'breakfast' with his kids' nanny, he always had the whole place to himself.

Jake first arrived on the private island of St Augustine's over three decades ago as a twenty-eight-year-old intern with dreams of becoming a hotshot producer. He'd been hired by legendary husband-and-wife team Tina and Harry Dean, who had a hunch that their new show *Falcon Bay* – set on the sandy shores where he was currently standing – would become one of the most successful soap operas in history.

And they were right. An instant success all over the world, it wasn't just bigger than all its rivals, it also outlasted nearly all of them. And as it grew, so did Jake. Realising that to scale the beanstalk you need to break some branches, he manipulated himself up the power ladder, allying himself first with Tina and Harry's sons, and then – when their sons sold the network – to Chad and Madeline Kane, the billionaire new owners who appointed him *Falcon Bay*'s showrunner. But even Jake, with his mega confidence, had never imagined that today he would own not only the production company that created *Falcon Bay*, but the entire private island of St Augustine's where it was filmed.

Jake raised his iPhone and inspected the wide smile on his recently veneered teeth. He'd had them done after he watched himself back on the live *Falcon Bay* finale – the one that YouTube was now calling 'the most shocking moment in TV history', with over 200 million views. He'd had a couple of shots of Botox then, too, just to ease the frown lines. His thick shock of silver-flecked blonde hair hadn't needed any work, and judging by his fan mail since his appearance in *Falcon Bay*'s final, live episode, he was as shaggable in his sixties as he'd ever been.

He took a selfie on his iPhone and opened the Instagram app. He had over 2 million followers. With the light hitting him in the right angle he didn't even need to use a filter. A smug smile crossed his face as he recalled the live episode in all its bloody and revenge-filled glory. As he had delivered his final monologue down the barrel of the TV cameras, he had the delicious pleasure of witnessing the five women he hated most in the world get arrested live on national television. Now the bitches were rotting in jail and he, Jake, was on his way to becoming a billionaire.

He typed out a caption and then posted the selfie.

'Another day in paradise. Come see us – if you dare...'
#StAugustines #FalconBay #ThemePark #MadelineKane

For some algorithmic reason he didn't understand, it always took a little while for the likes and comments to start flooding in. But there was already one that caught his attention.

'Bet these bitches be wishing they were there dude!'

The comment included a link to the clip of Catherine, Sheena, Farrah, Helen and his estranged wife Amanda being led away by police from the final episode. As Jake was waiting for the likes and comments to flood in, he let his mind wander to the trial, due to start next week.

The world's press were certain the five women had no chance of getting off – after all, there was a very public recording of their confession that Madeline Kane's death was no accident. The thought of them behind bars caused another smile to spread across Jake's cruelly handsome face. He ripped off his joggers, climbed up one of the rocks which spread along the shoreline and dived naked into the gorgeous sea. His cock twitched as it touched the cold water, reminding Jake pleasurably of the breakfast awaiting him after his morning swim.

He turned back, treading water, and took in the view of his island. He couldn't believe that Chad had given him the island after the live episode, but Jake wasn't one to dwell on the shattered dreams of others if it benefitted him. He congratulated himself on exploiting Chad's grief and persuading him of his deep respect for what the island meant to Madeline. In fact he had spotted the potential to turn the island into a goldmine. Now, the sandy beach, the old *Falcon Bay* sets, and the luscious woodland would be dwarfed by La Mirage, a skyscraper with glass elevators at each corner, from the top of which you could see for miles on a clear day.

Falcon Bay was the past, La Mirage was the future: a hotel for fans of the show to stay at after visiting the *Falcon Bay* theme park; luxury apartments for the filthy rich who want a tax haven near France; and a world-class spa for all the young wives on the arms of their bank-rolling husbands. And, on the very top floor, the pièce de résistance, Monroe's Bar. An open rooftop terrace laid out around a vast marble bar, full of hidden corners where VIP guests could relax away from prying eyes. The blueprints showed that there would be a glass dancefloor, incredible views and a secluded VIP roof garden where peacocks would strut against the skyline. This sanctuary could be accessed by elevator or helicopter, and stunning views from the top were guaranteed. Whether guests chose to feast their eyes on the coast of France in the distance or on the perfect arse of a nubile twenty-something on the beach below would – of course – be up to them.

Jake may have two actual children living on St Augustine's, but La Mirage was his true baby. It had taken almost a year of blood, sweat and tears to get the damn thing built – obviously not Jake's own blood, sweat and tears, but those of the architects, regulators and building firms he had bullied and bribed to get the foundations laid. He had originally been told that under no circumstances could he build on the sandy ground that bordered the Cove, but a few fistfuls of cash had solved that problem swiftly. The grandeur of the structure and the notoriety of St Augustine's had seen every apartment sell off-plan before a single foundation footing had even been dug. At 382 metres tall and 105 floors, it was as tall as the Empire State Building. And this was a fitting comparison: after all, this was his empire now. The island, the theme park, the skyscraper. All of it. They were just finishing the decorative elements of La Mirage now. He couldn't wait to pop that first bottle of vintage Bollinger high in the sky and toast himself on just how far he'd come.

He checked his Apple watch and swam out of the water, threw his joggers back on and began the walk towards the house where his kids lived with their nanny, Lauren.

As he passed the old *Falcon Bay* dockside, now surrounded with candy stalls, fairground rides and food kiosks, he paused to take in the enormity of what he had achieved with the *Falcon Bay* theme park.

Inspired by the success of the HBO show *Westworld* – about a futuristic amusement park where you could pay to kill and fuck life-like robots – Jake decided to create a world where fans of the show could live out their dreams, interacting with fake versions of its former stars. It hadn't been easy to achieve, because his best senior technician, Dustin, had quit *Falcon Bay* soon after Madeline died. Jake had somehow got away with paying Dustin a pittance of a salary for years, so when he had to poach one of Disney's senior prop masters to fill the gap, it had been eye-wateringly expensive. But it was well worth it. From the day tickets had gone on sale, they'd generated £50 million, so no expense was spared in restoring the exterior sets to their former glory, especially when it came to replicating the infamous Christmas Day live episode where actress Catherine Belle and CITV's network owner Madeline

Kane had gone to battle by the water's edge with a live shark circling, and only one had survived.

It was uncanny how real the Great White Death Experience seemed compared to that very night. A mechanical shark that made Jaws look like something out of a Pokémon game lay still in its tank. An industrial rain-and-thunder machine was poised overhead, ready to replicate the exact storm that had descended as the women had filmed that fateful episode on the slippery boardwalk. Unlike *Westworld*, though, real actors played out the parts of the stars of the show.

Legendary soap actresses Lydia Chambers and Stacey Stonebrook, playing the parts of Lucy Dean and Madeline Kane, provided almost as much of a draw as the highly realistic great white shark. With the shark swimming ominously around the dock, the dockside fight exploded between the girls. While an animatronic Madeline fell into the shark's razor-sharp teeth, a special trapdoor allowed Stacey to disappear. A trap door identical to the one that should have saved the real Madeline Kane.

It was so lifelike that by the time the animatronic Madeline was bobbing in the water screaming, the audience were always beside themselves. They'd had to make the ride's seats waterproof as many of the older guests had been known to wet themselves watching. Jake had felt sick at that, but knew that where bladders split open so did wallets, so he'd quickly arranged a brand of multi-sized clothing covered in 'I survived the Great White Death Experience' slogans, to flog to those who'd gotten a little too excited.

The new Madeline Kane was even more realistic than the shark. She'd been manufactured by a company that made sex dolls in San Francisco, using the latest cyborg technology from Japan. Even to the touch, she felt real, and the way her beautiful face moved, it was like looking at the real thing, only less sneery.

Because the dolls were attacked by a hyper-realistic shark every day, they had a single use before needing fixing, so they had ten in rotation, all hanging in a warehouse at various stages of repair. They were worth every penny though. A video of animatronic Madeline that Jake had posted was already the fifth most liked post on Instagram this year, just behind a photo of one of the Kardashian sisters' rear.

The first week the Madeline prototype arrived he'd had it delivered to his office saying he wanted official sign-off, but his true intentions were very different.

It had always irked him that Madeline had spurned his advances. Now he was about to get his own back. After she'd been unboxed and inspected by all, and everyone had left, he closed the blinds so none of the security cameras would catch him doing what he'd always wanted to do. Fuck Madeline Kane's gorgeous body.

As he lay the silicone body over his desk and parted her legs he studied just how perfectly the designers had made her. Her pussy felt so lifelike to the touch he was instantly hard. After taking his engorged cock out and pouring some lubrication on it, he slipped it in and screwed her so hard that an Emmy fell off his desk. He was so turned on that he barely lasted a few minutes before he'd shuddered deep in the doll – accidentally triggering the blood-curdling scream which was programmed to go off when the ride dropped Madeline into the shark's mouth. Thank God he knew where her kill switch was, even if he had to rip some of her hair out to access it.

The memory of shagging Madeline's replica made his cock twitch again. Luckily he was nearly at the bungalow where his son and daughter lived with Lauren.

When he'd got custody of his children, he'd told the world how much it meant to him to know they were safe with him instead of with their criminal mothers. In reality, though, being a dad wasn't his thing. He only visited for two reasons: to shoot footage with the kids to boost his career; or, for exactly the reason he and his throbbing cock were heading there now, to fuck the nanny. By agreeing to be his live-in escort as well as his nanny, she was earning about ten times as much as a regular Norland. As he opened the door to the main house, Lauren, who was doing yoga on the living room floor with the balcony open facing the sea, turned, and put her finger to her lips to gesture that the children were asleep. Jake smiled and took in her perfect body in her skin-tight leggings and crop top before dropping his joggers to reveal his rock-hard manhood. Lauren smiled and leaned towards him to gently take the tip in her mouth. She could taste the salt of the ocean, and she sucked him deeper until his balls were resting on her perfect chin. As Jake fucked her mouth her mind wandered to all the awful jobs she and her friends had endured in the past. Some of her friends were still working for men whose desires didn't bear thinking about. As far as sex-work went, she'd hit the jackpot: Jake was a pretty hot punter for his age, his kids were adorable and it paid well enough that in less than a year she'd have saved enough money to buy an apartment in London and then follow her ultimate dream of putting herself through law school.

She was aware that some people thought escort work was beneath them but the money was too good to give up. She'd tried to become an OnlyFans creator, but she found that being on a camera was strangely more degrading than being on the end of a stranger's dick. It wasn't long before she felt the familiar shudder as Jake thrust her head down hard as he climaxed. That was the bit she hated the most about his morning blowjob routine – he insisted on finishing down her throat. Still, at £10,000 a week, in cash, and with no expenses, she really couldn't afford to complain. So, although she gagged a little as he shot his load, she managed her usual fake smile as he pulled out.

'Now that is what I call a perfect morning,' Jake said with a wink.

'And that is what I call a perfect breakfast,' she lied, as he patted her on the cheek and pulled up his joggers.

As the door closed behind him, she grabbed a bottle of Evian and rinsed her mouth out then spat it in a plant pot. Once again, he hadn't asked about the children. Not even a mention, let alone popping his head round their door to have a look at them. What an arsehole. She really hoped that even if the women didn't get off in the court case, which she'd heard was impossible, they'd at least get visitation rights, which so far Jake had managed to block.

She couldn't imagine how it must feel for Farrah and Amanda, not only locked up less than two miles from their children, but knowing their babies were being 'brought up' by such a grade-A prick as Jake Monroe.

But she couldn't allow herself to get upset. She had to block it out and remind herself that this was just a job, the custody battle was nothing to do with her, and she was only three months away from having everything she needed to change her life forever.

She padded barefoot down the corridor to where Olivia and Max were still fast asleep. *Poor little mites* she thought again, and said a silent prayer for Amanda and Farrah that things might go just a little bit their way.

CHAPTER 2

Sheena

To her surprise, Sheena McQueen found she didn't mind prison. Yes, she had fallen far: in almost the blink of an eye she had gone from being the country's top showbiz agent to sharing a cell with a petty criminal. And yes, it was undignified to have been hauled into custody on live TV. But there were upsides to life behind bars. Gone were the pressures of living for others, constantly fixing things for her clients and never for herself. For the first time in years, she could spend time alone with her thoughts. And her room – to call it a cell would have been putting it too strongly – may have been far from her lovely home in Knightsbridge with its marble bathroom that ran the whole width of the top floor, but it was light, airy and modern. In fact, it might have felt like a detox spa break if it wasn't for her cellmate, Kayleigh, a thirty-something shoplifter with cropped hair and Chinese tattoos, who spoke in a strong northern accent and rarely gave Sheena the peace she craved. At least Kayleigh was friendly, though, bustling about, humming her favourite ABBA songs, making tea, and outlining the dos and don'ts of life inside: do get a job in the library and sign up for yoga; don't go near the mashed potato. Since Sheena rarely ate carbs, that last one was no hardship.

Sheena sipped her tea and stretched out on the narrow bunk bed. *Someone up there is looking out for me*, she thought, watching her roommate fuss over her. When she'd been remanded to custody pending trial, she'd pictured Sean Bean's brutal experience in the drama series, *Time*. She had imagined bullying and beatings, a paranoid cellmate who'd try to kill her in her sleep. Things really weren't as bad as she had feared. Her roommate was sweet, the inmates were on first name terms with the staff, the yoga sessions were amazing, and the low-security prison's grounds were quite lovely: a low white building flanked by manicured lawns and a formal rose garden. According to Kayleigh, it was a good deal nicer than the bedsit she'd had in St Helier before her arrest, perhaps about as nice as an Ibis Budget hotel, if Sheena had come across those? Sheena smiled at that. She had stayed in the best hotels in the world – the Georges V in Paris, Sandy Lane in Barbados, The Langham in London. She had never heard of an Ibis Budget, let alone experienced one. Thank God.

Yes, Sheena reflected, *if you're going to be locked up anywhere, Jersey's La Croix Prison is a pretty good place to be.* Especially if you had been through worse – and Sheena had.

Much worse.

As a teen actor, while starring in the TV series *Second Chances*, Sheena had suffered appalling abuse at the hands of Ed Nichols, the studio's main investor and a dangerous paedophile. Plied with drink and drugs, passed from one predatory man to another, she was soon broken and unable to act, with her future hanging by a thread. And yet despite the damage he wrought, she found a way back. Turned her life around. Made something of herself by carving out a reputation not as an actor, but as a fearsome talent agent: a steely negotiator and razor-sharp businesswoman whose clients always landed the best jobs in showbiz. She was tenacious, resourceful, not the type to give in to self-pity, never one to wallow.

Prison was not even rock bottom – it was merely a setback, a blip. As soon as she arrived here, she had begun to consider how she and her friends might come back stronger and even more successful than before.

They had all been arrested together. Sheena McQueen, Farrah Adams, Amanda King, Helen Gold and Catherine Belle. Once the beating heart of CITV, the company that made *Falcon Bay*, they were an unstoppable team: Farrah was a brilliant writer–director; Amanda, a producer with masses of creative flair; and Helen a gifted casting director. As for Catherine – Sheena's number one client – she had been *Falcon Bay*'s standout star for forty years. Sheena refused to accept that their arrest had consigned them to the scrapheap. After all, before all of this they'd had the world at their feet. Hundreds of millions of viewers around the world were on tenterhooks, ready to tune in to the live episode that would form *Falcon Bay*'s grand finale, the one that would cement its legacy, and that of all the women who worked on the show. Sheena sighed. They had come so close. What an almighty mess it had become.

While Kayleigh chattered on about the prison timetable for next week, Sheena let her mind wander to that fateful night on set. Catherine Belle was about to exchange wedding vows live on TV with her co-star and real-life love, Lee Landers. The ceremony was to be binding in real life, as well as providing a gripping final episode for the viewers at home. At that point, Catherine and Sheena hadn't realised that Lee was only after Catherine for her fortune, and Catherine was radiantly happy.

Apart from the fact that Catherine had looked a bit glazed – Xanax, Sheena suspected – everything had been going so well. Sheena tried to recall the clues that it would all come crashing down. Could she have prevented it? Had she been careless? She, who was usually so good at reading people and situations. Had she missed the first cracks as they started to appear? There was the unscheduled arrival of Chad Kane, who showed up in the Cove just ahead of filming; silent and grim-faced. That should have been a massive red flag.

Jake Monroe, too, wasn't supposed to be anywhere near the set, yet swanned in like he owned the place – a punch to the gut for his ex-wife, Amanda, who'd only recently had him fired. Then there was pregnant Farrah, who'd insisted on directing the episode even though she had started having contractions, only relinquishing control when she was in the late stages of labour, and about to give birth on the gallery floor. One thing on top of another, each more ominous than the last, as if a thick blanket of fog had rolled in from the sea and cloaked the Cove in an atmosphere of foreboding.

No, Sheena hadn't missed anything. But she had, for once, been powerless to intervene as events unfolded horribly before her eyes.

She had to hand it to Chad. His revenge for the death of his wife, Madeline, was flawlessly executed. The skill with which he picked his moment, hijacking the final ever episode of *Falcon Bay* to expose the women he held responsible for Madeline's grisly death was a masterstroke.

If only Sheena had managed to rein in Catherine, Chad would never have had the material to expose them. Catherine, who'd insisted on going to Madeline's funeral in New Orleans – expressly against Sheena's advice. Catherine, who'd cornered Sheena in the grounds of the Kane family mansion after the funeral to blurt out the guilt she felt, her need to tell Chad what she'd done. 'I had the chance to save Madeline from the shark, and I didn't.' Loud and clear for the secret recording devices that of course a billionaire like Chad would have all over his property, Sheena thought bitterly.

Every bit of their conversation had been captured, including what Sheena had said about why Catherine could never tell the truth: 'We all helped you cover it up. Don't make us all pay the price together.'

Sheena felt a sudden stab of fury towards Catherine. If only she'd kept her mouth shut. Stuck to her lines, like the experienced actress she was. Sheena groaned. That damning conversation outside the Kane mansion had given Chad all the ammunition he needed.

After the riveting climax of *Falcon Bay*'s last ever episode, their impassioned scene had aired everywhere. On news bulletins worldwide, splashed across the front pages of the tabloids in the UK and abroad. The slew of lurid headlines kept coming:

Falcon Bay Bitches Taken Down! Scandal on TV's Murder Island! Soap and GORY!

Anonymous users on Twitter ripped into Catherine: #Cove-Killer and #CatherineBelleMonster began trending within seconds of Chad's home video airing.

As Sheena sipped her tea and tuned out Kayleigh, her mind was whirring.

No use crying about it now.

No use thinking about the what ifs.

She just had to find a way to salvage things for her and the girls. She was the agent, after all, clear-headed, cool in a crisis. She was good at solving problems. Before long, a plan was beginning to take shape in her mind. As long as all the girls behaved rationally and predictably, there was no reason why it shouldn't work.

*

Sheena strolled through the gardens to the day room, her favourite part of the prison. The walls were painted a sunny yellow and hung with reproductions of old tourist board posters urging people to visit Jersey. There were rattan chairs dotted about, and comfortable oversized sofas, donated by some Jersey bigwig benefactor. Light streamed in onto the pale oak flooring, a bit like Sheena's hallway at home.

Amanda, Farrah, and Helen were in a huddle in the centre of the dayroom, the Scrabble board on the low table in front of them. Sheena's heart sank. Not Scrabble. Again.

'Where's Catherine?' Sheena asked as she sank into a plush velvet sofa.

'Seeing the priest,' Farrah told her. 'As usual.'

Since arriving at La Croix, Catherine spent all her time in the prison chapel.

'Do we need to worry about all this born again stuff?' Sheena wondered aloud.

Helen shrugged. 'It's a distraction.'

'It seems to keep her happy,' Amanda said. 'Not so... haunted. Less... troubled.'

Sheena raised an eyebrow. 'Let's not forget I've spent years bending over backwards to keep Catherine happy – and look where that got me.'

Farrah nodded in the direction of the door. 'Right on cue.'

Catherine was saying her goodbyes to the priest, a bony little man, his face all sharp edges. As he headed off up the corridor, Catherine pressed the palms of her hands together and bowed in his direction.

'Here she is,' Farrah said, as Catherine pulled a chair closer to the table. 'Mother Teresa.'

Catherine smiled. 'Not yet,' she said.

'Now we're all here, let's get started.' Amanda handed round the little bag of Scrabble tiles.

'So,' Catherine began, 'how's everyone feeling today? Are we all doing OK, holding things together?'

Farrah spluttered. 'Well, let me see. I'm in prison and have been for nearly a year, because of a false start to our trial in January. I'm due to find out in ten days whether I'm going to be spending many *more* years in this place. And if I am, then my son is either going to be brought up by a lying, sleazy, porn-mad, double-crossing, self-centred, serial shagging, manipulative prick, or by a nanny I've never met.'

Catherine winced. 'Let's not forget Jake *is* his father.'

Farrah glared at her. 'Ah yes,' she said icily. 'A father who uses his child as a weapon to cause maximum pain and distress to his mother.' Catherine opened her mouth to speak but Farrah hadn't finished. 'Do you have any idea what it's like for me, stuck here behind bars—'

'Oh, let's not exaggerate,' Catherine interrupted. She gestured at the bifold doors which opened onto a wooded walkway, a cool breeze wafting in.

'Behind bars,' Farrah said again. 'Having had my new-born baby ripped from my arms. By Jake!'

Amanda put a hand on her arm. 'I know how it feels.' Jake really was a low-life, scheming, ruthless snake. He was also her ex-husband. And now he had custody of her daughter Olivia as well as Max, his child by Farrah. It made her want to weep thinking of her precious child, conceived after so many IVF attempts, in the home of a man who'd shown not the slightest interest in her.

There was an uncomfortable silence.

Helen cleared her throat. 'I've got a Z, so do I get to start?'

Sheena gazed around at her friends. Their chances of getting through this depended on them sticking together, and yet their once rock-solid bond was starting to fray. She had always prided herself on her ability to read people, her years as an agent teaching her all she needed to know about power struggles, ego soothing and peacekeeping.

Farrah, she guessed, was about to blow a fuse. On *Falcon Bay*, Farrah had been the best writer, and a brilliant, controlled director. Nothing fazed her. Now, as she sighed loudly and swept a hand through her hair, she seemed to pulsate with undirected anger. Yet a light inside her seemed to have gone out. Her usually gleaming ebony skin was dull and sallow, her nails bitten.

Words had started to appear on the Scrabble board. Zen. Fever. Tart.

Helen was hunched over her letters. She rearranged them on the plastic rest, frowned, tried a different combination. In contrast to the worn-out Farrah, Helen appeared to be her usual unruffled self, but the way her fingernail tapped restlessly on the table told Sheena that beneath her cool exterior she was suffering too. Sheena felt for her. After a lifetime of casual sex and hot flings, Helen had finally fallen in love a few months ago – but there was no way her relationship could survive prison. Trust Helen to fall in love with a policeman and then get herself arrested. It had been nearly a year, and Matt hadn't come near.

Catherine broke into Sheena's thoughts. 'Your nails are looking lovely, I like the colour.'

'Thanks', said Sheena. 'Kayleigh did them. It's called Do You Lilac It? Opi.' Kayleigh had been a skilled manicurist in a high-cnd nail bar before she got caught slipping a bottle of Opi polish into her pocket. It was a dusky rose-tinted nude called Barefoot in Barcelona, the shade everyone wanted for their pedicures. It wasn't the first time she'd helped herself, and she was sacked on the spot. Kayleigh boasted that she had squirreled away about forty bottles by then, practically every shade there was. Sheena assumed Kayleigh had stolen cash from the till as well to end up in here – but had learned quickly that prison etiquette meant following a "don't ask, don't tell" policy when it came to inmate crimes.

'Bless her, she does a wonderful job,' Catherine said, her attention back on the Scrabble board.

Sheena studied her for a moment. Something about Catherine had changed, and it wasn't just that the usually glamorous star was in a grey prison-issue tracksuit, or that her once plump rosebud mouth, denied its regular contouring appointments, was now set in a thin hard line.

'How do you spell *chasuble*?' Catherine asked.

Amanda, six vowels to play with, having managed a paltry four points on her previous go, stared. 'You think you can make *chasuble*?'

Farrah scowled. 'What's a *chasuble* when it's at home?'

'It's the garment the priest wears,' Catherine informed her. 'The vestment.'

The penny dropped. Bless her. Chasuble. Vestment. The little gold cross she now wore. What was niggling Sheena about Catherine was the extent to which her religious obsession had taken hold since arriving at La Croix. She had written a letter to her ex Lee Landers quoting the Gospel of Matthew, in which she officially forgave him for trying to trick her into marriage. She had also stopped watching soaps, thanks to Father Padraic's insistence that they were wicked, full of immoral, shouty people who seemed incapable of seeing the error of their ways. In short, Catherine was being completely brainwashed.

'You know,' Catherine was saying, 'it's been a huge help to me to have God back in my life.' Her eyes were on Farrah. 'It might help, you know, to have a word with the priest.'

Farrah's expression was glacial. 'Sorry, me?'

'You do seem to be struggling,' Catherine said, aiming a pitying look at her.

'Struggling? Of course I'm fucking struggling! What do you expect? I mean, Christ almighty' – Catherine winced – 'how the fuck is it going to change anything, me speaking to some bloke in a dog collar? We're in here for the foreseeable, and all we have to look forward to is a trip to court when we'll be utterly humiliated all over again, then, most likely, properly banged up – for years, probably. Years.' Her eyes blazed. 'And who's to blame, I wonder? Ah, yes, that would be you.'

Catherine gasped.

'Hold on,' Sheena began. 'Let's not …'

Farrah rounded on her. 'Don't try and defend her, not when we all know who landed us in this shit in the first place.'

No one said anything. The air seemed to crackle between them.

'Look, we're all upset,' Amanda said after an awkward silence, 'but we'll only get through this if we stick together. We're all grown-ups, we make our own decisions. No one had their arm twisted. It was our choice as a group to get behind Catherine, after the ridiculous stunt Madeline pulled.'

'I don't remember having much choice at the time,' Helen pointed out.

Sheena looked around at her friends. Women who had known each other for what felt like forever, who'd always had one another's backs. If one was in trouble the others rallied round. Hadn't it been that way for as long as she could remember?

Sheena thought back to the night of Madeline's death. They were filming a live episode of *Falcon Bay* with a storyline in which Catherine's character would tumble off the dock into the jaws of a circling shark. Madeline, as the owner of the network, had insisted on using a real shark instead of CGI, and had refused to use a stuntwoman, under the guise of gaining extra PR for the show. It had made no sense to try something so dangerous, until it became clear that Madeline had a personal vendetta against Catherine and was trying to destroy her reputation. But in trying to save Catherine's career, Sheena and the others had unwittingly sentenced Madeline to death.

Sheena shuddered at the memory, the splash as Madeline fell, the awful screaming, the thrashing about in the sea. Whether or not Catherine could have saved Madeline was debatable. But – and it was a big but – she might just have managed to. Instead, she pulled away her hand at the very moment Madeline reached out to her on the dock. A decision which had dragged the others down with her when they agreed to cover up what she'd done. Or rather, what she hadn't done.

'We can set the record straight,' Catherine was saying, 'be honest. Isn't that best – for us, for poor Madeline's soul?' There was a faintly shrill note in Catherine's voice and Sheena could tell she was heading towards an emotional cliff edge.

Catherine drew breath, fiddled with the little gold cross. 'And, while we're at it, we can deal with the other matter as well.' Sheena became instantly alert. 'So that once we get out of here it's with a clean slate, nothing hanging over us. Then we can move on with our lives with a clear conscience.'

'My conscience is fine, thanks,' Sheena told her. 'If you ask me, Madeline engineered that whole crazy scenario on the dock to destroy you and create mayhem – and she succeeded. Only it backfired on her and that's why she died.'

'Yes, but it's not just Madeline we need to address,' Catherine said.

Sheena shot her a warning look. 'Yes,' she insisted, 'it is.'

Catherine waited a beat. 'I'm talking about Ross Owen.'

Helen snapped at her. 'Have you lost your mind? I told you that was sorted.'

'Meaning,' Catherine countered, 'you made it go away. Which doesn't make it right. A man died. Doesn't he deserve justice?'

Amanda listened, wide-eyed.

'Please, someone,' Farrah said, her head in her hands, 'tell me this is all a horrible dream, that I'll wake up and none of this fucking madness will actually have happened?'

'I cleaned up your mess,' Helen told Catherine. 'Again. We all did. And now you want to tell the world – what, so your conscience is clear?'

Catherine gave her an infuriating smile.

'That despicable reporter's death was accidental.' Sheena's tone was icy. 'Unfortunate, yes, but let's not forget he tried to rape you.' Her glare pinned Catherine in place until she looked away. 'Which was how he ended up staggering backwards and falling off the cliff.'

'Of course, we only have your word for that,' Farrah told Catherine. 'Perhaps there was more to it. Maybe he was at that little clifftop hideaway at your invitation. It was a big night, you were on a high, you'd just scooped the Best Actress Award. Maybe you fancied a bit of rough, and there was Ross, a vile hack who'd got it in for *Falcon Bay*. Maybe you lost control and gave him a beating, using your new trophy as a weapon.'

Catherine shrank back, horrified.

Amanda intervened. 'Look, we know what went on, we trust your version of events, Catherine.' She shot a warning look in Farrah's direction. 'Please, let's not fall out – not over this. Right now, we need each other.'

'We agreed the Ross Owen business was over,' Sheena snapped. 'There's nothing to tie us to it.'

'Thanks to me sticking my neck out,' Helen muttered. She had smoothed things over when phone footage of Catherine arguing with Ross, captured on Ross Owen's own mobile which had been recording the night from his pocket, found its way to *Falcon Bay*'s Lost Property office and then to the soap's PR, Candy Dace. Candy could easily have dropped them in it, had Helen not managed to get her on side then seen to it the footage was destroyed.

Sheena's gaze bored into Catherine. 'He was drunk, he fell off the cliff, end of story.'

'I just wish we could've come clean. But when someone hauled his corpse into the sea, I lost my opportunity to do the right thing,' Catherine lamented.

Sheena's jaw dropped. Yet another situation when she'd had to act on instinct to save Catherine – who now had the gall to fling it back at her. 'Is this what your sessions with your priest have taught you?' she demanded. 'How to be an absolute cow and turn on your friends, the very people who've stuck by you through thick and thin? Is he teaching you how to betray those who've shown you nothing but love and loyalty?' Her gaze slid to Farrah, lip curled in disgust, then Helen, her face rigid with rage, and Amanda – the peacemaker, eyes full of unshed tears. 'Look around you,' Sheena said. 'We're the ones who've put ourselves on the line, to keep you safe. Careers, happiness, families – all down the pan. For you.'

'And not just once either,' Helen said. 'Twice.'

'I've just remembered,' Catherine said, cool as anything, 'I've got a Bible session now, so if you'll excuse me.' She stood.

Farrah caught at her wrist. 'You can't drop a bombshell about revealing what really happened to Ross fucking Owen, then swan off to church. What exactly are you planning to do?'

She tugged her hand free. 'Do?' she said, sounding puzzled, as if there could be only one course of action. 'I'm going to do the right thing, of course.'

CHAPTER 3

Madame Anglaise

It was market day in the town of Saint Valery in Brittany. The sun was shining, music was blaring, and the streets were teeming with shoppers. Food, clothing, shoes and haberdashery were set out lovingly on stalls draped with colourful canopies. A queue had formed at a stall where sea bass, oysters and langoustines had been laid out like edible artworks, freshly caught in the port that morning. Greetings were called, half-hearted complaints muttered concerning the price of scallops, which were selling fast, nonetheless.

Among the shoppers was the English woman, who cut across the cobbled square in her customary dark glasses, red hair gathered in a Bardot-style up-do, a baguette poking from the top of her bag. At the fromagerie, she bought Camembert and a square of Pont-l'Évêque. Zigzagging through the market, she picked up fat green olives from one stall and garlicky peppers in olive oil from another. From the charcuterie she chose a selection of cold meats.

A bent old woman in a headscarf, carrying a shopping bag in one hand and a live chicken in the other, stopped to exchange a word or two, calling her Madame Anglaise, asking after her health. They chatted for a moment. The English-woman's French wasn't perfect, but it was good enough that the stallholders and the townspeople treated her with respect. Sufficient for her to feel at home in Saint Valery.

Then why did she feel so on edge? So increasingly restless?

It had been her choice to come here, to live in her elegant three-storey townhouse on the Rue Antoine, one of the loveliest streets in town. With its dark green shutters and a pretty courtyard at the back, it had become her bolthole. She had lived there just once before, the last time her life had reached a crossroads, and she was in need of privacy. For almost a year back then, she'd adjusted to a whole new way of being. Saint Valery had been kind to her, the people accepting, unquestioning. Once she was ready to return to the outside world and start afresh, she had been surprised by how much of a wrench it was to leave.

And now she was back.

Deep in her heart, she had always known she would return. What she hadn't predicted was how suddenly it would happen. The way in which things had crumbled was so sharp, so catastrophic, it had left her no option but to flee. So, here she now was, living alone once more, having left behind all she held dear. The reclusive Madame Anglaise LaRoche. Madame Anglaise. This time was different, though. She wasn't simply biding her time, waiting for the right moment to stage a comeback. This time her move was permanent.

After what she'd done, she had no choice.

She could never return to her old life. She couldn't even switch on a phone or a computer to find out what she had left behind. She didn't dare.

CHAPTER 4

Sheena

The next day, Sheena found Farrah in the TV room watching a real estate show.

'So, this guy,' Farrah said, not taking her eyes off the screen, 'he's set his heart on buying one of those romantic wrecks they sell in rural Italy for one euro – middle of nowhere by the look of it – not even nice countryside.' She frowned. 'They're dragging him round all these crappy little places you wouldn't be seen dead in – dilapidated, shutters falling to bits, not a ristorante in sight; I mean if you're going to live in Italy, you want a pizzeria nearby at the very least.' She drew breath and Sheena was about to speak but she hadn't finished. 'So far, we've not even seen a café, nowhere to get a cappuccino or a glass of Verdicchio. They're showing the poor guy ghost towns. He specifically said he wanted room for a pool, but their idea of a pool is what you or I would barely call a hot tub.'

Sheena watched for a moment. 'Who's the presenter?'

'No idea. She's something else, though, look at those heels – on a spiral staircase.'

A bedroom appeared, just about big enough for the bed and a single wardrobe pushed up against a wall. The man was looking around him, his face a picture of despair, the friend who'd come along for moral support hovering in the doorway, horrified.

'I was wondering how you're doing,' Sheena said.

'If that was me, I'd have told the production team where to go by now,' Farrah replied, her eyes still fixed on the screen. 'The last place they went to was awful, like a cheap ski chalet. Ask them where the nearest pizzeria is!' She gave Sheena a grim smile. 'How I'm really doing, you mean?'

Sheena nodded, and Farrah's face crumpled.

'I'm missing my baby.' There was a catch in her voice. 'Like really missing him, it's like a physical pain that gives me cramps, and that makes me snappy and exhausted and weepy and furious all at once.'

Sheena stayed silent.

Farrah sighed. 'I've got an investigator looking into Jake's childcare arrangements, watching his every move and compiling a dossier on anything we can use on to wrestle custody back once I get out.' She frowned. 'And I saw my lawyer this morning – he thinks I've got a good chance at getting out.' She shot Sheena a look. 'But he doesn't know yet that Mother Superior wants to screw it up for all of us. You know, I could fucking kill her for this.'

'Me too,' said Sheena. 'It might come to that if she carries on like this.'

The two women locked eyes.

*

She expected to find Catherine in the little chapel, in a huddle with the priest, but it was deserted. She tried the chaplain's office, the library and the rose garden. No sign of Catherine anywhere. Her roommate, lounging on the top bunk, barely looked up from her copy of *OK!* magazine, to confirm she'd not seen Catherine all afternoon.

In the end, Sheena gave up and headed to her room, where Kayleigh took one look at her and insisted on a healing facial massage treatment to ease her stress.

'You've got lovely hair,' Kayleigh told her as she pressed shea butter into Sheena's skin. 'Is that your natural colour?'

'Pretty much.' She was lucky with her hair, which was thick and shiny, a deep mahogany that verged on black.

'I'm finding a lot of tension in your jawline,' Kayleigh said, working her knuckles along the bone. Her massage technique was something else, and within about five minutes, Sheena was feeling considerably better. Once they were both out and all this was over, she planned to set Kayleigh up in business, an upmarket salon in Chelsea or Westbourne Grove. Or one of the chic London hotels. People paid a fortune for natural face-sculpting; Sheena knew a good business move from a mile away. She sighed. No point thinking too much about the future when she had no idea how long she would be inside.

'Your shoulders too,' Kayleigh remarked, 'all knotted up. Ooh, that's a nasty one.'

No wonder, Sheena thought, after what had gone on in the day room. What was Catherine thinking? She'd seen her like this before – stubborn, intransigent, refusing to consider any opinion but her own – and it never ended well. Sheena felt a surge of indignation at Catherine's dig at her for pushing

Ross Owen's body into the sea. Memories of that night flooded back; the shock of discovering the reporter dead, Catherine practically deranged, her dress torn and bloodied. Someone had to take control and dig Catherine out of yet another colossal hole. And from what Sheena remembered, she was the only one able to think straight, to grasp what the ramifications would be – for Catherine, especially – if events ever came to light. She'd had no option but to handle things as she saw fit to avert yet another scandal.

Now Catherine wanted to rake it all up again.

Well, if Catherine wanted to go nuclear, Sheena would have to fight fire with fire.

As things stood, Catherine was the only one facing the charge of involuntary manslaughter, while her friends were standing trial for conspiracy to pervert the course of justice. If they were found guilty, they'd likely be given a short sentence in an open prison like La Croix, or perhaps some hours of community service. But if Catherine told the truth about Ross Owen, things could look very different. Dragging a body into the sea to cover up the true cause of death was the kind of thing that got you locked up for a very long time. There's no way they'd get community service for that. Sheena sighed deeply. God, if only there was a way to make Catherine just shut up.

'All done,' Kayleigh said.

Sheena sat up. 'You're an angel, really. Put it on the tab.' Sheena intended to pay Kayleigh properly once she was out and life was back to normal. If that ever came about. She sat for a moment, breathing in the comforting scent of the shea butter, tension returning to her jaw and pulsing at the side of her temple. She needed a back-up option – something that would stop Catherine's revelations from coming out if she couldn't be reasoned with. Without warning, she hit upon the answer.

She glanced at Kayleigh. 'I don't suppose you could get your hands on some Temazepam?'

*

Sheena headed out into the grounds, taking the path that skirted the edge of the wooded area to the highest point of La Croix where a bench overlooked the sea. The sky was shot through with fluffy clouds, the sun shimmering on the water, its surface glittering like a carpet of crystals. In the distance lay St Augustine's, the island that had been home to *Falcon Bay* for forty years.

She breathed in the salt air, enjoying the peace. In her old life it had been vanishingly rare to have time like this to herself. She might be in the salon with her head in the basin, in a therapist's treatment room, her face encased in a hard clay mask, or at the dentist's having emergency treatment for an abscess she'd put up with until the pain was unbearable. Or The Ivy where mobiles were banned – having lunch with a network controller. Other than during these fleeting moments of peace, the phone was always ringing: tearful clients relaying dramas she alone could resolve; angry producers lashing out at her for something it would turn out was their own fault.

She squinted at the sea. Somewhere, in the distance, was the south coast of England, a short hop from there to her home in Knightsbridge. Out to the west lay the Atlantic. She found herself remembering a young woman who had rowed, single-handed, from Spain to Antigua, and set a new record. It hadn't seemed possible and yet she'd done it. Throughout Sheena's career she had held onto the idea that nothing was impossible. She was an optimist, a survivor, who knew from experience that, even in the darkest moments, there was hope. In all things it is better to hope than despair. Who said that? Jesse Jackson? Martin Luther King? She couldn't remember.

A voice broke into her thoughts. 'Mind if I join you?' Without waiting for an answer, Catherine made herself comfortable on the bench.

Sheena felt a flash of irritation. Even here, she was interrupted. 'I was just having a moment to myself,' she said a touch sharply.

'I know, it's good for the soul to get away from it all,' Catherine replied, oblivious.

Sheena said, 'Actually, I was looking for you earlier.'

'I was in the chapel.'

'I tried there.'

'In the little room at the back, Father Padraic was hearing my confession.'

Sheena felt an urge to get hold of her and shake her. What was she sharing with this priest? she wondered. 'Oh?' she said, managing with great effort to keep her tone mild. 'And you're finding it helps, all this unburdening?'

Catherine turned, eyes shining. 'It's quite transformative. Sheena, really, you should try it. It's utterly liberating. I feel so much better.'

Sheena was wondering if this feeling of "liberation" would extend to the trial if she chose to confess there too and ended up with a lengthy prison sentence. She glanced at her. Couldn't she see what she was doing? Perhaps she wasn't in her right mind.

'Have you thought any more about Ross Owen?' Sheena's tone was impatient. 'What you intend to do?'

Catherine took a moment before answering. 'As I told you, the only option for me is to do the right thing.'

'Right,' Sheena said. 'And that would be what, exactly?'

Catherine patted her knee. 'I appreciate this is difficult for you, after all, given your business dealings, the murky world of TV, the lines can sometimes get a little blurred.'

'You'd be surprised,' Sheena said, affronted. 'There's less blurring than you might imagine, which is why my standing in the industry has always been high.' She twisted round to face Catherine. 'I don't mean to be unkind but can't you see that all of this comes back to you? It was thanks to you Madeline was out for revenge in the first place. It was your actions that meant we all got dragged into covering for you when Madeline ended up in the jaws of a frigging shark. You were the one who took a swipe at Ross Owen.' She caught Catherine's look. 'I'm not saying any of it was deliberate, it's just the way it played out. And since then we've all tried to get you through it.' Her voice softened. 'Because we love you and we want to protect you. But if you tell the truth, you drag us all down with you. Can't you see that?'

When Catherine didn't answer, Sheena tried a different tack. 'Have you spoken to your barrister?' Catherine had engaged Rupert Flint, smooth, silver-tongued, an eminent defence counsel with a theatrical love of Latin and a habit of securing acquittals even when the accused was guilty as sin. A conjuror,

Sheena's defence barrister Eva Hope, exceptional in her own right, had told her. If anyone could secure a Not Guilty verdict for Catherine, it was him. And the catastrophic mental breakdown she'd suffered in the past, and her subsequent fragile mental health, would play well for both Catherine and Sheena, Eva had said. As an older woman, an actress whose status and livelihood were threatened, Catherine was under extreme pressure. And then the trauma of a shark attack right in front of her. People would understand, they'd sympathise. 'The jury will get it,' Eva had assured her. 'By the time Rupert's finished they'll think she's Joan of Arc.' Which seemed appropriate, given what was going on with Catherine right now.

'There's every chance you'll be acquitted,' Sheena now said. 'That we all will. We've got the best barristers, we're of previous good character… We just need to stick together. Isn't that our strength – our friendship? All for one, one for all. Think about what happens to your friends if we all go down. Helen will lose the love of her life for good! And who knows when Amanda and Farrah will get to see their children again.'

Catherine shook her head. 'Sticking together is what landed us in the mire. What about truth, honesty? Do they count for nothing?'

'Whose truth, though?' Sheena demanded. 'Life's not black and white, however much we might want it to be, there's no single version of right and wrong. It's shades of grey, interpretation. That's why we can't start throwing spanners into the works now. That's why we have to forget all about Ross Owen.'

'You're very good, Sheena, persuasive. Perhaps you should conduct your own defence, the jury wouldn't stand a chance.'

Catherine got to her feet. 'I've made my decision. I know what I must do.'

Sheena waited for her to leave, then turned to face the horizon. 'Then so do I,' she said ominously, her words caught in a sudden gust, the damp salt air carrying them out to sea.

CHAPTER 5

Amanda

Amanda waited in the visitors' room, sun flooding in from the vast picture windows. She could see a keep fit class underway on the lawn in the distance, the instructor jogging on the spot while her class did what they could to keep up. Amanda gazed at the instructor, lean and fit, in a cropped top and leggings, and felt frumpy. She had swept her hair into a messy up-do in an effort to look nice and rolled up the bottoms of her shapeless tracksuit which, she told herself, made it look marginally more flattering. But there was no denying she had gained weight at La Croix, thanks to the puddings on offer every day: jam roly-poly, treacle sponge, apple crumble. She glanced at the clock and smiled. Dan would be here any minute.

Amanda would never have coped with prison and being separated from her daughter had it not been for Dan's visits. Despite the damaging revelations that had emerged about her, the secrets she had kept from him, he had chosen to stand by her, to give her the benefit of the doubt. He loved her, he said, trusted her. Whatever she had done, she must have had her reasons. His goodness made her want to weep. He was the most decent, principled man she had ever met. Her second chance, when things fell apart with Jake.

Dan was her everything.

She just wasn't sure she deserved him.

Was she a bad person? She wondered. Was that why things had fallen apart?

Not so long ago her life on St Augustine's had been happy, settled. The island was her anchor. Whatever she thought of Jake now, she had loved him once, enough to marry him. And, for a time, they were good together. She had thought so, anyway. Working as a team, producing *Falcon Bay* – a series they both felt passionate about – then defying the odds to have a baby in her forties. Amanda felt a pang for her daughter, a knot forming in her gut. She would never have believed it was possible to feel such loss and longing.

If only she had done things differently. She had jeopardised everything she held most dear when she deleted the footage that implicated Catherine in Madeline's death, and for what? To save Catherine's skin? Catherine, who now seemed hellbent on destroying the very friends who had rallied around at her time of need.

Having made them her co-conspirators, Catherine had decided she couldn't handle the guilt. And now Sheena had gone all cold and steely, as she always used to when she was planning a huge negotiation or a dazzling deal for one of her clients. Amanda wasn't sure what she was plotting, but she knew it wasn't good.

She looked up to see Dan in a suit, a white shirt open at the neck, striding towards her. Her stomach did a flip. She got up and they briefly clasped hands across the table.

'I got you some flowers,' he said, smiling, as he settled into the seat facing hers. 'Those big cream lilies you like. I knew I wouldn't be allowed to bring them in so they're on the windowsill at home.' He peered out at the sea in the direction of St Augustine's. 'Don't think you'll be able to spot them from here…'

'I can picture them,' she said, smiling. 'Almost catch their scent if I concentrate.' She closed her eyes for a second and breathed in. It was his cologne she could smell, the unmistakeable citrus of Acqua di Parma Colonia. She gazed at him, felt a stab of desire.

He gave her a searching look. 'So, how are things?'

She nodded. 'Oh, not too bad.' No one could really complain about life at La Croix. 'Catherine's found God.' Dan raised an eyebrow. Amanda suddenly wanted to blurt out everything, the whole business with Catherine and Ross Owen, but she couldn't. It was too late. She'd had her chance to come clean ages ago, the heart to heart she'd had with Dan on his first visit to her in prison, when she'd owned up to her part in covering up over Madeline's death. That's everything, she had told him. I promise, there's nothing more to tell. And Dan, being the thoughtful, kind soul he was, had said he forgave her for lying, and that her crime didn't seem so bad. She had only done what she thought was in the best interests of her friend. She swallowed.

'Have you seen Olivia?' she asked.

Dan, once the finance supremo on *Falcon Bay*, was still living on St Augustine's in the house Amanda had bought after she separated from Jake. He shook his head. 'Jake's barred me from accessing the appalling theme park he's running, which means I can't get anywhere near his place.'

Amanda's shoulders slumped.

Dan touched her hand across the table again. 'But the good news is I've spoken to Farrah's private investigator, and bunged him a bit extra to keep an eye on Olivia.'

She gasped. 'What? Is she alright?'

'She's fine. She and Max were out with the nanny, on the beach. Making sandcastles, happy as anything.'

Amanda felt as if her heart might break open. A complicated torrent of love and envy tore through her. She would kill to be able to make sandcastles with her daughter. 'Oh, God,' she said, 'I don't think I can bear it.'

'My guy says the nanny's good. Young, twenty-something. From what he could tell, she seemed good with Olivia, so—'

Amanda cut him short. 'I don't want someone who's good with Olivia, I should be caring for my daughter, not some… hooker Jake's dug up.' Dan winced. 'Because I guarantee if she's working for Jake, she's not just the nanny – she'll be there to service him.' She was close to tears. 'I'm her mother!' Her voice had risen to a wail and one of the guards, a dumpy woman with bouncy blonde Farrah Fawcett curls, sent a warning look her way. Amanda lowered her voice. 'Sorry. It's just so upsetting.'

'I'm sorry my darling. I didn't mean to be insensitive, I wanted to give you some good news.'

Amanda nodded, miserable. 'I'm grateful. I just don't want Olivia being raised by Jake, who has never cared about anyone but himself, or by a twenty-something-year-old girl I've never met. It should be me there with her. And what about Farrah's baby? How's he doing?'

Dan nodded. 'He was in a buggy on the beach, sleeping, one of those fringed parasols shading him from the sun. So, my guy takes a peek, says what a great couple of kids, shows idle interest, and the nanny says they're not hers, it's a bit of a long story but they've got different mums and right now they're both away. It's complicated, she says, but – and wait for this – she hopes they'll be back on the island soon and reunited with their little ones.'

Amanda stared at the table, silent. When she looked up, her eyes brimmed with tears. 'I don't know what I'd do without you,' she said. 'Honestly, I think I'd have fallen apart by now.'

'You'll always have me,' he said, his voice serious.

Would she, though? What if Catherine were to pull the pin and detonate the Ross Owen grenade? Then what? Would Dan still love her? Would he pick his way through the debris, post-explosion, looking for her? Dan was her rescuer. Strong, independent, reliable. Honest. 'And you've got your friends,' he was saying. 'That makes such a difference. I've never seen such a tight bunch, there for one another, no matter what.' He smiled. 'Five amazing, ambitious, capable women – you'd think it would be a recipe for bitching on a grand scale, but the way you have each other's backs, it's quite something.'

Amanda looked away. If only he knew.

CHAPTER 6

Candy

Back on the island of St Augustine's, Candy Dace was trawling through La Mirage's social media platforms. She sat at a table on the terrace of the Heron Café, overlooking the Cove where *Falcon Bay* was once filmed and where now visitors swarmed over the set and shrieked at the Great White Death Experience, the hourly shark attack which saw a lifelike figure of Madeline Kane tumble into the waiting jaws of the beast.

When the drama was being filmed, this part of the island had been off-limits except to cast and crew. Candy used to come here and watch the nesting birds flying from the cliffs out to sea and back to their chicks. When the café had opened as part of the theme park development, Candy had feared it might ruin her favourite spot, but the building blended well into the landscape and proved popular with people who, like her, enjoyed the peace and the spectacular views. Now, she tended to work from the café rather than in the sterile office assigned to her by Jake. Marco, who ran the place, was originally from Australia's Sunshine Coast – just like Candy. He had bright blue eyes, tousled honey-blond hair, and made the best flat white on the island. She glanced up and Marco caught her eye, aiming one of his dazzling smiles at her. She beamed back at him. The coffee wasn't the only thing he was good at. She still tingled at the memory of their morning, when he had awoken her by nibbling her ankle, then tracing his tongue slowly up the inside of her leg. Languid with sleep, she had lazily parted her legs and invited him to discover how wet she was. His mouth found her pussy and he flicked his tongue across her clit just the way she liked it. She arched her back in pleasure, spreading her legs more widely, aching for him to come inside her. He made her wait, teasing her, circling a nipple with his finger and bringing his other hand up to stroke her inner thigh. Finally, she could wait no longer, and grabbed his bum, pulling him on top of her and inside her roughly. As his thrusts became harder and more rhythmic, her hands tangled in his hair, and she pulled his head down to bite his earlobe. Marco's breath quickened, and as he started to moan, a sunshine warmth started gathering around her groin, spreading out to the tips of her fingers and toes. They thrust together, shuddering, as they climaxed together.

Candy shook the memory out of her head and turned back to her laptop. She had to concentrate or she'd never get the job done. This morning she was doing her least favourite part of her job description as Jake's PR: to inform her boss about what was being said on social media about Amanda and Farrah. Pure poison, most of it. Over a period of months, she had compiled quite a dossier, although why Jake wanted to see all this stuff, posted by people who invariably shielded their own identities, Candy didn't know. It gave him a sense of warped satisfaction, she guessed. Something must have set the trolls off again because there was a ton of stuff this morning. She skimmed through the content.

Amanda was usually tagged #UnfitMother, while Farrah tended to be labelled #SchemingSlag. Candy copied and pasted everything she found into a folder as she went. During her search, she came across posts about the other arrested women too. As usual, there were nasty posts about Sheena from years back, pictures of her with the vile paedophile, Ed Nichols, unfounded insinuations that she had been a willing participant in his notorious sex parties. Candy hated all that and clicked on 'report post.' Strangely, Catherine drew less vitriol than the others. All those years playing *Falcon Bay*'s Lucy Dean – one of TV's most loved characters – seemed to count for something. As for Helen, a slew of salacious stories continued to surface about her liberal use of the casting couch at *Falcon Bay*. Usually, anything Helen-related was accompanied with something semi-pornographic, which, since Candy liked Helen, she routinely reported to Twitter. For all the good that did.

For a time on *Falcon Bay* Candy had harboured a bitter loathing for these women, but over the last few months she had started to feel a degree of compassion for their plight. Just before they got arrested, Helen had shown her kindness, made her see that they weren't the evil hags Jake claimed they were, but were simply women trying to survive; trying to protect themselves and each other in the face of utterly ruthless behaviour from the men in their life – mostly Jake. His relentless efforts to destroy them were enough to push anyone to extremes. Candy shuddered to think she'd once had a thing with Jake, and endured the worst, least fulfilling sex of her life. Gazing over at Marco, expertly shaking cocoa powder onto a cappuccino to create his trademark bird in flight, she thanked her lucky stars she'd seen the light.

Candy's gaze drifted out to the tranquil bay. Hard to believe that it was on this idyllic sandy shore that Ross Owen's body had washed up, his clothes torn and his skull smashed in. Candy hadn't wanted to get embroiled in anything unsavoury, but when his mobile phone unexpectedly came into her possession, she watched the footage on it nonetheless. The film revealed that on the night of the TV awards there was a violent altercation, in which Ross Owen attacked Catherine Belle just before he fell from the cliff. In Candy's view, Ross was a rapist snake who got what was coming to him. But no matter what he deserved, the women's subsequent actions, all recorded in technicolour, were definitely illegal. Her first thought was to hand the phone over to the police, and she would have done so if Helen hadn't stepped in and persuaded Candy to give it to her instead.

She glanced up at the clock and saw it was almost ten, time for her regular morning meeting with Jake. She finished her coffee, shut down her laptop and nipped around the counter to plant a kiss on the back of Marco's neck. He turned, smiling. 'Savings pot's looking good,' he said, indicating a bulging tip jar on the counter.

Marco and Candy had plans to go travelling together, to see the world. He was saving all his tips, and she was contributing the part of her salary she was paid in cash to cover her Jake-related expenses.

She headed down the hill. On the far side of the bay was the clifftop spot where Ross Owen had confronted Catherine. Attempted to rape her, from what Candy had seen on the phone footage. It remained vivid in her mind, the moment Catherine had lashed out, sending him staggering backwards, crashing through the rail and over the edge.

Giving Helen the phone so she could destroy it had definitely seemed the right thing to do at the time. Ever since, though, she'd wondered if she'd been a touch hasty. Such incriminating footage might well prove useful in future.

Which is why she had kept a copy. Just in case.

CHAPTER 7

Madame Anglaise

The little bell above the door of Coiffure de Rêve chimed as Madame Anglaise entered, announcing her arrival. The hair salon's interior was a blend of vintage charm and modern elegance. Gilded mirrors lined the walls, reflecting the chandelier's warm glow, while plush crimson chairs awaited their patrons.

'*Bonjour,*' the salon's owner, Claudette, greeted her with a warm smile. 'The usual style for today?'

'No. I've come here for a change,' Madame Anglaise said in accented French, her voice low and velvety.

'*Très bien,*' Claudette replied, gesturing to one of the empty chairs. As Madame Anglaise settled in, she caught her reflection in the mirror, the fiery red locks framing her porcelain skin.

As Claudette applied the new colour, Madame Anglaise closed her eyes, and thought back to what had happened that morning.

At breakfast, she had sipped disconsolately at the café au

lait served by her housekeeper Mademoiselle Hubert, a tiny woman who dressed every day in a pencil skirt and crisp white shirt, and was as bright and intelligent as the birds that visited the courtyard. Madame Anglaise had never been able to work out her age – sixty? Seventy? With her blonde wavy bob and discreet make-up, it was impossible to tell.

Mademoiselle Hubert had placed a fresh coffee on the table and gently removed the old one, which had gone cold. 'Pardon,' she began. 'Is Madame… quite well? It seems you are a little,' she frowned, searching for the right phrase, '… *triste*. Melancholy.'

Without warning, Madame Anglaise felt tears prick at her eyes. She blinked them back. 'I accidently saw something about St Augustine's in a paper yesterday evening. Something that made me realise I have to leave here.'

Mademoiselle Hubert nodded sympathetically. 'It's been a long time since you asked me to lock away your items in the safe. Shall I use my password and retrieve them for you?'

After a long silence, Madame Anglaise agreed. Mademoiselle Hubert tactfully took away her coffee, and replaced it with an old phone. As soon as she connected the phone to the villa's wheezing old Wi-Fi, Madame Anglaise felt a pang of terror, mixed with exhilaration. Was this a path she wanted to tread? Once she Googled the headline she had glimpsed, she would not be able to turn back the clock. But after so long hiding in the shadows, of severing all connection with the world she left behind, perhaps it was time to come into the light. She clicked into the search bar, and typed in the headline she had seen in the café: '*St Augustine's Theme Park Passes 1 Million Visitors*.' She scanned the article that came up in the results, and read it through twice. The picture that accompanied the piece seared itself onto her brain: a handsome but arrogant looking man in leather trousers striking a pose on a sandy cove while a monstrous building reared up behind him. The caption read: *Jake Monroe, owner of Falcon Bay theme park and skyscraper La Mirage.*

She had asked Mademoiselle Hubert to book her into the hair salon for that very afternoon.

The minutes ticked away, and soon enough Claudette returned to rinse the dye from Madame Anglaise's hair. As the water washed over her, Madame Anglaise felt a thrill of anticipation. The new colour felt like a rebirth. With a flourish, Claudette unveiled the transformation, and then gave a little gasp of recognition.

Madame Anglaise caught the hairdresser's shocked expression in the mirror and realised at once that her true identity had been glimpsed. Her eyes brimmed with tears. It had been a long time since anyone had seen her as she truly was. '*Merci*, Claudette. It's perfect.'

As she left Coiffure de Rêve, the hairdresser clasped her hands in hers. 'My dear girl,' she said, looking into Madame Anglaise's eyes, 'you have been through so much. Are you sure you are quite alright?'

Madame Anglaise considered. The last time she had felt so transformed was the moment she finally stepped out of the clinic, and into a new chapter of her life. She looked out of the doorway at the late afternoon sun casting long shadows on the streets of St Valery. She had peace here, but not freedom. She had to leave.

'Yes, Claudette,' she replied. 'I'm more alright than I've been in a long time.'

As soon as she got home, she found the rest of the items from the safe arranged carefully on her desk by her housekeeper. She flicked through the passport, noting how much she'd changed since her last photo. She pocketed the bundle of cash, and turned on the phone she had used that morning, watched it come to life. Then she dialled a number, one she made sure she'd learned by heart. On the second ring it was answered.

'It's me,' she said. 'I'm coming back. Time to dig up that dirt and send it to you-know-who.'

CHAPTER 8

Tabitha

Tabitha Tate was running late, and in her hurry she nearly crashed her car as she careened into the parking lot of the *LA Leader*. Her morning had started badly. When she had yanked the milk from the fridge to froth for her coffee, it had spurted out, soaking her new silk top and cargo pants, and run onto the brand new rug she had paid nearly two grand for at a store on Rodeo Drive the week before. She was furious with herself – she never left the top off the milk – but, pressed for time, she dumped her ruined clothes on the floor, took a quick shower and got dressed again.

Then she couldn't find her car keys, which she always left in the bowl on the table just inside the hallway. She turned the place upside down before finding them on one of her bookshelves, next to a half-read book she could have sworn she had left on the side of the sofa last night. By the time she finally set off, a throbbing pain at her temple, she was nearly two hours late.

Now she cursed as she climbed the grubby stairs to the

newsroom in her stilettos, the soles of them blood red. This stairwell was not where she had imagined the career ladder taking her when she decided to return to America – but no matter how far she fell, or how far she had to climb, she refused to give up her Loboutins.

Tabitha wondered what Sandy would have for her today. The brutish news editor of the *LA Leader* seemed to delight in putting Tabitha in her place, sending her out to cover non-stories in parts of downtown LA Tabitha wouldn't be seen dead in. What she would give for something juicy, a front page splash with a picture by-line. The kind of stories she used to cover. She sighed. Thanks to her smash-hit book last year *The Curse of Falcon Bay*, she had enough money in the bank never to work again. But she didn't want to be out of the business, so even though this rag was the lowest of the low, she'd rather be here than an outsider.

In her less rational moments, she pinned the blame for her misfortune on *Falcon Bay*, the now defunct drama that had once fuelled her success. The real-life scandals, backstabbing, deaths, and intrigues had provided her with exclusives and front-page headlines. She became a media darling and *Falcon Bay* expert, her face plastered across TV and social media. It was while researching for the book that she had discovered the sensational story of what happened to actress Honey Hunter, after she disappeared from the show on the eve of her screen debut. Tabitha tracked her down and finally discovered her – drugged, abused and traumatised – in a rehab clinic run by a sadistic doctor, Andrew Durand. Working the story into her book made for a sensational page-turner, hailed as "sizzling but important" by *The Sunday Times*, who ran a six-page spread featuring photos of Tabitha in extravagant ballgowns. The interview with her was titled: Meet the New Star of Cutting-Edge Entertainment Journalism.

But ever since the night of the Columbia Prize award ceremony, Tabitha's career had been in tatters. The audience's silence after her speech still haunted her.

Tabitha entered the newsroom, spotting Sandy on a call with his back turned. Hoping to slip by unnoticed, she scurried to her desk and hid behind her computer screen.

'Nice of you to join us,' Todd, a mediocre feature writer, shouted across the room. Tabitha shot him a glare.

Sandy turned, spotted her, and ended his call. He marched over, hands on hips, sweat patches under his arms. 'I told you – shift starts at eight,' he said, pointing at the clock. It was just past ten. 'You're lucky we even hired you. You'd think the least you could do is turn up on time. Don't you have a watch?'

Tabitha glanced at her Rolex, its rose gold strap bright against her jet-coloured skin.

Sandy continued, not waiting for her reply. 'I'm sick of you strolling in here whenever you want, in your fucking suits and power purses like this is *Vogue* magazine.' He glanced at her Louboutins. 'I'd love to see you run in those.' Leaning in, he said, 'You need to try harder, Miss Columbia Prize. Make an effort to fit in. Start by arriving on time.'

Across the newsroom, Todd whistled, rubbing his hands together. 'Amen to all that,' he jeered.

Tabitha felt like going over there and wiping the smile right off Todd's stupid face, but this was LA, where assaulting a work colleague wouldn't just lose her a much-needed job, but would probably result in a multimillion dollar lawsuit.

She swallowed her fury and apologised. 'I had a problem at home,' she told Sandy.

Sandy waved dismissively. 'I don't care if your building catches fire. Just be on time, or you'll be out, and I'll expose you as a lazy, arrogant bitch.' He returned to his desk, satisfied with his outburst. 'On top of all the other stuff.'

Tabitha stayed silent, feeling bruised, watching Sandy bustle back to the desk, a spring in his step. What a prick. And yet, didn't he have a point when it came to what he called "the other stuff"? The other stuff was why she was at the *Leader* in the first place. *The Curse of Falcon Bay* had won the Columbia Prize, and the night she collected the award should have been the highlight of her career – probably of her life. But she'd blown it.

She'd had advance notice that she'd won and had rehearsed her acceptance speech in private, over and over, until it was polished and slick and word perfect. She hadn't thought to run it past anyone to get another opinion, before delivering it in public. She was too caught up in all the offers coming her way, too concerned about what to wear on the night – Alexander McQueen, lots of skin on show, Jourdan Dunn meets Michaela Coel, she told herself. Which was why, when it came to it, she had got the tone of her speech utterly, diabolically wrong.

In hindsight, she should have paid tribute to Honey Hunter; thanked her; been empathetic to her trauma; called her an inspiration to other women. Instead, she had self-indulgently praised her own achievements. She'd gone on a self-indulgent rant about how she'd clawed her way to the top, how she hoped she'd inspire young journalists to follow in her footsteps. She hadn't expressed humility or gratitude for her award. Before the night was over, offers of work from Netflix, ABC and Apple were withdrawn. Social media and trolls ripped into her, saying she was a bloodsucking vampire. She was journalist scum.

Tabitha Tate was cancelled.

*

She scanned the news agenda on her computer, and saw that her name had yet again been assigned to the smallest stories: a local neighbour dispute, and a fender bender on the Pacific Coastal Highway. Life was fucking unfair.

Just then, a headline caught her eye. The brief report, sparse on detail, mentioned a home invasion. The victim's name, Antony Earl, rang a bell. She concentrated hard, and remembered he had worked at the clinic where Honey Hunter was abused at the hands of the deranged Dr Durand. Antony Earl had agreed to an interview for Tabitha's tell-all book, but it never happened. He'd backed out, citing his wife's illness.

Tabitha sat for a moment, deep in thought.

Antony Earl.

Honey Hunter.

Interesting.

She looked over at the news desk. No sign of Sandy. Todd was gone too. One or two reporters were tapping at their keyboards, and a girl with red hair whose name Tabitha didn't know was talking too loudly into her phone. Tabitha logged out, snatched up her jacket and bag, hurried down the back staircase to the car park, and left.

Maybe she could get a scoop in this godforsaken job after all.

CHAPTER 9

Tabitha

Tabitha drove to Studio City, to the address she had for Antony Earl, although she couldn't get near because police cars had blocked off the street at both ends. She parked half a mile away and walked back in, passing a TV truck and a glossy-haired reporter in a lime green jacket with ferocious shoulder pads, frantically re-doing her lipstick before she went on air. Tabitha walked on. On the outer perimeter of the cordon, a cop leaning against the door of his car called out to her. 'Hey, Tabs, that you?'

She turned. It was a guy from her spinning class, Cornell, his name was. Cute. She had no idea he was one of LA's finest. 'Hey,' she said, going over. 'You're a cop.'

Cornell smiled. 'Is it that obvious?'

She smiled back, channelling her inner Gale Weathers. 'Kind of.' She figured she could get away with a few questions without him realising she was a reporter. Nodding up the street at the forensics vans, she put on her most innocent expression and said, 'So what's going on around here?'

Cornell looked around, made sure no one was in earshot. 'I shouldn't really tell you, but it'll be on the news soon enough. It was a home invasion. The homeowner was tied up, their throat was cut and…' he hesitated, pulling a face, 'mutilated. It's like a slaughterhouse in there.'

Tabitha felt her heart racing. 'Did he or she have a family?'

'He had a wife and kids. But they were out of town. Just as well.'

She sensed something big about to break. 'It doesn't sound like your standard home invasion…' she said.

Cornell shook his head, glanced up the street, lowered his voice. 'He had the word 'Sadist' scratched into his forehead with a scalpel.'

'If you had to guess, who would you say did it?' she asked.

'I don't know but it's not your average crime. This is serial killer shit. It's a proper horror scene in there.' Cornell said.

Tabitha thanked him and promised she wouldn't spread any rumours – hoping he didn't buy the *Leader* and wouldn't see her by-line in it tomorrow. After she left she called Sandy and told him what she'd found out. She thought he'd be pleased, but instead he tore into her for taking off without checking with him first. 'Get out of there now,' he said.

'But it makes sense for me to stay and do the story – I mean, I'm here,' she said.

'I've already assigned someone to cover this,' he snapped. 'A senior crime reporter.'

'But…'

'I decide who covers which story, not you. Is that clear?'

*

65

She got on the freeway, furious with Sandy, and drove straight to Carlito's Way, her local hangout. She was in need of a drink, and Leon was working the bar today. He wouldn't usually be her type – barely out of college, hair dyed blond – but he was witty and self-deprecating, and a writer like her. Screenplays. Looking for his first break. Everyone in LA, it seemed, was on the hunt for a break – but something about Leon made her think he just might find it.

He smiled when he saw her, asked how she was and what he could get her. Friendly but not too familiar, Tabitha was pleased to note. Just because they'd had wild sex on the floor of her apartment last week didn't mean he could take liberties. She ordered an Absolut vodka and tonic and took it to the other end of the bar where the TV news was reporting the same few details about Antony Earl in a loop.

Home invasion gone wrong. Suspicious death. Appeal for witnesses. And so far, the cops weren't giving much away.

'I knew the victim,' Tabitha told Leon. Antony Earl had wanted ten grand for the Honey Hunter interview, she remembered. Said he could blow the lid on all kinds of dodgy stuff that had gone on at Durand's clinic.

'Wow, sorry… Any idea what happened?'

She shook her head. 'They're not saying.' Cornell had told her the graphic details, but she wasn't going to share them. Besides, she couldn't bear to think of them. She finished her drink, ordered another. She could tell Leon wanted her to stay until he'd finished his shift, but she had a sudden urge to be alone at home, to think everything through.

*

Back in her apartment, she changed into a vest and shorts and cleaned up the morning's spillage in the kitchen as best she could. She poured a glass of Zinfandel and nibbled at a hard lump of Parmesan. She'd not eaten all day, she realised, and had nothing in. She ordered takeout: noodles, teriyaki prawns, dumplings.

When the delivery came the guy handed her a package, a small envelope with her name scribbled in untidy handwriting. It was on the step, he said.

She took it, wondering why it hadn't been put in her mailbox or handed over personally. Nothing on the envelope gave away who the sender was. Hate mail from Sandy, probably. Telling her she was fired. She opened the package and found a memory stick inside.

She plugged it into her laptop and clicked to open the content. It was a video of some kind. A poor quality recording, the light was so dim it was almost impossible to make anything out. Then a sudden beam of light revealed a face: big, distorted, close-up, wide-eyed. She frowned. The camera swung away and made a jerky sweep of the room. Now she could see an unmade bed, a robe tossed at the foot of it. Shoes and clothes strewn on the floor. A single lamp was on, and it was hard to see much more, but she could make out the outline of a person sitting on a chair at the end of the bed. Tabitha peered more closely at the screen. Tied up, it looked like. Eyes like saucers. And was that a gag? She frowned. What was going on – some weird sex game she'd rather not know about? Then why send it to her? Was it a celebrity sex tape from someone hoping she'd leak it? Fascinated, she kept watching, looking for clues.

The camera steadied on a wide shot of the room and a tall figure stepped into view, wearing what looked like latex. A mask covered his face. Oh God, it *was* a sex tape. The figure in latex moved towards the guy in the chair, stroked his hair, undid the buttons on his shirt. Tabitha felt a bit sick, as if she were spying. If this was what got them off, then OK, but what did it have to do with her? Did she know them? Each to their own, she told herself. What went on between two consenting adults was their business. Where was the harm? And then, at the end of that thought, the latex figure plunged a blade into the neck of the man in the chair, sending a spray of blood into the air, which splashed against the walls, the ceiling, the bed. Tabitha gasped. Not just with the shock of it all but because something about the guy dying in front of her felt familiar. His eyes were frantic as he thrashed, desperately trying to free himself before the life ebbed out of him, his eyes closed, and his chin dropped onto his chest. Tabitha's heart was hammering, as if it might burst open. Suddenly, she realised who she was she watching: Antony Earl.

The figure in latex stood over him, not yet finished.

Outside, a car backfired, and Tabitha almost jumped out of her skin. Her head was spinning. Who'd delivered the memory stick to her door? Could it have been the killer? She swallowed. Why? And how did they know where to find her?

On screen, all she could see now was the figure towering over Antony Earl. Oh, God. It seemed an age before they stepped aside to reveal an even bloodier scene, Antony's forehead dripping blood, his pants pulled down, more blood between his legs. Tabitha's hand flew to her mouth. The screen went fuzzy then filled again with the masked face of the attacker: grotesque, grinning, rubber spattered with gore. Something was thrust into the camera, like a trophy.

Earl's severed dick.

Tabitha rushed to the bathroom and heaved.

CHAPTER 10

Tabitha

Tabitha spent most of the night at the police station. She'd gone in as soon as she could to hand over the memory stick and its hideous footage to the people who might be able to catch the killer. Once the cops had passed the evidence to forensics – along with the envelope it came in and even Tabitha's laptop – they had a lot of questions for Tabitha about her history with Antony Earl. They also wanted to know if Tabitha knew where Honey Hunter was living these days. It was rumoured she was back in her mansion on the shores of Lake Geneva but Tabitha knew that wasn't the case. She had spoken to the housekeeper, paid her to tip her off if Honey returned so that Tabitha – who was truly ashamed of how she'd behaved – could apologise to her in person.

Although the police officers who interviewed her seemed sympathetic, and glad of Tabitha's full cooperation, she guessed her mugshot was now on a wall of the incident room under 'POSSIBLE SUSPECTS'. The interviews took so long that by the time an LAPD patrol car finally brought her home it was just getting light, the neighbourhood deserted. Feeling uneasy about returning to her apartment, Tabitha headed to the diner two blocks down and sat at the counter with a coffee until LA began to wake up.

She wished there was someone she could call, a friend who'd come and be with her, an ex, but there was no one in LA she was close to. She considered calling Leon, but she didn't want to blur the lines; their relationship couldn't be too familiar. She needed to focus on her next scoop.

It struck her that she had nobody. Nobody who'd drop everything and race to her side in a crisis, willing to take her in. And now not even her own home felt like a safe space. Even before her life had gone so wrong, she had been single-minded, focused so much on success that there hadn't been time to cultivate friendships, to forge lasting relationships.

She had been too self-absorbed.

In desperation, she went home and called Sandy. To her surprise, he seemed genuinely concerned and sympathetic as she explained about the video. 'It's just shocking,' Sandy said. 'Are you OK? How long has it been since you received the footage?' he asked. It was a relief to talk and she was touched by his kindness. Maybe she'd got him wrong.

She felt wired, and at the same time worn out, her limbs like lead. A soak in a hot bath infused with her favourite neroli and geranium salts would help. Only she couldn't find them. How could she have mislaid a glass jar that weighed about a kilo? She checked the bathroom cabinet, her wardrobe, even the kitchen cupboards. Had she done something stupid, like put them in the glass recycling? She seemed to be getting increasingly scatty. In the end, she resorted to a seaweed bath brew she'd paid a ridiculous amount for at the local health store. Her head ached but she was out of Tylenol – there was just an empty box on the shelf in the bathroom. She couldn't remember finishing those. She really was losing it. Tossing the box into the trash she clambered into the water, wrinkling her nose at the smell of the bath brew, which brought to mind something gone bad rather than the salty tang of the ocean.

Every time she closed her eyes, Antony Earl's face swam into view. His frantic eyes. The gag over his mouth… Oh God. She shuddered. Unable to relax, she got out, dried herself and put on a robe, thinking she'd get some sleep. But the moment she stepped into her bedroom, where the blinds were shut and the room in shadow – just how she liked it, usually – she felt jumpy and knew she wouldn't be able to switch off despite having been awake all night. She wondered how long it would be before she felt normal again. She'd seen some bad things in her time as a reporter but the sight of the killer mutilating Antony Earl, in that gruesome grinning mask, would be with her forever.

She threw on some clothes and opened the blinds, allowing sunlight to flood the room, and headed out into the world. The postman wheeling his trolley along the opposite side of the street, the neighbour's dog stretched out asleep on the veranda, the woman cleaning her front windows in the Gothic pile on the next block: the everyday ordinariness of life made her feel better. At the park, she watched the skateboarders for a while then called at the drugstore for a pack of Tylenol. Finally, she stopped at the deli and bought a sandwich she wasn't sure she would manage to eat. Feeling a bit brighter, she went home.

She powered up her desktop and went online to see what the papers were saying about Antony Earl. When she clicked on the front page of the *Leader*, she thought her heart might stop. Her own face jumped out at her, over a headline that screamed:

'I Watched Slasher Kill My Friend!'

She checked the by-line.

EXCLUSIVE! by Sandy Moran, News Editor.

She scrolled through the text: everything she'd told Sandy earlier, word for word, was laid out in stark black and white. She felt sick. Sandy, all sympathy and understanding, getting her to open up, share every gory, distressing detail, then turning it into a salacious tell-all interview. She would never have put her own face on that story, but that's not what the trolls thought. She reluctantly checked her DMs. As she suspected, they were full of messages accusing her of appropriating victimhood.

> Once again, you've managed to make someone else's trauma about you. I hope that one day you are a victim of horrific abuse, so you can see how messed up it is for you to be profiting from the pain of others.

> Boohoo poor Tabitha Tate, forget the family of Antony Earl, let's all shed a tear for a blood-sucking asshole whose never had any hardship in her pathetic little life!!

She felt furious – mostly with herself. He was a better reporter than she'd given him credit for. And hadn't she worked out on day one in the newsroom that Sandy was a devious little shit, who was not to be trusted?

She picked up her phone, intending to call Sandy and tell the fucker exactly what she thought of him, then thought better of it. He probably recorded all his calls. Whatever she said could end up distorted and in print. For the rest of the day, she lay on her sofa and binge watched *Grey's Anatomy* for the third time.

At around 8 p.m., the doorbell went. It must be Sandy. He had a nerve. She flung open the door about to let rip, only to find a delivery guy facing her.

'Noodles, teriyaki prawns, dumplings,' he said.

'That's what I ordered last night,' Tabitha told.

'And we got the same order for tonight. Must have been good.' He gave her a winning smile.

'No, it's a mistake.'

He checked his phone. 'Order came in this afternoon, delivery specified for 8 p.m.' He reeled off a number. The landline Tabitha rarely used. 'That your number?'

She shook her head bewildered. 'No, I mean yes, I…'

He handed her the food. 'Oh, and the dude next door asked me to give you this.' He pushed an envelope into the bag.

'What dude next door?' Her neighbour, a retired professor, was away in Venice.

'Dude came up as I was about to ring your bell, said he had something for you. Assumed it was your neighbour.'

Tabitha pushed past him out into the street. It was deserted.

*

It hit her like a blow. Someone had been into her apartment, ordered food from the phone at the side of her bed – the same order as the night before. She tensed. Her thoughts turned to the weird stuff that had been happening lately: the cap left off the milk, her car keys in the wrong place, the missing bath salts, that empty Tylenol pack. Someone was watching her, playing with her. Coming into her own house! Who, though? Why? How? She shuddered, suddenly terrified. This was supposed to be her sanctuary and yet she wasn't safe.

A shiver crept the length of her spine. What if whoever was doing this was here now, hiding?

Picking up a heavy lamp, she advanced towards the bedroom, snapping on bright overhead lights as she went. She held her breath, then checked under the bed, opened up the wardrobe. In the kitchen she stepped into the narrow corridor that led to the basement. There were bars on the windows, the door that led out to the yard at the back was bolted. She rattled the handle. It was secure. She checked inside the top loader. Empty. Feeling slightly foolish, she let out her breath in a long slow sigh, and headed back upstairs.

At her desk she stared for a long time at the envelope. It bore the same poor handwriting as the other one. She guessed she would find another memory stick inside, and she knew she ought to call the cops, hand it over before she opened it, and tell them about the weird stuff that had gone missing from her house. Would they believe her, though? She imagined their faces when she explained what had gone missing: a few painkillers, her bath salts. Still, they'd have to take her seriously once they saw what was in the envelope. Wouldn't they? She picked up the phone to call the sergeant who'd questioned her about Earl. She hesitated, the reporter in her saying that maybe she should check what was in the envelope first. Besides, she'd feel stupid if it was nothing. She tore it open and was surprised to see that there was no memory stick in the package. Instead, a single sheet of paper fluttered out. The handwriting was so bad it was almost indecipherable, but she managed to make out that it was a list of some kind. The name scrawled at the top was Antony Earl. His name had a line through it. Second was Mickey Taylor, who'd published Honey Hunter's autobiography as well as Tabitha's tell-all epic, *The Curse of Falcon Bay*. Mickey, who'd blanked her since the Columbia Prize debacle. She frowned. Jake Monroe was the third name. How was the sleazeball from *Falcon Bay* mixed up in all of this? A scrawl above the list was almost impossible to read. Tabitha could make out the phrase "justice for Honey", and the words "killings" "stop" and "suffering". Then a last, chilling sentence: "Vengeance will be mine." Tabitha shuddered again. Her eyes slid to the bottom of the page where there was another barely legible scribble. One last name.

She stared at it for a long time: Tabitha Tate.

CHAPTER 11

Jake

On St Augustine's, Jake Monroe was admiring his baby, La Mirage. At a meeting with the site engineer that morning he had been assured that everything was on schedule, that the glass lifts positioned on each corner of the towering 105-floor structure would be working within days. He had been warned from the beginning that his plans for La Mirage were overly ambitious, and the foundations were not quite as deep as they should be for a building of this size. A snooty architect with a double-barrelled name had suggested that a more modest structure – low rise, discreet – would be more in keeping with the surroundings. 'In any case, I doubt what you're proposing is safe,' he'd said. 'You're looking to build something as big as the Empire State building and you want half of it dug into sandy foundations! And the style of it, all that glass... I know bling's a thing, but we're not in Dubai.'

As it happened, Jake loved Dubai: the flashy hotels with vending machines that dispensed champagne; where no one batted an eye if you ordered caviar and a Bellini for breakfast. He sacked the smart-arse architect on the spot, and got on with finding a team who would understand his vision and do as they were told. It had been surprisingly easy in the end. He was paying good money, and it was clear to all that the planning authorities had been bribed, which soon attracted the right kind of people for the job. Jake hired a project manager and an engineer who'd completed an enormous skyscraper for a notoriously wealthy Sheikh in the Middle East in record time. They shared Jake's distaste for UK building regulations and – crucially – they knew how to get around them. Before you could say seven-star luxury, the foundations were being dug, and the 382-metre building was on its way skywards. Jake couldn't believe how fast it was all happening. Now he needed to start throwing ideas around with Candy for a fabulous launch. He had dreams of creating a wall of fire and a frozen waterfall in the vast lobby, but couldn't work out how to make it happen. Not for the first time he mourned the loss of Dustin, *Falcon Bay*'s Executive Producer. His replacement had done a good job restoring Dustin's work, and adapting it for a theme park audience, but he didn't have the same creative flair. Dustin had always been incredible at turning a crazy idea into reality, using animatronic props, or the magic of CGI technology. Perhaps Jake should have tried harder to keep him when he handed in his notice months ago, but then he never had much time for whiny employees who got above their station.

He looked up. Candy was heading his way. She was wearing a trouser suit in the kind of electric blue that hurt his eyes, with some of her blonde hair peeping out from underneath her jazzy head scarf. Her stiletto heels, utterly unsuitable for a building site, were slowing her down.

Jake gave her an appraising look. 'I take it Elizabeth Taylor's back in fashion.'

Candy frowned. 'Who?'

Jake flushed. It was infuriating how she always managed to make him feel ancient.

Candy's cool blue eyes bored into him. 'I have no idea what you're talking about,' she said, but her mouth twitched.

Jake glared at her. He could never tell if she was joking or not. She had a real attitude on her sometimes. Time of the month, he supposed.

'What are you doing out here, anyway?' he asked.

'You're not answering your phone,' she said sharply.

Jake shrugged. He was his own boss now, and he decided what phone calls to make or to answer. The world of TV with its schedules and meetings, its whingeing actors and moaning execs, its daily crises and fires to put out, was well and truly behind him, and it felt fucking fantastic.

He gazed lovingly up at the glass tower growing in stature above them. 'What do you think?' he asked Candy.

'Great,' she said, scrolling through her phone, not looking up.

'I hope you can muster a little more enthusiasm when it comes to selling this to the press,' he snapped, annoyed.

'Have you seen the Honey Hunter story in the States?' Candy asked.

Jake shrugged. The last thing he wanted to be reminded of was Honey. He still felt bad about enabling her slide back into alcoholism ahead of making her debut on *Falcon Bay*.

He could have done something – checked her into a clinic or whatever – but instead he kept on fucking her. Until she finally broke, and ran off to LA instead of making her much-anticipated appearance on screen. Still, he told himself, it wasn't as if he'd made her hit the bottle. It was her choice.

He arranged his features into an expression of bland interest. 'Why, what's Honey done?'

'She hasn't done anything. She's still in hiding, but look – its on TV. All the major news channels received the same clip in their mail boxes. Watch this.' She held up her phone and clicked 'play'.

Honey Hunter appeared on the screen, looking bereft and lovely, her makeup a work of art, her voice full of pleading. Jake thought she looked just as fuckable as ever, and reflected that whoever the lighting director was had done a terrific job. She looked radiant, glowing, nowhere near the fifty-something she actually was.

'I have been informed that a man has been murdered in the most shocking circumstances,' she said, her eyes brimming with tears, 'and that the person responsible for taking his life claims to be doing so on my behalf.' She paused, blinked, and looked up again. 'I can only say how horrified I am to think a life has been taken in my name.' A single tear rolled down her flawless cheek. 'I appeal to whoever is doing this to stop right now before any more lives are lost. Please, whoever you are, turn yourself in so that you can receive the help you need.' Her voice softened. 'I know you think what you're doing is for me, but I am opposed to all violence. In any form. It is anathema to me. So please, if you truly want to help, let there be no more of this senseless killing. I beg you.'

It was an eloquent, polished speech, delivered with just the right amount of concern, shock and bewilderment. Jake figured there was no way Honey had written it herself. He turned to Candy.

'So what? I mean it sounds horrible – a nutcase in LA bumping people off in her name – but what's it got to do with me?'

Candy hesitated before she answered. 'There's a list of people who've hurt Honey. All the people linked to Honey's downfall.' She paused. 'They're calling it a hit list. It's just been leaked to the press.' She took a breath. 'And you're on it.'

Jake flinched. It was a moment before he felt able to speak. 'Me?'

Candy was watching him. 'You've gone pale, are you OK?'

'Why would I be on a list?' Jake said, feeling frantic all of a sudden. 'What am I supposed to have done?'

Candy studied her phone screen for a moment. 'It doesn't say. But the first two people on the list are dead. Nurses from that horrible clinic Honey went to after she left here. You didn't have anything to do with sending her there, did you?'

'No!' Jake's voice had risen to a shout. 'Of course not! I knew nothing about what she was planning. She left without a word to me or to anyone, dropped us right in it. Just left a post-it note on the desk saying "I'm sorry. I can't. Don't hate me."' He gave Candy a defiant look. 'Let's not forget it was thanks to her running off that Madeline ended up dead!'

If only Honey had showed up for her *Falcon Bay* debut, Madeline would never have taken on the role herself, quite literally stepping into Honey's shoes and gate-crashing the scene with Catherine. And if Madeline hadn't appeared in the scene, she would never have tripped and landed in the water, her life snatched away by the shark she herself had insisted they use on the show. Jake had tried to warn her against using a real shark – tried to persuade her that their senior technician, Dustin, could make a CGI one that looked identical – but she wouldn't have it. Well, that had certainly backfired. Although then again, Madeline's death was the reason his ex-wife Amanda and her hareem of HRT-riddled banshees were now banged up in jail, and also the reason that he was now the fabulously wealthy owner of St Augustine's. Every cloud, he told himself.

Candy was still scrolling through the article. 'So far, all the victims have been in LA, so maybe you don't have to worry,' she shrugged. 'I just thought I'd mention it.'

'Thanks,' he said stiffly, already thinking about how he might beef up security on the island without putting off the thousands of tourists who visited the Great White Death Experience every day to make memories, and line Jake's pockets.

Jake gazed out to sea where a sailing boat tacked around the bay. He'd always wanted to learn to sail, but had never got round to it. Perhaps he would now, get himself a luxury sloop and hunker down on it. It might be safer than living on the island.

'These killings, they're brutal,' Candy said, with some relish. 'The police aren't revealing all the details but from what I can gather there's an element of... mutilation.' She allowed her gaze to drop to his groin and linger there. 'The killer scratches something on their forehead and then takes a body part. I mean, it's horrific. The killer chops off their—'

'Alright, alright,' Jake interrupted, uneasy. 'As you say, it's thousands of miles away, I don't suppose we need to get too worked up.'

'Why do you think you're on that list?' Candy persisted. 'What happened with Honey?'

'Nothing happened with Honey. What are you getting at?'

She held his gaze, waited for him to say more. Jake stayed silent.

'What went on, Jake? Were you fucking her?' Her eyes stayed on him.

He looked away, muttered something inaudible.

'Was she drinking? Before she went AWOL from the show?'

'She was drinking before she even got back on the island,' he snapped.

Candy gasped. 'And you did nothing? You didn't tell anyone? The production team could have intervened if you'd just got the poor woman some help.'

'I'm hardly an expert in addiction, how was I supposed to know what to do?' It sounded feeble even to him.

The look on Candy's face was pure contempt. 'Really? That's your defence? Not good enough, Jake.' She pointed a talon in his face. 'You enabled a recovering alcoholic to slide back into addiction. I think we've discovered why you're on the list.'

Jake refused to meet her eye. Everything would be fine as long as people thought that the reason he was on that list was just because of the booze.

CHAPTER 12

Sheena

In the grounds of Jersey's La Croix prison, Sheena, Farrah, Helen and Amanda had gathered next to a bare-looking patch of earth once home to soft fruits and runner beans.

Farrah dug a spade into the ground and leaned on it. 'Remind me why we're out here weeding when we could be inside working on our defence?'

'It's the only way we can guarantee privacy,' Sheena told her, dragging a rake across the soil.

Farrah rolled her eyes. 'For fuck's sake. We're running out of time. In a week from now Catherine intends to stand up in court and tell the world we bumped off Ross Owen.'

'We didn't,' Amanda protested. 'It was an accident.'

'Hardly accidental when we decided to launch him into the English Channel,' Helen said, giving Sheena a pointed look.

'Ross was a threat,' Sheena said coolly. 'To all of us.'

'I wanted to call the police, remember,' Helen said.

'Oh, and that would really have helped,' Sheena snapped.

'Get a grip, Helen. You'd slapped him, remember. Our DNA was all over him.'

'I wasn't the only one.' Helen aimed a foul look at Farrah.

Farrah looked daggers at her. 'He was drunk, abusive. Asking for it.'

'Any detective worth their salt could have made a case for every one of us having our reasons for wanting rid of him,' Sheena said.

Amanda cleared her throat. 'Well, that's not exactly true.'

The others turned to face her. She bent and retrieved a handful of withered plants and dropped them into the garden waste bag before putting down her trowel. 'I wasn't even there. I don't see why Catherine would want to make me a part of it.'

Helen gasped. 'You definitely had a run-in with him that night! Came to blows if I remember rightly.'

'Actually, he ran into me,' Amanda said. 'Grabbed me and caught himself on my bracelet.' Her Robert Lee Morris cuff. It had drawn blood. 'I didn't actually touch him.'

Sheena looked at Helen, who was pink with fury. Farrah was frowning, an expression of outrage mixed with disbelief. Amanda kept her eyes fixed on the ground. She dug around in the soil for a moment before looking up at her friends. 'And I don't see why I should carry the can for any of it. I've got Olivia to think about. And Dan. There's too much at stake, I can't risk losing them.'

Farrah grabbed at her shoulder. 'And what about me? I'm a mother too! I've just as much to lose!'

'Oh, I see where this is going.' Helen was incensed. 'Those of us who don't have children don't matter as much? Unbe-fucking-lievable!'

'Let's all calm down and think clearly,' Sheena said. She knelt down and unearthed a bulb, pressed it back into the soil. 'As you all know, I've been working on Catherine. I hoped our relationship, all the years of loyalty I've shown her, would count for something. But she won't budge. So we have to do something drastic.'

'What exactly do you mean by that?' Farrah said.

Sheena sighed. 'We can't just sit back and let her wreck our lives all over again. Agreed?'

She waited a moment. 'Because, make no mistake, that's what she plans to do. Whatever's going on inside her head, she's clearly gearing up for some dramatic *Silks*-style big reveal.'

Sheena pushed her trowel into the border, yanked hard at a withered root and tossed it onto a small pile. She stood up and beckoned the others closer. 'Which is why we have to silence her. For good.'

'You want us to commit murder? In jail?' Helen scoffed.

'Keep your voice down, Helen!' Farrah said sharply.

No one spoke for a moment.

Helen was forthright. 'And how exactly do you suggest we do that?'

Sheena explained her plan, and there was a long pause.

Eventually, Farrah spoke. 'I'm in. It's the only way I'll see my son again.'

She caught Helen's look. 'Oh, don't be so prim and proper, it's our best chance. Our only chance right now. We've no idea what Catherine might say when she gets on the stand.' She took a deep breath. 'At the risk of causing offence, all I care about is my baby. Anything that gives me the best shot of getting home, and getting my child back, is alright with me.'

After a lengthy silence, Helen said, 'I think Sheena's right. It's our only way out.'

Amanda, who'd returned to digging her trowel into the earth, turning the soil over with no apparent purpose, looked up. She didn't know what to do. If Catherine successfully accused them of killing Ross Owen, she and her friends could end up in prison for ever. But if she went along with Sheena's plan, she'd be making a cold-blooded decision to end the life of a close friend. Could she live with the knowledge of what they'd done? Could she conceal such a dreadful secret from Dan, who was so loving and trusting? From Olivia, who was so innocent? How, with blood on her hands, would she manage to raise her daughter? She would be worse than Jake, she realised. 'I can't believe you agree with this,' she said to Helen.

'You're not the only one who wants their life back,' Helen told her.

Sheena nodded. 'Me, too. And I'm willing to take care of the… practicalities.' Thanks to Kayleigh, she had enough Temazepam stashed away to do the job.

'You're talking like it's nothing,' Amanda said, appalled. 'As if you're booking a cab! The methods you're using to kill Catherine are more than just a *practicality*. Please, for God's sake, just stop for a second, will you, and think about it?' Her voice dropped to a whisper. 'We're talking about murder. Of our friend!'

'Some friend she is,' sneered Helen, 'willing to bring us all down for fucking helping her.'

Sheena pointed a purple fingernail at Helen. 'Stop it! Let's not fall apart now, girls. We have to stick together. Look, it's the worst decision I've ever had to make but it's the only one I can live with.' Her voiced hardened. 'I'm not going to lose everything because Catherine's had some kind of religious awakening.'

'Amen,' Helen said.

'About fucking time,' Farrah nodded.

'Won't it look suspicious?' Amanda said. 'On the eve of going to court, Catherine dies.'

'People die in prison all the time,' Sheena said. 'Suicide or accident. And she does have a history of popping pills. Maybe, having found God, the guilt of failing to save Madeline was too much for her conscience to bear. Who knows what they'll think? They can speculate all they like but I can't see why it would come back on any of us. Not if we handle it right.'

Amanda shook her head. 'I can't accept that this is the only way.'

'Fine,' Farrah said. 'Why don't you think of something, then, Snow White? We're all ears.'

'I could speak to Catherine, try and talk her round...'

Farrah snorted. 'That's your big idea, is it?'

Helen took Amanda by the shoulders and brought her face close to hers. 'Haven't you been listening?' she hissed. 'Sheena's tried that. Catherine's on a fucking mission to expose us – and we're the only ones who can stop her!'

She let go of Amanda, and the women all fell silent.

Amanda, shaken, stared at the ground where a worm, disturbed by her digging, was trying to burrow its way out of sight. Finally, she spoke. Her voice was small. 'I'm in.'

CHAPTER 13

Jake

A storm was coming. Jake stood on the terrace of his villa staring out to sea, the air heavy and humid, the sky threatening, streaked with grey. The wind was getting up, catching at the tops of the trees, making the leaves rustle. A security light came on in the garden and he jumped. Someone was out there. He craned to see, his heart beating too fast all of a sudden, as his kids' nanny, Lauren, stepped onto the lawn, talking into her mobile. Relief flooded through him.

What Candy had said about Honey Hunter and the so-called hit list gnawed away at him. It was outrageous that his name should be mixed up in all this. Hadn't he done everything he could for Honey? Handed her a gold-plated opportunity to get her non-existent acting career back on track? It was hardly his fault if she chose to throw it away and drown herself in booze. Or if she chose to run away and end up in the arms of some nutter.

The sky flashed bright, a jagged bolt of lightning over the sea. A low growl filled the air. Thunder. Jake padded back into the kitchen and topped up his wine, the bottle done. He took another from the fridge, in the mood to get tipsy. When he looked up Lauren was hovering in the doorway.

'I took a call for you,' she said. 'On the house phone.' Jake frowned. 'It was Candy. She says she needs to see you, it's urgent.'

'Why didn't she call me?'

'She tried, she said, but you didn't pick up.'

Jake glanced at his phone. Strange. No missed calls.

'She wants to meet you on the jetty.'

'When?'

'Now.' It was late, almost 10 p.m. 'She said it's something that can't wait – but she wouldn't tell me what it was.'

*

Jake headed out in a foul mood. The wind had strengthened, and a few drops of rain were falling from the air. He had one of his good leather jackets on. If the heavens opened it would be ruined. What was Candy playing at, dragging him out like this? Was she going to try and blackmail him about Honey? Let her. She'd soon realise he was more than a match for an amateur like her.

Fat drops of rain splattered his hair and his face. He cut through the deserted theme park, stumbling slightly in his Cuban heels as he approached the wooden beach bar where so many of *Falcon Bay*'s dramas had once played out. He felt a bit drunk. He'd had cocktails, a bottle of Margaux and a couple of brandies over dinner with his producer, and it was all making him feel woozy. Cursing Candy, he staggered on towards the jetty, the rain now almost horizontal, whipping off the sea, seeping into his clothing. His leather jacket, a new Belstaff Gangster, was soaked. He shivered. Usually the island he had spent so much time on felt like a familiar haven, an old friend. But tonight, standing by its waters in the dark, swaying slightly from all the booze in his system, he felt ill at ease. He glanced about him, called out Candy's name. There was no answer. The wind gusted, almost lifting him off his feet and into the rolling waves. He swore. 'Where the fuck are you?' he yelled.

Behind him, a husky female voice said, 'Mind you don't go too close to the edge, Jake. I'd hate to see you fall in.'

He spun around and peered into the darkness, trying to locate the voice. Strange. It didn't sound like Candy, with her distinctive Antipodean twang. Was she playing a prank on him? 'If this is your idea of a joke, Candy, I'm not finding it funny.'

The voice laughed, a hard, mirthless sound. 'Oh, it's no joke, Jake.'

The wind blew hard, scattering her words. He craned his neck, straining to catch a glimpse of her. His eyes finally adjusted to the dark, and a figure emerged from the shadows.

'OK, you've had your fun. What's going on?' He waited for an answer. Silence. 'If this is about Honey Hunter, I already told you, that's nothing to do with me. Stop trying to spook me out, or else you can pack your stuff and get off my island tonight.' His voice sounded genuinely annoyed.

When she laughed again, the sound clicked in his mind. He recognised that deep, mirthless laugh – and it wasn't Candy's. For a second, Jake froze. Then he let out a gasp of surprise. A Madeline Kane automated robot was moving towards him, slinking through the shadows like a cat. He watched, mesmerised. It was creepy but impressive. Was that why Candy had got him down here? To see an upgraded Madeline Kane robot in motion? It looked – and sounded – utterly lifelike.

'Wow!' he said as he approached it, and called out to Candy one more time. No doubt she was watching in the dark, wanting a raise for her work. 'OK, very impressive,' he said with a smile, already calculating how much he could put the admission prices up with this new invention. But as he reached out to touch it, it jerked away suddenly, one arm flailing out and slapping him hard across the face.

'Don't you fucking touch me!' it hissed.

'What the fuck…' Jake mouthed. His legs turned to jelly, and his cheek began to sting.

'You look like you've seen a ghost,' said the robot mockingly, as their eyes met.

He stared at the creature, fearing for his sanity. Perhaps he was hallucinating? He'd smoked some weed earlier – no more than usual, but maybe this was some sort of bad trip?

There was a pause which seemed to last an eternity before it spoke again.

'I get it, it's a shock.' Its hand rested on his arm and he almost jumped out of his skin. The hand was warm on his cold arm, just like a real human. He screwed his eyes closed and resolved to change his dealer as soon as possible – whatever he had smoked must have had something freaky in it. Silence fell, and after a couple of beats he reluctantly opened his eyes. The robot's sharp eyes and contemptuous smile were just inches away from his face. He allowed his gaze to drop down, taking in the clinging dress that accentuated her curves. He knew that the animatrons were exact reproductions, intended to make visitors feel they were looking at the real thing, but this felt different. There was something alive in the way the wind whipped at her raven-black hair, the way her eyes glittered. She looked wild, dangerous. A Medusa.

'I'm not one of your disgusting bots. And I'm not a ghost Jake, I'm real. Flesh and blood. Your worst nightmare come back to haunt you.'

Reality hit him like a truck. This was no doll.

'But… it… can't be… You're dead…' Jake stuttered.

She moved right up to him, her face almost touching his, her breath warm on his cheek. 'Now you're starting to get it.' She tilted her head on one side. 'Mad-e-line. Remember me?'

He swallowed. 'But how… I saw you. That night… The shark.'

She gazed at him, amused. 'Ah, yes. The magic of the television edit. Even when it was supposed to be live.' She smirked.

Jake's head was spinning. He felt sick. The lobster he'd had for dinner, followed by Danish pastries, swilled in his gut, bathed in Margaux. If that lot came up now it would make quite a mess.

'But I saw you die,' he tried again.

'You and the world saw what I wanted you to see. What you missed was me dropping into the second safety tank,' she said. 'And what you and the viewers – not to mention that sanctimonious ex-wife of yours and her edit-suite cronies

– didn't notice was at that very moment, the live action switched to smart CGI footage.' Her full glossy lips parted in a smile. 'A sleight of hand from an insider that worked even better than I hoped.'

Jake was reeling, trying to replay the live episode in his mind.

'Let me save you the brain ache, God knows you don't have much to work with. It was all done through the power of distraction, Jake,' she replied. 'And you and the whole world fell for it'.

For once, Jake was speechless as his mind whirred. How had she pulled off such an audacious trick? And who had the skills – and the inclination – to help her?

Madeline took a triumphant step back. It looked like she was enjoying the moment, congratulating herself on just how well her plan had succeeded.

Jake finally found his voice.

'But… but nobody knew you were going to play Honey's role in the live finale. That was a last minute substitution.'

'Ah, Jake. I'd been plotting it since I arrived on St Augustine's. I knew I wouldn't be able to control everything, so I came up with several different plans: one for each eventuality but the same outcome: me, live on screen, confronting that snake Catherine Belle about how she ruined my life when I was a child. In the end, the ruses I'd invented to ensure Honey never made it on set were never needed. Honey ran off to LA, playing right into my hands.'

'But the shark… The body… The police…' he stuttered.

'Ah yes,' she laughed again, genuinely enjoying herself. 'Let's take them one by one, shall we? Jaws first.'

'You'll remember that when I imported the Great White, our insurers insisted on a back-up, a failsafe, to be used in the event of any health and safety breach? And you and the team – now savour this, Jake, because it's the only compliment you're getting – had already created an excellent CGI shark scene. I knew that for the right price, I only needed one ally in place, ready to switch the feed to the fake footage at the perfect moment.'

Jake's head was spinning. Who on *Falcon Bay* would have that level of Machiavellian plotting in them?

Madeline laughed. 'Let's move this along shall we? Save what's left of your grey matter. As for the body and the police – I'm amazed you haven't figured it out already Jake. We're on a private island, with private police, private hospital and a private coroner. She gestured to Jake's half-built skyscraper in the distance. 'Haven't you found recently that all this privacy makes money very persuasive, when it comes to getting what you want on my island?'

The mention of La Mirage seemed to shock Jake's brain back into action. Madeline might have thrown him for the biggest loop in his life, but he wasn't going to let her threaten his pride and joy. He took a step back, and eyed Madeline from head to toe.

'I think you'll find it's my island,' he replied firmly. 'Chad gifted his shares in it to me.'

'They were my shares,' she snarled, a hint of perfect teeth flashing in anger, 'and it's my island. What the fuck were you thinking turning it into a freak show?'

'I don't need to explain myself to you. After all, you don't exist anymore. And, as impressive as all this is – and I'll give you that, it's a plot twist worthy of *Falcon Bay* itself – you have a big problem.'

Madeline looked at him contemptuously. 'Which is?'

Jake smiled. 'The whole world thinks you're dead, and your precious husband does too. I imagine you want him to know you're alive, but how can you? Soon the women you hate most in the world will be tried for your murder. The minute anyone knows you're alive, they'll be freed, and you – my undead darling – will be left rotting in a cell instead of them. How will you and Chad be reunited then, which I'm guessing is your next plan?'

Madeline's face twitched at the mention of Chad.

'And even if he does find you, how do you know he'll forgive you? Those of us who haven't been hiding in a hole for the last year know that you've broken his heart so completely he's gone totally off-grid. So, yes. If you want to announce you've risen from the dead, you'll be royally fucked. And not in the sort of way I'd have enjoyed, if you weren't so faithful to that stupid man you claimed to love so much.'

Madeline was silent. Sensing he had regained the upper hand, but with his stomach still in knots at what was one of the most bizarre nights of his life, Jake barrelled on. 'So, I suggest you crawl back to wherever you've been hiding and we pretend this never happened. I won't tell anyone – I mean, who would believe that you've been alive all this time?' He let out a laugh as he pushed past her roughly and started walking back towards the beach.

Madeline stood perfectly still, the moonlight highlighting her beautiful face, a single tear welling up in her stunning green eyes.

Without turning around, Jake added a kicker. 'Just stay dead.'

Madeline watched him walk out of sight then turned her eyes back to the sea. The waves crashed, and something inside her broke. Her breath came in short, painful gasps as the reality of what she had done sunk in. She had fled from the man she loved because she couldn't bear for him to discover her secret past. She had feared that once Chad realised that she had been born in the wrong body, he – and the rest of the world – would shun her. It was only when reading the article in France that she had finally understood the truth: Chad had always known her secret. And he loved her anyway. He had stated it publicly, and proudly. And now to hear from Jake that Chad had disappeared! She closed her eyes and let out a wail. The island would always be in her heart, but she could live without it. She couldn't live without Chad.

She let the sobs come until she felt composed. She wiped the last tear from her eye and felt icy resolve fill her veins once more. Jake would pay for humiliating her, and she would find a way to track down Chad and convince him to understand why she had done what she had. She prayed to the sky above that he would forgive her. She'd do anything to earn back his love.

Jake's shadow had left the boardwalk, but she spoke aloud to him nonetheless.

'When I'm done with you, Jake, you'll wish I really was dead.'

PART 2

CHAPTER 14

Jake

Jake woke up with a splitting headache. He ordered the housekeeper to close the curtains to keep out the light, and prepare him a three-egg omelette for breakfast. Then he called Candy and told her to reschedule his day.

'Are you ill?' she said, not sounding the least bit sympathetic.

As well as the headache, he had thrown up – although that was more to do with the vast quantity of alcohol he'd got through the night before and the richness of the steak and lobster he had guzzled. But he also felt feverish.

'I'm definitely coming down with something,' he told her.

'Can you get out of bed?' Candy asked. 'Because there's a journalist from *Le Monde* coming in this morning, in around,' she checked her watch and tutted impatiently, 'two hours, which I had to move heaven and earth to set up.' She was silent a moment. 'Have a shower,' she instructed, her voice brisk. 'Do the Wim Hof Method: a blast of freezing water for the last sixty seconds at least. Just stand there until you feel like screaming. And get some coffee inside you. You'll feel just fine in no time.'

He could be dying for all she knew. Ordering him around like she was in charge, bossy little bitch.

'Now just a second…' he began.

Candy cut him dead. 'See you at 9 a.m. sharp.'

He sighed loudly, got out of bed and went into the bathroom. He needed a comforting shower, hot. Screw Wim Hof and his fucking Method.

As sharp needles of scorching water prickled his skin, the events of the night before clicked around inside his head.

Madeline Kane.

Back from the dead.

He struggled to take it in. How had she faked her death? She'd said she had help on the inside – but from who? And where had she been hiding all this time? It couldn't be the UK. Her face had been splashed across too many newspapers for that. He felt suddenly nauseous as he considered how much time she would have had in exile, with nothing to do but plot her revenge on him. What if everything he was working on to transform St Augustine's was about to come crashing down? An image of his glorious skyscraper in ruins came to him and he almost cried out. Fucking bitch.

He wouldn't let it happen.

He shut off the water, grabbed a towel and opened the French windows to let the sun stream in. Now, with the sound of birdsong in the air, the sky a glorious sapphire blue, what had unfolded between them in the rain and the wind last night seemed faded and unreal. He perked up further as he admired his own reflection in the mirror, watching him dry himself. His luscious blond hair was attractively flecked with grey, his blue eyes still twinkled above a smile that was both warm and filthy. No one would guess he was in his sixties. He felt some of his energy come back to his limbs, and his determination hardened. Madeline couldn't take the island from him even if she wanted to. Chad had gifted him those shares in St Augustine's, and the contract was watertight. He finger-gunned his reflection and sauntered over to the wardrobe to get dressed.

His phone buzzed on the bedside table, and he picked it up. He had a new WhatsApp. He opened the chat, from a number and a message format he didn't recognise. It said 'Photo (1)' which he clicked, and was confronted with a photo of sharp red fingernails clutching a piece of paper with the word "contract" written on it. He shut the message, not realising it had been sent as a disappearing photo and he couldn't click on it again. Damn it. His phone buzzed again, with another photo message of a piece of paper. This time it read:

> You stole my island and I can take it back any time I
> want.

Jake screenshotted the message, but when he went to his camera roll there was a message about how you can't screenshot disappearing photos. He knew who this was now. He saved her number as MK. He wrote a reply:

> Jake: Bitch

She continued messaging him by taking a snap of a piece of paper she'd written on, and sending it as a disappearing photo.

MK: Check your contract. It's only your island if I'm dead.
And I'm very much alive.

Jake recovered some of his composure. He would call her bluff. That was the only way to deal with a fucking madwoman like this.

Jake: You faked your death. I could tell the authorities
and send you straight to prison.
MK: If you do that I'll bring you down with me. You see,
I know your secret...

Jake hated that his heart-rate sped up while he waited for the next message to come through. What did she know? He focused his eyes on the phone screen, and held his breath.

MK: I know what you did to Honey Hunter...

Jake let out a sigh of relief. OK, the booze and drugs he had shared with Honey didn't paint him in the best light, but he was far from the only one who had a hand in her downward spiral. Ultimately, Honey had to be responsible for her own addictions.

But the messages were still coming:

MK: Not just the booze...
MK: Not just the drugs...

Here she left a pause just long enough for Jake to wonder if she was bluffing, trying to get him to confess to something more. After all, how could she know what he did? Unless Madeline had installed cameras inside the private houses on *Falcon Bay*, and that would be completely illegal, wouldn't it? He stayed silent.

MK: I know what you did before she fled to Dr Durand.

Jake felt suddenly cold and clammy.

MK: And if you don't give back the island...
MK: I'll tell the world.

Jake swore loudly, and threw the phone across the room so hard it bounced off the mirror, leaving a large crack where he had smiled at his reflection just minutes earlier.

What the fuck was he going to do now?

He had to keep his cool for the interview about La Mirage, so he took three deep breaths, smoothed La Prairie cream onto his forehead and slipped into a dark navy Paul Smith shirt. On the leather desk in the study, a pile of official-looking letters awaited his attention. One seemed to be stamped by St Helier Police. Most likely some busybody had complained about the lack of planning consultation for La Mirage. He swept them into a drawer – he would deal with them later. Then he picked up the villa's landline, and speed-dialled his lawyer.

CHAPTER 15

Tabitha

Tabitha strutted into the wood panelled bar in Chateau Marmont, turning heads in her shocking pink Dolce and Gabbana trouser suit. She eyed Mickey Taylor from across the room. Despite their tumultuous history, she couldn't deny the grudging respect she had for the publisher of Fonda Books. Like her, he was an outsider who had had to fight for his career, a self-made man with a no-bullshit attitude. Mickey stood up as she approached the table, pulling out a chair for her. His outfit, white jeans and a garish striped blazer with oversized gold buttons, made him look ridiculous. But she supposed that, like her, he dressed to stand out.

'Nice jacket,' she said sarcastically.

His face lit up. 'Got it on Melrose. Clothes for the older gent who wants to make a statement, according to the bloke in the shop. A celebration of longevity if you like – of growing old disgracefully. "Do not go gentle into that good night" and all that. Dylan Thomas?'

She gave him a blank look.

'Ah, you're much too young to worry about the dying of the light. Only oldies like me obsess about death. Let's have a drink.' Mickey signalled to the waiter, and two Negronis appeared on the polished mahogany tabletop.

'So,' said Mickey, raising his glass, 'Quite the phenomenon at the moment, aren't you?'

Tabitha bristled. 'Hardly. Haven't you heard? I've been cancelled.'

Mickey brushed off her concerns by holding up a cheque. Tabitha could make out a three, followed by a lot of zeros. 'Your royalties for *The Curse of Falcon Bay* are rolling in – this is a three million quid cheque! Forget the haters, sweetheart. They actually make you more money. And speaking of money, I asked you to meet me today because I have a new project for you.'

Tabitha raised an eyebrow. Mickey had shut her out after the Columbia Prize fiasco, and at the time she had sworn never to work with him again. But Mickey had a knack for finding scoops, and she couldn't help being curious. 'What kind of project?'

Mickey leaned forwards, a glint in his eye. 'Can't say too much right now, but let's just say it's another book, and its right up your alley. It involves your friends at *Falcon Bay*, particularly a certain deceased woman, whose life was even more colourful than people would think.'

'Is it Madeline Kane?'

'I couldn't possibly say. I'm meeting a source tonight who needs to confirm a few things to do with this woman's parentage. If I'm right about what the source knows, this book will be explosive with a capital E.'

Despite herself, Tabitha felt a flutter of excitement. She didn't exactly have any friends at *Falcon Bay* – not since she burned her bridges with Candy, anyway – but she wasn't about to tell Mickey that.

'I'll do a bit of research into Madeline Kane's past, just in case,' she said with a wink. 'Is there budget to send me over to St Augustine's?'

'You bet,' Mickey replied. 'This is a big one. Fly over tomorrow, if you like, and expense it afterwards. I'll phone you in the afternoon with the results of tonight's meeting.'

Tabitha was tingling with excitement. It had been a while since she'd been on the trail of a properly juicy story. Even though her previous one had ended in disaster for her, she was still proud of the book she had written. 'Any news from Honey?' she asked next, trying to sound casual. 'Have you managed to get hold of her?'

Mickey looked briefly guilty, like he was keeping a secret from her. Tabitha wondered if he felt sorry for pushing the actress into the addictive spiral which ended in a rehab centre run by a doctor who drugged her and abused her. Only Mickey would think it was a good idea to lie to a recovering alcoholic that 'just one glass won't hurt.' He made her gulp champagne at a book signing so the paparazzi could get their pictures. And only Mickey would pay a writer a small fortune to track down his missing star and then write about her horrific experience at the hands of the man the tabloids had called 'The Psycho Physician'. In hindsight, Tabitha should never have allowed Mickey to persuade her to make Honey's story the focus of *The Curse of Falcon Bay*, instead of the deaths of Ross Owen and Madeline Kane. She should have been more wary of the evil flash in Mickey's eyes when Tabitha first told him that she'd found Honey, and described how Honey had been kidnapped, tortured, and was close to death. But the lure of the story had proved too much for Tabitha. She had allowed herself to be persuaded to throw human decency out of the window, and watch the book fly off the shelves. And now Tabitha and Mickey had been watching the royalties roll in, while Honey had disappeared in the wake of her trauma.

'I've been trying to track Honey down myself,' Tabitha said. 'I'm desperate to apologise for what I did. For what we did. We allowed the publication of *The Curse of Falcon Bay* to come before everything else. But she clearly hates me. She won't accept my apology. Won't even return my calls.'

Mickey took a long swallow of his drink, dabbed at his mouth with a napkin bearing the Chateau Marmont crest. 'Honey's a sweetheart. She doesn't hate anyone, even you. Honestly, she wouldn't hurt a fly. That psycho vigilante has got it all wrong if he's killing in her name. But look, back to this new project: the woman whose past I want you to dig into. I'm excited, and I think the book's perfect for you. It's not just about one person, it's about secrets, lies, cover-ups… the whole *Falcon Bay* shebang. I'll be in touch straight after my meeting tonight.'

'Going anywhere fancy?' the reporter in Tabitha was curious.

'Just some villa up in the hills,' he said, a touch too casually. 'Owned by some flash producer, runs one of the major studios.' He gave Tabitha a self-deprecating shrug, as if to say it was beyond him to understand why one of the studio bosses in LA would want to host a meeting between him and a source. Something about his performance seemed off, and Tabitha gave him a suspicious look.

'Trust me, Tabitha, you're a great reporter and this book I want you to write? It's got everything. Drama, suspense, twists, secrets, and a ton of heart. I'll brief you fully as soon as I'm done with tonight's meeting. So long as this source gives me what I'm hoping for, you and me are going to get even richer than we did from Honey.'

Tabitha took another sip of her cocktail and started to unwind. The buzz of alcohol was mingling pleasingly with the low murmur of the chic clientele of the Marmont. Wasn't that Madonna sitting over there in a discreetly darkened corner? She had to admit, it felt good to be back among people that mattered. And she knew it would feel damn good to be on the trail of a juicy story again. She needed a distraction from the haunting image of Antony Earl's mutilated face. Plus, she was pretty certain, based on the little Mickey had told her, that it was indeed about Madeline Kane. Some kind of explosive revelation about her childhood? Her parentage? Even if Mickey couldn't tell her more until after his meeting, she'd start digging around right away.

She raised her glass to Mickey and flashed him a smile. She hadn't forgiven him for dropping her when she got cancelled, but she sensed this was his way of making amends. And she trusted him to know a good story when he saw one. 'Great to be in business again.'

CHAPTER 16

Sheena

Among the drably dressed visitors at La Croix Prison, Riley Clarke's lime green suit stood out like a peacock in a flock of pigeons. Sheena rolled up her grey prison-issue sweater sleeves and looked her lawyer in the eye. Riley was the most determined woman Sheena knew, and her eyes were narrow and dangerous, flecked with amber to match her flame-coloured spiky hair.

'Well, what do you think? Can you make Chad pay up?' Always hedging her bets, Sheena had employed two lawyers. Eva Hope to fight the charge of conspiracy to pervert the course of justice, and Riley Clarke — a ferocious negotiator, as famous for her clownish suits as for her near 100% win-rate — to sue Chad Kane for invading her privacy by recording her incriminating conversation with Catherine.

'He's in the wrong, without question,' Riley said, folding one milk-white hand over the other. 'Chad Kane lured you into a trap, subjected you to intrusive and covert surveillance without your knowledge, and then broadcast it on TV to an audience of millions. It's a clear breach of privacy law.'

Sheena nodded, grateful for Riley's confidence. She had first met the lawyer years ago, emotionally shredded after the Ed Nichols abuse scandal had destroyed her career. It was Riley who had secured her a huge financial settlement, helped her get back on her feet.

'Now, don't panic,' Riley said. 'But Chad's gone missing. I reached out to his legal team and they say he took off after the final episode of *Falcon Bay* went live. They say he went off for a digital detox a year ago, to help him cope with grief. He never said how long he'd be away – but nobody's heard from him since.'

'What the fuck?' Sheena grabbed Riley's arm, her sharp nails digging into the flesh. 'How can we sue Chad if he's not there?'

'I told you not to worry,' Riley said, removing Sheena's hand. 'We've pivoted. We're now suing the Kane Foundation, not Chad personally. It's worth billions, and his sister is still at the helm. Trust me, you'll get a much better pay-out this way, and I'm confident we have a strong case. You and your friends are about to be seriously, seriously rich. So you'd better make sure you get off on your other charge,' she flashed a predatory smile, 'or you'll be pretty limited on where you can spend it.'

*

Sheena went outside to think. She breathed in the sea-scented air, and started walking along the woodland path, cutting up through the trees. A blackbird scurried out in front of her, sending up an alarm call. Ahead, perched high up in a sycamore, two crows flapped and screeched at one another. She breathed in the cool, still air. Her mind was racing. In just three days they'd be in court, charged with conspiracy to pervert the course of justice for the investigation into Madeline's death. The evidence was circumstantial, and their characters were good: most likely, they'd be told to go and clean the graffiti off a bus shelter. Meanwhile, her lawyer was sure they could get a fat pay-out from the Kane foundation – the kind that would allow them all to get on with their lives.

This was all on the assumption that nothing else would come to light, such as Catherine telling the world that she pushed Ross Owen off a cliff, Sheena tampered with the body, and Helen and Farrah hid crucial evidence of the circumstances of his fall.

Sheena felt inside her pocket, and her fingertips brushed against a carefully folded handkerchief. Inside were ten Temazepam pills she'd got from Kayleigh, crushed into a fine powder. The kind of fine powder you could stir into a hot drink – particularly if it had a tot of whisky in it to hide the taste. Sheena took a deep breath in. Was she really going to do this? But she had to. For the good of her friends, as well as for herself. Catherine had to be silenced.

She cut through the rose garden, her heart heavy. The sun was going down, the sky aflame, a brilliant orangey red. She stopped for a moment, reflecting on how few times in recent years she had paused to notice the setting sun, or the sound of birdsong. It was a strange irony that it had taken prison to tune her in to the world. She had spent most of her old life glued to her phone.

'There you are.'

Sheena turned with a start. Catherine was striding towards her. She seemed agitated. Could she know what was about to happen? Sheena braced herself.

'Catherine! I was just thinking about you. It's freezing out here – let's go in and have a hot toddy. Kayleigh smuggled me in some of that single malt I know you like.' Her hand went into her pocket once more, and closed around the Temazepam. Amanda's appalled face flashed into her mind, and she felt suddenly seized with doubt. Could she really end the life of one of her oldest, dearest friends? She chased it away. This was about survival, not just her own, but the others' too.

Once they got to Sheena's room, Catherine sounded as if she was about to cry. 'I need to tell you something,' she said, as Sheena busied herself boiling water in the kettle and slicing wedges from a lemon.

'Sure, what is it?' Sheena asked vaguely. She got out two mugs, one red, one blue, and cast around for the whisky. Where would Kayleigh have hidden it? She felt around under Kayleigh's mattress and her hand closed around a glass neck.

Catherine shook her head. 'Oh, it's nothing,' she said, getting up and switching off the kettle, which had started to whistle. 'I was just thinking – isn't the world wonderful?'

'Stop that!' Sheena snapped, as Catherine spooned honey into each mug, added a lemon wedge, and poured boiling water over both. 'Sorry, I just meant… You sit down and relax. I'll bring you the drink once I've added the best bit!' She brandished the whisky bottle.

Catherine raised an eyebrow, surprised by Sheena's sudden shift in mood, but she sat down at the little table in the corner, and waited for Sheena to join her.

Sheena turned so that her back was between Catherine and the mugs. Her fingers fidgeted with the hanky in her pocket. She would lose her nerve if she didn't do it soon. She needed to keep Catherine talking so she didn't see what she was up to. 'What did you mean before, about the world being wonderful?' Sheena drew the hanky out of her pocket, and tipped its contents quickly into the red mug.

'I had an epiphany,' Catherine said quietly. 'Something Father Padraic said. About justice and retribution.'

Sheena felt a twinge of irritation at the mention of the priest. 'What about it?' she asked, sloshing whisky into both mugs. Catherine took a deep breath. 'He had a sister,' she said. 'She was attacked and raped, and the man who did it got off. The jury believed him when he said it was consensual. He never faced justice.'

'That's terrible,' Sheena said, feeling awful for the girl, but only half listening, focusing instead on stirring the contents of the red mug until the powder had dissolved. She set both drinks down on the table, the red mug close to Catherine, and sat down.

'And then he did it again, to another girl,' Catherine continued, 'and Padraic's sister killed herself because she couldn't cope with the idea that he was still out there. She hadn't been able to stop him.'

Sheena felt anger swell in her stomach. All thoughts of what she was intending to do vanished, displaced by the thought of yet another man committing a hideous crime without ever facing justice. 'I'm so sorry,' she said, putting a hand on Catherine's arm.

'And it made me think,' Catherine said, tears welling up

in her eyes. 'About Ross Owen. About what he did to me.' She raised the red mug towards her lips, and Sheena held her breath. Was she really about to go through with this? But before she had a chance to speak, Catherine looked her directly in the eye, and put the mug down.

'You know, Sheena, I've been so focused on what we did to him, feeling so guilty for our actions. But I've got it all back to front. What matters is what he did to me. Everything we did afterwards was in response to his crime. He deserved everything he got. And you, my friends – my rocks – you helped me! Even though it was a huge risk.'

Sheena felt sudden relief bubble up through her body. She let out a long breath she hadn't known she was holding. 'Oh Catherine, thank God you see that now. Has it changed your mind about what you'll say in court?'

Catherine nodded, wiping away a tear. 'Yes. I won't say a word about Ross Owen. I won't let that snake damage us any more than he already has.' She picked up the mug again, and tilted it towards Sheena like a toast. 'This smells heavenly, darling. Let's drink to us. To friendship!'

Sheena snatched the mug away and laughed nervously. 'Oh darling, silly me, you can't drink from that!' She tipped the contents down the sink and ran the tap. 'It's Kayleigh's mug, she goes ballistic if I use it! Here, share mine.'

As the two women sipped companionably from what was – Sheena congratulated herself – a delicious hot toddy, Sheena offered up a silent prayer of thanks to whoever was listening. For the priest, for his poor sister. And for Catherine and her eleventh-hour epiphany.

Thank God.

CHAPTER 17

Candy

On the terrace at the Heron Café, Candy Dace was typing away on her laptop, drafting a press release about the wall of fire and cascade of ice that would soon grace the lobby of La Mirage, when a shadow fell across her screen. Looking up, she saw Tabitha Tate standing before her, dressed to the nines in a scarlet military-style jacket, cigarette pants, and ankle-strap peep-toe shoes with monstrous heels. They made Tabitha's legs look endless – but quite how she had made it up the hill in them was a mystery. A couple sat on another table, dressed in windcheaters and with binoculars slung around their necks. They twisted around in their seats and gawped at Tabitha as if she were some sort of exotic bird.

Candy glared at her. How dare she turn up on her island, in her favourite bar? Last time they saw each other, Candy was leaking juicy exclusives about the cast and crew of *Falcon Bay* to Tabitha. In return, Tabitha had promised to bring Candy to America, introduce her to all the movers and shakers in LA. Then she had left without a word. Traitorous bitch.

'I thought you were in the States,' she said coldly.

'I was, but now, as you can see, I'm back.' Tabitha grinned at the twitchers on the next-door table, and gave a small bow.

'Sit down, will you?' Candy hissed. 'People are looking.'

She glanced inside the café where Marco was behind the counter, apparently entranced. 'Hey, can I get a coffee?' Tabitha called, turning and aiming a megawatt smile at him. 'Cappuccino, please. Oat milk if you have it.'

Candy's eyes were like daggers. 'Fuck off, Tabitha. I don't want to speak to you.'

Tabitha's expression became serious. 'I'm here to apologise,' she said. 'I bailed on you.'

'Bailed?' Candy said, incredulous. 'You fucked off, broke our agreement, didn't even tell me you were going. And why? Because bigger things beckoned. Your Honey Hunter book. And we all know how that turned out, don't we?'

'I did a great job,' Tabitha told her. 'It won me the Columbia Prize—'

'And cost you just about everything else, am I right?' Candy cut in.

Tabitha looked away. 'It was unfortunate what happened.'

'Unfortunate? From what I see, you've been fucking buried.'

There was a frosty silence. Marco appeared with the coffee. 'Oat milk,' he said, setting it down, keeping his eyes on Tabitha. Candy watched, livid, as he gave a little salute.

'Cute,' Tabitha said, turning back to Candy, after he'd gone.

Candy fumed. 'If you've finished flirting, can you just tell me what you want so I can get on with my day? It must be something big to bring you all the way from glamorous LA.

Oh no, wait, I forgot. LA isn't glamorous for you right now, is it? What's that rag you work for that no one's ever heard of? The *LA Wiener*? Don't expect to be on the guestlist when we open La Mirage.'

'If you mean that ugly glass thing I spotted on the way here then no thanks,' Tabitha said, secretly seething at the idea that Candy was working on a project that the *New York Times* had dubbed 'visionary'. 'Cheap champagne, caviar on too-hard blinis, bite-sized burgers made from wagyu beef, so-called celebs no one's ever heard of...' Tabitha suppressed a yawn. 'I'd rather die than have my name on the list.'

'Looks like you're probably going to die because your name's already on a list,' Candy shot back. 'A hitlist.'

'Oh, that?' Tabitha said nonchalantly. 'You know what the media are like. It's just stupid gossip. Anyway, the cops are all over it. It's some psycho vigilante. He'll make a mistake soon and they'll catch him.' She picked up her coffee spoon and licked off the froth, but Candy didn't miss the flicker of fear that ran over Tabitha's face.

'Why are you here then if not to lie low?' Candy challenged her. 'Although it's not like you're incognito in that outfit.'

Tabitha leaned in and smiled conspiratorially. 'I'm here for the burning of the witches. You know, the *Falcon Bay* trial? My publisher reckons everything links up – Honey Hunter's disappearance, Madeline Kane's death, the four women who conspired to cover up the part they played in it... and then there's Jake Monroe, of course. Also on the hitlist – but no one knows why. I'm writing a book about it all – starting with what happened to Madeline Kane and spiralling out from there. You know everything that goes on in this island. Help me out and I'll make it worth your while.'

'You mean like you did before?' Candy snapped. 'That was a fucking joke. I'm not trusting you after that. Besides, my life's good now. I'm living on a sunny island, my job pays great, and I'm getting laid every night,' she gestured towards Marco. 'Why would I risk all of that?'

Tabitha held her hands up in surrender. 'Twenty grand,' Tabitha said casually. 'You'll get that today. Regard it as a gesture of goodwill for letting you down before. And five times that, if you can dish some serious dirt on the *Falcon Bay* gang, starting with the late, great Madeline Kane.'

'Twenty grand?' Candy looked outraged. 'You've no *idea* what I'm sitting on. You think your last book was explosive? Wait until you see what I have.'

Candy's eyes had lit up, and Tabitha pounced. 'A hundred grand then. And five hundred after you show me what you have. Come on, Candy. Say yes. We were good together before, and we'll be good together again.'

'What's in it for you?' Candy asked. 'You're rich enough from your book royalties, aren't you?'

Tabitha sighed, and Candy caught a fleeting glimpse of the exhausted woman behind the expertly applied red lipstick. 'I need to take back control of my story,' she said. 'Right now, the column inches are about me, not by me. I need a juicy exclusive to get my career back on track.' She looked up and met Candy's eyes. 'Oh, and I want to become so fucking successful that those Twitter trolls wish they had never been born.'

Candy laughed despite herself. She knew it was dangerous to get tangled up with Tabitha again, but she had that explosive

Ross Owen footage just sitting in her desk drawer. And she didn't even need to hand it over right away. A hundred grand would give her and Marco nearly enough to elope to Bali and set up a beach bar like they'd talked about. Five hundred would be more than enough. But once she gave the Ross Owen footage to Tabitha, she wouldn't have it as leverage any more. Plus, a lot of lives would be ruined. She needed some time to consider her options, maybe to negotiate with Tabitha on the price.

She drained her coffee and gestured for the bill. 'Pay me the hundred grand first. Then we'll talk.'

CHAPTER 18

Jake

Jake paced back and forth in his study, the setting sun casting long shadows across the room. The sky outside was a deep shade of purple, and the empty beach looked eerie in the fading light. Ever since that stormy night, he'd been convinced that Madeline Kane was still hiding somewhere on St Augustine's, plotting her revenge on him. But where? And who was sheltering her?

He ran through a list of possibilities, but none made sense. Candy was too lazy to pull off a stunt like this. The *Falcon Bay* hags probably wanted revenge on him enough to team up with their other enemy, Madeline – but they were still banged up in prison. Could it have been Chad? Might he have helped his wife fake her death for some obscure reason? But Jake was sure his grief at the funeral had been genuine. And why would he give Jake shares in the island if Madeline was coming back?

He shook his head and sat down at his Porada desk, where a Moleskine notebook sat neatly on top of the butter-soft leather. It didn't help brooding over "who" and "why" and "what if", he told himself. All that mattered was that he didn't lose the island that Chad had gifted to him last year.

He had written down in the notebook everything his lawyer had said to him on the phone – a phone call he later discovered had cost him five hundred quid – and he read it back to himself now. He'd underlined the words "ambiguity" and "deceased". The contract was almost watertight, the lawyer had said. But there was one clause, referring to Chad's deceased wife, which was a bit murky.

Jake had asked for clarification: 'It says here that the shares are only Chad's to sell if his wife is dead. What if she isn't?'

The lawyer had chuckled then, tried to make a joke. 'We lawyers never deal in certainty, but I can tell you this is highly unlikely to prove awkward. Unless you believe in ghosts of course.'

Jake leaned back in his Eames chair, and let out a howl of frustration. This was the last thing he needed on top of everything else.

Earlier that day, he had almost jumped out of his skin when another ghost from his past showed up. Tabitha Tate, lounging coolly on his villa's terrace, in a lemon-yellow jumpsuit with shoulder pads that could put your eye out, and a pair of stiletto Louboutins that should have been classed as dangerous weapons.

'What's up Jake? You look rattled. Aren't you pleased to see me?' She was smiling, but her words put Jake on guard. Tabitha Tate may have been a cold, unfeeling bitch but she had an extraordinary ability to sniff out scandal. If she was here, it meant she knew something about him he'd rather keep secret.

'What the fuck are you doing here? Aren't you meant to be cancelled?' Jake stood in his doorway, blocking her from entering.

'Haven't you heard, Jake? I'm part of a news story. And you've got a starring role too! Well, we both do. Now, I know why I'm on the vigilante hitlist for crimes committed against Honey Hunter. But what about you? What did you do to Honey, Jake?'

He'd slammed the door in her face and double locked it, waiting until Tabitha had left. She clearly didn't know the truth yet about what he'd done. But Madeline knew, and that was dangerous. What if she'd got in touch with Tabitha somehow, and let slip? Or worse. What if she'd tracked down Honey and told her? Tabitha would hang him out to dry. He needed to think, so he took the remains of a bottle of vodka down the path that went directly from his terrace to the beach and went for a long, cold swim.

He thumped his desk in anger and the Moleskine notebook tumbled to the floor. Until Tabitha had shown up, Jake had been just fine. He had convinced himself Madeline wouldn't dare to show her face in public, and he'd been sure the mad bastard killing people in Honey's name in LA would never make it as far as St Augustine's. What if neither was true? What if a murderer was lurking in the shadows, right now, ready to pounce? Jake couldn't bear to think about what the killer had done to those other victims: the knife, the mutilation. He picked up the notebook and flicked back to the notes from the call with the lawyer, but he couldn't focus. What if Tabitha coming to the island prompted the killer to follow her? Put a line through both their names at the same time?

A grinding headache started to press behind his eyes. He went into the kitchen to get some water, but instead took a bottle of wine from the Smeg fridge and slopped some into a tumbler. The ice-cold liquid made him feel better. He finished the glass, poured another, knocked it back, felt his swagger return. He was just letting things get on top of him, he decided. He just needed to get a grip. After all, his life was exactly where he wanted it: the theme park was raking in cash, La Mirage was almost ready to launch, his hag ex-wife was in jail where she belonged. He wasn't going to let those ruthless bitches Madeline or Tabitha get the better of him.

He permitted his mind to dwell on the upcoming court case where that clan of venomous vipers would be publicly shamed once again. Even if the barristers got them off, their reputations would be ruined. They'd never shake off the taint of Madeline's death and they'd probably never work in TV again. He smiled evilly as he thought of the women, deprived of their lucrative careers, sinking into poverty.

He frowned. Unless, of course, Madeline revealed to the world that she was still alive, like she had threatened in her disappearing messages. But she'd never risk that, would she? If she showed her face in public, she'd be locked up. A criminal who faked her death. No, all Jake had to do was hold his nerve and wait. The trial would be over in a few days, and whatever the outcome, his revenge on Amanda and her cronies would be complete. *Falcon Bay*'s scheming bitches would finally get what they deserved. The trial was going to be a media circus. And he would have a ringside seat.

CHAPTER 19

Madeline

At Café le Clement, in Saint Valery, Madeline had just been served an omelette aux fines herbes and a glass of vin rouge supérieure. The omelette was just right, soft, oozing, its herby filling fragrant and delicious. On the far side of the square, the church bells rang out, a sign that Mass was about to start. Mademoiselle Hubert, Madeline's housekeeper, was among the women who made their way towards the gothic structure that dominated the little town, fastening a headscarf as she ascended the stone steps to the main door.

Madeline thanked the chef who had come out to check that 'Madame Anglaise' found the omelette to her liking. She took care to be respectful to everyone she encountered, whether that was the chef who cooked her omelette, or the woman on the passport control desk when she'd travelled to St Augustine's to scare Jake. Her life as a busy network controller, criss-crossing all over the world, had taught her it paid to be nice.

Certainly it helped smooth her journey to St Augustine's, on a private plane followed by a luxury chartered yacht. She smiled wryly as she remembered the distinctly unglamorous Fiat that had picked her up from the airstrip and driven her through narrow, twisty lanes to a secluded clifftop on the wild and undeveloped north-eastern tip of the island.

The car had swept through the gates of a wisteria-clad villa and her driver jumped out to hold open the door for her. 'Welcome back to St Augustine's,' he said with a tiny bow.

She had removed her Dior shades and given him a dazzling smile. 'Thank you, Dustin.'

Madeline settled back in her chair in the sunny square and wondered what she would have done if she hadn't met Dustin. Things could have ended very differently.

Madeline had noticed Dustin as soon as she became the network controller for *Falcon Bay*. He was an awkward, geeky producer who existed on the margins but had ambition – and she knew all too well what that felt like. His technical skills, particularly when it came to CGI, were second to none. Realising immediately how useful he might be, she made a point of striking up a conversation when they were alone together in the edit suite. She asked what he was working on, hinting that she might have a special project he could be a part of. Something sensitive, confidential, and extremely well-remunerated. She had fixed him with those clear green eyes. 'It wouldn't just be a life-changing amount of money.' Dustin had swallowed nervously. 'It would be the one thing you've always wanted. Power. But the stakes are high.' She had kept her gaze on him, unflinching. Chad had once described her eyes, one a slightly deeper shade of emerald than the other, as the kind that looked into men's souls. When she finally explained her plan, Dustin had barely paused to think about it.

'Yes,' he'd told her. 'Count me in.'

Unlike Jake and the rest of the crew, who behaved as if Dustin was invisible, Madeline treated him as an invaluable ally. And so he had done exactly what she asked: created the seamless CGI footage that convinced the world she was dead, helped arrange her escape from St Augustine's, and gone to live in the secluded clifftop villa that Madeline had built as a hideaway to be used in desperate circumstances. From here, with a pair of strong binoculars, he could watch the island undetected, waiting patiently for Madeline to get back in touch. It had taken more than two years of living in France under the guise of Madame Anglaise LaRoche before Madeline was ready to hear about what she had left behind. And when Dustin had told her how Jake was destroying St Augustine's – the disgusting theme park that made a fetish of her death, the giant skyscraper built far too quickly on dodgy foundations – she was furious. She knew Jake was ruthless, but for him to make a spectacle of her death for his own profit was a new level of low. She wanted to punish Jake before she and her lawyers figured out how to take her island back.

Dustin had come up with the idea of the confrontation on the jetty, and – with the storm raging, and Jake being drunk and stoned – it had worked even better than expected, shaking Jake to his very core.

She had enjoyed sending Jake those disappearing messages on WhatsApp, too. In reality, she would never tell the world what she knew about Jake and Honey. That would be for Honey to decide – if she ever came out of hiding. But Jake didn't have to know that.

Madeline took the last bite of her omelette and sipped her wine. Sunshine streamed into the square, adding to the sleepy feeling that always settled on the village around lunchtime. The tabac opposite Café le Clement was closing for lunch, the owner fastening the wooden shutters while a ginger cat wrapped itself around his ankles. The door to the church had opened, the congregation drifting away after the service. From the tower, the bells once more rang out, and Madeline felt a sharp pang for Chad, remembering their wedding day: him in a tuxedo, her in cream silk, the scent of freesias filling the air from her bouquet.

If only she had truly believed him when he vowed that day to love and cherish her "come what may, all the days of our lives". Oh, she never doubted that he loved the woman she had become: the ambitious, resourceful, glamorous Madeline. But she had always been terrified that if he ever found out about her past – if he discovered that she had spent eighteen years trapped in the wrong body – he would be disgusted. She'd been certain that it would sound the death knell for their marriage. And so, when the truth was about to come out, in the depths of her despair, she had convinced herself that only through her own death would Chad escape the shame of being married to a lie.

How wrong she had been.

He knew.

He knew, all along.

And he loved her all the same.

What she yearned for more than anything now was to have him back. A second chance – was it too much to hope for?

Perhaps it was, given that Chad had disappeared.

Dustin told her he had made enquiries as soon as he knew she wanted to return. Chad had left his home nearly a year ago, for what everyone assumed was a sabbatical to process his grief.

But now no one – not even Dustin – seemed to know where he was.

CHAPTER 20

Tabitha

Tabitha had gone for an evening swim in the cold ocean and got out just as the sky started turning from pink to purple. She'd been sitting at home all day, trying to watch *Grey's Anatomy* and stay calm, but the image of Antony Earl's slashed face kept popping into her head, tormenting her. Every time she thought of him she involuntarily covered her eyes with her hands, as if her subconscious was telling her that if she couldn't use her eyes then the image would go away. She wished it would work like that. When she wasn't plagued with thoughts of Antony Earl's face, she couldn't help but feel on edge, like she was being watched.

Now she was using a microfibre towel to dry her hair in the bedroom of her woodland cottage. Her first day researching the *Falcon Bay* cast and crew hadn't gone as well as she'd hoped. She'd got titbits of gossip out of Candy and a few others on the island she contacted, but there was so much that had been written about the show in recent years that it was impossible to find anything genuinely new and shocking.

It was clear from her meeting with Mickey that Madeline Kane was where the real story lay – but where? What was she supposed to be uncovering? She cursed Mickey – he said he'd phone her yesterday after his meeting, but he hadn't, and when she'd rung him it had gone straight to voicemail.

The doorbell rang, and Tabitha jumped. She told herself not to be silly – she had to shake off the fear of someone tracking her down and doing to her what they'd done to Antony Earl. But when she opened the door, she felt a chill travel down her spine. Sitting on the doormat was a white padded envelope, with her name scrawled in black marker on the front. She knew instantly what it would contain, and, hands trembling, she bent down to pick it up. A memory stick rattled inside. She ran out and looked left and right across the beach, but it was empty. The sand was too soft for footprints and the crash of the waves was too loud to call out. Not that anyone would have answered.

She knew she should call the police, but she was like an addict. She had to watch the footage, even though she knew it would haunt her dreams – and make her look over her shoulder for the rest of her life. Her heart racing in her chest, she double-locked the door, grabbed her laptop and sat down at the table. She plugged the stick into the computer, and pressed 'play.'

A grainy, black and white image came into view. The person holding the camera was standing in the grounds of a huge house – no, a mansion. The timestamp on the footage read 7th June, 12.30a.m. The camera panned around and Tabitha caught a glimpse of a sprawling white building set around a lush garden and a heart-shaped swimming pool before the camera paused, and zoomed in on a private driveway flanked by towering palm trees. Beyond the electric gates, the hills of Hollywood rose up; Tabitha could see the famous sign glinting in the distance. A movement caught Tabitha's eye. The electric gates were opening, first slowly and then gathering speed. Tabitha held her breath as a figure emerged, and strode confidently into the grounds. A figure wearing an unmistakable striped blazer. Mickey Taylor.

Tabitha longed to reach out, warn him that something terrible was about to happen to him, but all she could do was watch helplessly as Mickey's face came into focus, his expression changing suddenly from confusion to fear. Whoever was wielding the camera must have had it strapped to their body, because the next thing Tabitha saw was a hunting knife, glinting in front of the frame, held by a hand wearing a black leather glove.

'Look out, Mickey!' she screamed hopelessly. But of course, he could not hear her, and before she could pause the footage and gather herself together, the video went black.

Trembling, Tabitha reached for the memory stick and unplugged it from the computer. She felt a wave of nausea, followed immediately by a surge of guilt. Should she have pressed for more information in the bar? She had known in her heart that Mickey was lying to her. He'd been so cagey about who he was meeting that night. If she had grilled him about where he was going, could she have saved him from this monster?

She breathed deeply, trying to calm her nerves, but at that moment the phone rang, and she nearly jumped out of her skin. The screen had a picture of a hairy gorilla – the image she'd put into her contacts for Sandy.

'What is it?' she said, but she was pretty sure she knew.

'Bad news,' Sandy said at once, his voice grave but tinged with excitement. 'There's been another killing. Mickey Taylor.'

Tabitha stayed silent.

'The police got a tip-off about a Hollywood mansion,' Sandy continued, 'and when they arrived they found him floating face down in the swimming pool like a scene from *Sunset Boulevard*. The body had begun to bloat.'

Tears pricked at Tabitha's eyes. She hadn't exactly been friends with Mickey, but he'd made her a very rich woman. And they'd had a fun evening at the Marmont, swapping gossip over their Negronis and competing to spot celebrities in the darkened booths of the bar. He had even showed her a picture of his wife, a glamorous brunette who looked like J-Lo.

She blinked. Emotion never helped anything. She needed to find Mickey's killer, and bring him to justice. The reporter part of her brain clicked into gear.

'What exactly is this house?' Tabitha asked Sandy. Maybe his answer would help her figure out who Mickey had been going to meet. He'd mentioned a studio boss, and someone who had information for him – presumably about Madeline Kane. She cursed herself again for not pressing him harder over drinks.

'It's called Castillo del Amor. Nine bedrooms, two swimming pools, marble terrace. It's empty because it's up for sale, on the market for £30 million. It used to be owned by the studio boss Caspar Felix. Did you read his obituary? He died last year. He was famous for his A-list parties – but there were rumours he was linked to the mob.'

Tabitha's mind whirred as she processed the information. Did Mickey's murderer choose this place as a statement, to create maximum glamour and maximum impact? Or were they personally connected to the mansion and its dark past? And how – if at all – did this fit into the other hitlist killings?

Tabitha swallowed before her next question. 'Sandy. Tell me straight. Was Mickey…' she paused. 'Mutilated? Like the others?'

Sandy hesitated. 'Yes. I'm afraid so. It was…'

The line crackled, and Tabitha shook her phone in frustration. The signal was terrible. She unlocked her front door and walked out to the beach, glancing over her shoulder as she did so. She flinched as a seabird flew out in front of her towards the waves. God, she was jumpy.

'Say that again, Sandy? My signal's just come back.'

'I was saying his mutilation followed a similar pattern to the last victim. His tongue had been cut out, and the word "liar" was scratched into his forehead – with a scalpel, they reckon. And that's not all. The cops found a copy of the hitlist in the house. Mickey's name had a line through it. And folded under the list was a newspaper cutting, the story we splashed all over the *Leader* after the Antony Earl killing. About the video you'd been sent.' Sandy paused. 'We're going to run a big piece tomorrow about it. The cops are calling him the Hitlist Killer. But there's something else.'

'What is it?' Tabitha pressed, though she had an awful feeling she knew what was coming.

'The killer had scribbled something across the picture we ran of you.' Another silence.

Tabitha kept her voice steady despite the fear that was beginning to grip her. 'What did they write?' she asked.

Sandy cleared his throat. 'You're next.'

CHAPTER 21

Tabitha

Tabitha Tate arrived at the Royal Inns of Court in St Helier around 4 a.m. She'd barely slept after the call about Mickey the night before, alert for every tiny sound outside her cottage, certain that she was next. She scanned the crowd of reporters and TV crews until she spotted the perfect place. Somewhere that no one could sneak up behind her with a scalpel, but somewhere that gave her a clear view of the entrance to the courthouse.

St Helier's legal system was different from America's, and even separate from the UK's. Tabitha had been brushing up on how this trial was expected to work, so she could begin reporting on it in the US before the trial had even began. After the trial had had a false start in January, they still accepted the women's plea: not guilty. Because of how high profile the case was, they'd been held since their arrest, so that evidence couldn't be tampered with. They'd been held at La Croix, a facility more like a retirement home than a prison, because they had not been found guilty. Elsewhere, they would be held in a far less luxurious prison. Still, it gave the women's critics joy to think of them playing board games and tending to flowers in trainers, something they were bound to loathe. Though the trial would likely last a couple of weeks, today would be the most interesting day for the press, other than the day of the verdict, as the entire case would be outlined: by the judge, the defence and the prosecution. However, unlike elsewhere, the judge can dismiss a jury at any point and deliver the verdict themselves, if they see fit.

The accused would be whisked in the back entrance, in a prison van with blacked-out windows, but from this vantage point, she could be the first to report on what the women were wearing on this most important of days. She shivered in the early morning chill, and pulled the sleeves of her charcoal pinstripe jacket down over the hands. She'd made a conscious effort to dress down today.

The memory stick delivered to her cottage yesterday had shaken her to the core. Someone out there knew where she was living. St Helier Police had stationed a sergeant outside her cottage, but didn't have the funds to stretch to a permanent bodyguard. If there was a killer on the island, she didn't want to draw attention to herself.

A voice made her jump. 'What time did you get here?'

Tabitha turned to see Candy Dace, dressed in a flamboyant orange trouser suit paired with cream cowboy boots and a bright silk turban. So much for being anonymous in pinstripe, Tabitha fumed. Candy handed Tabitha a coffee and yawned. 'I thought I was early,' she said. 'You must have got here when it was still dark.'

Tabitha shrugged and took a sip of the mediocre coffee. She and Candy had agreed a fragile truce, but it didn't mean she had to like her. 'The early bird gets the worm,' she said vaguely, her eyes scanning the crowd for any sign of movement.

Candy looked at her. 'The early snake gets the first scoop on the rats you mean,' she muttered darkly. 'I can't think why you dragged me out here so early. So you can sell a story on what their designer outfits are supposed to symbolise? "Catherine Belle's suit resembles one that Lucy Dean wore in an episode of *Falcon Bay* where she was found not guilty of fraud, symbolising that she is not guilty." Give me a break.'

'I hardly dragged you out here, Candy,' Tabitha said sharply, ignoring her curt and true words. 'You're here because I'm paying you to give me some background on these women, remember? Anyway, I've got a feeling things are going to get pretty exciting today. Before he died, my publisher hinted there was something newsworthy about Madeline Kane. And I'm now realising there's a lot more than just the scandal of her death to uncover on the island. You know she was adopted as a baby? I think I have a lead about her birth mother. I'm hoping something comes up in the trial when they're discussing her life.'

Candy was silent, and the two women stood sipping their coffee as a minibus pulled up at one end of the square, unloading a group of people passing placards around.

As they watched, a man wearing a blonde wig and makeup, with a bulge at the front of his leggings, strutted towards them.

'Where did you get the coffee?' he asked, his pink puffer jacket wide open to reveal a t-shirt that read: Self ID! I'm with Madeline!

Candy gestured towards the street behind them and the man swaggered off. 'What's that about?' Candy asked.

'Don't you read the news?' Tabitha scoffed. 'Madeline Kane is a trans icon now. The wider community are using her name to claim that anyone can be a woman if they say so. But it's literally the opposite of Madeline's idea of femininity. All those huge hairy thighs squeezed into little dresses. She'd be turning in her grave.'

'I loved Madeline Kane, and I'm not trans!' piped up a small voice just behind Tabitha. She turned to see a young woman with long auburn hair, weaving her way through the group waving placards, looking at Tabitha's press pass longingly. 'I'm a huge fan of *Falcon Bay*,' she said. 'I've watched all the shows, and I've read all their memoirs. I even moved to St Helier to be closer to the set! I don't suppose you could get me into the trial, could you?'

Tabitha shook her head. 'Sorry. It's press and relatives only. But if I could, I would – because actually you're just the person I need. I'm writing a book about *Falcon Bay* and I need some local colour. Would you be interested in giving me an interview?'

The woman flushed pink, clashing with her hair. 'I'd love to. My name's Hannah Price. You can reach me at St Helier police station most days. I'm one of their call dispatchers.'

Tabitha handed her a gold and white business card. 'Tabitha Tate, reporter. Keep this safe and I'll be in touch next week?'

Hannah Price floated off into the crowd, looking like she couldn't believe her luck. Tabitha turned to Candy, who was looking amused. 'What? I might as well widen the net since you're being so stingy with information.'

Their sniping was interrupted by a sleek people carrier with smoked glass windows, which pulled up on the end of the street opposite. The passenger door slid open to reveal Olivia and Max, strapped into their car seats, and Jake facing them on an expensive looking leather seat. He was clearly basking in the attention from the paparazzi, who were already sprinting towards them with their cameras. Tabitha had persuaded her boss to hire her a freelance cameraman to get some footage for the website, and she was pleased to see that he wasn't part of the throng, but had his lens trained on the courthouse steps, as instructed.

'What's Jake doing here?' Tabitha asked.

'Come to gloat that his ex-wife is on trial, and he's got custody, I expect,' Candy replied with a scowl.

As they observed from a distance, a pretty young woman in a uniform joined them on the pavement. She was dressed modestly, in a beige knee-length dress, a prim little hat and a pair of white gloves.

'Who's that?' Tabitha asked.

'Lauren, the kids' nanny.'

'What's with the fancy dress?'

'Apparently, Lauren's a Norland nanny,' Candy told her. 'A prestigious qualification, so Jake says. I've only ever seen her in a vest and cut-offs. The whole Mary Poppins vibe is for the press.'

Lauren posed for the photographers, jiggling Max on her hip, and ruffling his hair with her white-gloved hand. Olivia was in a cotton dress with a billowing skirt and cute red patent T-bar shoes, while Jake was beaming with pride, standing next to them. The kids looked like Prince Louis and

Princess Charlotte, and the crowd of snappers went wild.

'It's the first time I've seen him have anything to do with his kids,' Candy said, shaking her head in disgust. 'Lauren has them 24/7 – except when she's blowing Jake off when the kids are asleep. All Jake can think about is his sodding skyscraper. La Mirage is his baby, not his children.'

Tabitha watched Jake carefully. As he posed and joked with the press, she thought she could see a hint of fear in the way he carried himself: upright, alert, scanning the crowd just like she was. It looked like she and Jake were both looking out of the audience for the same person: the Hitlist Killer.

CHAPTER 22

Sheena

Sheena took a deep breath and tried to ignore the heady cocktail of emotions swirling around the day room. Farrah was in a defiant mood, ready to fight tooth and nail to see her son. Amanda was tearful and anxious, afraid of seeing Dan in court and worried about what might happen if she did. Helen appeared stoic, as if the worst had already happened and she was ready for whatever came next. Catherine, on the other hand, exuded a serene stillness, her 'que sera, sera' attitude giving her an air of unflappable calm. Sheena felt only a sense of relief that the day of resolution had finally come.

But did she even want it to? Sheena felt a sudden rush of panic. She had been happy in prison, free from day-to-day decisions and responsibilities. She muttered something to the others and strode out of the day room, towards the rose garden. She paused next to a luscious pink climber and breathed in its fragrance. Constance Spry. Who would have thought that she would leave prison knowing the names of five different varieties of English rose? Perhaps she could plant one in her garden when she got home.

As she looked up, she saw the others coming towards her, exuding power and ready for battle. Her barrister Eva Hope had managed to sweet talk the governor into allowing a stylist into the prison, and she had chosen the women's outfits perfectly, selecting well-cut clothes in muted tones that were unusual but not ostentatious. Amanda wore taupe, Catherine wore blush pink, Farrah wore delicate apricot, and Helen wore creamy yellow. Sheena smoothed her own outfit — a sharp suit in a shade of purple so dark it was almost black — and reflected on how good it felt to be out of the grey tracksuit she'd been wearing since she arrived at La Croix nearly a year ago. Perhaps going home wouldn't be so bad after all.

'You look amazing,' Sheena told them as they approached. 'As if you've stepped off the set of one of those slick American crime dramas where the women chase down criminals in six-inch heels without a hair out of place.'

Catherine took hold of Sheena's hands. 'This is the best I've felt for ages,' she said, her eyes shining and her smile warm and relaxed.

'You aren't going back on what we discussed are you?' Sheena asked her anxiously.

Catherine shook her head. 'The Ross Owen secret dies with me. Let's go be free!'

'We can do this,' Farrah said, her voice wavering slightly.

Amanda nodded. 'All for one.'

'One for all,' Helen added, a fierce determination in her eyes. With that, they linked arms and walked down the wooded path, to where the prison van was waiting.

*

The courtroom was packed to the brim, the gallery over-flowing with journalists eager to be the first with the scoop. Every seat was taken. The tension was palpable, a thick cloud of anticipation that hung heavy in the air.

The five women took their seats in the dock, a united front against the accusations that had been levied against them. Sheena sat in the centre, flanked by Catherine and Helen to her left, and Amanda and Farrah to her right. They intertwined their fingers, holding on tight for support. 'All for one, one for all.'

Amanda's heart sank as she searched the faces in the public gallery. Dan was nowhere to be seen. Sheena squeezed her hand, and mouthed 'Hang on in there.' Amanda nodded in gratitude.

Finally, the judge entered the courtroom and everyone rose to their feet. Mr. Justice Godfrey Walker settled into his seat and took his time polishing his glasses before turning his attention to the defendants. 'No one told me we were expecting a fashion parade,' he quipped drily.

The women remained impassive. Sheena caught the eye of her barrister, Eva Hope, who was just about managing not to glare at the judge, and focused on the natural pink of her freshly painted nails. They were off to a bad start if Mr Justice Walker was already complaining about their outfits. Maybe the trial wouldn't go their way, after all.

Sheena felt a little better after hearing Justice Walker's opening remarks, which outlined the case in a dispassionate manner, and then passed over to the counsel for the prosecution, a barrister who looked to be in his early twenties and whose suit was a size too large. His voice faltered as he drew the jury's attention to the few pieces of evidence that implied Madeline's death was no accident: the argument between Sheena and Madeline earlier that day; the broken high-heeled shoe that tipped Madeline into the water; the ever-so-slight withdrawing of Catherine's hand, when Madeline reached for it. As he spoke, he continually referenced a bundle of A4 notes clutched in his trembling hand, often backtracking, his eyes flicking to the jury as if to seek approval that he was doing a good job. He wasn't. The expressions on the faces of the jury ranged from indifferent to unimpressed, The case against the defendants in the dock was being articulated by someone who needed more defending than they did.

The jury sighed audibly in relief when the young barrister finished his speech, and passed over to Catherine's lawyer. Rupert Flint KC, the silver-haired King's Counsel employed at great expense by Catherine, stood up before the jury to make his opening statement. His voice resonated with the kind of authority that could only be forged in the halls of Eton, the quads of Oxford and the cloisters of the Middle Temple.

'Ladies and gentlemen of the jury,' he intoned, 'we are gathered here today to examine the tragic events surrounding the death of Madeline Kane. My client, Catherine Belle, finds herself unjustly accused of involuntary manslaughter in connection with that incident. However, I submit to you that the evidence will reveal a far more complex truth.' Flint nodded toward Catherine, who squeezed Sheena's hand and bowed her head. 'Catherine Belle is an innocent woman caught in the treacherous currents of fate. She was present during the tragic incident, yes, but she bears no responsibility for Madeline Kane's death. We will demonstrate that this was a case of unforeseeable circumstances, an act of nature beyond Catherine's control.' Rupert kept talking, painting a vivid picture of the events leading up to that fateful evening on the jetty at *Falcon Bay*. The jury nodded, spellbound, as he wove his story: the risks of working with live animals, the unpredictable nature of live television, and, at the heart of it all, an older actress whose livelihood – whose very world – was under threat. 'A woman under huge pressure, dealing with the trauma of a shark attack right in front of her. A woman whose mental health…' he paused for effect, 'was crumbling. A woman who was not responsible for her actions.'

Catherine flinched, and Sheena squeezed her hand again. She knew Catherine would hate playing the mental health card, but as Eva had told her, it was their best shot at getting off. She kept her hand wrapped around Catherine's, and allowed Rupert Flint's mellifluous voice to wash over her. The jury seemed to be lapping it up.

But just as Sheena was allowing a tiny sapling of hope to take root, the mood in the courtroom shifted. A woman in a navy peplum skirt, who had been standing by the door, now lifted her palm as if to halt the court. The jurors took notice, and started to whisper. Rupert paused his speech, looked around and addressed the judge.

'Your honour, please advise me. What is this commotion? My client deserves a fair trial.' The judge raised his own hand for silence, as the woman in navy walked down the aisle, leaned over the bench and delivered a whispered message to the judge.

Mr Justice Walker's voice took on a grave tone. 'An urgent matter has been brought to my attention. One which must be dealt with before concluding the statement of Mr Flint.'

Sheena tensed, Catherine's grip on her hand tightening to the point of pain.

Amanda looked at Sheena, a silent plea in her eyes. Eva Hope, their barrister, seemed equally bewildered. Sheena's mind raced. What was this urgent matter? Had Catherine turned traitor after all, ready to reveal everything about Ross Owen? What if they had to spend life in prison after all? It would likely be a real one this time, not the cushy low-security open prison they had got used to on St Helier. On the other side of her from Catherine, Amanda's nails now dug painfully into her palm.

The women looked at each other, panic mounting, a sudden gleam of accusation glinting in their eyes. Had one of them done a deal with the courts? Had someone ratted them out in exchange for immunity? What happened to one for all, and all for one?

The official in navy beckoned to a stout woman wearing a barrister's wig, who had entered the courtroom from the wide panelled doors at the back, and now approached the bench. 'Your Honour,' she said, giving a slight bow. 'Ladies and gentlemen of the jury. New information has come to light which is highly relevant to these proceedings. With your permission, I would like to introduce a new witness.'

The crowd seemed to hold its breath as the doors to the courtroom swung open. In walked a tall woman wearing a white fitted Chanel suit, and a pale blue hat with a white polka-dotted half veil. A diamond cross hung just below her shapely neck, and under the veil Sheena glimpsed a pair of huge dark sunglasses covering her eyes. Her hair was long and black, with soft waves framing full lips, set in a heart-shaped face. Whoever it was exuded elegance and poise. There was a hint of ethereal Hollywood glamour in her bearing. Whispers rippled through the courtroom as the spectators and the jury strained their necks to catch a glimpse of this vision in white who seemed somehow familiar.

Sheena felt an ice-cold fist clutch her heart. Beside her, Catherine gasped aloud. Amanda's hand went limp; she seemed speechless. 'What the actual fuck?' Farrah exclaimed. Helen stared, wide-eyed, mute, feeling as though the wind had been knocked out of her. After a moment she managed to regain her breath and utter the unthinkable. 'It's Madeline Kane.'

Back from the dead.

The eyes of the women widened. They looked from each other to the woman in white stood at the back entrance of gallery. Were they hallucinating? No, they knew that body, and that slight sway as she walked, all too well. But how could it be her? Madeline was supposed to be dead. Millions of people around the world, had seen her death happen in real time! Sheena and the women had seen the shark tank, which had been placed under the water that lapped at the edges of the exterior studio set of *Falcon Bay*. They had screamed alongside viewers as Madeline had been torn apart by a shark, live on television. Then, as police and medics swarmed the floor and the shows live feed was pulled off air, they'd witnessed the retrieval of what was left of Madeline's severed body, pulled from the water onto a stretcher. Later, in Louisiana, they had attended her funeral for fuck's sake! Where her beloved Chad, so wracked with grief, could barely get his words out during his eulogy for the woman he'd been robbed of living his life with. And now here she was, not just alive but breathtakingly glamorous, not a hair out of place. It was completely impossible, wasn't it?

Amanda and Farrah had spent years coming up with outrageous plotlines during their reign as the world's most watched soap, but never in a million years could they have pulled off a stunt like this.

Had it all been faked? But if so, how? And what about them? Sheena's fury started to build. She and her friends had spent nearly a year in prison waiting to declare their innocence after being accused of being behind Madeline's tragic demise. And she wasn't even dead! If this truly was her, what would that mean for Catherine? Sheena's head spun and she could see that the women felt the same way.

A camera flash dazzled her eyes, and she tuned back into the room. The courtroom was buzzing, the murmurs from the press bench so loud the judge was banging his gavel and calling for order. The echo made Sheena's ears ring. She glanced at her friends. Amanda and Farrah were holding hands in perfect silence. Catherine's face had gone a terrible waxy colour, with beads of sweat appearing on her brow causing her carefully applied makeup to run.

Deadly silence fell over the court. An official whispered something inaudible in the judge's ear, and Mr Justice Walker nodded at the stout barrister. 'You may proceed.'

'Thank you, your honour. Rather than presenting an opening statement, I think it would be best if I went straight ahead to call my client, Madeline Kane, to take the stand,' said Madeline's lawyer.

'Very well,' Justice Walker replied.

Madeline's six-inch stilettos clicked on the wooden steps as she walked up them into the dock, where she stood facing the court, head slightly bowed.

Catherine stood up as if to object and Sheena grabbed her hand and pulled her back down. 'Don't do anything stupid,' she whispered in Catherine's ear. 'Just listen. This could go well for us. How the fuck she pulled off this Jesus stunt is beyond me, but we can't have played any part in the death of a woman who is very much alive. Just keep quiet. If there's no death, there's no charge.'

Trying to take it all in, Catherine sat back down, shaking. Sheena could see that her mind was racing through possibilities, just like her own. Maybe it wasn't her. Maybe she had a sister? After all, they still hadn't seen her full face. But just as she had the thought, the judge turned to the witness and gestured for her to remove her veil and glasses. She placed her hat and glasses on the stand next to her and slowly raised her gaze to meet the crowd. As she did so, her piercing green eyes, one a slightly darker shade of emerald than the other, met with the packed court room. There was no doubt left in anyone's mind. Madeline Kane was alive.

'Mrs Kane, could you begin by telling the court why you are here today?' Madeline's lawyer asked.

In a low, quavering voice, barely above a whisper, Madeline began to talk. 'Of course. Firstly, before I explain why I did what I did, of which I am deeply, deeply ashamed, I want to apologise to everyone in this room and around the world.

I need to explain what desperation and fear was driving me towards my decision.' When Madeline paused to draw breath, two journalists tried to shout out, and were silenced immediately by court staff. After another pause, where she hung her head as if in shame, she lifted her chin and began to speak again. Her tone was uncharacteristically soft; nothing like her normal voice which could cut through the chattering hub of a packed meeting room with no more than a single word.

'Before the night of my apparent death, I had been living a nightmare,' she continued. 'Somebody I did business with – a wicked person who cared only for their own gain – had discovered a secret from my past. It was one that I had done everything in my power to hide, so ashamed of it being exposed, that I'd hidden this secret even from my own husband for fear he couldn't love me, if he knew my hidden truth. I had succeeded in keeping this secret until one woman sitting in this courtroom revealed that she had discovered that I was born in the wrong body. She intended to blackmail me, with the threat of revealing it to the world'. Madeline's brimming eyes flashed towards Sheena, making it clear to the entire room whom she was talking about.

She aimed a tearful gaze towards the judge and jury, dabbed at her eyes with a silk hanky, and continued. 'She discovered I only became the woman you see before you when I was eighteen. She threatened to expose me to my husband, and the world, if she didn't get what she wanted.'

Madeline paused dramatically, and Sheena rolled her eyes. This whole exchange had clearly been expertly choreographed. She took steady breaths, trying to keep her anger under control while this Oscar-worthy performance played out.

'And do you see this woman in the courtroom today?' asked Madeline's barrister.

'I do,' said Madeline. She pointed a perfectly manicured finger straight in Sheena's direction. The women locked eyes for a second before Madeline turned back to address the court. 'It was Sheena McQueen, agent and manager of Catherine Belle. She proceeded to share that information with the others sat alongside her today. Together, they blackmailed me.' Madeline's voice was steadier now, filled with resolve. 'They said they'd tell the press about who I really was if I didn't hand over control of my show, *Falcon Bay* to them. They bullied me into believing the whole world would turn against me. With the media back then being so toxic towards trans people, they said I'd be vilified; hunted like a wild animal. I was terrified for my life. I knew I couldn't handle being exposed. Not only would I be hated by the public, but I would lose my husband, who I love more than anything in the world. I just wasn't strong enough to lose him.'

Sheena saw Helen roll her eyes, and then plaster an apathetic expression on her face after Farrah nudged her in the ribs. Sheena knew that if Farrah had to listen to a pack of lies from one of the most vengeful women she'd ever met – and boy had she met a few during her life in showbusiness – there was no way she was going to react if doing so took her even an inch further away from being reunited with her baby boy.

Cameras flashed again as Madeline swept a lock of her luscious hair away with her hand. Sheena could tell it was done deliberately to reveal the massive eighteen carat gold diamond wedding ring Chad had given her. The crowds seemed to be lapping up Madeline's performance like one of their highest-rated episodes: well, the trial was being televised, after all. A camera panned around the courtroom, and Sheena kept her face neutral, though she could feel a muscle twitching in her cheek. Beside her, Amanda surreptitiously adjusted her Spanx, clearly worried in case the viewers back home caught sight of the weight she'd gained in prison.

'I thought about killing myself,' Madeline continued, in what Sheena could now see was the kind of six-page one-hander script Farrah had always excelled at writing, 'but then I would never have been able to hang on to my dream that, one day, when the dust had settled, I could reunite with my husband and beg him to accept and love me as the woman I truly am and was always meant to be. So, I... I...'

'Yes?' said her barrister encouragingly.

'I did the only thing I could think of that would give me a chance to possibly gain his forgiveness if it came out. I faked my own death.' Madeline's voice wavered. 'That day I intended to kill Madeline Kane, and so escape the torture and fear those women forced me into. But I never, ever expected everything that I did to bring us all here today. For as much as I despise these women for making me give up the love of my life, I would never want to separate any woman from her family, or send anyone to rot in prison for a crime they didn't commit. So I had to take the risk of the world turning on me today by turning up here, your Honour, to tell you the truth, the whole truth and nothing but the truth. I only pray that you, and everyone in this courtroom, and everyone watching around the world, are able to forgive me for the trouble I have caused.'

Sheena glanced over at the jury. Three of them were in tears, and neither their faces nor the judge's showed a glimmer of awareness that they were not witnessing a penitent woman, but the sheer brilliance of Madeline Kane's raw acting ability. Helen was clearly having the same thought. She was gazing at Madeline with an expression of pure admiration. Despite her disgust for Madeline's actions today, Helen was impressed by her performance. She remembered all those years ago when she first cast Madeline in *Falcon Bay* to play the troubled teenage boy, Calvin. She silently congratulated herself on her casting eye, which had never been wrong.

Back in the witness stand, Madeline appeared to be coming to end of her speech. She leaned forward, clearly searching for the red lights which would indicate which cameras were beaming her live around the world. Like Sheena, Madeline would know only too well that the world would have stopped what they were doing to watch what was probably the biggest televised trial since O. J. Simpson. Madeline turned her head slightly so that her most flattering angle would be picked up by the cameras.

'I know I've taken up too much of your time, your Honour,' she said, giving him a rueful smile. 'So I'll end by saying that the crime I committed that led us all here today truly was my only choice. I hope and pray that you can understand I was out of my mind. All the time I was hidden away in France, I never once looked at any news or media. I locked my phone in a safe and I tried to block the whole incident out, start a brand-new life.' Her voice cracked, and she began to sob. 'Since I decided to come out of hiding, I realised that the whole world knows my secret anyway, including my beloved Chad. To think I'd spent decades too frightened to tell him, terrified to face his disgust, when it turned out he knew all along, and loved me anyway, is the worst of it. Now he has disappeared, and all of this has been for nothing. I did all of this to protect the man I love, but knowing what I know now I will regret my actions for the rest of my life. I am so sorry. I hope that you all, and most of all my darling husband, can forgive me.'

As the cameras moved off her to get reaction shots from the crowd, Madeline caught Sheena's eye and gave her the ghost of a wink.

That was it. Sheena finally snapped. 'You're a fucking liar!' Sheena was up on her feet, and the cameras span to catch her reaction.

'Leave it!' Amanda hissed, pulling her friend back down. 'Let her lie. We can't be convicted if she's alive! No matter what bullshit she's spouting, keep your mouth shut!'

'Silence in court!' The judge spoke sharply, and Sheena fumed silently. Would the judge really take pity on Madeline after that saccharine performance? Madeline had faked her death, which was a crime in itself wasn't it? And what about wasting police time and prison resources? Surely she would go down for this?

Sheena held her breath as the judge stood up. The court-room's large clock ticked loudly in the silence as Justice Walker pronounced: 'We will have a brief recess. Court will resume in fifteen minutes.'

The atmosphere in the room was electric. The spectators burst into a cacophony of loud whispers as Madeline glided out of the witness stand with a blank expression. Rupert Flint and Eva Hope, the lawyers representing the stunned women, motioned for them to follow. They strutted out in their high heels, moving through the back door of the courtroom and into a small, stuffy consultation room with a wooden table and a few chairs, a stark contrast to the grandeur of the courtroom. The women sat down, their faces clenched with shock and anger, underscored by a hint of fear. Catherine's hands were trembling, and she clenched them into tight fists. Amanda stared blankly at the wooden grains of the table, while Sheena's eyes were ablaze with fury. Helen and Farrah whispered to each other, disbelief staining their words. Sheena was the first to speak. 'This is insane!' she spat out, slamming her fist on the table. 'She's manipulating the court, turning them against us with her damned sob story!'

Catherine, her voice shaking, replied, 'Sheena's right. This is a carefully crafted ploy. She must have been planning this for months...' Her voice trailed off, the truth feeling too absurd to utter aloud. They'd witnessed her violent death, hadn't they? Catherine had even felt responsible for it – the guilt weighing her down constantly.

Rupert, always the calm in the storm, lifted his hand, a signal that they had to simmer down. 'Listen,' he began, his voice firm yet reassuring. 'If Madeline is alive, that changes everything for us, legally. Catherine, they can't convict you of killing someone who isn't dead. And my learned friend Ms Hope will surely agree that the rest of you won't have to face perjury charges either.'

Amanda wasn't pacified. 'But what about Sheena? Sounds like Madeline is trying to pin a blackmail charge on her!'

Rupert nodded solemnly. 'Yes, that is a concern. But we can fight that. Mrs Kane's credibility is in tatters. She faked her own death. Any claim she makes is going to be scrutinised against that backdrop.'

Farrah voiced the question that had been in Sheena's mind too. 'How did she do it? How did she fake her own death so convincingly?' No one had an answer. The image of Madeline being torn apart by a shark, witnessed by millions on live television, was etched into all their minds. A heavy silence enveloped the room.

Sheena was still simmering with anger, and her tone was venomous. 'She needs to pay for what she's done. She's dragged us into hell. Especially Catherine.'

Eva looked at Rupert and sought his silent agreement before replying. 'As your defence lawyers, our priority is ensuring that none of you face charges for a crime that never occurred. Revenge or retribution against Madeline has to wait.' Eva's gaze held them all, instilling as much reassurance as she could. 'Ladies, this is good for us. They can't charge you for killing someone who's sitting right there in the courtroom. We need to sail these rough waters together, and make sure that none of you drown in the process.' The women nodded, and clasped each other's hands as they prepared to re-enter the courtroom together.

'All for one, and one for all,' Sheena whispered, and they strode back into the room, radiating a confidence they didn't feel.

Sheena held her breath as the jury filed back in, and the judge cleared his throat, ready to deliver his summation. The atmosphere in the courtroom shifted once more as he spoke.

'Ladies and gentlemen of the jury, a remarkable development has unfolded in this trial. Madeline Kane, the alleged victim of manslaughter, has reappeared before us, undermining the very foundation of this case. And while I do not condone her actions or think lightly of the great strain this has put on the resources of our beautiful island's police and justice system, it is clear Mrs Kane was undergoing considerable emotional suffering at the time of her actions. Because of the judicial complexity this poses to the case, I have made the decision to dismiss the jury at this time and deliver a verdict for which only I am responsible. I thank you for your time and your service. You may now leave the court.' The jury began to file out.

'All rise for the verdict,' the judge said, once they'd left. Sheena and the others stood up, still reeling, but holding hands tightly.

'It is clear from Mrs Kane's testimony that while you may not have committed the crimes you have been charged with, you ought not be proud of your actions. You threatened a mentally vulnerable woman with the exposure of her gender transition, which forced her to take drastic action. Mrs Kane, your lawyers have informed me that the Kane Foundation will reimburse the entire cost of the investigation, of the women's incarceration, and any further costs that come to light that led us up to today. Is this correct?'

Madeline nodded. 'It's the least I could do, your Honour.'

'Given this offer, and since none of us wish to waste more court time, I will sentence you now for your own crimes, Mrs Kane.' Madeline went pale, and Sheena grinned.

'For the crime of misleading law enforcement, how do you plead?'

'Guilty,' Madeline replied.

'For that you will receive a fine of ten thousand pounds, in addition to the reimbursement we just mentioned.' The judge said. 'And for the crime of wasting police resources, how do you plead?'

'Guilty,' Madeline repeated.

'Very well. For that I am sentencing you to a community service order of one hundred hours.' Madeline found comfort in imagining herself wearing the same silver dress that Naomi Campbell wore during her community service. 'Given the extraordinary changes you have made to your life, creating an ambitious and successful woman from such humble beginnings, I suggest your community service involves filming seminars for those younger visitors to this court who don't seem to believe they can change their destiny.'

Sheena dug her nails into Helen's hand while a huge smile flashed across Madeline's face. 'Thank you, your Honour. I love to give back and motivate. I'd be delighted to show those who've had a bad start in life that you can turn things around if you really want to.' The expression on her face was nothing short of angelic, and Helen wanted to stick her fingers down her throat. Like Sheena, she was absolutely raging, and Madeline's performance was enough to make them want to be sick.

'In that case,' Judge Walker said, happy at her response, 'I believe we can wrap up what has certainly been one of the most interesting cases of my career.' He smiled at Madeline again, and Sheena gritted her teeth. She'd gotten away with the whole thing while they lost eleven months of their lives in prison.

As the judge got out of his chair to leave, he delivered his final words to the women who were itching to get out of the building, and away from this madness. 'You may not be leaving this court charged as guilty, but you are certainly ruthless, vengeful women. I'd advise you to take a long hard look at your conduct and just how far you were willing to go to get what you wanted.' He left the courtroom.

Sheena seethed with anger. Madeline had unjustly locked them up for nearly a year, and was being treated as a victim, while they had been framed as ruthless bitches who would do anything to get ahead. She took several deep breaths and counted to ten, then stood up with the other women and filed out of the courtroom, heads held high and still holding hands.

As they were being ushered into the side lobby used for defendants and court staff, Sheena spotted a smirking Madeline making her way for the exit. She tried to go after her, but Amanda grabbed her arm with all her might to stop her. 'Let me go,' Sheena growled as Madeline watched on amused.

Helen was also fuming. 'You fucking cow!' she spat in Madeline's direction. 'You had us locked away! For something we didn't do! You've just been alive all this time? And no one seems to think that's illegal? You're the one who should be in prison, not us!'

Farrah and Catherine pointed death stares at Madeline as she sashayed out of the building to what seemed to be a million flash bulbs going off from the waiting press.

As soon as Madeline had departed, Eva Hope and Rupert Flint hurried over to their clients.

'Bloody hell,' said Rupert, running a hand through his silver hair, 'that was a turn up for the books. Congratulations!'

'No one can tell me that bastard judge wasn't in her pocket.' Farrah looked furious. 'She must have paid him off to let her stage an entrance like that.'

'I'm sure of it,' hissed Sheena. 'She fucking winked at me when she was pretending to cry.'

'That bitch!' said Helen.

'Careful with your words until we leave the building. There are cameras and microphones everywhere,' said Eva. 'Accusing one of the most respected judges in Jersey of corruption will land you right back in here for contempt of court. You've got what you wanted haven't you? You're free! So zip it.'

'She's right,' said Amanda. 'Let's not open a can of worms. Please, I just want to see my daughter.'

'But we're innocent, and she's not,' Catherine exclaimed. 'Don't you want to fight this so the world knows it?'

Rupert raised an eyebrow. 'Whether you fight it or not, after the performance in there, you'll never be innocent in the eyes of the baying mob out there. So you need to prepare yourself for that. Listen.' The women strained to hear, and cries of 'Bitches! TERFs! We love you, Maddie!' reverberated through the court's old windows.

'Shit,' said Helen.

'I'm afraid so,' said Eva. 'You need to prepare yourselves. Rupert and I have arranged cars for you, but you're going to have to run the gauntlet first.' She led them towards a small door which was a side exit off the court, just beside the main steps where Madeline had exited to soak up her moment of glory.

The women hugged for a second and said their mantra. All for one, and one for all.

Then Sheena kicked the door open with her spiked heel, and they headed out, into the light.

CHAPTER 23

Amanda

The protest outside the courthouse was in full swing. The air was thick with tension as the women made their way through the crowd with their barristers as fast as they could towards the cars which stood open, waiting. But suddenly their exit was blocked. They were surrounded on all sides by placards and angry chants. Someone yelled: 'Turf out the TERFs!' and the cry went up all around them as they struggled to make it to the cars. Catherine turned to Helen, confused. 'What are they calling us?' she asked.

'TERFs,' Helen replied grimly. 'It stands for Trans Exclusionary Radical Feminist. It means they think we're opposed to trans people.'

'I'm not opposed to trans people!' Catherine exclaimed. 'None of us are.'

'I'm opposed to that bitch,' Sheena spat.

'Yes, but not because she's trans!' replied Amanda. 'None of us think like that. It's disgusting.'

Helen shook her head. 'Doesn't matter. If today's taught us

anything it's that the truth means fuck all. No matter what we say or believe, TERF is a label we're going to have to get used to hearing.'

The women huddled together, instinctively feeling the need to stay close to each other in this new hostile world. As they struggled through the crowd to reach their cars, Amanda broke away as she spotted Dan, waving and blowing her kisses. As she went towards him, she caught sight of Jake with Olivia in his arms, standing next to a woman in a brown dress and white gloves carrying a baby boy. Her heart threatened to crack open, and she started pushing her way through the crowd, calling her daughter's name. Someone barged into her shoulder; it was Farrah, shoving people aside, desperate to reach the woman carrying her son. But before they could make it through the scrum, Jake gave a cheery wave and a salute, and ushered the woman in the brown dress into a people carrier before climbing in behind her. The door slid shut behind them and the vehicle started pulling away. Just as Farrah and Amanda managed to break through the crowd, a window opened a few inches. Jake stuck his hand out and gave the press a backhanded wave, but Amanda could have sworn that he had arranged his fingers for a brief instant to flick her and Farrah the V-sign. Farrah's eyes narrowed and she was breathing hard, two spots of white appearing high on her cheeks. Amanda wouldn't forgive Jake for snatching away her daughter when she was practically in arms' reach, and it looked like Farrah wouldn't either. Thank God they were out of prison now. It was time for the women to team up, get their children back and punish Jake as much as they possibly could in the process.

The other women caught up with them. 'Let's get out of here,' Sheena said, as a ring of police officers began herding them towards the fleet of cars. But as they followed, Amanda noticed that the crowd was suddenly swarming away, back to the steps of the courthouse, where Madeline had re-appeared, still flanked by her barrister but now dressed in a totally different outfit. Gone was the saintly white suit, replaced by a flame-red jumpsuit, six-inch black heels, and her hair in a high ponytail. She looked like she'd stepped off the catwalk rather than out of the court room, yet the simplicity of the outfit, with her full face on show, was powerful: at once fierce and fragile, it was impossible not to look at her.

Amanda hesitated, torn between getting to St Augustine's as quickly as possible to see Olivia, and desperate to find out what Madeline had to say.

'I'm overwhelmed by your understanding and forgiveness,' Madeline began, her eye catching Sheena's, giving her once more the ghost of a wink. 'I'm just truly sorry that our society makes it almost impossible for a woman like me to live in the manner of their own choosing, without fear of harassment, exposure, and censure.'

'She's fucking unbelievable,' Sheena muttered to Amanda. 'She doesn't even want to be classed as LGBTQI+, she's using these activists as protection. She's a disgrace,' she spat.

Amanda didn't answer, but watched in silence as the placard-wielding protestors roared their approval, first to Madeline, then to the cameras. Reporters were swarming everywhere, filming live links while press drones overhead captured the bird's eye view of Madeline, surrounded by the adoring crowd. But as one of her supporters – a person with a beard and a bald head, squeezed into a tight dress and high heels – leaned in for a selfie, Amanda saw Madeline flinch as their bodies made contact. Ever the performer, she gritted her perfectly porcelain veneers and smiled for the cameras, but Amanda, who'd spent years working on TV sets with co-stars who hated each other, could tell that she had positioned her body so as to keep some distance between them. She could see the effort it took Madeline not to recoil as she was forced to clasp her bearded supporter's hand in hers, and raise it aloft, as the chants grew louder.

'You're one of us! Self-ID! Self-ID!' they shouted.

Helen looked on in amusement. Like Amanda, she didn't have any prejudices herself, but she knew that Madeline would have given anything to snatch her hand away: not even her best acting could convince her otherwise. 'Well,' she said, 'She got us locked away in St Helier prison, and now it seems to have landed her in gender prison. She's gone from taking the most extreme steps to never be linked to her past, to becoming the face of transgender activism. Now that, for her, is a prison sentence'. Helen let out a low cackle, and Amanda smiled wryly.

The crowd was quieting, and it looked like Madeline was about to make another speech.

'Thank you – all of you – for understanding my struggle.' Madeline said, disentangling her hand from the bearded protester, and waving at the roaring crowd like Madonna playing Eva Peron.

'Can't they see she's faking it?' Farrah was exasperated. 'Given half the chance she'd spear anyone who didn't fall under her version of gender perfection with her Louboutin.'

Amanda looked over at the press pack, who were clamouring for Madeline to look over at them so they could get the money shot: a direct, to-camera question and answer. She caught sight of Tabitha Tate, making her way through the chaos and climbing onto one of the courthouse's large pillars. It looked like she was the only reporter whose shot was clear. She was almost eye-to-eye with Madeline now, which Amanda knew would make the shot look exclusive and pre-arranged, like photoshoots of Obama on the steps of the White House. Amanda gasped as Tabitha jumped the two-foot gap to the courthouse steps and landed without a wobble despite her ridiculously high heels. She winced slightly as she strode over to Madeline, and Amanda saw another cameraman zoom in on a two-shot while Tabitha thrust her microphone closer so whatever she said would be crystal clear.

'Tabitha Tate, the *LA Leader*. Madeline Kane, may I ask you what the whole world wants to know now you're back from the dead?'

Madeline's face flickered, and Amanda could sense that her confidence was wavering. Amanda guessed Madeline was hoping to be in the car and away from it all well before she said anything that might trip her up. But now, with Tabitha's microphone jammed in her face, there was nowhere hide.

'What's next for you, what do you want now this is all over?' Tabitha asked, to Amanda's surprise. Tabitha had a reputation for being a merciless journalist. Getting cancelled must have softened her.

The microphone picked up a small sigh of relief from Madeline. It seemed that of all the questions to be asked, this was one she could answer easily. Her voice was infused with a rare honesty as she answered. 'There is just one thing I want. To be reunited with my beloved husband, Chad. All my life, I've gone to great lengths to shield my journey. Fearing I'd spend my life alone, feeling like damaged goods after all I'd been through to be my true self. Then a miracle happened. Love struck us like a lightning bolt, and from the first moment I met him, I knew he was my soulmate, my reward for all the pain I'd suffered.

'I longed to share my story with him. I yearned to be honest and explain my past but I loved him so much the fear he might reject me kept me silent. And so, the revelation remained buried, simmering beneath the surface, and now after watching the live broadcast of last year's *Falcon Bay* where he revealed he knew all along, and he loved me anyway, feels like the biggest blessing and the most awful curse. A curse because he's disappeared. Because of what I did, he ran away to mourn my passing. And now I might never see him again.' A stream of tears ran messily down her perfect cheek bone. For the first time that day, Amanda believed her grief was real.

Tabitha Tate was silent for a moment, as if she too had been thrown by Madeline's raw honesty. But then she came back to her journalistic senses, and seized the chance to grab some footage she knew would be syndication gold. 'Take the mic, and look down the barrel of the camera,' she instructed Madeline, and gestured to her cameraman to zoom in. 'Speak to your husband.'

Madeline took a deep breath, and turned her beautiful green eyes down the lens. 'Chad, if you are watching, please believe me. I wanted to tell you. And I pray you can forgive me. Please, Chad. Come home.' Madeline dabbed her eyes with her silk handkerchief, handed the mic back to Tabitha and began to make her way down the steps and away from the crowd with her head bowed.

Tabitha darted after her. 'Just one more question before you leave. Do you have anything else you'd like to tell the millions of people who've been following your story?'

Madeline, who had now reached the final step, turned back, and spoke into the microphone and looked down the camera lens once more. 'Once again, I'd like to thank you all for your support. And remind you all that my one wish now is to find my husband. If Chad isn't listening, I'm appealing to anyone who might know how to find him. If you can help, please come forward.' Her eyes stared down the barrel of the lens intently. 'I promise to make it worth your while.' Flanked now by bodyguards in crisp black suits, she walked away, stepped into a black Range Rover with tinted windows, and sped away from the courthouse at speed.

Amanda was confused. She had assumed Madeline's marriage to Chad was one of convenience, to make them each a part of the ultimate power couple. But that speech had been heartfelt.

'What a performance,' Sheena scoffed.

'She'll say anything for the column inches,' said Helen, rolling her eyes.

'No,' Amanda said. 'She meant that. I could tell.'

'Whatever,' Sheena said. 'I've had enough of this charade. Come on ladies. Let's get out of here whilst their attention is diverted. We're free, right? So let's fucking go!' She turned to push her way through the crowd, strutting confidently on her gold Jimmy Choo heels. Suddenly the shouts of

'TERF! TERF! TERF!' seemed to be coming from everywhere again.

'What the fuck!' Helen stopped suddenly and looked down at her beautiful yellow suit, now stained with a viscous liquid and flecks of something orangey-brown.

'What is that?' Amanda asked, but before Helen could answer, she felt something hit her shoulder and shatter, leaving something wet and gloopy behind.

'They're throwing eggs,' Sheena yelled. 'Hurry, just get in the car!'

Amanda ducked, and saw an overripe tomato fly over her head and graze Farrah's ear. She grabbed her friend's hand and pulled her away, and together they and the police moved through the angry crowd, ducking and weaving, until they reached the sedan with blacked-out windows waiting beyond the police cordon.

Amanda settled back in her seat and caught her breath. Despite the car's soundproofing, she could hear the chants of 'Madeleine! One of us!' coming from the throng outside the courthouse.

'They worship her. She's their new icon,' Catherine said, her voice tinged with disbelief.

'What does that mean for us?' Farrah asked.

'It means,' said Sheena grimly, brushing a stray piece of eggshell off her dark purple jacket, 'that no matter the verdict, and no matter how insane the stunt Madeline pulled, in the eyes of the people, and especially that shitty judge's damming remarks, we're still considered guilty. And to those activists and millions who follow their views', she gestured in the rear view mirror, 'we always will be.'

Amanda closed her eyes and let her head sink back into the seat rest as the car pulled away. It was like a horrible nightmare. All she wanted was for everything to be over. She wanted to be held in Dan's arms, with Olivia cuddling up to them both on the sofa. But with Jake taunting her by keeping her daughter away, Madeline back from the dead and no doubt plotting revenge, and her supporters wanting to tear Amanda and the others apart, it felt like the worst was still to come.

PART 3

CHAPTER 24

Candy

Candy was just turning up the hidden stone path that led off the beach to Jake's villa when she heard a deafening crash from inside the house. On instinct, she started running. After all, Jake was in his sixties and the stress of the revelations at the trial couldn't have been good for his heart. Breathing heavily, she clambered up the steps to the terrace, where a roar of frustration, followed by another smashing sound, stopped her in her tracks. She peered through the billowing white curtains into the dining room, saw Jake raise a whisky glass above his head like a baseball, and fling it at the wall. Judging by the shards of glass around his feet, he had been at this for some time.

'Snap out of it, Jake!' Candy strode straight in through the ornate French windows and grabbed her boss's arm.

Jake turned to her, his face set in a snarl, his body coiled like a wiry boxer ready to throw a punch. She had never seen him look so angry.

'I just took a call from my lawyer. There's an issue with my ownership of St Augustine's. That bitch Madeline Kane has triggered a clause that means it will revert to her. And she wants me out of my villa by tomorrow!'

Candy tried to stay calm and think fast. She didn't want to be the next target for the Waterford crystal. Neither did she want to lose her lucrative job as Jake's PR – not until Tabitha's money came through anyway – and if Jake had to give up La Mirage, he sure as hell wouldn't keep her on the payroll.

'Let's be rational, Jake. We're nearly there with the launch. You need to contest her claim. Get it stuck in the courts, buy yourself some time. Once you've launched La Mirage, and caused a huge buzz in the press, you can move on and say it's your choice to leave the island and it won't look like she's kicking you out.'

Jake furrowed his brow, as if paused in thought. He straightened up, and put the crystal tumbler down carefully on the sideboard.

'All right,' he said grudgingly. 'Maybe we can still pull off the launch. And thank God for the sheikhs. They've paid me for most of the apartments in cash, and it's all offshore so no one can touch it but me. There's no way I'm paying any of it over to that hag. And I'll make a public statement saying I would never stay on an island with such a deceitful, disgusting woman. I'll damn her with my exit and go out on a high.'

Candy wrinkled her nose in disgust. So Jake would make his escape with piles of cash, probably set himself up as a billionaire out in the Middle East like nothing ever happened. 'Well that's just great for you,' said Candy wearily, suddenly keen to get back to work and leave Jake's despicable orbit for the day. 'Let's have our meeting in the living room – I'll put on some coffee.' She picked her way over the broken glass to the next room. Jake should be bloody thankful she'd arrived when she did, or there'd be nothing left in the house to drink from.

Once Jake had settled himself into the white Versace sofa in the corner of the living room, he looked much calmer. Candy served him an AeroPress espresso in his favourite Hermès coffee cup, and calculated her best way forward was to pretend everything was fine. She snapped open her clipboard. 'Where were we?' She consulted her notes. 'Ah yes, you were saying you wanted a French theme. Bastille Day?'

'I've changed my mind,' Jake said, taking a sip of espresso. 'I want a masked ball. You know, like they have in Venice, or wherever.'

Candy gritted her teeth. 'But I've already briefed the press—'

'Lavish costumes,' Jake said, ignoring her. 'Elaborate masks, so nobody knows who's who. That will make things interesting.' He put down his coffee and clapped his hands, all thoughts of the island's ownership apparently forgotten. 'Yes – masks will encourage debauchery, scandal. The launch night for La Mirage needs to be an event extravagant enough to make the whole world take notice.' He paused. 'A nod to France would be good though. Give it a Versailles theme. Marie Antoinette. As long as it's lavish and glamorous and spectacular.'

Candy's irritation bubbled over. Didn't he realise the storming of the Bastille was an act of revolution? That Marie Antoinette was beheaded for her lavish tastes? 'Maybe we could have a guillotine,' she suggested sarcastically. 'Mock decapitations alongside the Dom Perignon fountain.'

Jake looked excited. 'Now you're talking.' He grinned. 'And we need a firework display. The biggest anyone's ever launched from a building.'

Candy sighed. 'I already told you, the New York Plaza did that last year. Any bigger and there'd be a serious threat to life.' Candy had seen the pictures marking the hotel's one hundredth birthday and there was no way that Jake could top it. Crowds had gathered below to watch the series of brilliant explosions, golden flames that shot high into the night sky.

'Don't be a health-and-safety Nazi. Ours is going to be bigger, and it's going to be better.' Jake was sitting up straight and smiling now. 'Once I've launched La Mirage, I'll be happy. And that bitch,' he snarled, 'can keep this fucking island and this house. I'll be in Dubai in a bigger and better one.'

Candy made what looked like a series of dutiful notes on her clipboard. She knew that, from his perch on the white leather sofa, Jake couldn't see that she was writing just one word, and underlining it several times: Arsehole.

CHAPTER 25

Sheena

Life after prison had been a mixed bag for Sheena McQueen. The first night of freedom had been suitably euphoric: she and the girls had gotten drunk on a case of Cristal that Sheena had received last Christmas from a client, and ordered a midnight delivery of Haribo for dinner. But the next day dawned flat and empty. Although Sheena was glad to luxuriate in her super-king bed made up with the softest sheets, as soon as she got up, she realised she missed the routine of La Croix, the simplicity of life, the ease with which one day flowed into another. She kept her promise and added £5,000 to Kayleigh's commissary to account for all Sheena's beauty treatments in prison. But in doing so she realised how much she missed Kayleigh, with her gravelly voice and healing massages. She even missed the Scrabble sessions with the others in the day room.

For the next few days, Sheena had prowled restlessly about her vast house. She emptied every cupboard in the kitchen, cleaned them, rearranged the contents. She rummaged through her wardrobe and pulled out items of clothing she'd never been fond of, including an Azzedine Alaïa dress and a pair of unworn Gucci loafers – what she was thinking buying flats? – earmarking them for a charity shop. Returning to her office was equally depressing. No one had been in since her arrest and during the months it had lain empty, a fine layer of dust had gathered on every surface. When she drew the blinds to let some light in through the grubby windows, she had stood for a moment, feeling disorientated, as if she were in the wrong place. That night, wallowing in a deep, scented bath in her vast marble bathroom that ran the whole width of her Kensington townhouse, Sheena reflected that while in jail, almost all she had thought about was her freedom. Now that she had it, she didn't know what to do with it.

Catherine seemed to be having the same problem. After forty years of celebrity, of having her days planned for her, everything done to a schedule, she was at a loss. She tried to find solace in religion, but outside of prison, she realised it wasn't her calling. She booked a few beauty treatments, but couldn't find any fulfilment in facials and seaweed wraps. Ill-equipped to be alone, she had even gotten in touch with her old co-star Lee Landers to dangle the idea of re-kindling their relationship. Sheena wasn't surprised when he didn't reply. Lee was a gold-digger, and Sheena knew he would never allow his lust for Catherine's body to override his desire to find an uber-rich wife. Poor Catherine, rejected and alone, couldn't think of any ways to fill her time. She phoned Sheena twice a day on the pretence of enquiring about acting work, even though Sheena had explained over and over that her work contacts would no longer take her calls. All her clients had left her, and her inbox was filled only with toxic, hate-filled emails. After Madeline's performance at the trial, the media had labelled Sheena as a TERF, and in her industry that was akin to being cancelled.

While Catherine occupied herself with beauty treatments, Sheena toyed with the idea of taking a holiday, somewhere exclusive and hugely expensive like the La Prairie spa. She still had millions in the bank from her ex-clients, after all. But now that she was in a position to go, she didn't really want to. Drifting, purposeless, lacking the kind of clear goal she had been focused on in prison, she found she couldn't settle to anything. And even on the rare occasion she managed to flop in front of Netflix or flip open a magazine, she was still taunted with the knowledge that Chad, Madeline and Jake were all out there somewhere, living their lives, having ruined Sheena's business and her reputation and gotten away with it. Sheena wasn't proud of her desire for revenge, but she couldn't avoid it. Being a vengeful woman was part of who she was. She vowed that she would take them down just as soon as she had shaken off her lethargy and sorted her own life out.

This morning though, Sheena woke in the mood to grab life by the scruff of the neck once more. She'd had excellent news yesterday from her prosecution lawyer Riley Clarke. The Kane Foundation were prepared to settle the civil suit she and Catherine had brought against Chad Kane for broadcasting their private conversation. Sheena had messaged Helen and Catherine at once, telling them to come and meet her at the Palm Court restaurant at London's Langham Hotel at 1 p.m. today, and to dress for celebration.

*

Sheena decided to arrive half an hour early, in the hope of bumping into her favourite waitress, Alicia. She strutted in through the grand entrance to the hotel, causing two sharply dressed men and an attractive blonde woman to do a double take. She smiled. She was dressed to kill after all, in a RIXO backless suede jumpsuit, Dries van Noten heels, and a Birkin crocodile bag that cost more than a London flat.

Tammo, the maître d', greeted her with genuine delight, showing her to her favourite alcove table and reassuring her it had remained unoccupied ever since what he sweetly referred to as 'that unfortunate misunderstanding'. As he fussed and led the way through the restaurant, she felt more heads turn, and the sensation of all those people looking at her made her nipples harden.

'Is Alicia here today?' she asked.

Tammo smiled. 'Of course, Madam. The moment she saw you were booked in, she swapped her shifts.'

A warm, soft voice floated over her shoulder. 'Cristal? On the house of course.'

Sheena turned to see Alicia approaching, bearing a bottle of champagne and two glasses. Tammo strode briskly off.

'So good to have you back with us, Ms McQueen.' Alicia smiled flirtatiously at Sheena. 'Can I take your coat? Or your... jumpsuit?'

Sheena stood up and returned the smile. 'Do you know, Alicia, I think I've forgotten the way to the coat room. Could you remind me?'

Alicia placed her hand on Sheena's bare back, as if to guide her forward. As the two women moved out of the restaurant and into the corridor, Alicia dropped her hand lower, then lower still, until it was just touching the top of Sheena's bottom under her jumpsuit.

'Did you miss me?' she murmured, one finger circling lightly over Sheena's skin.

'You have no idea,' Sheena sighed. Alicia's mouth was hot against her earlobe.

They had stopped in front of a locked door, and Alicia swiped a card against a metal plate to open it. Once they were inside, Alicia spun Sheena around to face her, and pressed her against the door. 'I have an idea,' she said. She reached behind Sheena's neck to undo the halter. The jumpsuit slithered to the floor, and Alicia kissed Sheena on the mouth, bringing one hand up to stroke her breast, the other down to graze the edges of Sheena's La Perla lace knickers.

Sheena moaned, and Alicia slipped a finger under the lace, and her tongue into Sheena's mouth. Sheena felt her orgasm building, and put her own hand up Alicia's neat black skirt to find the spot where her stockings met her smooth thighs. Alicia's breath caught, and Sheena moved her fingers higher, tracing the line of Alicia's thong, teasing her, until Alicia couldn't resist any longer and thrust herself against Sheena's hand. They climaxed together, and fell, juddering, against the door, Alicia's skirt pulled up to her waist, Sheena's jumpsuit still pooled around her feet.

'I needed that,' Sheena said when she had caught her breath.

Alicia laughed and kissed her again. 'That makes two of us, Ms McQueen. But you'd better find your way back to your alcove before your guests arrive or the boss might complain.'

Sheena returned to her table on wobbly legs just in time to greet Catherine, who looked the picture of elegance as she strolled through the restaurant in a vintage YSL white trouser suit, a shiny red Hermès Kelly bag in the crook of her arm.

'Where's Helen?' Sheena asked.

'A huge crowd was at the front of the Langham so I snuck in the back – I told Helen to come with me but she said she wouldn't be bullied.'

Sheena was about to ask what sort of crowd it was when Helen stumbled in from the lobby, looking bedraggled, and furious. She was wearing a huge green necklace from one of her beloved Hollywood estate auctions, paired with what had once been a pristine pink bandage dress. Both were now spattered with red paint, and the dress had a vicious tear running down one side. Just before the lobby door swung closed, Sheena caught the roar of 'TERF!' from the crowd outside.

'I don't know who tipped them off, but they're fucking following us everywhere we go!' Helen sank heavily into her chair and gestured at her splashed necklace and ruined dress. 'These emeralds once belonged to Marilyn Monroe, and the dress is Balmain! Don't they have any respect for fashion?'

'Were the press there too?' Catherine sounded sympathetic, but Sheena detected a trace of satisfaction that she had avoided the baying mob.

'God, yes,' said Helen. 'I got papped wearing this and I just know I'll be in the *Daily Mail* sidebar of shame tomorrow. I'm desperate to start things up again with Matt and if he sees me in the papers like this... Well. It's not exactly the quiet, stable life he was hoping for once I finally got out of prison.'

'Has he replied to your letters yet?' Sheena asked.

'Just one.' Helen looked miserable. 'It was waiting for me when I got home. It was a reply to the one I sent just before our trial, the one where I finally said the L-word. He said he understood, but his job made things complicated. He said I shouldn't contact him again unless I was acquitted at the trial, and the press vultures have stopped hounding me.' Helen twisted the cap violently off a bottle of fizzy water and sloshed it into her glass. 'He says he can't risk being seen with me when there's an angry horde of activists after my blood. As if it was my choice to go to prison, or to get my dress ripped to shreds in front of a hundred paparazzi! What I don't understand is why Madeline doesn't have all this harrassment from the press. She's the one who faked her own death, for crying out loud!'

'Look,' said Sheena, 'I've been going over this myself, and I know Catherine has too.' She glanced at Catherine, who nodded. 'I'd like nothing more than to take revenge on Madeline for what she did to us. But right now, she's untouchable. She's got a forest of bodyguards on St Helier, and the world's media thinks the sun shines out of her pert little arse. She's on every magazine cover all over the world – I even heard her on an Oprah podcast the other day. It's unbelievable.'

'So what can we do?' Catherine was twisting her napkin, looking anxiously towards the lobby where the crowd was still calling Helen's name.

Sheena signalled for the champagne to be opened, and another glass to be brought. 'Luckily for you, I've found a way we can get close to Madeline, but keep our distance at the same time. So we watch and wait. Then we strike when we can – not at her directly, but at those she loves.'

'What about money?' Helen asked. 'I'm totally broke. I never needed to save my *Falcon Bay* salary, and now I can't get any work. No one in the industry's returning my calls.'

'Don't worry, Chad's paying.' Sheena winked. 'He – or at least his sister – has agreed to settle the case brought by Riley Clarke on behalf of Catherine and me. We've secured two hundred million dollars to stop us taking the Kane Foundation to court for breach of privacy.'

'Two hundred million! Fuck me!' Helen was stunned.

'It's a drop in the ocean to the Kane Foundation,' said Sheena, waving her hand airily. 'And I know just what to spend it on.' She leaned over to pour the Cristal into three flutes. 'My idea will give Catherine something to do, get Farrah and Amanda their kids back, and give the press something real to write about. Which should push you, Helen, out of the limelight so you can win back Matt.'

Helen sipped her champagne slowly as Sheena explained her idea. The hum of conversation, the lilting sound of the pianist playing Cole Porter, and the buzz of the alcohol was softening her animosity. The crowd's roar was receding from her memory. It was a mad plan, but it might just work.

'What about you?' said Helen when Sheena had finished. 'What do you get out of this?'

'Darling, a return to St Augustine's gets me everything I want.' Sheena raised her glass. 'My agency's dead. I need a new challenge. And most importantly, I must have vengeance on those who have crossed me.'

Catherine clinked her flute to Sheena's, then to Helen's. 'I for one love the idea. I miss St Augustine's like anything. So here's to us. All for one. One for all.'

'Here's to us.' Sheena raised an eyebrow. 'To vengeful women. And to our biggest comeback yet.'

Helen raised her glass to her lips. 'I'm not sure exactly what we're signing up for. But what I do know is that what Sheena McQueen wants, Sheena McQueen usually gets.'

Sheena downed her glass of bubbles in a single gulp. 'Trust me. This is going to be big.' She waved at gorgeous Alicia to bring them another bottle.

CHAPTER 26

Jake

Jake woke early, as he always did these days. His night had not been restful, tormented as he was by two alternating images flashing in his mind: the Hitlist Killer, standing over him with a scalpel, and Madeline Kane, arriving on his island trying to steal it from him. He couldn't decide which was more terrifying. He had to get a grip, and needed to wash away the headache which seemed to be a constant presence behind his eyes. He reckoned a bracing swim in the ocean was the best way to do that. Taking a soft yellow beach towel from the driftwood chest in the living room, he stepped out of the French windows and started walking down his private footpath to the beach. It took him a few moments before he saw it: an enormous yacht, anchored a short distance from the cove. It must have sneaked into the bay under cover of darkness. He gazed at the sleek hull, the shiny white deck, the helipad at one end. He could just about make out two deckhands, each carrying a mop, swabbing what looked like a raised swimming pool near the bow. The owners were presumably still sleeping, and Jake itched to know who they were. Judging by the size of the thing, it was someone with a taste for the flashy and money to burn. Perhaps one of the sheikhs who had reserved an apartment in La Mirage and was waiting to move in.

Jake reached the water, and plunged in. With each firm stroke, he felt his worries from the night before begin to melt away. He reminded himself that things weren't so bad. His ex-wife and her hag friends were penniless and living far away in London. The Hitlist Killer was in the States, and would surely be caught by police well before he could make it over to Jersey. And would it be so bad if Madeline got the island back? So long as he could stall the takeover for long enough to launch La Mirage, he could probably leverage himself a cushy job in Dubai. Yes, the situation wasn't so dire at all.

He swam out a bit further, until he could just make out the boat's name. Nemesis. The Greek goddess of revenge. He chuckled. It was probably a celebrity who had pissed off a few people in their time. Simon Cowell perhaps? But no, Simon Cowell was in Portofino, summering with Kylie Minogue if he remembered correctly from Candy's RSVP list for the launch party.

He swam back to shore, towelled himself dry and, with a spring in his step, went back up the footpath to retrieve the binoculars that hung on a special hook next to the daybed, in the wisteria-covered pergola on the terrace. He trained them on the yacht and focused in on the stylish swimming pool. It was tiled in black, and the water shimmered like ink. There was a fully stocked bar at one end of the pool, and next to it, a booth-style table bearing three empty bottles of Cristal, five champagne flutes and what looked like a discarded pair of crystal-studded Jimmy Choos. Maybe the rich owner had hired some floozy last night, made her dance on the table for him.

As he watched, a woman in a polo shirt and tailored shorts appeared to clear up the debris. Now he came to think of it, the two deckhands he'd spotted earlier had both been female. It wasn't unheard of for a boat to have all-female crew, but it was certainly unusual. Intrigued, he swept his binoculars along the boat, looking for more clues as to its inhabitants. His eye caught on a row of swimsuits, drying in the early morning sun. Three string bikinis, a structured fifties-style two piece, and a dark green one-piece with a jewelled neckline. His blood froze in his veins. It looked identical to one belonging to his ex-wife, Amanda. He remembered it because she usually wore bikinis, but had a one-piece specially commissioned – to hide her saggy mum-tum no doubt – from some up-and-coming fashionista which had cost a fortune. But Amanda couldn't be here, on a ridiculously luxurious superyacht, could she? She was tainted by scandal, no one in the industry would work with her; she could never afford this. His mind flew to her hag friend Sheena, their puppet master. She always had her dirty fingers in lots of pies. Fuming, he grabbed his laptop and searched Sheena McQueen + Amanda King + Nemesis. He clicked on the first news article that came up.

Riley Clarke's Legal Triumph: Massive Settlement in Baton Rouge Case

In Baton Rouge, Louisiana, Attorney Riley Clarke's courtroom brilliance prevailed as she secured an extraordinary settlement for her clients, Sheena McQueen and Catherine Belle. The case centred around Chad Kane's illicit recording of the two women, which violated privacy law and contributed to their false imprisonment.

Renowned for her fearlessness and legal acumen, Clarke negotiated a nine-figure, out-of-court settlement from the Kane Foundation. In the wake of this unprecedented victory, the claimants and their companions Helen Gold, Farrah Adams and Amanda King have chartered the superyacht Nemesis, at a rumoured cost of £60,000 per week. Sheena McQueen commented: 'We intend to celebrate our newfound financial security with a girls-only holiday on a beautiful boat near our old island home. We're here to have a good time, and to clear our names after some recent unfortunate events.' When questioned as to why the yacht was named Nemesis, McQueen answered, 'That's just a coincidence.'

A sense of impending doom took hold of Jake. What the hell were they plotting? He speed-dialled his lawyer to demand the yacht be served with an exclusion order; given notice to sail into the sunset pronto. His useless lawyer informed him there was nothing to be done, it had every right to be there. Jake could feel his headache starting up again, intensifying with his lawyer's parting words: 'Furthermore, I'd advise you to review your arrangement for your two children, Mr

Monroe. While the mothers awaited trial it was very difficult for them to contest custody, but now they've been acquitted, it's a different story. I can of course recommend a barrister if you'd like to sue for full custody in court?'

Jake slammed down the phone and knocked back three paracetamol. He desperately needed his public image as a decent family man to deflect attention from how he'd got La Mirage built in record time and without planning permission. The zen calm he had achieved with his morning swim was totally shattered. It felt like everything was crumbling around him. He took a deep breath, and tried to hold on to the fact that not everything he feared had yet come to pass. La Mirage was still standing tall, and the building work was nearly finished. There was still a chance that Madeline wouldn't carry out her threat to take back the island anytime soon – after all, he'd heard she was totally focused on tracking down Chad. Did she really have time to come and reclaim an island which – let's be honest – surely only held terrible memories for her?

Eventually, he managed to calm himself down. The negotiations with Madeline's lawyers were nearly at an end, and he was fairly confident of getting most of the things he wanted. Later today he would find out what the final settlement would be. And until then, he just had to remain cool, calm and in control.

CHAPTER 27

Tabitha

Tabitha Tate was on the terrace of the Heron Café, sitting in the far corner so that no one could sneak up behind her, when a foghorn sounded loudly. She jumped, nearly knocking over her coffee cup, before her brain caught up with her body. A serial killer was hardly likely to announce their arrival on the island by foghorn. She took one last sip of her flat white – Marco's coffee was the best she'd ever tasted, dark, smooth and strong – before curiosity got the better of her and she moved to the railing to look out to sea.

Moored in the distance, not far from the cove, was a vast, hulking yacht that hadn't been there yesterday. But that wasn't what had made the noise. A sleek, wooden sailing boat was heading towards the island's marina at speed, and it had just passed the superyacht with what looked like inches to spare. As the sailing boat neared, Tabitha could make out a lone woman, standing at the prow, so still and upright that at first, Tabitha mistook her for a figurehead. The woman was tall and curvaceous, and was wearing a clinging dress that matched the colour of the dark blue sea. Her raven black hair blew in the wind as the boat gathered speed. Presumably there was a skipper and some crew hidden somewhere on the boat, but, aside from the woman at the front, the ship's deck was completely empty.

Tabitha knew exactly who the woman was, and she had to hand it to her: Madeline Kane certainly knew how to stage a dramatic entrance.

The reporter in her clicked into gear, and she grabbed her notebook and made her way to the marina. She was just in time. A crowd of press had gathered – Madeline must have tipped them off in advance – and flashbulbs were popping as Madeline appeared regally at the top of the gangplank leading to the pontoon, like a queen about to address her subjects.

'Good morning, St Augustine's!' Madeline's honeyed voice carried beautifully over the water. 'As many of you know, this island belonged to my beloved husband, Chad. What you may not know is that, deranged by grief, and without *Falcon Bay* to run, Chad gave the island away to Jake Monroe – a known fraudster and cheat – and then he disappeared. I have now returned,' she paused dramatically, 'to reclaim our island – *my* island – and to find my darling Chad, wherever he is.'

In the rustles and whispers that followed this announcement, Tabitha caught a stealthy movement out of the corner of her eye. It was a man dressed in white, trying to escape the crowd unnoticed.

'Ah, Jake Monroe!' Madeline's voice had a hint of victory, but stayed steady. 'The man of the hour.' A paparazzo stepped forward and snapped a picture of Jake looking stony. Madeline addressed the crowd again. 'Mine and Mr Monroe's lawyers were up all night, working towards an amicable arrangement.' Jake winced, but didn't move. 'I must congratulate Mr Monroe for the work he's done to bring tourists and sightseers to St Augustine's. Though parts of the theme park were in poor taste, I think we can agree that his huge building is starting to look quite special.' She gestured towards La Mirage, which rose majestically out of the woodland, the sun glinting off its glass facade. 'We've agreed that Mr Monroe will remain on my island until he has achieved his goal of launching La Mirage. After that, he plans to move to Dubai.'

A reporter in a garish sun visor raised his hand. 'Where will you be living on the island, Mrs Kane?'

'Mr Monroe has graciously agreed to move out of my villa and into one of the woodland cottages and I shall be moving back in.' Madeline stepped aside. Four burly men appeared, carrying two Louis Vuitton trunks which they manoeuvred over the gangplank and onto dry land with surprising ease. Tabitha scribbled down the image in her notebook. This kind of detail was gold dust, and an on-the-ground story about the world's darling Madeline Kane kicking some lowlife out of her home so she could reclaim what was rightfully hers? Now that was a scoop even Sandy would be happy with.

Madeline strode regally towards Tabitha until they were face to face. 'Ah, Tabitha Tate, reporter extraordinaire. I have a proposal for you.'

Madeline took her arm and guided her away, out of the press pack. Tabitha was puzzled. Did Madeline know that Tabitha was writing another book about the *Falcon Bay* cast and crew, and that this time Madeline was at the heart of the story? She couldn't imagine who would have told her. After all, Mickey had commissioned it, and he was dead.

Madeline looked Tabitha in the eye. 'I admired how you tracked down Honey Hunter the last time she disappeared and didn't want to be found. Now I want you to do the same for Chad. You'll move into my villa today, and we'll start work immediately. When you find him, I'll pay you enough that you never have to work again.'

Tabitha cocked an eyebrow. 'I already have enough money that I never need to work again.'

Madeline placed a hand on her shoulder. 'In that case, I'll give you back your credibility and clean up your image. I imagine you'd love the world to stop calling you a heartless bitch? Find the love of my life for me, and I'll make sure the global press knows that under all that Christian Lacroix, beats a heart of gold.'

CHAPTER 28

Jake

Jake was so angry as he hurried away from the crowd of onlookers and towards his pathetically small new home, he didn't notice the figures in his way until he almost bumped into them. Amanda and Farrah stood shoulder to shoulder blocking his path, looking like a pair of heavies with their oversized sunglasses and grim expressions. He stopped, turned around, and tried to stalk off without saying a word. He wasn't going to speak to them without a lawyer present. If they wanted custody of the brats, they'd have to go through the courts.

'Mummy!' A cry of pure delight shot through the air. Jake looked ahead of him to see three-year-old Olivia toddling towards them, as fast as her chubby little legs could carry her. Lauren, carrying Max in her arms, was striding behind her, trying to keep up. Jake fumed silently. So now Lauren had betrayed him as well, making a deal with the mums behind his back. He made a mental note to withhold this month's salary. That would teach the bitch the meaning of loyalty.

'My darling girl!' Amanda rushed past Jake and swept Olivia off her feet, covering her with kisses. 'I've missed you so much!' There were tears in her eyes as she snuggled Olivia into her neck. 'You'll come home and live with Mummy now!'

Farrah was already running towards Lauren, her stupid heels clattering on the flagstones, reaching out for her baby boy. As soon as she had him nestled in her arms, she closed her eyes, and breathed in his smell. There was a moment of stillness. Then Max blew a loud raspberry and the spell was broken. Farrah started sobbing, clutching her son to her as if she would never let him go.

Even Jake had to begrudgingly admit that the children looked happy to see their mothers – Olivia was bouncing up and down in Amanda's arms, and Max was squealing while his mother tickled his tummy. He plastered a scowl on his face and squared up to the three women.

'If you want custody, you have to go through the courts,' he snarled. 'And as for you,' he looked at Lauren, 'this is grand insubordination and I'll be withholding your pay – and your bonus – unless you take the children back to my cottage this instant.'

Farrah lifted her head from Max and looked Jake in the eye. 'Haven't you heard? Sheena and Catherine have paid Lauren in full and we've hired her on the same pay, but without the sex work, to come to our yacht and look after the children until they're settled. They need some consistency in their lives after all your fuckery.'

Lauren spoke up. 'It's just business, right, Jake? Isn't that what you used to say to me when you came into my bedroom without knocking?'

Jake adopted an icy tone. 'I didn't see you refusing any paycheques. And what makes you think you can take them? I have custody until the courts say otherwise. What you're doing here is child abduction!'

Farrah handed Max to Lauren, and took a step towards Jake so that they were in touching distance. It went through his head that they'd just come out of the nick, having been banged up for months. Who knew what kind of violent, psychotic criminals they'd been mixing with, giving them ideas about how to solve their problems. God knows they were capable, regardless of what the court had decided. He felt an urge to run away, but forced himself to stand his ground, not wanting them to know he was intimidated.

'What's up, Jake?' Farrah said, giving him a nasty smile. 'Not scared, are you?'

What was it with these harridans? he wondered. Their uncanny knack of being able to see right through him. Was he really so easy to read?

Farrah reached inside her jacket. Oh, God, the bitch had a gun!

She produced an envelope and tapped him hard on the chest with it. 'Don't you think that the fact you are literally on a serial killer's hitlist might affect your ability to care for your children?' Another whack with the envelope. 'There's a court order in here. Our children are to come with us, to safety, until there is no longer any chance they would be abducted to get to you.'

Jake's mouth gaped open. 'I...'

'Haven't you been taking this seriously?' Amanda said. Her huge eyes held an expression of genuine concern. 'There's a killer on the loose – and he has you in his sights! Aren't you meant to be under police protection?'

Jake thought back to the official looking letters piling up in the villa. He hadn't opened any of them, too frightened they would be a court summons for one of the many dodgy deals he'd done to get La Mirage off the ground.

Now he shivered, looked around nervously, as if the Hitlist Killer was hiding behind one of the ornamental palm trees that flanked the path to the beach.

'I've been too busy working, providing for my family,' he told them, lamely.

Farrah nodded. 'Ah, right.' She withdrew another envelope, this time from her rose gold Birkin handbag. 'Working. Is that why the private investigator we hired provided all these photos of you drinking, snorting, and,' she lowered her voice so as not to be overheard by Lauren or the children, 'fucking the nanny?'

Jake gasped. 'You had me followed?'

'Too right we did. And it would only take one click on my phone for these to be all over the internet. Would you and your Instagram followers like that, Jake? No? Didn't think so. Then be a good boy and let us take our children out to the yacht now. We'll see you in court. Unless of course the Hitlist Killer gets you first.'

The three women turned and walked off towards the shore, Amanda still cooing over Olivia, Lauren pausing to blow a kiss over her shoulder towards Jake, then share a laugh with Farrah who had Max clutched in her arms again.

Jake watched until they climbed into a tender bobbing in the shallows, and zoomed off towards the Nemesis. He hated these women with an intense passion. He had never felt so alone. He looked over his shoulder again, paranoid now. Not just scared that a crazed killer might jump out of the bushes brandishing a scalpel, but afraid that his time was up. No one was on his side. Not Lauren, not Madeline, certainly not his exes. Could Candy still be counted on? Or was she as evil as the rest of them, making pacts behind his back, stitching him up, having him followed for Christ's sake!

A terrible thought struck him. What if Madeline had done the same, three years ago, on the set of *Falcon Bay*? If she'd had him followed, it was conceivable that she knew exactly what he'd done to Honey. Could Madeline have employed someone at *Falcon Bay* to watch him? If so, who? Perhaps the same person who helped her fake her death and escape the island?

But then he returned to the thought he always came back to. He made sure he'd closed the blinds. He was sure of it. If there was one thing Jake Monroe wasn't, it was an idiot. He was careful to make sure no one could see him. For the life of him, he still couldn't figure out who the traitor might be. And on top of everything else, that grade-A cow Tabitha Tate was no doubt about to run a hatchet job on him in the press after the scene at the marina. Shit.

He felt outnumbered, isolated, afraid.

Who would be there if it all came crashing down around his ears? He glanced up at the towering edifice of La Mirage, the sun gleaming off its glass, and felt suddenly superstitious, wishing he'd not thought about things crashing down. It seemed like an omen, one that could turn out to be very bad indeed.

CHAPTER 29

Tabitha

Tabitha couldn't believe the speed with which Madeline's entourage transformed Jake's villa. Within two hours, all Madeline's Louis Vuitton trunks had been unpacked, and the villa had morphed from a playboy mansion into something that resembled a beautiful Italian palazzo. One of the moving staff confided in Tabitha that this decor was much more in keeping with the penthouse on the island that Madeline had originally occupied when she lived with Chad, which had been knocked down in order to build La Mirage. New art had been hung on the walls, the heavy whisky tumblers had been exchanged for delicate fluted glasses. Even the naff white Versace sofa was gone, replaced with an antique chaise longue upholstered in gold silk.

Amidst the hustle and bustle, Madeline had installed Tabitha in a quiet corner, at a leather-topped desk overlooking the sea that had – for now at least – been spared the cull. She'd instructed Tabitha to start work right away, reeling off a list of details she'd need to start her search: the colour and make of

Chad's car; the kind of hotels he would stay in; the places that Madeline and Chad had visited together, where they'd been happy enough that he might want to return.

It was rare for Tabitha to fall in line with another person's instructions so completely, but Madeline had such an authoritative air, and was so single-minded in her desire to find her husband, that Tabitha quickly formed a sneaking admiration for her. Yes, she was a ruthless operator who didn't care about treading on people's toes. But she was passionate and focused too, if the £500,000 Madeline had already transferred into Tabitha's account 'to show she meant business' was anything to go by.

Tabitha opened her laptop and glanced at the notes she'd made from her conversation with Madeline. The first and most important was Madeline's certainty that Chad was alive, and had disappeared on purpose. If he had died or been abducted – wealthy men in Chad's circle had been kidnapped and held to ransom in the past – they would have heard about it. As it was, his disappearance had left no trace: surely, then, it was something he had planned, and executed flawlessly. Tabitha deduced that, assuming he was alive, it was also a safe bet to assume that he was living somewhere off-grid, somewhere the world's media did not reach. Otherwise, wouldn't he have got in touch as soon as Madeline's resurrection was splashed all over the news?

She started her digging by investigating Chad's network. Someone had to have helped him disappear, and she hoped the numerous articles and photos of him online would give her some clues as to who he might rely on in a secret but important situation like this. She wasn't sure exactly what she was looking for, but as she scrolled through photos of Chad at corporate events, TV awards ceremonies and the like, she noticed that the same man kept cropping up in several of the pictures. He was short and wiry, but otherwise non-descript, and seemed to be dressed in the same plain black suit each time. Was it some sort of uniform? He wasn't the focus in any of the pictures, but a figure in the background. He always stood apart from the group, and Tabitha wouldn't have noticed him if it weren't for the fact that he looked so alert and watchful. She double clicked on a photo of Chad shaking hands with Hillary Clinton at the World Economic Forum in Davos, and zoomed in. There he was again, and this time it was unmistakable: he was looking right at Chad.

Tabitha called Madeline over, and showed her the photo. 'Who's that?' Tabitha asked.

Madeline frowned, puzzled. 'That's Ashton Rockwell, Chad's chauffeur. They've worked together for years. His face is blurry, but I can tell from the uniform. I don't know why he'd be in on a private conference in Davos, though. I thought his job was to stay with the car.'

Tabitha clicked through the other shots. 'Do you think there's a chance Chad was employing him as a bodyguard as well as a driver? If so, would he trust him enough to help him escape?'

Madeline's face lit up with a rare and dazzling smile. 'I knew there was a reason I hired you! After a kidnap attempt last year I begged Chad to have a bodyguard, and all he would say is that I shouldn't worry, it was taken care of. I thought he was fobbing me off, but he must have promoted Ashton and kept it secret. Ashton used to be a driver with special forces, Chad would trust him with his life. It all makes perfect sense.'

Tabitha's skin started to tingle in the way it often did when she was about to crack a story wide open. She tapped at her laptop. 'All we need now,' she said to Madeline, who was now perched on an elegant hardwood chair at Tabitha's desk, 'is to contact Ashton.' Her fingers flew over the keys as she searched profiles on Twitter, LinkedIn, Instagram, TikTok and Facebook at lightning speed. But 'Ashton Rockwell' drew a blank each time.

'Another dead end, then.' Madeline's voice was steady, but Tabitha saw how her polished red nails tapped urgently on the leather.

'Not at all,' Tabitha said. 'The fact we can't find him is a good sign. It means he has something to hide. Now let's think logically. He's a chauffeur, right? So he knows about cars. And he's ex-special forces, so he knows about staying off-grid. If I were him, I'd rent a car, pay in cash, and then drive my boss somewhere far away. Across state lines for sure. Across a national border if I could.' Tabitha was already bringing up Google Maps and running a search. 'There are three car hire companies within five miles of Baton Rouge. Eight if we widen the search to ten miles. All we need now is a little sweet-talk, and a lot of patience.'

She picked up the phone, keyed in a number, and asked to speak to the manager. She added a Southern lilt to her usual New York accent: she was a good mimic, something that had always given her an edge as a journalist.

'I'm so sorry to bother you, Sir, but I lost a diamond earring in one of your cars. It was about a year ago and – silly me – I only just realised! I'm offering a thousand-dollar reward for its return. Can you help me?'

'Of course, Madam, can you let me know which car you hired?'

'Well, that's just it. I'm no good with cars,' she simpered. 'I can't even remember the colour! My husband takes care of everything. He can't know I lost the earring – he'll be furious – they were his wedding present to me! He booked the car sometime around July 10th, last year, and he paid cash, I remember that because he'd just had a big win at the casino. His name is Ashton Rockwell.'

There was a pause, and Tabitha held her breath. But no one got this lucky on the first try.

'I'm terribly sorry, Madam...' Of course he was sorry, Tabitha thought. He had probably already spent the thousand dollars in his head. 'No one of that name rented a car that week.'

Tabitha apologised, said she would try the other rental companies, and hung up.

An hour later, and five rental companies down, she thought she'd scream if she had to do that fake Southern simper one more time. But, gritting her teeth, she picked up the phone and prepared to do the charade all over again. This time, the pause at the other end while the manager scoured their database felt different. Tabitha's skin tingled again.

'We did have a gentleman who paid cash on 11th August last year,' the manager sounded hesitant. 'But the name is different. Does your husband go by any other name?'

Tabitha thought fast and took a gamble. 'His middle name is Chad. He uses it for work. Come to think of it, that's the name on his driving licence! Silly me,' she let out a tinkling laugh.

The manager sounded relieved. 'Of course, Madam. Yes, Chad Rockwell. It was a black Buick LaCrosse, wasn't it? It's in our parking lot right now and I'll have one of the team look for your earring immediately.'

'Well that's just wunnerful,' said Tabitha, drawing out the word. 'You have a great day now!'

Madeline looked at her, impressed. 'You are a serious operator.'

'Takes one to know one.' Tabitha winked.

'What happens now?'

'Now is where I reach the limit of my powers. I used to have a contact at ANPR who'd run a search for me, but he got a bit handsy and I had to cut him loose. Do you know anyone techy who can access closed websites? Ideally someone who's prepared to... bend the rules a little.'

Madeline smiled. 'I've got the perfect man.'

*

An hour later, after a delicious lunch of Jersey crab salad served with a chilled glass of Sancerre, there was a knock on the French windows. Madeline gestured for the man outside to enter, and when he did, Tabitha did a double take. It was Dustin, the producer she remembered from her time digging into the scandalous events at *Falcon Bay*. But he looked somehow... different. He used to be geeky. Squeaky clean. Dull, she'd concluded back then, of no interest to her. But he didn't look nearly as dull as she remembered. Dustin's hair was longer, his sunglasses were Ray-bans with cool tortoiseshell frames. His shirt clung attractively to his muscled arms, and his skin was tanned. Tabitha was surprised to find her hand going to the neckline of her yellow Commes des Garçons tank top, pulling the zip just a fraction lower.

Madeline's mouth twitched in amusement. 'This is Dustin. He's my right-hand man and he knows his way around a firewall. He'll be your tech support.'

Madeline stood up and gestured for Dustin to take her chair. He sat down and pulled himself in next to Tabitha, so close she could feel the warmth of his thigh against hers. He took off his sunglasses and looked at her. His eyes were dark green, flecked with orange.

'So, you're the one who finally cracked it. I've been searching for days.' Dustin sounded impressed.

'We aren't there yet,' said Tabitha. 'But we're making progress.'

Dustin opened his own laptop next to hers and pressed a fingerprint to the screen to unlock it. 'JetCar Baton Rouge?' he asked. Tabitha nodded, and he typed rapidly, lines of code appearing on the screen, white against blue.

'Bingo,' he said softly, as the code started to dissolve. 'We're in.'

Tabitha peered over his shoulder. It was grainy CCTV footage. 'Is that the parking lot?' she asked, unable to stop a hint of admiration creeping into her voice.

'Yup,' said Dustin. 'It's a live feed. Looks like there's just one black Buick in the carpark – here.' He zoomed in, until the number plate was visible. 'All we need to do now is run this number through ANPR—'

'You can do that?'

'Sure. How do you think I smuggled Madeline out of St Augustine's?' Dustin smiled at Tabitha, showing surprisingly good teeth. His fingers flew over the keyboard and in under a minute he had opened a database, run a search, and clicked on yet more grainy footage. It was the black Buick, leaving the parking lot on the day Chad disappeared. Dustin clicked out of the footage and scanned a list of files. His voice was tinged with excitement. 'See here? Those are all the clips that show the car crossing state lines.'

Tabitha squinted at the screen. 'Alabama, Tennessee, Kentucky, Ohio, Michigan. He headed north?'

Dustin nodded. 'If I had to bet, I'd say he took the Windsor-Detroit tunnel from Michigan into Canada. And this clip,' he scrolled to the very end of the list, 'should prove it.' Dustin clicked theatrically, and Tabitha and Madeline watched, silent and alert, as the Buick disappeared into the tunnel.

Tabitha let out a breath she didn't know she'd been holding. Madeline, usually so composed, blinked back a tear that had gathered in the corner of her eye. She cleared her throat, regaining control. 'I'm going to call it a day for now. You two carry on without me.' Her voice cracked, and Tabitha could tell that emotion was getting the better of her. 'We seem to be getting close. Excellent work both of you.'

As soon as she'd gone, Dustin nodded at Tabitha. 'I think we deserve a break, don't you? Care for a celebratory swim?' He walked out to the terrace, taking off his shirt as he did so to reveal a toned torso and muscular upper arms.

As Tabitha followed him down the stone path to the beach, she reflected that Dustin looked extremely good for someone who sat in front of a computer all day. Nor did it escape her notice that Dustin's eyes lingered just a beat too long on her own body, clad in a fuschia Melissa Odabash bikini that she'd just happened to wear underneath her clothes, and that left little to the imagination.

When she glanced back up the footpath to see if Madeline was following, she got the distinct impression that her new boss was leaving them alone together on purpose.

'Wait up!' she called to Dustin, and sped up until she was keeping pace with him. 'Would you mind putting a little suncream on my shoulders?'

She turned to look out to sea, enjoying the feeling of his hands on her skin, rubbing the cream into her shoulders and then lower, down her back, and around her waist. Dustin was close enough that she could feel how aroused he was. She reached back and stroked his thigh. He caught his breath and moved closer, pressing against her from behind. But she'd never been one for a quickie; she liked her pleasure long and drawn out. She let him bring a hand up over her stomach to graze the soft underside of her breast, but when he tried to slide the other hand between her legs she pushed it away, turned to face him and ran her tongue very gently over his lips.

'You don't want it enough yet,' she murmured. 'I like my men to beg.'

Dustin groaned, and Tabitha smiled.

'Race you to the sea!' She ran ahead and plunged in, feeling more alive than she had in months. The excitement attracing Chad, the memory of Dustin's hands on her waist and the cool water lapping at her skin made her worries about the Hitlist Killer melt away. In any case, in Madeline's mansion, with round the clock security, she would be safer than ever.

Dustin swam towards her, and she splashed water at him flirtatiously. She swam back to the beach and walked out of the shallows, making sure he got a good view of her glistening gym-toned body as she strolled up the sand, and back to the villa.

CHAPTER 30

Helen

After two days of raucous parties celebrating the women's freedom, new-found prosperity and the return of Amanda and Farrah's children, a soporific mood had descended on Nemesis. Catherine had retreated to her opulent cabin to sift through the bombardment of messages she'd received from Lee Landers. Ever since the announcement in the press about Catherine's win against the the Kane Foundation, Lee had been in touch daily.

He had left voicemails, sent text messages and had even arranged for a handwritten letter to be delivered to the yacht by drone. Each missive started by declaring his love for Catherine, went on to apologise for his silence while she was in prison (to write to her would have been far too painful, he said) and ended by outlining in graphic detail how he would worship Catherine's body if she would ever allow him to see her again. As much as Catherine enjoyed his fantasy of laying her out naked on the edge of the yacht's swimming pool so he could kiss and caress every inch of her, she knew that Lee's love for her was dependent on her bank balance. And she wasn't going to fall for his lies again. When she'd shown the messages to the others, Helen and Sheena had both suggested that she use the situation to her advantage, and engineer a way of humiliating Lee in the way that he humiliated her. Based on the smile that had curved on Catherine's lips, Helen was sure that Catherine was now plotting some kind of fiendish revenge on the hapless Lee.

Amanda and Farrah were sunbathing beside the black-tiled pool on the upper deck, taking some time for them-selves while Olivia and Max were napping in a gorgeous pink-and-yellow nursery with a connecting door to where Lauren was.

Sheena was on the sitting room balcony on the upper deck, gazing at the white sandy shores of St Augustine's, lost in thought. Helen came and stood beside her. She was still tingling from the memory of Matt's hands last night. Now that she was no longer a criminal, and the world's press had stopped hounding her, he had agreed to rekindle their relationship. Helen had sent a helicopter to pick him up, and had greeted him off the chopper wearing a G-string bikini, gold stilettos and a pair of diamond earrings that had once belonged to Ava Gardner. Taking in the vast yacht and his freshly waxed statuesque girlfriend, Matt had looked like all his Christmases had come at once. As soon as the helicopter pilot had disappeared below deck, Helen had taken Matt's hand, led him into the helicopter cockpit, and straddled him.

She smiled at the memory. He would be back tomorrow, and had promised to visit her twice a week until she was back on dry land and they could start a 'real' relationship. But

Helen wasn't sure when that would be. Sheena had pretty fixed ideas about their schedule.

Helen touched Sheena's arm, jolting her out of her reverie. 'Now we have our money, and the mothers have their kids, what are you planning on doing next?' Helen asked.

Sheena took a while to reply. 'I've been giving it so much thought. I've decided to relaunch the agency.'

Helen looked surprised. 'You're going back to work?'

Sheena smiled, ruefully. 'It's what I know.' She looked at Helen. 'Pretty much *all* I know.' She gestured at the yacht. 'What we're doing now is fun, sure, but there's a limit to how many times I can hear Catherine sing Cher songs after a bottle of Cristal. Anyway, I'm the best in the business, haven't you heard?'

Helen smiled. 'Actually, I have.'

Sheena glanced at Helen conspiratorially. 'If I told you I was pivoting from agenting to producing, and thinking about resurrecting *Falcon Bay*, what would you say?'

Helen grimaced. 'I'd say it's over. No one wants to work with us. And does anyone even watch soaps anymore? Another three were cancelled while we were in prison.'

Sheena shook her head. 'That's why it's brilliant. We could be practically the only one! The audience is still there. Just not the networks. But we'd do it in a modern way: Netflix, Amazon, Apple. It's all about global streaming.'

Helen sat up. 'I hear what you're saying, Sheena, but seriously – I've been cancelled. No one's taking my calls.'

'Showbusiness is fickle. It'll forget our scandals so long as we have a good proposition. We just need a backer who has industry clout. Then I think we could do something real –

a reboot. Bring back Honey, Lydia, Catherine – the whole gang. The fans would love it.'

'Are you mad?' Helen said. 'Honey's disappeared and there's a crazed killer slaughtering people in her name. Lydia's washed up. Catherine's head is full of her revenge plans against Lee. And what about Jake? He's still got it in for us.'

Sheena shuddered. 'According to Lauren, that prick's being chucked off the island as soon as that monstrosity is launched.' She nodded over to the Cove, where the towering bulk of La Mirage glimmered in the sun. 'We have Madeline Kane to thank for that. Who knows, maybe she's on our side after all. I'm wondering if she might be ready for a collaboration again.'

'Madeline might hate Jake, but that doesn't mean she likes us. Why would she agree to go back into production with her arch-enemies running things? Especially as we've just taken Chad and the Kane Foundation for a fortune.'

Sheena shrugged. 'Chad's nowhere to be found, and the amount the foundation paid out was small change to them. Anyway, the settlement was business, which I'm sure Madeline will understand. If the boot – the Manolo, in her case – were on the other foot, she'd have done the same. If we came up with a proposal that made financial sense, I can't see Madeline objecting. And after everything that's happened, I think she may well have a different outlook now, a less vindictive take on things, if you like. You heard what she said outside court, she's not looking to settle scores, all she cares about now is finding her husband.' Sheena was quiet for a moment. 'I need to speak to Madeline, woman to woman, before any of this is certain. For now this is just me thinking out loud so keep it to yourself.' Helen nodded. 'I just can't imagine a world where the five of us aren't making telly. I mean, will any of us be happy putting our feet up for the rest of our days? We're going to have to find something to do, why not something we're good at?'

Helen sat down next to Sheena and looked out to sea. A gull cawed and dived into the waves, emerging with a wriggling fish. They fell into silence, and Helen considered everything Sheena had said. It was true that their leisurely champagne lifestyle would soon wear off. She missed the cut and thrust of television, and now she no longer had the threat of a trial hanging over her, she wanted to be back on the mainland so she could enjoy her freedom and try for a proper relationship with Matt. Could it really be as easy as Sheena said? Would Madeline play ball? Would Jake back off? Would they be able to track down Honey? Sheena seemed certain it was possible, and mostly, what Sheena wanted, Sheena got.

Helen smiled and closed her eyes, letting the sun warm her skin. She had the sense that the things she'd been craving – freedom, success, love – were finally near, just around the corner, so close she could almost touch them. *Yes*, she thought. *So long as nothing else went wrong, the future looked very bright indeed.*

CHAPTER 31

Candy

Candy had arranged to meet Helen at the Oyster Bar, a smart new haunt on the island. Candy got there first and chose a marble-topped table by the window, framed by two soft velvet banquettes. She ordered a bottle of champagne. She needed a drink. She was sick of Jake and his ludicrous orders. Just that morning he had summoned her to his cottage in the woods and informed her he wanted the launch of La Mirage to involve wolves in suits scampering up and down the walls of the lobby.

'Wolves?' she said, incredulous. 'In suits?'

Jake nodded. 'Holograms or avatars, or something, they did it in Dubai, you'll have to find out.'

Candy suppressed a sigh and wrote something on her pad.

'And the fire and water thing I already told you about – blue fire reaching up the walls of the lobby, water streaming down at the same time.'

She gritted her teeth. 'Yes. I'm looking into it like you asked. We're setting fire to the building on its opening night.'

But Jake was too wrapped up in his ideas to catch her sarcastic tone. He waved his hand, impatient.

'It's some kind of special effect,' he said. 'I'm not actually planning to burn the place down'. He gave her a sly grin. 'Not unless I'm advised to do so for insurance purposes.'

Candy's thoughts were interrupted by the clang of the restaurant's old-fashioned wrought-iron gates. Someone who clearly didn't like to wait had wrenched open the door to the Oyster Bar and was now striding purposefully over to Candy's table.

Candy sized up Helen as she approached. She was looking gorgeous. Not as much makeup as usual, her hair in soft waves that framed her face. She was wearing a floaty Pucci dress, and she seemed younger, full of energy. Was that what prison did to you? Or was it the fat pay cheque Sheena had scored from the Kane Foundation?

Helen beamed at Candy and bent to hug her, and Candy felt a twinge of guilt for what she was about to do. She liked Helen. Had even promised her, once, that she was on her side. But she'd have to forget about that, give herself a stern talking to. After all, now Helen and her friends were stinking rich, why shouldn't Candy share in their good fortune? The money she had got from Tabitha was good – but it wouldn't stretch that far.

'It's great to see you,' Helen gushed. 'How are things?'

Candy considered how much to reveal. 'Well, as you probably heard, Madeline's back on the island and Jake's got the sack. After the launch of La Mirage, I'll be out of a job. So unless I suddenly become a millionaire...' She paused meaningfully. 'I guess I'm about to become unemployed.'

Helen waved a hand breezily. 'Don't worry, something else will come along. It always does.'

Candy frowned. Just because Helen always fell on her feet, it didn't mean everyone else did. She clutched the memory stick under the table. The footage it contained was the only thing that stood between her and a share of Helen's millions. Candy thought back to the first time she'd seen the clip on Ross Owen's phone. A handheld video recording of what happened after the awards ceremony, the night Ross Owen met his death. The footage showed Sheena, Helen and Ross arguing; Helen slapping him after he called her "a show bike". But it was what came next that was really explosive. Ross Owen, drunkenly trying to force himself on Catherine at the top of a cliff. Catherine, terrified, fighting back, pushing Ross away until he lost his balance and fell over the cliff's edge onto the rocks below.

It was a desperate act against a hideous predator. No one would be sorry for Ross's death; he was a lowlife of the worst kind. Candy couldn't blame Catherine for protecting herself, nor Sheena for dragging Ross's battered body into the sea, allowing it to be washed up the next day and his death pronounced a tragic accident. She'd even shown the footage to Helen long ago, and willingly handed over the incriminating phone, promising she'd keep silent. She'd simply omitted the fact that she'd kept a couple of copies, as insurance.

Candy gave Helen an appraising look. 'Your hair looks nice like that. It suits you.'

'Thanks, it's good to try something new.'

Candy poured the champagne into two flutes, and they clinked glasses.

'This is nice,' Helen said, 'are we celebrating?'

'From what I've read, you certainly are,' Candy said meaningfully.

Helen raised a perfectly plucked eyebrow. 'We're thrilled to be free, if that's what you mean. Even my gorgeous Matt has finally forgiven me.' Helen pulled out her phone and showed Candy some recent pictures of the two of them: Helen in a skimpy gold bikini, Matt in plain blue trunks, posed on the diving board of a stylish black-tiled swimming pool. The white railing of a boat was visible in the background, slicing through a blue cloudless sky.

Matt's return explained the new, softer, happier look, Candy realised, and felt the twinge of guilt once more. But her resolve hardened when Helen scrolled through a few more photos of the ostentatiously luxurious yacht that was her home for the time being.

'I wasn't talking about celebrating your acquittal,' Candy said. 'I was talking about celebrating your windfall. I gather you've all received a hefty pay-out from the the Kane Foundation.'

Helen, catching the edge in Candy's voice, put her glass down and gave her a long look. 'What's this really about, Candy?'

Candy leaned in close, and explained her proposition.

CHAPTER 32

Sheena

The sinking sun cast a faint fiery glow on the horizon, and the water lapped gently against the hull. Occasionally, there was a splash as a cormorant dived into the depths. But on board the Nemesis, inside the elegant sitting room hung with vibrant David Hockney water paintings, the scene was anything but calm.

'She's fucking blackmailing us?' Sheena said, her voice tinged with disbelief. 'For two million pounds? That bitch! I thought she hated Ross! I thought she was on our side.'

'Me too,' Helen replied, sounding desperate. 'She gave me Ross Owen's phone months ago – she said that was an end to it. She promised.'

Sheena was sharp. 'She lied and you fell for it. She kept a copy of the footage, like most of us would.'

Amanda looked stricken. She was sitting on the edge of a red velvet sofa, dangling a brightly coloured toy above Olivia. 'I've only just got Olivia back! If this comes out, Jake will have no trouble getting custody again.'

Farrah, in a dark blue leather armchair that was big enough for two, placed a hand over Max's tummy. Her expression was that of a tigress protecting her cub. 'Don't worry, Amanda. Hell will freeze over before I let that rat get his disgusting claws on our babies again.'

'I told you we should have come clean.' The colour had drained from Catherine's face, and she was picking anxiously at a gold tasselled cushion on her lap.

'That was never an option,' said Farrah. 'If we'd admitted to a crime they would have locked us up and thrown away the key!'

'Well, what do you propose?' Catherine looked petulant.

'Farrah's right. If we had come clean, we wouldn't be on this yacht right now.' Sheena removed the cushion from Catherine's hand before she tore it apart. 'We need to stop squabbling, keep a clear head and work out what to do.' She stood up, walked purposefully across the pale oak floor and opened the doors onto the balcony, which protruded out over the side of the boat, directly above the sea. A light breeze was stirring but the evening was still warm, and the cry of seabirds pierced the air. She looked out to the horizon, her mind racing, while the other women sat for a long while in silence, struggling to take in Helen's news.

'Why is Candy doing this?' Amanda said at last.

'She's worked too long for Jake,' Farrah said bitterly. 'It was bound to rub off.'

'She tried to explain that it isn't personal,' Helen said, looking bereft. 'She told me that Tabitha Tate's writing another book about *Falcon Bay*. It's mostly about Madeline Kane, but she's offered to pay Candy to dish whatever dirt she's got on any of us. So if we don't pay Candy, she'll sell the footage to Tabitha – and that would be game over for us.'

Farrah laughed, mirthlessly. 'And obviously she knows we're rich because somebody blabbed to the press.'

'If you're referring to my interview about Nemesis,' Sheena said coldly, 'you know as well as I do that we have to control our narrative. Someone was going to write about a big fat yacht turning up in the bay. It might as well be us.'

'Maybe she just really needs money?' Even to Amanda's own ears, it sounded like a lame excuse.

'Oh, come on,' said Farrah. 'Don't be naive. We knew she was a bitch back when she was shagging Jake, feeding him gossip about what the rest of us were doing. We never could trust her. And now she's blackmailing us, the backstabbing cow.' She gazed at the others. 'Why we ever thought she'd keep her word with something this explosive, I've no idea.'

Helen was silent while the others glared at her.

Sheena turned around to face the room again, leaning back against the white railings to feel the breeze in her hair. 'Well, girls, what do you think we should do?'

'I say we pay her the two million to go away, as much as I hate the idea in principle,' Farrah said, jiggling Max on her knee. 'It's a drop in the ocean to us, and it's really our only option.'

Helen nodded. 'Let's just do it. I want this to be over. I can't have anything else come between me and Matt.'

'I agree. We can afford to,' Amanda said, Olivia on her hip. 'And we can't afford not to.' She stroked a lock of hair back from Olivia's forehead. 'There's too much at stake.'

'How can we be sure that's an end to it?' Catherine said. 'Maybe she's kept multiple copies. We only have her word to go on.' She glanced at Helen, who looked away. 'And look where that got us last time.'

Helen refused to be cowed. 'I know she's not been trustworthy in the past, but I really believe two million will do it. It's a lot of money to her. And what's the alternative? Let's get her on side. Invite her here, make her part of our team, give her a reason to stay loyal.'

Amanda looked doubtful. 'I get what you're saying, Helen, I just don't know if we can trust her, not now.' She sent a pleading look around the group. 'If we're not careful, the footage of Ross Owen could become a tap to drain our funds forever.' She blinked away the tears that threatened to come.

Farrah nodded. 'I'm with Amanda. We can't trust the bitch. I don't want to spend the rest of my life having to keep her sweet with more and more cash, worrying she might tell the police about what we did.'

Sheena looked thoughtful. 'So, we agree,' she said at last, 'that this is a problem we need to make go away for good. And I agree with Helen – we need to get Candy 'on board', if you'll pardon the pun. Let's do exactly that. We'll invite her here, on board Nemesis, and we'll sort this out once and for all so she never asks us for money again.'

The women were so relieved that Sheena was solving their problems once again, they failed to notice the small smile that played around her lips, or the fact that her hand, with its huge emerald ring that glinted in the fading light, tightened its grip on the balcony rail as she spoke.

CHAPTER 33

Tabitha

It was early in the morning and Tabitha and Dustin, both early risers, were sitting out on the terrace of Madeline's villa, drinking coffee and discussing the next stage of their hunt for Chad. Using a combination of Dustin's tech skills, Tabitha's ability to charm information out of strangers and Madeline's intimate knowledge of her husband's state of mind, they had traced him crossing the Canadian border into Ontario. Then – via three flights, six train rides and another car hire – they tracked him to Bali, where the trail went cold. He had really gone out of his way to cover his tracks.

While Dustin explained how he was now trying to trace Chad through Bali's satellite GPS system by implementing a spoof request on something called an SSL certificate, Tabitha's mind wandered. She still hadn't let Dustin fuck her, and the tension was delicious. She extended her leg under the table and ran her foot up the inside of Dustin's calf, then his thigh, pausing when she reached the edge of his dark green shorts. Dustin trailed off, losing his thread. He caught Tabitha's foot in his hand under the table, and massaged her sole urgently with his thumb.

'Please,' he groaned. 'See? I'm begging. Isn't that what you wanted? I can't wait anymore. I want you, Tabitha.'

Tabitha leaned forward slightly, subtly pulling her arms together so her breasts spilled out over the edge of her fuschia bikini. 'Let me see how much you want me.'

By way of an answer, Dustin took her foot and placed it on his crotch. She could feel his erection straining through his shorts.

'Good. Then get under the table.'

Dustin crawled under the table until he was kneeling in front of her, an expression of pure lust as he looked up at her face, and then down to her thighs. Tabitha leaned back in her chair, eased her bikini bottoms off and hooked one knee over his shoulder. She took Dustin's head in both hands and pulled him between her legs. He moaned loudly, and tentatively flicked his tongue over her smooth pussy.

'Harder,' ordered Tabitha, and pushed herself against his mouth. As he licked and sucked her clit, she felt a current of electricity building from her toes. But it was too soon.

'Stop,' she said, and Dustin groaned aloud.

'Please, I'm begging you, I can't hold...'

'You can if you know what's good for you.' She pressed herself against his mouth once more, then stood up and bent over the table, her breasts pressed against the cool marble, her pussy exposed to the sea air.

'I want you to stand behind me and fuck me slowly,' she said. 'If you go too fast before I tell you to, I'll stop – and this time for good.'

He eased himself into her, inch by inch. She could feel his cock throbbing inside her as he plunged deeper, setting her nerves on fire as he pulled out and then, exquisitely slowly, pushed back in. Dustin was breathing hard, one hand exploring her bottom, the other tangled in her hair. Tabitha let out a moan, and it was as if something inside Dustin snapped. Suddenly he sped up, ramming into her, faster, harder, slapping against her with each thrust, pinning her down on the table so she couldn't slow him down any longer. Not that she wanted to. She thrust against him too, finally letting her orgasm build, so much deeper than before, electricity spreading through her body until such an intense pleasure exploded between her legs she thought she would melt. Glad of the table beneath her, she moved her hips one last time and Dustin cried out and came, hard, then collapsed on top of her, shaking like a leaf.

They both startled at a noise from inside the villa, and scrambled back into their clothes. Dustin gave the table a hasty wipe with his shirt, and not a moment too soon. Seconds later, Madeline emerged from the French windows, looking poised and elegant in a black Chanel swimsuit and a green kaftan that matched her eyes. She removed her sunglasses and raised an eyebrow at the pair.

'Up early, are we?' She smiled knowingly. 'How wonderful to see the two of you getting on so well.'

Dustin blushed. Tabitha thought it suited him.

Madeline sat down at the table and poured herself a coffee. 'I've had a thought about Bali,' she said. 'You know I told you we went there once, and it was paradise?'

Tabitha nodded. Madeline had explained that two years

into their relationship, a conference in Bali they were meant to be attending had been cancelled, leaving them with a rare chance for a spontaneous holiday. She and Chad had stayed at a remote resort on a far-flung, unspoilt island, where they were the only western tourists the island had seen in years.

Tabitha waited a moment, confused. 'But Madeline,' she said gently, 'we've called that resort already. They closed down last year – and nobody we spoke to on the island remembers a foreigner visiting since the two of you.'

'But did I tell you about the horses?'

Tabitha looked bemused.

'There were wild horses, you'd see them galloping along the beach. And the resort kept horses too. The woman who took care of them was extraordinary. They loved her, you could tell. They'd trot over when she appeared and cluster around nuzzling her, and she'd whisper back. It seemed they shared a secret language. Chad said it made the hairs on the back of his neck stand on end. We'd never ridden before but we learned quickly. We both said that one day we'd have horses, and that when we did, we'd create that special relationship with them too.' Madeline's eyes shone; her lips were parted in a smile. She seemed miles away suddenly. Then she seemed to remember Tabitha and Dustin, and came back down to earth. 'Sounds crazy, I suppose, but it could be a lead.'

Tabitha shook her head. It didn't sound crazy, not one bit. She herself had learned to ride in Australia as a teenager, and the feel of the animal's powerful muscles moving beneath her, carrying her into the outback, was hard to beat. In the wild emptiness of the Australian bush it had felt like she was the only person in the world.

A thought struck her suddenly between the eyes. Australia was not so far from Bali, after all. 'Madeline, did you and Chad ever go to Australia?'

Madeline shook herself out of her reverie. 'Several times, on business trips. We didn't see much more than our hotels.' She sighed. 'We always said we'd go back one day, but we never got that far.'

Tabitha's mind whirred. Maybe Chad did.

CHAPTER 34

Candy

Candy leaned back against Marco's chest and sighed happily. They were sitting on a sun-lounger on Marco's little balcony outside his flat above the café, watching a pair of warblers circle above the sea before returning to their nest in the side of the cliff. During nesting season there were so many birds, jostling to occupy their tiny bit of ledge. Raising a family under such difficult, overcrowded conditions looked perilous: several of the young kept falling off the ledge into the sea, to be rescued – or not – by their parents.

Marco slid his arms around her waist, nuzzled the back of her neck. 'We'd do a better job of raising chicks than these gulls, eh? When will all that money you've been raking in from Jake be enough to get our own place?'

Candy took his hand and placed it under her bikini top, enjoying the feeling of his fingers exploring her warm skin. 'It's funny you should say that,' she said. 'Once the launch of La Mirage is out of the way we can leave the island for good. Go wherever we like.'

'A vacation, you mean? A trip round the world?'

'I was thinking more a permanent move. Maybe back to Sydney, snap up a nice little waterfront property in Pont Piper.'

He turned her around so she was straddling his lap, facing him. He gave her a curious look. 'Those houses go for millions of dollars. Your salary's good but it's not that good. Where will we get that kind of money?'

She traced her finger down his chest. 'I'm due a windfall – a bonus, if you like. Enough for us to start over anywhere in the world.' Her hands reached his swimming shorts, and eased them down over his slim hips. His cock sprang up, ready for her. 'But it doesn't have to be back in Australia. Anywhere you've ever dreamed of going. Petra, Easter Island, Antarctica, Java. That beach bar in Bali you always wanted to set up. You name it, we can do it.'

Marco moved her closer, pushing aside her bikini bottoms and sliding himself into her. He groaned as she moved on top of him, grinding her hips and matching his rhythm. She took his hand and placed it between her legs, rubbing herself against him until she came, hard. He moaned again and thrust into her one final time.

They lay in silence, entwined on the chair, while they got their breath back.

'Babe, are you serious? About the money I mean?'

She looked him in the eye. 'Deadly serious. It's not Jake the money's coming from though,' she said, and looked away. 'He's a tightwad and anyway, any money from him would be tainted. It's... owed to me. From before. When *Falcon Bay* was still being filmed here. The women who were in jail, they'd racked up a debt and, to be honest, I expected I'd have to write it off but...' she trailed off, gave a shrug. 'The point is they still owe me and now they're in a position to pay up.'

Marco sat thinking about this. 'How much?'

'A lot.'

He nodded. 'OK. What's it for, this "debt"?'

Candy hesitated, then said, 'I did them a favour. A really big one.'

'What kind of favour?'

She sat up, gave him a broad smile and slid her hands around his neck once more. 'One worth two million pounds.'

CHAPTER 35

Jake

Jake slammed the door to his cottage and swore loudly when he realised he'd left his keys inside. Used to his fully staffed villa, where there was always a housekeeper or a cook to let him back in after a morning swim, it felt like confirmation that the whole world had turned against him. Now he'd have to call a locksmith when he got home. Probably a good idea to change the locks anyway, he thought, as he walked down the forest path towards the café.

He needed to beef up his security now he was in a cottage on the part of the island usually reserved for workmen, which was lacking in the kind of high-tech surveillance cameras Madeline had installed for the execs at the classier end of the island. He thought with a pang of his beautiful villa, now inhabited by Madeline and that cow Tabitha. He'd seen a man going in and out of the villa too, when he'd trained his binoculars on them just yesterday. Something about his stance reminded him of someone, but he couldn't think who. Probably some fuck-buddy of Tabitha's, he thought.

Maybe if he timed it right with the binoculars he could watch them at it. He wasn't getting any action since Lauren had betrayed him – and he'd enjoy the feeling of getting one up on Tabitha, after she'd stitched him up horribly in the online press. The humiliating headline was still burned in his brain:

MONROE'S MELTDOWN: Disgraced Theme Park Boss Loses Villa, Stalked by Killer

By-line: Tabitha Tate

Jake Monroe, creator of the Falcon Bay Experience theme park on St Augustine's, has been on a downward spiral ever since owner Madeline Kane returned from the dead to reclaim her island home.

The once thriving Great White Death Experience, famous for its tasteless recreations of notorious scenes, now lies in ruins. Monroe has lost his grand villa from which he surveyed the island. He has poured his energies into La Mirage, a gigantic skyscraper that dominates the idyllic island. But will he live to see it launched? The so-called Hitlist Killer, the predator who has evaded the LA police, has named Monroe as his next victim.

As La Mirage's unveiling nears, Monroe stands in the spotlight. Will he be next, or will he defy the odds? His doomsday countdown begins. Only time will tell if he escapes the clutches of fate.

It was typically sensationalist, exactly the kind of thing Tabitha always wrote for whatever rag would stoop low enough to hire her. But it put him on alert, nonetheless. Tabitha had delivered the article in person, strolling right in through his front door in her ridiculous heels, clutching her iPad, no doubt loving the fact she was living in his villa with Madeline while he'd been banished to this tiny cottage with a flimsy lock.

'When you've read this, you might want to think about beefing up the personal protection,' Tabitha had said, thrusting her iPad under his nose. 'Wouldn't want the next person who walks in here to be the Honey Hunter vigilante, would you?' She laughed. 'Mask, latex.' She leaned over him and made a stabbing motion. 'Blade.'

'If he's here then he's after you too,' Jake spat back. 'You're just as much part of the list as I am. If it even exists that is.'

'Oh, it exists,' said Tabitha breezily. 'I was sent it, remember? And LAPD has verified it. But their theory is that I'm only on it to guarantee a media frenzy. Besides, if the killer is after me, then you're first. They're bound to catch the maniac before he gets to me.'

She'd strutted off, flashing her red soles – how she walked on the forest paths in six-inch Louboutins was beyond him – and left his front door swinging ominously.

Jake pushed the memory away and carried on walking towards his meeting with Candy. Not for the first time, he wished he had never set eyes on Honey. When the newspaper had called him for comment, he'd said stiffly, 'I don't see what I can add. I shouldn't even be on that ludicrous list. I did nothing wrong.' In his heart, he knew that wasn't true. But – so far anyway – the world didn't know what he'd done. Maybe he had got away with it after all.

*

He was still deep in thought when he arrived at the Heron Café to find Candy in an unusually good mood. She was perched on a balcony table overlooking the sea, and started updating him on progress right away, ticking things off her clipboard as she went.

'The RSVPs are in. Cardi B is a yes; George and Amal are a no. Harry and Meghan are a maybe if she can make it back from her talk show in time. The budget can't stretch to Beyoncé, along with everyone else.' She paused, looked closely at Jake. 'Are you alright? You look quite pale.'

'I'm fine,' he said tersely. Didn't she realise his whole life was in ruins and he was possibly being stalked by a nutcase? 'Tell me about the cake.'

'All confirmed. They can do fifteen feet but no higher. It will still be taller than the Plaza's, though.'

'Special effects?'

'All in-hand. The pyrotechnics team promise the fireworks will be the grandest ever seen at a private event. And there'll be holograms on the front of the building, packs of wolves loping up and down–'

'Guetta?'

'Yes – he's being flown in for a three-hour set. The other guests are mostly coming by chopper, but a few by boat. It seems the Nemesis being moored in the bay has encouraged the jet set to think of us as something of a superyacht destination,' she looked at him slyly. She was rubbing it in, the cow.

Still, he had to admit she'd done good work so far on the Versailles-themed bash. The hashtag #MirageMask was trending as celebrities showed off the elaborate masks they were planning to wear to the party in only a few weeks. A horrible thought struck him. In a sea of masks, how would he be able to spot a killer? He swallowed, and Candy paused again.

'Are you sure you're OK? You're not listening, and you seem distracted. Are you looking for someone?'

Jake didn't want to admit that his mind was on a killer who probably didn't exist so he said the first name that came into his head. 'Tabitha Tate.'

'Really?' Candy wrinkled her nose. 'Well, she's not far away. She came here to write a book about Madeline Kane, and now she's brown-nosed her way into working for her, haven't you heard?' She fixed him with an infuriating smile. 'With Dustin. Remember him from our *Falcon Bay* days? The three of them are searching for Chad.'

Jake gawped at her. That meant the man he'd seen going in and out of the villa must have been Dustin. Awkward, geeky, porky Dustin. *Falcon Bay*'s former producer. He couldn't believe it! Did that mean Dustin helped Madeline pull off her death-by-shark stunt? Yes, he was the best technician they'd ever had, and he was a wizard at CGI. But he was one of life's wallflowers. The man he'd glimpsed walking into Madeline's villa seemed confident, attractive, powerful. Candy had to be winding him up. 'Pull the other one,' he scoffed.

She laughed. 'It surprised me too. I've always thought of him as a speccy geek. But from what Marco says, they're making progress with the search, and now Dustin and Tabitha are an item.' She raised an eyebrow.

Jake was speechless. He swallowed down a stream of expletives, but the truth was, he felt more betrayed than ever. Everywhere he looked there were enemies: the hags on the yacht, who'd hit the jackpot with their settlement and managed to nab back their kids and steal Lauren from him, and now the unholy trio in Madeline's villa, doubtless plotting his downfall when they weren't trying to track down Madeline's idiot of a husband.

He felt a great wave of self-pity wash over him, and Candy must have picked up on it, because she adopted a sympathetic air, put down her clipboard, and asked again if he was alright. Then, a bit nervously, she asked, 'I know you don't have many friends left on the island, Jake. Would you like to have dinner one night? With Marco and me?'

Jake was taken aback. He certainly hadn't thought she'd offer that. 'Dinner?' he said on instinct. 'With you? And Marco?' Articulating each word with enormous care, as if attempting a new and particularly tricky language.

'Why not? Somewhere special – that new place in Le Touquet everyone's raving about.' She smiled. 'Our treat.'

Jake could barely get the words out. 'Just to be clear, my PR and her barista boyfriend want to treat me to dinner at a restaurant where the beautiful people go? No, no and no.' He infused his voice with as much contempt as he could muster. 'I don't socialise with the help. Not now, not ever.'

Candy shoved her laptop into her bag and got to her feet. She looked furious. Jake felt a moment of remorse. He would actually have liked to have dinner with the two of them. But she'd never respect him as a boss if he did that. And with nobody around to love him, respect was all he had.

'Do you know what,' Candy said. 'I only invited you for dinner because I felt sorry for you. Nobody cares about you, Jake. You're a nobody. Have you noticed how there's a delay between when you post on Instagram, and when your followers interact with you? That's because I've been paying for your interactions for the past year. Your video of the Madeline doll is the fifth most liked post on Instagram because I worked my *ass* off to get it there. You've lost the island. You're finished. Nobody wants you anymore. Well, apart from the Hitlist Killer. I'll complete my work on the launch because I'm a professional. But after that, I quit. Enjoy your fifteen-foot cake, you fucking prick.'

Jake let her walk away, his towering silver skyscraper glimmering in the distance.

CHAPTER 36

Tabitha

After exhaustive enquiries through her network of contacts, Tabitha was fairly certain Chad had not made Bali his final destination. In any case, she reasoned, if he missed his dead wife so much that he decided to disappear from the world, would he really go somewhere haunted by memories of their happy moments together?

As soon as Madeline told her about the horses, she widened her search to Oceania. Dustin had tried his best, but he couldn't hack into the passenger manifests for any of the airlines that flew those routes. Madeline was deeply disappointed, but Tabitha was undaunted. She still had her own tools to track him down. Logic, charm. And a third, rare thing: a journalist's hunch. She knew Chad would have to be somewhere remote enough that western news wouldn't reach him, big enough that local people wouldn't bother him, and she knew he would need to fill his time with something. She dismissed the islands quickly: they were small places where everyone knew everyone and western tourists abounded.

Chad wouldn't go there if he wanted to escape. She turned to Australia. She felt certain that if she found somewhere that had horses, but no internet, she would find Chad.

She started by charming an exclusive travel agent into believing she was a high net-worth individual ready to splash millions on her next holiday, and received six brochures by email immediately, advertising various 'wellness' resorts in the Australian outback – all places that boasted of being Wi-Fi-free, perfect for a digitally detoxed, back-to-nature experience. She had emphasised to the travel agent that it had to be in a location that was genuinely without internet (her simpering Southern drawl returned as she explained how addicted she was to her iPhone), and was assured that these places were so far in the back of beyond that they used satellite phones, and those only in emergencies. She ran internet searches for all six, looking for any which mentioned horse-riding as a local activity. Finally, armed with three distinct areas in western Australia, she rang up a property lawyer in Sydney who owed her a favour.

He agreed to look into recent property sales in each location, focusing specifically on places with stables. He came back with just one candidate. It was a smallholding in a place called Rainbow Creek, roughly 300 kilometres north of Sydney. Purchased within the last six weeks by a guy who spoke English, though no one seemed sure where he was from, and who was now living there on his own. The town – if you could call it that – had a couple of hundred people, a gas station, a store that sold basics, and a bar. But it had beaches, wilderness, wildlife – koalas, raptors, parrots – all practically on the doorstep. And the smallholding had stables, half a dozen horses, and a couple on site who took care of the day-to-day running of the place.

No one seemed to know anything about the new owner, where he'd come from, how long he intended to be there. The lawyer had spoken to the land agent who'd handled the sale and had met the new owner only once. Private, a man of few words. Reclusive, the agent said. Like Howard Hughes. Seemed to be a keen horseman, was all anyone knew.

Might be worth looking into, the lawyer told Tabitha. Just in case.

When Tabitha told Madeline, she sat very straight and very still for a long while, not speaking a word.

Tabitha waited, the certainty with which she'd presented her findings starting to seep away. She had tried not to sound overconfident because, mostly, she was going with her instincts rather than anything that constituted hard evidence. The longer Madeline sat in silence, deep in thought, the more Tabitha began to fear she was way off the mark.

'It could be anyone,' Madeline said at last. 'What makes you think it's Chad?'

Tabitha steeled herself to face Madeline's derision. 'I'm not sure… it's a gut feeling as much as anything.' She placed a hand on her middle. 'In here. Does that make sense?'

Madeline held her gaze for what seemed an uncomfortably long time. Tabitha anticipated a dressing down.

At last she spoke. 'Listening to you just now,' she said, 'I got that same feeling.'

A sense of giddiness surged through Tabitha, a feeling she knew well, one that took hold whenever she was on the brink of breaking a big news story, 'I think I should go out there,' she said, 'take a look. See if the loner at Rainbow Creek is Chad. If it's not, we'll move on. But. I think we need to find out.'

'Yes,' Madeline said, her eyes sparkling with excitement, 'but I don't want you to go. If my husband is there, I have to be there too. I have to see him. I need to go and find him myself. You stay here and explore other options. I'm getting on a plane tomorrow.'

CHAPTER 37

Candy

Candy hadn't told Marco she had arranged to meet the women on Nemesis tonight. She suspected he might try and talk her out of it. Whenever she mentioned getting the money the women owed her, he became wary and suspicious, wanting to know what could possibly merit such a large amount. Two million, he kept saying, incredulous. A fortune, a life-changing amount. People don't just hand over that kind of cash. What had she got herself into?

Candy was vague, saying only that it was a debt to do with *Falcon Bay*, a few favours that had added up while the women were in prison. Marco shouldn't worry. After all, Candy told him, this is showbusiness. Two million is nothing, these women are loaded, it's a drop in the ocean to them. Smiling at her deliberate pun. She had read that the yacht they were on cost £60,000 per week. No matter what she said, it didn't seem to make a difference, he still wasn't reassured. And if she tried to bring up where he fancied going once things were sorted – anywhere he liked, she said – he changed the subject.

It would be different once the cash was in the bank, she told herself.

Candy wasn't sure what to wear on a superyacht. What if she turned up in a gorgeous floor-length gown and a pair of killer heels, and found the others in kaftans and Havaianas? She laughed. Hell would freeze over before Helen and the others ever wore flat shoes. How must they have coped in prison issue gear? She'd ask them later. Once they had a few glasses of champagne inside them and were kicking back, enjoying the satisfaction of the kind of business deal where everyone feels like a winner.

She concentrated on drawing a feline flick at the outer corner of each eye, then pulled on her favourite Rat & Boa dress. She looked in the mirror, admiring the plunging neckline, the slit which ran from ankle to thigh, the way the sheer fabric showed just a hint of her skin beneath. Red, the colour of passion, of danger. She put on a pair of gold Tom Ford sandals. She felt a thrill. No one was going to mess with her, not looking like that.

She took one final look at herself in the mirror, then slipped the all-important memory stick inside her La Perla lace bra. This time, she hadn't kept a copy. She was going to end this saga once and for all.

The tender was waiting when she arrived at the jetty. The captain – Nikki, she said her name was – took her hand and helped her on board, wobbling slightly on her heels. She hoped there wasn't a rule against spike heels on deck – the dress wouldn't look nearly as good without them.

The sun had gone down a while ago and the decks of Nemesis were lit with strings of twinkling fairy lights. Once the tender was moving, it was cool on the water, and she was grateful for her cashmere Celine wrap. In just a few minutes they had arrived, the pilot tying the boat to the stern and helping her onto the yacht, leading her along a corridor with a glass wall that overlooked an indoor pool, up a sweeping staircase to the upper deck where the women were chatting, drinking champagne around an outdoor pool whose water was an inky black. Candy shivered and drew her wrap closer around her shoulders. She assessed the scene: five impossibly glamorous women, whose strength lay in their bond of friendship as much as anything. Helen, in a slinky silk and lace slip dress, came to greet Candy, beaming, planting an air kiss on each cheek. She caught hold of her hand and tugged Candy towards the others. 'Look who's here,' she said.

Candy wondered how much champagne Helen had drunk – she seemed to be a little tipsy.

Amanda leaned in for a hug, saying how good it was to see her, that her dress was gorgeous. Were those tears in Amanda's eyes? How odd. It wasn't as if they were particular friends.

Candy had been expecting a cooler reception, given she was here to relieve the women of a large amount of cash, so she was thrown by what appeared to be a genuine welcome. Catherine told her she looked quite lovely, Farrah thrust a champagne flute into her hand. All the women were talking at once, overwhelming her with questions, so when Candy saw Sheena slip away to tell the pilot of the tender that she and the cook should take the children ashore to Lauren's cottage and then have the night off, she didn't think anything of it.

The girls drew her by the hand over to a red velvet sofa in a beautiful sitting room lined with what looked like

David Hockney originals. Amanda sat next to her on one side, Helen on the other, and Farrah topped up their glasses as soon as they sat down. Catherine proposed a toast – 'to new beginnings' – and they all clinked glasses. Candy hadn't intended to drink tonight, thinking she would need a clear head to negotiate for her money, but it was hard to say no when they'd opened a magnum of Cristal in her honour. She knew she needed to bring up the money as soon as she could, get them to hand over what Helen had agreed – then she'd relax and let her hair down.

Before she could do so, they adjourned to the lower deck for dinner. Candles flickered on a table laid with crisp white linen, set with dazzling chinaware in blue and gold. Long-stemmed wine glasses sat next to heavy crystal tumblers, already filled with sparkling water. The table was groaning with delicious looking Middle Eastern dishes. Stuffed vine leaves, smoked aubergine, tzatziki, bowls of bulgur wheat mixed with walnuts, celery and parsley. Olives and flatbreads on wooden boards.

'Should we get the matter of Ross Owen out of the way before we eat?' Sheena said, fixing Candy with a cool look.

'Oh,' Candy said, looking around the table at the five sets of eyes now boring into her. No longer smiling.

'I gather from Helen you had a sum in mind,' Sheena went on, helping herself to a glass of rosé, this time placing the bottle back in the ice bucket without offering Candy a drink. The temperature in the room seemed to plummet under Sheena's icy gaze. Candy wished she had her cashmere wrap, which she'd carelessly left on the sofa upstairs. She shivered, and hardened her resolve.

'Well, I…' Candy began, suddenly feeling out of her depth under the scrutiny of the women. She sent a pleading look in Helen's direction.

'She wants two million,' Helen told Sheena, not taking her eyes off Candy.

'Well,' Sheena said, 'I suppose that's not unreasonable.'

Candy felt a rush of optimism. It was going to be alright. They'd agree and then things could go back to how they were before, everyone relaxed and smiling. The atmosphere had been bound to change once they got down to discussing business. 'I'm not greedy,' Candy said.

Sheena arched a brow. 'Hear that? She's not greedy.'

'Not greedy,' Farrah echoed. 'Well, that's a relief. For a moment, I thought she said… two million.'

There was laughter around the table. 'Surely not,' Catherine said, sipping at her wine.

'Because some might think that was greedy,' Amanda said.

There was a horrible moment when no one spoke. Candy was feeling more and more like the women had staged this. Had they invited her here to turn her down? Or just to talk tough to scare her out of doing the dirty on them again? Then Helen said, 'In the circumstances, you could say it's a fairly modest sum.' Candy gave her a grateful smile. 'Given what's at stake here,' Helen said. 'I suppose my only question is, can you be trusted, Candy? I mean, this footage you say you've got, wasn't even supposed to exist. You promised you'd given me the only copy.' She sighed. 'Disappointing. All this time you've spent working for Jake, you've become a real chip off the old block.'

'I promise you,' Candy said, 'this is an end to it.' She pulled out the memory stick from her bra and held it in front of her. 'This is the only copy. I promise you.'

'I thought that was the case the last time we had this conversation,' Helen said twiddling the stem of her wine glass.

Candy looked around the table. The air seemed to crackle with hostility. Was it all just an act? She was suddenly desperate for a drink, to steady her nerves, but she couldn't reach the wine. 'If we can just agree, I'll give you the footage and we're done,' she said.

'Oh, I think we're done,' Sheena told her. 'You know, before you came to us with this — what do you call it, a proposal? — we were going to hire you to work on our massive new TV show. You'd have made that two million in a couple of years! But you've blown our trust now. One thing experience has taught me is never to do business with people you know are capable of double-crossing you. Too risky.'

Catherine was nodding. 'I was thinking of that quotation: "Betray a friend, and you'll often find you have ruined yourself." Aesop's Fables.'

'I'd like to think you can be trusted, Candy,' Amanda said. 'Because what you're doing puts in jeopardy my ability to keep my child safe from Jake.' She glanced at Farrah.

'Same here,' Farrah said. 'So, you can see, it's quite a conundrum.'

'Let's say we pay you,' Catherine said, 'and you go on a bit of a spree, run out of cash and come back for more... and more. Because, just like before, you've kept another copy of Ross Owen meeting his unfortunate end.'

'I promise,' Candy said. 'This is truly the only copy. I want this to be gone, just like you do.'

After a moment, Helen broke the tension. 'OK, Candy. I believe you.' She glanced at the other women in turn. 'Girls, we can relax now. I don't think she'll do this again. We'll deposit the money in your account now, Candy. Do you have your details?'

Candy let out a long, low breath. God, they were a tough bunch. But it made sense that they'd want to frighten her a bit just to be sure she wouldn't betray them again. They looked a lot more friendly now, though Sheena's gaze was still a bit distant. She took the pen Helen offered, wrote out her account details, and passed them to Sheena. Sheena tapped something into her phone and flashed Candy a screen that confirmed an electronic transfer of two million pounds would be made, the money landing in the account within the next two hours.

'Does that sound OK?' Helen asked.

Candy nodded, but she couldn't be sure it wasn't a trick. She made to leave, the memory stick still tucked beneath her bra. 'I'll come back and hand the footage over tomorrow, as soon as the money lands in the morning.'

'Why not wait here for the next two hours?' Sheena said. 'The money will be through by then, and the staff have gone ashore with the tender, so you're stuck with us for the time being anyway.' She gave Candy a brilliant smile and poured her a glass of rosé. 'Might as well have a drink, and toast our deal.'

The atmosphere had changed completely, and Candy started relaxing into the women's company once again. Everyone was chatting and laughing, knocking back the wine, passing bowls of plump green olives around. Candy felt a bit unnerved, but it was only two hours before she could go home, and then she and Marco could start their new life, far away from all this. She couldn't wait to see the look on Marco's face when she came home and presented two million dollars in their bank account as a *fait accompli* she had achieved all by herself. Candy, feeling slightly woozy from the wine, said she needed to use the bathroom, and Sheena said the one off the sitting room balcony had to be seen to be believed. 'It's all done in gold and rhinestone, and has an incredible view,' she told Candy, guiding her along a dimly lit corridor, catching hold of her elbow when she stumbled.

'Heels,' Candy muttered, and Sheena took hold of Candy's arm and steered her towards a set of glass doors that opened onto a balcony.

They stepped out into the cool night air. Above them the moon, a brilliant crescent, cast its light onto the sea. Candy felt her stomach lurch. 'I'm feeling a bit light-headed,' she confided to Sheena. 'Don't think I've eaten enough to soak up the wine.'

'We've all had a bit too much,' Sheena agreed. 'Fix your eyes on the horizon and take a breath. That always helps me.'

Candy placed a foot on the lower rail and levered herself up for a better view. 'It's so calm here. Peaceful. I can see why you love it.'

Sheena leaned back against the rail and narrowed her eyes. 'Do you feel at home on the water, Candy?'

'Not really,' Candy said with a rueful grin. 'I'm probably the only Australian who never learnt to swim!'

CHAPTER 38

Tabitha

As soon as Madeline left for Sydney, Australia on her private plane, Tabitha turned her attention back to her other two projects: the Madeline Kane book, and the Honey Hunter vigilante case.

The first was easy to progress, she simply had to fire off a few emails to a few contacts in her rolodex, fact-checking various dates before she moved onto the interview phase. She made a mental note to contact the fan she'd met outside the court case first – she had a hunch Hannah Price would be something of an expert in her field.

The vigilante case was more complex. Weeks had passed since she had been handed the hideous footage of Mickey's murder, and despite her warning to Jake about the hitlist, she was beginning to wonder if the heat was coming out of the case. She'd been following the US news obsessively, and the media had been gradually losing interest. The consensus was that since there had only been two killings (not enough to be counted by the police as carried out by a serial killer) it was a random maniac, using what Honey went through as an excuse to perpetrate fetish killings, probably adding Jake and Tabitha's names to the list to ensure the media coverage was global.

She put in a call to her news editor, Sandy, who gave her an earful. 'You've been gone for two weeks, and you've barely given me any stories. You better get your skinny ass back here the moment that skyscraper is launched. And if you don't write me the best goddamn article about the party, you'll be back on celebrity cats faster than you can say Choupette.'

Tabitha was riled. 'I'm working my ass off right now, writing a piece on the Hitlist Killer for you. I'm close to uncovering a new lead.'

'Whatever, the story is dead,' Sandy told her, and then, with relish, 'unless, of course, the killer goes after the last two names on the hitlist after all.' Tabitha flinched. She couldn't help thinking of the message the killer had left at the scene of Mickey's murder: 'You're next'. 'I mean,' Sandy said, with a touch of disappointment, 'you're the other side of the pond on some island no one's ever heard of, so probably the killer wouldn't even know how to find you.' Tabitha decided not to point out that, thanks to *Falcon Bay*, St Augustine's was world famous. 'You know, most Americans never go outside their own state, their own town, let alone overseas,' Sandy said, making it sound like outer space. 'More than half of us don't even have a passport. I don't.'

Tabitha was shocked. He was supposed to be a cultured, worldly journalist for Christ's sake. She wasn't as convinced as Sandy that the killings had simply stopped. What about

Jake? He was on St Augustine's too. She shivered. If the killer decided to travel over here, they'd be getting two for the price of one.

She itched to know what Jake had done that was bad enough to put him on the list. She resolved to confront him about it herself – but first, she had to get a bit further with the Hitlist Killer. If the media really had lost interest, the police would soon follow. That meant it was in Tabitha's interest to solve the question of who was killing in Honey's name – and why.

She took her laptop to the Heron Café, where the terrace was drenched in late afternoon sun and busy with twitchers, several pairs of binoculars trained on the cliffs, Nemesis still anchored in the bay. She found a quiet table inside at the back of the restaurant. Marco brought her a cappuccino topped with his signature bird sketched in cocoa powder. 'Marco, you're an artist,' she said, admiring his handiwork. He frowned, seeming distracted, miles away. As he turned to leave, she said, 'Hey, is everything OK? Where's Candy?'

'Fine,' he said. 'Well, a bit off, to be honest. She's got these grand plans to call in some debts and then splash the cash on travelling the world – I'm not so sure it's a good idea. But she's at a work dinner tonight so I haven't seen her.'

Tabitha was impressed. Candy was not as daft as she thought – sounded like she was screwing money out of the women as well as from her. But she'd set aside this time for Honey, and she wanted to stay on track. She fired off another email to the address Mickey had given her months ago.

Dear Honey, please answer my messages. As you know
I am offering a sincere apology for all the things I've got
wrong. I am truly sorry for my many blunders in terms
of writing about your shocking experiences. You're very
much on my mind as I'm now on St Augustine's. I know
your time on the island was difficult and unhappy, and
I see that now. Everything I've been through lately has
taught me some big lessons and, hand on heart, I'm not
the brash, self-absorbed bitch I used to be. Please, call
me, and give me a chance to prove it.

She added her cell number and pressed send.

For a moment she sipped at her coffee, thinking. She
scanned through her notes about the killings in LA and
focused in on Mickey. His body had been found at Castillo
del Amor, the mansion once owned by the old mobster and
studio boss, Caspar Felix. Why had the killer gone to all that
trouble to make sure Mickey died there? Tabitha knew it was
where some of Hollywood's biggest, most star-studded parties
had taken place, but she couldn't help wondering if there was
a greater significance. She started digging into Felix, trawling
through photos online. He was a big, bulky man, like Marlon
Brando after he got fat. He'd been married four times, and
had nine children by seven women, including one with his
former housekeeper. Practically every star of note had been
pictured with him at some time or other, but their stance
always suggested they'd rather be somewhere else.

Marco came over, put a fresh coffee in front of her. She
had barely touched her last one, and it had gone cold. Tabitha
smiled at him. God, he was gorgeous. Candy was a lucky girl.

She returned to the laptop, carried on picking her way through hundreds of images of Caspar Felix with various famous people. She didn't recognise all of them, but she assumed they were all old-school Hollywood royalty. She spotted Elizabeth Taylor, Audrey Hepburn, Janet Leigh and – as Caspar got older and the photographs became more recent – Anna Nicole Smith, and Gene Wilder.

Almost two hours went by before she finally found the photograph she had been looking for.

*

Once Tabitha had gone and Marco had closed up, he waited up for Candy in his little flat above the café until after midnight. It was unlike her to come back so late from a business meeting. She was usually in and out of those in the little time it took to gulp a glass of champagne and pick at a crab salad.

He tried her mobile, but it went straight to voicemail. Then he called the Oyster Bar, which was where she normally went for business dinners, and got hold of someone who was just about to lock up. Candy hadn't been in that night.

He phoned Jake, feeling slightly foolish, not even knowing who Candy was meant to be meeting. Jake was scathing, said he knew nothing about any meeting Candy was supposed to be having, but then why would she tell him what she was doing? She claimed to quit her job yesterday but maybe she was just being hormonal. For the next few minutes he ranted about the vast sums she'd been splashing on expenses recently – his money – on meetings to finalise the launch do. 'I haven't seen many of the receipts. Some people call that fraud, you know,' he said bitterly. Marco hung up.

Finally, he got in the car and drove down to the Cove. There was no one about. Out in the bay, Nemesis was in darkness, only its anchor lights on. He couldn't see the tender – perhaps the women on board had nipped over to France for an evening of debauchery.

He went home, tried Candy's mobile again, left another message, then tried to sleep. At around 5 a.m., still awake, alert for the sound of a key in the door, he got up and made his way downstairs to the café. A lone bird watcher was on the grass, binoculars trained on an elegant guillemot that swooped in the air below the cliffs.

Marco tried calling Candy again. It went straight to voicemail. Hours passed. He made a double espresso for himself, and a cappuccino for the birdwatcher. He went out and sat with him for a while, gazing out at the cliffs.

When it got to 8 a.m. he made another call. 'Police,' he said, when prompted to say which service he required. Moments later, a woman's voice asked how she could help. 'My girlfriend's gone missing.'

PART 4

CHAPTER 39

Sheena

It had been a spur of the moment decision to push Candy overboard.

What else was she going to do? Candy said she couldn't swim then leaned precariously (provocatively, some might say) over the balcony rail. The obvious thing to do – the only thing – was to push her into the water. Candy had splashed around for a few seconds then disappeared as Sheena watched, holding her breath, waiting for her to surface, not sure what she'd do if she did.

Only Candy didn't appear.

Last night, Sheena waited a long time on that balcony before going back to the others. They were still sitting around the mahogany dining table, talking and drinking, surrounded by the debris of the night. They didn't even seem to notice that Sheena had been gone for so long.

Amanda looked up. 'What's happened?' she said. 'You look pale.'

'I don't want anyone to panic,' Sheena said calmly, sitting

down, refilling her glass, and taking a long drink. She looked up at the curious pairs of eyes all now trained on her, the expectant looks on the faces of her friends. 'There's been an incident.'

No one spoke for a moment, then Helen said, 'Where's Candy?'

'That's the weird thing,' Sheena said. 'I waited for her on the balcony outside the bathroom because she seemed pretty drunk. When she came out the bathroom, we ended up chatting for a bit out there – you know I love to talk to pretty women – and I got the impression she was a bit overwhelmed. The yacht, the booze...' Sheena shrugged. 'Giddy, too, thinking about her get-rich-quick scheme. So, we were looking out at the sea and she was kind of hanging over the edge of the railing...' she trailed off, a faraway look on her face. 'I left her there to get her a glass of water from the bathroom...'

'Then what happened?' Farrah prompted.

'When I got back she was... She was gone. I think she went overboard.'

'Oh my God.' Catherine had gone white.

Amanda pushed her chair back. 'We can't just sit here and do nothing! We need to try and find her!'

'Trust me,' Sheena said. 'We're not going to find her. I've searched as much as I can for her. She's not on the boat, and I can't see her in the sea – unless by some miracle she's swum to shore. She told me on the balcony that she can't swim. Can you believe that? We're in a pocket of deep water here, it's something like fifteen metres to the bottom, and I'm with a drunk girl who can't swim.'

'We have to call the police! The coastguard!' Amanda was pacing up and down the room.

'We can't call the police,' said Farrah. 'They'll never believe we didn't push her in.'

'Fucking hell,' Helen said, her voice rising. 'We're in huge shit! Up to our necks in it. People will know she was with us — Nikki, for one. She picked her up on the tender and brought her out here, but never took her back. Shit.'

'Listen,' Sheena said. She intuitively understood that the girls needed to believe that it was an accident. 'Here's what we say when we're asked, which we will be.' She fixed them with a penetrating look. 'We invited Candy to have dinner with us. We'd heard she was miserable working for Jake, looking for a change, which explains the calls to you, Helen, the fact you'd already met with her in the Oyster Bar. She gets here, it's a boozy night,' she said, indicating to the ice buckets, the empties strewn across the table. 'We're all in good spirits and we drink a hell of a lot.' She looked again at the mess of bottles in front of them. 'We leave things exactly as they are now, including the empty champagne bottles on the upper deck. It's all evidence to back up our story.'

No one spoke for a moment.

'What about the money we sent her — won't they be able to trace that?' A muscle flickered in Farrah's jaw.

Sheena picked up her phone. 'Oh,' she said calmly. 'It looks like the payment didn't go through. I suppose the signal is sometimes dodgy in the dining room.'

Farrah narrowed her eyes. 'That's pretty convenient.'

There was a pause while the women considered her meaning.

'Sorry, but leaving the money aside, how the fuck do we explain our guest went overboard and we didn't do a thing about it? Once they find her body, they'll be able to tell the time of death.' Helen seemed ready to explode.

'Calm down, Helen,' Sheena said sharply. She looked at Catherine and Amanda, still nervously pacing the room. 'We have to get a grip. Luckily for all of you, I've thought this through.' She walked to the blue brocade chair at the far end of the room and turned to face the women. 'Listen. Our crew are off duty and they've got the tender. There's no one to disprove what we say happened, which is this: Candy was drunk and asked if she could stay here for the night. She says she's going to bed and we all turn in.' Sheena paused. 'So, now I'm thinking about what we do in the morning. We all sleep late because we're hungover, right? We leave Candy in her room, not wanting to disturb her, then when someone eventually goes to wake her, we find the bed's not been slept in. That's when we search the yacht and raise the alarm.'

'It sounds plausible to me,' Farrah said.

Amanda was shaking her head. 'What if the police search the boat? They're bound to. What if they find the memory stick with the Ross Owen footage? We're finished!'

'I'm getting to that,' Sheena said. 'We need to hide it. Somewhere it can't be found.'

'What, like up someone's twat? We're not still in prison you know.' Farrah looked mutinous, but Sheena could tell that her mind was racing, thinking through options.

'No,' said Sheena, still keeping her cool. She walked over to Helen and placed a hand on her shoulder. 'This one's on you,' she said, looking her in the eyes. 'You need to leave in the morning, first thing, go to London, take the USB stick with you. And get rid of it.'

'How?' Helen said, her voice shaking. 'Anyway why me? I'm not involved in this, I didn't push her in–'

'None of us did.' Sheena's voice was steely. 'But you're the only one with a reason to go to London tomorrow.'

'What?' Helen was confused. 'Why? Won't it look like I'm fleeing the scene of the crime?'

'Think about it, Helen. When's your mum's anniversary?'

Helen looked surprised. 'June, Midsummer's Day.'

Sheena nodded. 'I thought so. That's why you're going back tomorrow, because you always visit her grave on that day.'

Helen opened her mouth to say something, then closed it again.

'It sounds to me like you've got it all worked out,' Catherine said bitterly. 'Did you plan all this before Candy set foot on the yacht? Right down to tying in the anniversary of Helen losing her mother?'

Sheena's expression softened, as if she was about to make a confession. Then the shutters came down again and her gaze was as steely as before. 'Of course not. It's just fortuitous that we can explain things in a way that makes sense. As long as we stick together.' Sheena looked around the table.

'Why am I getting a feeling of déjà vu?' Farrah said, looking pointedly at Sheena, and nodding her head towards Catherine.

'What do you mean?' said Amanda, and then her eyes widened as the truth dawned. 'Oh.'

Helen raised an eyebrow and snorted.

'What are you talking about?' Catherine was puzzled.

'Don't worry, darling,' said Sheena, patting Catherine's hand while glaring at Farrah. Now was definitely not the time to talk about her plan to put Temazepam in Catherine's hot toddy. 'What's done is done. We've got to think about the bigger picture now.' She gazed out of the dining room window towards her own reflection, as if she was trying to see through it to the inky midnight sky beyond. 'A tragic accident has freed us from a blackmailer who might never have left us alone.' She took a breath. 'We talked about this. We agreed we needed to deal with Candy. Get her on board, if you'll pardon the pun, and then off our backs. Well, now we have. It might not be in the way you planned – I mean, we planned – but what's done is done. Let's move on.'

As the women staggered off to bed, all of them carrying the weight of knowledge that once again they were complicit in something terrible, Sheena stayed motionless in the dining room, replaying in her mind the sound of the splash as Candy hit the water. She felt conflicted, but not remorseful. At this stage in her life – and in her friends' lives too – it was dog-eat-dog out there. Kill or be killed. She had probably saved them all from being slowly bled dry by Candy over the next few years. But did that make her a pragmatic opportunist? A ruthless operator? Or simply cold-blooded, vindictive? Like Marco, Sheena didn't sleep that night. And at 10.30 a.m. the next morning, she too picked up the phone and called St Helier police.

CHAPTER 40

Hannah

In St Helier's tiny police station, Hannah Price sat at her desk and twirled one end of her long auburn hair tightly around her finger. It was a habit she had picked up in childhood, and always meant she was deep in thought. As the island's only dedicated police call handler, Hannah had been involved in many incidents over the years, and she had a good instinct for how a case would turn out.

Today, as she answered a call from a man called Marco Ricci about his girlfriend Candy Dace, who he said had gone missing from St Augustine's. Hannah's heart had sunk towards her feet. Hannah knew that people sometimes went missing for mundane reasons, but the circumstances surrounding Candy's vanishing were unusual. She'd gone out for a business dinner, and her partner couldn't find her at her usual spot, or anywhere else on the small island. Despite Hannah's fears, when she relayed the information to the ageing Police Sergeant on duty, he insisted that it was most likely couple problems and the woman was bound to turn up soon.

A nagging feeling in the back of Hannah's mind suggested that there was more to the story than an aggrieved girlfriend staying out all night to punish her boyfriend for whatever he wasn't telling them about. So when a second call came in, this time from the superstar soap agent Sheena McQueen, Hannah was immediately on the alert. She had been an avid viewer of *Falcon Bay*, and she had read all the press following the trial of Sheena and her friends.

When Ms McQueen explained that a woman called Candy Dace had been on her yacht Nemesis last night, but this morning had completely vanished, Hannah's concern rose quickly. Her mind raced with questions. Why had Candy kept her visit a secret from her boyfriend? What was she doing on board Nemesis? Hannah couldn't shake the feeling that something was terribly wrong.

Hannah didn't trust her lazy sergeant to start searching for Candy quickly enough. She wasn't supposed to do anything either, except write up a bland report, and log it on the computer system.

But she felt she had to do something. So she picked up the phone, and called the reporter who'd tried to interview her before the *Falcon Bay* trial. The one who had given her a shiny gold and white card, with looping script that read Tabitha Tate.

CHAPTER 41

Tabitha

Tabitha and Dustin were sat on Madeline's terrace, enjoying the mid-morning sun. When Madeline left for Australia, she had told Tabitha to dismiss the staff if she and Dustin wanted the villa to themselves. 'It's such a secluded, romantic place,' she said, raising an eyebrow pointedly at Tabitha. Tabitha hadn't needed telling twice. Once the staff had gone, she and Dustin had explored every inch of each other's bodies in every inch of the villa's garden, especially the turquoise infinity pool positioned so the water appeared to tumble into the sea and the linen hammock – big enough for two – that swung lazily under two shady palm trees.

Tabitha's favourite spot, though, was the large, canopied daybed, tucked away in a sunny corner, bordered by pink hydrangeas. Earlier that morning, all she'd had to do was tilt her head towards it, and Dustin gave her his hand and let himself be led to bed.

When she'd got there she teased him, lying down on her back, stroking her own hands over her body, giving him glimpses of a nipple or a flash of thigh as she slowly took off her clothes, one by one. By the time she was nearly naked he'd begged her to let him touch her. Finally, she'd extended a foot and invited him to suck one of her red-painted toes, the journalist in her hoping there wasn't a paparazzo in the bushes ready to splash the moment across the front pages. But the groan Dustin had let out as he took one in his mouth had taken away all her fears of going the same way as the Duchess of York, splashed over the papers in a moment of pleasure. When Dustin had flicked his tongue down between her toes, she could've screamed with pleasure.

But she'd controlled herself, instructing Dustin to move his hand up her leg slowly, stroking the back of her knee, caressing her thigh, until finally – when she could tell from his breathing he couldn't wait any longer – allowing him to slide two fingers inside her, feeling how wet she was, how much she wanted him. After that, she'd let him take control, enjoying how his desire made him urgent, hungry. He'd torn off his own clothes and pushed her down on the daybed, spreading her legs wide and holding both her hands above her head as he plunged deeply into her, at first slowly and then faster and harder, until both of them came together, shuddering.

Tabitha smiled at the memory and took a bite of food. Dustin had made them a simple omelette and a rocket salad for brunch, and they were talking, as they often did, about tracking people down. The success they'd had tracing Chad's movements had encouraged Tabitha to seek Dustin's help in tracking down the elusive Honey Hunter.

'I don't understand why you want to find her, though,' said Dustin, taking a sip of coffee, and not quite meeting

Tabitha's eye. 'Hasn't she been through enough? Shouldn't she be allowed to stay out of the public eye for a while?'

'I'm convinced she knows more than she's saying about the killer though. The consequences of that are too big for us to simply ignore,' replied Tabitha. 'There was something off about that video she shared of her appeal to the killer. It felt too staged.'

Dustin furrowed his brow. 'You mean like maybe she knows the vigilante is a crazed fan, and Honey Hunter doesn't want her fans to get a bad reputation?'

'Maybe,' said Tabitha. 'But my reporter's hunch tells me it's something more involved. Look at this,' she said, turning her laptop to face him. 'That's a piece from the *LA Times* about the arrest of someone in Caspar Felix's circle, published about ten years ago. I discovered it yesterday, but I had to trawl through Google for hours. Look at the photo they ran with the article – do you see who it is? Check out the caption: 'The defendant is pictured here at a film premiere, with studio boss Caspar Felix, 74, and friend, Honey Hunter, 49.' I did a bit of digging on some Reddit threads about the LA mob, and it turns out Honey was Caspar's goomar. It was well-known at the time.'

'Her what? Is that an American term?'

Tabitha ruffled his hair. 'You're so unworldly. It's what you call the mistress of a married mobster.'

'Ok…' Dustin was trying to catch up. 'So, the killer lured Mickey Taylor to a mansion which once belonged to Honey's ex? I guess that's the kind of weird statement a crazed fan might make.'

'You're not seeing it, Dustin. Don't you think it's weird that Caspar and Honey's relationship has never been public knowledge? Especially with all the press attention around the killings, you'd think it would be everywhere by now. Instead, it feels like it's been buried.'

Dustin's face lit up with understanding. 'Christ, do you think it's the mob who are ordering the killings? Either to take revenge on those who wronged Honey, or to hush-up the connection with Caspar? Either way, maybe the police are too scared to take them down for it – or it's part of a bigger operation. It would make sense that Honey's gone to ground too. It's not exactly on-brand for her to be involved with a mobster.'

Tabitha nodded slowly, and shivered despite the sunshine. She hadn't told Dustin what it had been like to watch the footage of Antony and Mickey's hideous murders unfold before her eyes, powerless to stop it. She also hadn't told him about the intruder in her apartment in LA, or the feeling she had on St Augustine's that she was being watched. The words scratched into the victims' foreheads flashed into her mind. Sadist. Liar. What would her epithet be? Traitor? Gossip? Coward?

'Tabitha, look at me,' Dustin said. 'I can see you're scared. But you have nothing to be afraid of. The two men who died abused Honey. You just wrote a book about her! There's no way anyone – even the Mafia – would want to bump you off for that.'

'Let's not sugar coat it,' Tabitha replied, thinking about how she had hounded Honey, exploited her pain for her own stardom, 'there's every reason I'm on that list. Besides, what about Mickey?' Tabitha's huge brown eyes widened. 'He never abused her.'

'He persuaded her to drink alcohol when she was in

recovery,' Dustin said gently. 'To many people, that is abuse. Besides, it was his action that ultimately led Honey to Durand.' He paused, as if suddenly struck by an idea. He took off his glasses, and fixed Tabitha with a penetrating stare. 'Did you ever figure out why Mickey was at Castillo del Amor that night? Who did he think he was meeting?'

'No. He said it was a studio boss, that he'd tell me more after the meeting. But it can't have been Caspar himself. He died last year. Mickey hinted that the person he was meeting had information about Madeline Kane's parentage. Information that would make my book really explosive.'

Dustin put his coffee down. 'Have you ever considered that he might have been meeting Honey herself?'

Tabitha paused, then shook her head. 'I don't think so. The figure in the footage was masked and in a latex suit, but I'm sure it was a man. He was tall and strong and – well – he was just too angry to be a woman. You know?'

'You might think Honey is sweet and fragile, but abuse does terrible things to people. It changes them.'

Tabitha was frowning. 'No. I don't think so. I just can't imagine Honey a cold-blooded killer. But I could be going down the wrong path with the Mafia stuff. Maybe it's a nurse from the clinic? Someone in a lowly position at Durand's place who witnessed the horrible goings on and was powerless to do anything to change them. And now they're on a mission to eradicate their guilt.'

'If it is,' said Dustin, 'then there's no reason for you to be on that list.'

Tabitha suddenly felt drained, grateful to Dustin, the voice of reason. No wonder Madeline had spotted his potential, wanted him on her side. 'You could be right. I'm just seeing things that aren't there, letting paranoia creep in. Right?' She was asking not because she thought it was true, but because it was what she needed to hear in order to get through the day.

'Right.' Dustin smoothed her hair away from her forehead with his thumb. 'I'm sure you're safe on the island. Besides,' he said, cocking his thumb towards the villa, 'you know how obsessed Madeline is with CCTV. If a stranger came over these walls you'd be alerted in a heartbeat.'

Tabitha tried to feel relaxed, but as her eyes scanned the shoreline below the villa, she still couldn't shake the feeling that, somewhere along the forested beach, someone's eyes were staring back at her.

Her mobile phone buzzing on the table made her startle. God, she had to stop being so jumpy!

'Is it Madeline?' Dustin asked, hopefully.

'Unknown number,' Tabitha said, glancing at the screen. 'I'd better take it.'

When she did, all thoughts of Honey and the hitlist were chased out of her mind. After listening to the woman on the other end of the phone, she hung up, looking grimly at Dustin.

'That was Hannah Price – she's a call dispatcher at St Helier Police. Candy Dace is missing.'

'What? How?'

'It sounds like she went overboard. On Nemesis.'

CHAPTER 42

Helen

Helen was still at the cemetery when Matt called. She laid the tulips she'd brought for her mother's grave on the grass and took several deep breaths before answering. Sheena had said she had to act and sound as normal as possible today. Well, that was no problem when it came to Matt.

'Hey, sexy,' she said, purring down the phone. 'Still thinking about that cockpit?'

'This isn't a social call, Helen.' Matt sounded weary, as if this wasn't a call he had wanted to make.

'What's wrong?' Helen said, trying to sound less anxious than she felt.

'I've been summoned to St Augustine's by St Helier police,' he said, matter of fact. 'A woman went missing last night. And that bloody hack Tabitha Tate, determined to meddle with the police investigation, has published an online article with some pretty serious allegations.' He paused, allowing the silence to stretch between them.

'That's terrible,' Helen said, keeping her voice steady.

'Who's the woman? Do we know her?'

'Yes,' Matt sounded grave. 'She's a friend of yours. Candy Dace. And I gather you met her recently, at the Oyster Bar. I've been asked to notify you to return to the island immediately, for questioning.'

Helen remembered how Sheena had coached them all last night. 'God, that's awful. But you know, she wasn't a friend, exactly, more a work colleague. She was going to do some work with us. She was miserable working for Jake, she wanted a change.' Helen paused, praying that the girls had all stuck to the same story. 'But how can she be missing? I only saw her last night. She came aboard Nemesis for dinner. We all hung out and discussed how we could work together.'

Matt took his time before saying, 'Helen. You really don't know what happened to her between last night and this afternoon?'

'What? No. I mean, she'd had a fair bit to drink – we all had – and she decided to crash in one of the spare rooms. I left early for London, and everyone was still sleeping.'

'And why did you leave early?' Matt sounded sharp, in full interrogation mode rather than talking to the woman he was falling in love with. Helen's stomach plummeted and she felt tears prick the back of her eyes. She so wanted to be with Matt properly, and she had dared to hope that their intimacy on the yacht, the two of them entwined under the stars, was sowing the seeds of a meaningful relationship. If it ever came to light that Sheena – and by extension, Helen – was involved in Candy's disappearance, she'd never be with Matt. She glanced at her feet, at the headstone with its simple inscription, and at the little metal vase set into the grave. A little metal vase in which she had secreted the memory stick which showed Ross Owen in his final moments, and then filled the vase with tulips.

'I always visit my mother's grave on her anniversary,' Helen said a touch defensively. In the silence that followed, she tried to gauge Matt's expression, hoping it might be compassionate.

'Well, you have to come back to St Augustine's straight away,' he said, her hopes dashed by the harsh tone of his voice. 'This is serious, Helen. We're looking for a body and once again you and your friends are caught up in it all. I'm beginning to worry that this isn't an unfortunate coincidence.'

CHAPTER 43

Madeline

Madeline lay back in the super-king four-poster bed in her Sydney hotel room, and flipped open her laptop to watch another episode of the Kardashians. She had been here for five days, sleeping fitfully, watching TV, ordering room service she had no appetite for. Occasionally she would dip her feet in the private pool on her balcony, with its spectacular view of Sydney Harbour Bridge, but nothing brought her any joy.

She had tried to get excited about other things on the horizon, such as the interesting email from Sheena McQueen last week, suggesting that they put their differences aside and unite in the one thing they knew they both loved and cared about: rebooting *Falcon Bay*. But even the thought of working with her old nemesis to resurrect her favourite show and launch it for the modern age on a global streaming service wasn't enough to thrill her. She felt uncharacteristically lost, adrift, and totally without courage. She was only supposed to stay here for two nights, before travelling to Rainbow

Creek with a driver booked for her by Dustin. But when the time had come to walk outside and get into the car, she had completely lost her nerve, and instead booked three more nights in the penthouse suite. She'd told herself that there was no point going to track down Chad if she was a bundle of nerves. She needed to be feeling strong, self-possessed; ready to face whatever decision he had made about his future. But instead of spending the time empowering herself, she simply idled away the days, and now she was feeling even lower than when she arrived.

Anyway, what if Chad wasn't in Australia at all? What if the stranger at Rainbow Creek was some other horse-loving expat? What if – even worse – Chad *was* there, but didn't want to be found, least of all by Madeline? She couldn't stop thinking about what she'd done by faking her own death and running away. Would he understand why she had felt unable to reveal her true self to him, to the world? Would he forgive her for misjudging him so completely, for not realising that he knew about her past all along, and loved her anyway? Would he ever be able to overcome the fact that he had hosted a gorgeous, extravagant funeral for her, which he had said, in the article about it, was the hardest thing he had ever had to do? Would he say it was too late for apologies?

As she imagined the scenario over and over, Madeline experienced a rollercoaster of emotions. Her hopes leapt at the fantasy of running into his arms in a stable block, to be covered all over by his ecstatic kisses. Then she plunged into despair moments later, when she imagined herself turning up in the horse ranch, and Chad looking at her aghast, then sending her away, furiously angry. Surely this was the most likely scenario. After all, he had practically lost his mind with grief when she died. Would he understand why it had been necessary for her to disappear from his life? Would he forgive her? Would he give her a chance to explain? Perhaps by now he'd met someone, a new woman, sweet and kind, who was helping him heal. Madeline almost wept at the thought.

Her laptop pinged on the bedside table. It was an email from Dustin.

> Just checking in again. Remember I can book you transport at a moment's notice. Tabitha and I really think it will be worth the trip.

She sighed. She knew she had to make a decision. Listlessly, she started typing out a reply saying he should fly over and take her home to St Augustine's. She had made a mistake. But just before she hit send, a video folder on her desktop caught her eye. It was labelled 'Business Trip Blues' and she knew exactly what was inside. For the first time in five days, she smiled. She desperately needed a distraction, especially one that reminded her of how much Chad had loved her, once. She clicked on the first video, and an image of her gorgeous Chad appeared, naked to the waist, his stomach taut and his abs toned. In the days when they both had to travel for work, they'd book in regular video sex sessions, which Madeline often recorded so they could play them back later.

She pressed play, and Chad's honeyed Southern drawl filled the room. 'I'm in my hotel room, and I'm imagining the first time I met you.'

Madeline's voice replied over the airwaves. 'Tell me about it.'

'The moment I saw you, it was love at first sight. You were wearing a blue dress. It hugged your ass, and my God I wanted to touch you straight away.'

'I'm touching myself now. Can you see me?'

Chad groaned. 'Yes. I can see you stroking your nipple. It's making me hard.'

In her Sydney hotel room, Madeline placed two fingers in her mouth, moistened them and then ran her hand down between her legs. She heard her own voice float out of the screen again. 'Keep talking, Chad. What happened next? What else did you want to do to me?'

'I invited you for lunch in my hotel. We sat down. You ran your naked foot up my leg under the table and that was it. We didn't even make it to the aperitifs.'

'My nipples were hard when we got in the lift. You ran your hands over my body. You lifted up my skirt—'

'You were so wet already. I slid a finger inside you in the elevator. I wanted to fuck you so badly.'

'In your hotel room, you pushed me on the bed. You asked me to touch myself. I put my hands between my legs and you went wild.'

'I'm going wild now, baby.'

Madeline kept up her rhythm, stroking herself, her eyes fixed on Chad. As he moaned her name, and brought himself to orgasm on the screen, the desire for him surged through Madeline, until she too arched her neck. She allowed waves of pleasure to crash over her, again and again, blotting out everything except Chad calling her name.

She laid her head back on the forest green silk pillow, and closed her eyes. She sighed gently, smiling to herself as a blissfully heavy feeling crept through her body. She fell into a deep and dreamless sleep, and awoke eight hours later. For the first time since she arrived in Australia, she felt completely refreshed and ready to face the world. Maybe, just maybe, she would hear Chad call out her name like that again.

The cursor was still hovering over the send button on the email she had planned to send to Dustin. She deleted everything she'd written, and typed out a single line:

Book the cab now. I'm going to Rainbow Creek.

CHAPTER 44

Amanda

Almost a week had passed. Interviews had been conducted, Nemesis had been searched, police divers had spent hours exploring the seabed around the yacht. Four days after Candy was last seen, a detective confirmed that Candy's fingerprints were on the railing of the balcony outside the yacht's main sitting room, and a smudge from a shoe was on the bottom rail. On day six, a birdwatcher called up St Helier police. They had found a body, washed up on the beach at Corey Point, half a mile from where Nemesis was anchored.

It was the moment Amanda had been dreading. Somehow, without a body, she had been able to persuade herself that Candy might've survived, that perhaps she had swum to shore and then run away. Amanda knew deep down that she was being ridiculous, but her hope of the impossible had sustained her over the last week, allowing her to spend time with her daughter and not view herself as a monster. Now, though, there was no avoiding the truth. Candy was dead, and Amanda and her friends were the last to see her alive.

The next day, Amanda, Helen and Sheena were gathered outside on the upper deck, one of the few places on the yacht that wasn't closed off with police tape. They all felt too sombre to swim in the black-tiled pool, but they sat on its edge, legs dangling into the water that looked like tar.

'There'll be a post-mortem now,' Sheena said. 'It will confirm how much she'd had to drink, and that death was by drowning. All we need to do is sit tight, stick to our story, and wait for things to go back to normal.'

'Normal!' Amanda spluttered. 'We're at least partly responsible someone's death, how can anything be normal again?'

'I don't know how you can be so... unaffected by all of this,' Catherine told Sheena.

Sheena looked away. Far from being unaffected, she was haunted by what she'd done. She longed to confess that when she closed her eyes and tried to sleep, Candy appeared. Smiling, tipsy, confiding that she couldn't swim. Leaning on the balcony rail, clearly at ease with Sheena at her side. Never suspecting that she was her enemy.

Her killer.

Although Sheena constantly reminded herself that tipping Candy overboard was her safest bet at no one ever knowing what had happened to Ross Owen, her subconscious wasn't having it. When Sheena did manage to sleep, it was fitful, filled with nightmarish images: Candy, hollows for eyes, mouth twisted in a silent scream, clawing at the seabed in her red dress which billowed in the water, disturbing a shoal of black and silver fish.

She didn't tell the others because she knew they needed to be able to tell themselves that maybe – just maybe – it was an accident. They needed her to be strong. Any sign she was crumbling, any crack that might let the truth pour out, could lead to everybody falling apart.

She couldn't risk it. For all of their sakes.

'Did Matt believe you had a reason to go to London?' Sheena asked Helen.

Helen nodded, miserable. 'I think so. But I think he suspects we're hiding something.'

She had returned to the island as instructed, and gone straight to the mobile incident room in the harbour. Matt had taken her statement in the presence of a skinny, silent detective who looked to Helen like a schoolboy on work experience. Helen had confirmed what she'd told Matt on the phone about Candy drinking a lot, about her leaving for London early the next day; about the tender being out because the all-female staff had been given the night off.

'Well, that tallies with what we've already been told,' Matt had said.

Helen had nodded, relieved.

'A little too closely for my liking.' He sounded sceptical. 'Five women, all with the same near identical version of events. Quite remarkable really.' He leafed through his own notes. 'Right down to the last time you all saw Candy, where she'd left her jacket and bag, and how much wine she'd had.'

'I don't see how our recall would differ, given we all had the same experience.'

'As for the tender being unavailable,' Matt had continued, 'the crew given the night off. Some might say that was very convenient. And why didn't anyone know she was seeing you that night?' He'd fixed her with a look of incredulity. 'Some might find it all rather suspicious.'

'We asked her to be discreet because we were talking about poaching her from Jake, that was the only reason. No one asked her to lie to her boyfriend.'

'So you weren't aware that she handed her notice into Jake Monroe the day before? Funny that she didn't share that information with you, given you were about to hire her.'

Helen had blinked nervously. Had Candy told Jake she was coming into money and didn't need her PR job anymore? 'I expect she wanted some leverage,' Helen lied. 'We wouldn't have paid her nearly so much if we thought she was unemployed.'

'And how much were you planning to pay her?'

Something about Matt's tone put Helen on the alert. She made a quick decision, figuring that sticking as close to the truth as possible would be the safest option. 'It was somewhere in the region of two million – once you factor in bonus, share options and things like that. It sounds like a lot but Jake was paying her well so we had to pull out the big guns. Sheena's the finance whizz, she has the details.'

Matt had written something on his notepad, and his expression had softened slightly, showing Helen a glimpse of the carefree man who had wooed her on the yacht just a week before.

'Thank God you said the same when you were questioned,' Helen now told Sheena. 'But I don't think he's totally buying it. Not least because police never think there's such a thing as coincidence. What are the chances that we've just been released from prison after a mistrial, and here we are, slap bang in the middle of another suspicious death inquiry?' She paused. 'And, I didn't tell you this at the time but… he brought up Ross Owen.'

Sheena looked like she might pass out. 'Why? What's that got to do with Candy?' She caught Helen's look. 'Obviously, we know there's a connection but no one else does. Do they?'

'Oh, God,' Amanda said. 'I knew this would backfire. We've had it!'

'Calm down,' Sheena told her. 'What exactly did he say about Ross?'

Helen shrugged. 'Just that it was yet another unexplained death on St Augustine's.'

'In other words, he knows nothing,' Sheena scoffed.

'It was more like he was putting me on the spot, trying to make me squirm,' Helen said. 'In the end, he just looked at me as if I was a terrible person, bad through and through. It was awful.'

'What about you, Amanda?' Sheena turned to her friend. 'How's it been with Dan?'

'I hate it,' she confided. 'He keeps asking me what Candy was doing on Nemesis, and why I hadn't mentioned I was planning to see her.'

'And what have you been saying?' Sheena's voice was sharp.

Amanda sounded huffy. 'Obviously I'm sticking to our story! That our great negotiator Sheena McQueen wants to bring back *Falcon Bay* and we thought Candy might be an asset.'

What she didn't say was how it felt keeping this huge and horrible secret from her beloved Dan. She had so nearly blurted everything out yesterday, when the two of them were walking together on the beach, Olivia snuggled up fast asleep in a carry-pouch on Dan's chest. They had been informed at lunchtime that Candy's body had washed up on Corey Point, and after the initial shock had worn off, Dan had suggested going down to a part of the beach that wasn't cordoned off, where Candy had liked to swim, to say goodbye.

It was early evening, the sun was going down, and Amanda had slipped off her flipflops and was paddling at the edge of the shore. The water was freezing, and when a wave broke against her ankles and drenched the hem of her sun dress, she turned to Dan, expecting him to laugh. But instead his expression was serious.

'I have to ask you, Amanda. What really happened on Nemesis that night?'

'Nothing happened,' Amanda swallowed. 'I can only tell you what I know – which is that Candy was drunk, and ended up in the sea.' She gave a helpless shrug. 'I don't know what else to say.'

Dan muttered something she didn't catch.

'What was that?'

He gave her a hard look. 'Listen, I've stood by you through everything. I've believed you through everything. But something's not adding up. Do you promise me you're telling me the truth? Is there something you're not telling me?'

It had been a glorious, warm day and yet Amanda felt a cold shiver on the back of her neck. Dan sighed. 'It's not like you to be so cold, so unfeeling. A young woman you'd spent an evening with loses her life a few hours later in mysterious circumstances, and it's a case of not my problem.' He looked at her perplexed. 'Just one of those things.'

Amanda sat down on the dry sand, and Dan squatted down to join her, Olivia still sleeping soundly in her pouch. Amanda gazed out to sea, her eyes filling with tears, wondering how to square her guilt with her fierce desire that she, Dan and Olivia would finally be a proper family together. What's done is done, Sheena had said. But a life had been snatched away and Amanda couldn't stop thinking about the young woman, so beautiful in her long red dress, sinking to the ocean bed, unable to save herself. Did she have time to panic, to understand what was happening, or did she die at once, as the water closed over her head? It may not have been Amanda's own hand that had sent Candy plunging into the sea, and Sheena may still be insisting that it was simply a tragic accident, but Amanda's initial suspicion that Sheena was culpable had now hardened into certainty. And here she was, a supposedly innocent wife and mother, covering up her friend's crime. Whatever happened next, the repercussions of that night would be with her for ever.

Was she even fit to be a mother? Did she even know who she was anymore? She suddenly wanted to tell Dan everything, let all her secrets spill out onto the sand, into the sea. But she couldn't. They weren't just her secrets, they belonged to the others too, and she had promised to keep them safe. And there was Olivia's happiness to think about, too. If she went back to Jake, that could wreck the life of this happy, sweet girl.

All for one, one for all.

'What is it?' Dan said, breaking into her thoughts, kneeling beside her. 'You can tell me.'

If she did, that would be it. Dan being such a good and honourable man would have no option but to inform the police. They would never be a family, and Olivia would have to go back to the custody of vile Jake. She steeled herself.

'Has it even crossed your mind how hard it's been these last few months?' she said. 'What being in jail has done to me?' Her voice was shrill, and Dan seemed taken aback. 'Perhaps you're right, I am cold. Perhaps that's what being in prison does to a person. I'm sorry I'm not quite my old self, but until recently I had no idea when – or even if – I'd get my freedom back. And just as I was released – when I shouldn't even have been locked up in the first place, I might add – and was hoping life might finally return to some kind of normal, this tragic accident happens. I'm heartbroken about Candy. But her death is nothing to do with me.' She turned to face him. 'And I don't want to say this, and I really hope you don't take me up on it, but if you don't believe me, and you want to leave me, I will respect it. I hope you don't, but I would understand.'

Sheena nudged her in the ribs, bringing her back to the present. 'Have you been hearing anything I said?'

Amanda shook her head. 'Sorry, I was miles away. Thinking about Dan.'

'Well, we have to get our heads back in the game, girls. I know we're all sad about Candy but there's nothing we can do about it now. All for one, remember? Rebooting *Falcon Bay* and relaunching it on Netflix is going to be our saviour, I know it is. It'll be big, and it'll be different, and it will keep us sane, and give us purpose. On which note, I finally had a reply from Madeline. She hasn't said yes exactly, but it's a start. She says she's open to the idea if we can present it to her in a way that works and is fresh. It's not her priority right now, but if we can launch the franchise with a big splash, she's in. And she's already given me a great idea of how to do just that.'

CHAPTER 45

Jake

Jake was beginning to think someone up there had it in for him. On every front, he seemed to be putting out fires, every day some new horror. As if it wasn't bad enough having that harridan Madeline Kane breathing down his neck, sending her lawyers after him to take back his shares in the island, and Tabitha Tate, hideous hack that she was, popping up at every turn to give him the creeps about the Hitlist Killer, now, with the launch of La Mirage almost on top of him, he'd had a sticky conversation with his project manager, raising concerns about how they'd ignored the building regs and dug half the foundations into the sandy beach. Jake was furious, and sacked him on the spot. Hadn't he been clear from the outset that he wasn't going to be bound by stupid regulations designed for the sole purpose of causing delays to the construction? And hadn't his project manager, the recipient of a whopping great bonus Jake had paid into an offshore account, agreed wholeheartedly that the regulations were indeed a waste of time?

On top of everything, the island was swarming with police, which was just wonderful for the tourist trade. Come to St Augustine's where you're never far from a suspicious death! Actually, he was being unfair there. The murder mystery was good for tourism, visitors pouring onto the island in near-record numbers. If only Madeline hadn't shut down his main attraction, the Great White Death Experience, he'd be coining it.

In Jake's opinion, the cause of Candy's death was so obvious that a baby could solve the case. Which was a good thing, given the spotty policeman who interviewed him in his pokey cottage looked like he was barely out of nappies. Jake summed matters up for him in two succinct sentences: Woman boards superyacht full of ex-prisoners with an axe to grind. Woman 'accidentally' goes overboard.

'But what could possibly be their motive?' asked the square-jawed fool of a detective, Matt something, who seemed to be the boss of the spotty sergeant.

'They want to sabotage my launch party. I'm telling you, they're out to get me. I mean, is she even dead? Or is this just some stunt, like the one Madeline Kane pulled, intended to derail me? That lot have sunk to new depths,' Jake said, smiling at his pun, 'including murdering my PR so my big moment is ruined. I mean RIP and all that, but it's plain to me that this was less about Candy than it was about ruining my big night.' The detectives looked appalled, but this was the truth, as far as Jake was concerned. They thanked Jake and left.

He was determined to show them all. His launch – the biggest night of his life – was going ahead in a fortnight no matter what. There was no way he would put something that important on hold. Not for anyone.

Despite his bravado about the launch party, Jake couldn't help but allow a few worries to worm their way into his head. He had left all the event details to Candy, and he could only pray that she was good enough at her job to have confirmed everything at least three weeks before launch day. What if his highest-profile guests didn't show up? What if the bespoke bottles of Cristal with toppers shaped like Marie Antoinette hadn't been ordered? What if the walls of ice and fire in the lobby turned out to be – quite literally – a damp squib?

On the plus side, after the launch he'd be away from the witches on the yacht. He'd disappear to Dubai in a cloud of fame, and all the annoying things about running St Augustine's would become Madeline Kane's problem.

Feeling a bit more cheerful at the thought of his glittering future in the Middle East, he took a beach towel from a hook by the door, and set off down the dark forest path to the beach for his daily swim. Things weren't really as bad as they looked, he thought, as he plunged into the water and swam out towards the depths. Still, he made sure to swim in the opposite direction from the hulking yacht Nemesis, which loomed ominously in the distance.

CHAPTER 46

Helen

It wasn't Helen's idea to meet at the Oyster Bar, a venue that brought back difficult memories of the last time she was there, seeing Candy. That horrible realisation she had been taken in, double-crossed. That she and the others were about to be blackmailed.

She sat out on the terrace, at a table screened by triffid-like plants. She had asked to be seated there as it offered a degree of privacy but now, engulfed by greenery, she felt hemmed-in. She was on the point of asking the waiter to move her when a voice broke into her thoughts. 'I almost didn't see you,' Matt said. 'Hidden away in the rainforest.'

He sat down next to her, his knee grazing her bare leg as he settled into his seat. 'Thanks for coming,' she said, still not sure whether their meeting was a date or a police interview.

He nodded. 'I thought we should talk. Properly.'

The waiter appeared, poured him a glass of Chablis, and topped up Helen's drink. 'I wasn't sure what to order,' she said nervously. She'd had no idea whether Matt would arrive in detective or off-duty mode. With the cool, slightly detached way in which he scrutinised her now, she still couldn't tell. 'Is white wine OK?' she asked. 'Or… a coffee, if you're working?' She cursed herself for feeling so shy around him. What happened to the confident, self-assured casting director she had been this time last year? So much had changed. She had changed.

'This is fine,' Matt said, giving nothing away about why he was there, managing to sit so close his knee was still touching hers under the table, making her heart race.

She gazed at him. What was this? Work? Or play? She really couldn't judge.

'Any news?' she said at last.

'There is, actually.'

Her racing heart almost stopped. Had he discovered what they'd done? Did he know about Ross Owen, about Candy? Someone had seen them. Someone had found the memory stick hidden under the flowers on Helen's mother's grave. The one that showed what really happened to Ross Owen. She swallowed, feeling her mouth suddenly dry, certain that she and the others had been discovered, that Matt was here to arrest her. Tears pricked at her eyes.

'Are you alright?' he asked, peering at her.

'Yes, I'm… it's…' she picked up her glass and drank down half her wine. 'I'm nervous around you now.'

'Am I really that bad?'

'Yes,' she said. 'No. I don't know. It depends why you're here. I'm not sure if it's work or pleasure. It would help to know.' She attempted to smile. What would really help was knowing if he had something on them. If their brief taste of freedom was about to be snatched away.

'A bit of both, I suppose.' He sipped his wine. Helen drained her glass. In the silence that followed, the officious waiter appeared through the curtain of foliage and filled it up.

'We've had the results of the post-mortem,' Matt said, once the waiter had retreated again.

'Oh.' Helen hated the idea of Candy being sliced open by strangers, her insides removed, her internal organs weighed, slivers of brain tissue probed. She glanced at Matt. Science didn't lie. Unlike people. She felt a ripple of panic. What if it showed something untoward? Sheena kept claiming it was an accident, but Helen had her doubts.

'Are you sure you're alright?' Matt asked.

She nodded. 'The thought of a post-mortem makes me queasy,' she said. 'A body being cut open.'

'No worse than drowning, I imagine,' he said. 'Which is what happened to your friend.'

Friend. The word felt like a punch to the gut. Helen nodded. 'No, of course.'

'So, what we now know is that death was by drowning. She'd had a lot to drink. She was eight times over the limit to drive a car.'

'I suppose we'd all drunk too much.'

Matt frowned. 'You need to watch the booze, Helen,' he said. 'You're in your sixties.'

Ouch. Another blow. She hung her head.

'I'm not having a go,' he said, his voice softening. 'It's because I care.'

Helen looked up, suddenly hopeful.

'It seems like you and your friends have a death wish, drinking yourselves stupid on a boat, no crew on hand should you need rescuing. It's so irresponsible.' He caught hold of her hand. 'Any one of you could have ended up in the water that night.'

She laced her fingers through his. Her eyes brimmed with unshed tears. 'I know,' she whispered. 'And I'm sorry. I feel awful about what happened. Awful. I think Candy was just so overwhelmed – by the plush surroundings, all that delicious food, champagne on tap.' Matt's eyes were on her. 'We all overindulged and you're right. I need to cut back.' She hesitated. 'At my age.'

They were silent for a moment.

'I loved reconnecting after you were acquitted,' Matt said at last. 'Our time on the yacht together was blissful. It was like we were in our own private bubble, it felt magical, unreal.' He gave her hand a squeeze. 'Then, suddenly, Candy Dace went missing and you and your friends were involved. You can understand why I had to cool things while I ran the investigation, don't you? I'm a detective. My job is to uphold the law. So I had to be certain you'd done nothing wrong before we could be together. Do you understand?'

Helen nodded. It made perfect sense. And now, if she had grasped what he was saying, he seemed to be ready to give their relationship a proper go. Matt took her hand in his, and stroked her palm with his thumb. As his leg pressed against hers, every sinew in her body was screaming, telling her that a relationship with Matt – a real relationship – was what she wanted more than anything. And yet. He had said they could only be together if he was certain she'd done nothing wrong. That meant being with Matt would involve lying to him – not only now, but for ever. She felt the weight of it pressing on her. She longed to fall into his arms and tell the truth. Let everything spill out: Ross Owen, Candy, everything. Let Matt make up his mind based on the evidence, rather than on the untruths she'd been feeding him and he had swallowed. Didn't he deserve that? But she knew she would never, ever tell him the truth. His job meant he could never keep her secret. He would have to report it, and then her and her friends would go to prison. And this time it wouldn't be a cushy open prison on a beautiful island. She eased her hand free of his.

'Matt, I love you,' she said, looking into his calm blue eyes.

'That's all I've ever wanted to hear.' He was smiling, gazing at her with such tenderness, that finally a single tear brimmed over and started snaking down her cheek.

Helen steeled herself. She couldn't be with him if it meant deceiving him, never letting him glimpse the darkness hidden away inside her. It would drive her mad, and him too in the end.

'You're the only person I've ever loved,' she told him. 'But I can't do this. I'm sorry, Matt. I love you, but you're a policeman. I can't be your girlfriend, and a suspect in your case. And I only ever bring you bad luck. You don't deserve this. I don't deserve you. I don't deserve to be loved.' She got to her feet and his hand shot out, catching her wrist and stopping her in her tracks.

'Helen! No, don't. Please.'

She shook her head. Tears ran down her face.

'Marry me,' he said. 'Please.'

Helen stifled a sob, turned her head, and hurried away.

CHAPTER 47

Chad

Chad was in the stable block, grooming Storm, his white mare. When his beautiful wife was alive, he had used to brush her hair for her sometimes after a long day at work. She would relax under his hands, tell him it was so soothing, and it was for him too. It was a rare moment of peace for them both. He remembered it now, as he ran the curry comb over the horse's body in a slow circular motion, the animal at ease, utterly relaxed. For the first time in months, he managed not to cry at the memory of being with Madeline. As he finished brushing out Storm's thick white mane she turned her head and leaned into his chest.

When he lost Madeline, he thought he would never feel anything again other than loss and grief and pain, but he'd been proved wrong. He stroked the horse's neck, found a mint in his pocket, and fed it to her. She crunched it noisily, watching him closely, her expression knowing. It had been the right decision to come here, to cut himself off from friends, family and all the news, from any mention of Madeline. Before he moved away, he'd done his best to honour her memory. He created a beautiful funeral, spoke publicly about his love for her, and took revenge on the awful women who could have saved her, but didn't, by arresting them on live TV. After that, though, he cut off his connection to the outside world. No TV, internet, newspapers, or social media. Only by doing so could he preserve all his memories of her – so pure and real – without the hideous taint of tabloid gossip, or the TV industry's rumour mill.

That morning, he had ridden Storm out along the deserted beach at Bloody Bay, which was almost impossible to reach on foot. The path was steep, the vegetation thick, and a notorious riptide meant swimming was forbidden. He had been out riding for almost three hours, his time on horseback instilling in him the sense of peace that he craved, which had previously only been sated by holding Madeline in his arms.

At night, he still struggled to sleep, his mind filled with images of his wife in the water, begging him to save her, reaching out to him. Every time, he failed her. He wanted time to unspool, to return to the moment before she strutted onto the jetty. A moment where he would intervene, sweep her up in his arms, tell her he would hold her tight forever. But instead he woke every morning in a sweat, his heart pounding, feeling as if he couldn't go on. This is the day I die, he would tell himself. And then I can finally be with her again. Then he'd get up and go out to the horses and press his face into their soft muzzles, feel their calming energy. It was miraculous, their transformative power. Without them he wouldn't have survived. Now he was building himself back together, piece by piece.

He couldn't have carried on at home as he was. Not without Madeline.

He checked the horses all had water, made sure there was hay; had a word with each of them. He would be back again last thing before he turned in. 'Might as well just move into the stables,' he tried to joke to his pinto, Betty. He was half serious. The house was too big for him: the only rooms he ever used were the kitchen, bedroom and bathroom. Four other bedrooms, a sitting room, dining room, sunroom and study were all surplus to his requirements.

But just as he turned to trudge back to the house, Storm stamped a foot and whickered. It was rare for her to make a sound unless she was anxious. 'Hey, what is it, girl?' Chad said, turning back around and putting a calming hand on her neck. He noticed that the other horses, too, had become restless. One was snorting, one was making a soft whinnying sound. Chad tensed. Outside, a car door slammed. Someone was there.

Chad didn't get visitors. Ever.

It couldn't be Steve, his farm manager, could it? He wasn't due in today. It must be someone who was lost, had driven up the farm track by mistake.

A sudden fear clutched at his heart. It wasn't a journalist, was it? Come to track him down and say nasty, hurtful things about his wife in the hope of a response? Well, he wouldn't dignify any hack with a response. He had already shared his message publicly and there was nothing else to say. He had always loved Madeline, and he had always accepted her, as exactly who she was.

He stood still, not sure what to do. He had become so used to the lack of human contact; the few conversations he had to have with Steve were brief and practical. Everything else that he thought and felt he shared with the horses he had come to love. The idea of having to deal with a stranger filled him with ice-cold dread.

If he kept quiet, maybe they'd go away.

But they didn't.

Instead, the door to the stable block creaked open. A figure stepped inside. It was a woman. A tall woman, with long hair.

He stared at her, dazed, as if he had woken up in the middle of the most precious dream. Was he hallucinating? Was the figure in front of him real?

For a moment, he was utterly speechless.

'It can't be,' he said.

'It is,' she replied, and her words spoke directly to his heart.

'Is it really you?'

'It really is, my darling.'

'No. It can't be,' he said again. But his voice was full of hope.

'Chad,' she said. 'Oh, God, Chad.' She breathed his name like a sacred incantation. One he had heard in his dreams so many times, and had thought he would never hear again.

Wordlessly, he rushed towards her and held her tight. She raised her face to his and her eyes were wet. He let his own tears fall, and her hands reached up to tangle in his hair.

They stood there entwined for a long time, until the horses around them whinnied, then quieted, and all was calm and still.

CHAPTER 48

Sheena

Sheena couldn't sleep. Each time she felt herself drifting off it was as if the bed dissolved beneath her and she found she was falling, plummeting downwards into a gaping abyss. She would jolt awake, gasping for breath, heart hammering inside her ribcage.

She lay for a while thinking, waiting for her heart rate to return to normal, images of Candy flashing in front of her. The pictures she saw were ones conjured by her imagination; Candy, eyes wide with terror, arms and legs thrashing, the red dress a tangle, the sea pulling her into its depths. Madeline haunted her too. Even though her death turned out to be a performance, she couldn't shake the memory. In Sheena's dreams Madeline's face contorted with terror as she reached out and the shark closed in on her. Her hand withdrew out of Madeline's reach.

Her mind whirred. It wasn't surprising that the no-longer-ghost of Madeline was troubling her now. They'd exchanged a few more emails, and it looked like Sheena's master plan was going to come off. She was going to become Madeline's business partner, and reboot the show they both loved. But she felt guilty – horribly guilty – for once threatening to unmask her, and reveal details of a past life Madeline was entitled to keep private. Although, on the other hand, if she hadn't done that, she and the girls wouldn't be sitting on a pile of millions, and a big fat yacht. She sighed. She admired Madeline for many reasons, not least her incredible rise to glory after an appalling childhood. But she had left Sheena with little choice when she threatened to cut Catherine from *Falcon Bay*.

And then two years later, along came Candy. With pound signs in her eyes, she naively believed she could get the better of them. Well, she had been proved wrong there. Now her body had been recovered and a post-mortem carried out. No suspicious circumstances.

Once again, they were off the hook.

The problem was it didn't feel like it.

Sheena got up, pulled on a peach silk robe, and made her way to the upper deck. The moon was full, casting a beam of bright light onto the sea. It had been easy to ensure they'd silenced Candy. All she'd had to do was nudge her over the rail as she leaned over it.

In the end, it had been easy to take a life. The hard part was living with it.

'You couldn't sleep either?' Sheena turned to see Catherine. 'It must be the moon, all that energy keeping us awake.' *And my conscience*, Sheena thought. 'I don't feel like taking a sleeping pill, though.'

Catherine came to stand next to her. 'No, me neither.'

They were quiet for a moment.

'I was thinking,' Catherine said, 'about leaving.'

Sheena looked at her, surprised. In the moonlight, she looked pale, ethereal, still a beauty. 'Leave and go where?' she asked.

'I might go on a retreat,' Catherine replied.

Sheena smiled. 'Good idea. Why don't we both go? We could go to California, stay at Golden Door?' She had always dreamed of going to the exclusive spa once popular with Elizabeth Taylor and Judy Garland. She was drawn not just by the seaweed serums and microcurrent anti-ageing treatments, soothing massages and red-light therapy, but also by the philosophy of the place. Golden Door was more than a spa; it promised to change lives, help guests find their way back to themselves. 'It looks wonderful,' she told Catherine. 'It would do us the world of good to be looked after, spoiled... healed. Don't you think? We could stay as long as we like, until we feel back to our old selves. How about it?'

Catherine put a hand on her arm. 'That isn't what I meant, Sheena. I need spiritual food, not a facial.'

'And you'll get it there. Golden Door has everything.'

'I was considering going on a religious retreat. To a convent.'

Sheena digested this. She didn't want to say anything to antagonise Catherine. 'You don't have to run away, you know. We're in the clear. You heard what Helen said – the post-mortem found nothing suspicious about Candy's death.'

'Maybe I don't need to hide from the law. But I feel like we're all running away from what we've done, and that we'll never be able to stop unless we confront it in our souls.'

Sheena changed tack. 'What about the La Mirage launch? You can't miss that! I'm arranging something spectacular for the world's press.' That was the condition for Madeline to agree to the reboot. 'I promise you, it's going to be huge. We're hijacking Jake's party to announce *Falcon Bay* – there will be literally millions of people tuning in from around the world – it's going to be glorious. You have to be there!'

Catherine managed a small smile. 'I'm not going to the launch. I can't.'

'But you must! It's the launch of our show. And a chance to take revenge on Jake.'

Catherine gazed at her. 'Are you planning to remove him too? Push him off the top of his skyscraper?'

Sheena gave a grim smile. 'If anyone deserves to be wiped off the face of the earth, it's Jake. But no. I can't tell you the detail because Madeline made me sign a watertight NDA. But let's just say that a surprise guest is flying in. Madeline's helped me secure her for the show. But what Madeline doesn't know is that she's going to announce, in front of hundreds of celebrities, something terrible that Jake did. Like, really terrible. Then it will be his turn to be locked up.'

'That's great for you, Sheena. But I don't have any particular vendetta against Jake. The only man I'd want to crush into the ground is that gold-digging snake Lee Landers. But I know it wouldn't be right. It would be better for my soul to find a way to forgive him.'

Sheena's eyes glittered. 'But what if we *could* punish Lee? What he did to you was evil, Catherine. Truly ungodly.' She raised a perfect eyebrow. 'You could invite him to the launch, make him think you're ready to get back together, and then humiliate him live on air, just like he did to you. Madeline's arranged tons of press to live stream the event. We just need one of the cameras to follow you and him and then you can get your revenge on Lee. Then you can go on your retreat.'

Catherine's lips began to curl up into a smile. 'That is tempting. He isn't one of God's children, so he does deserve punishment,' she said thoughtfully. 'And you're right that we should all be there for the launch of the show.'

'Exactly,' said Sheena, congratulating herself silently for clinching the deal. 'We need each other now, more than ever. You've always been the heart of us, the glue that holds us all together.' It wasn't quite true but Sheena sensed it was what Catherine needed to hear. She took Catherine's hand and squeezed. 'We'll all go to the launch of La Mirage together. All for one, one for all. We'll announce the show, take revenge on Jake, humiliate Lee, then get away on retreat. Golden Door, a convent … wherever you like. We'll deserve whatever we want if we pull all that off.'

The two women stood side-by side. Catherine laid her head on Sheena's shoulder.

'You really are good at your job, you know,' she murmured.

'I know,' said Sheena, and smiled down at her friend.

They stood like that together for a long while, looking out to sea as the sun rose over the horizon, washing the sky in blush pink. Finally, they each went off to their cabins, and for the first time since Candy had gone overboard, Sheena fell into a deep and dreamless sleep.

CHAPTER 49

Madeline

When Madeline first saw her husband in the stables in Rainbow Creek, she wasn't certain it was him. So much about him had changed. He was leaner, hardened. His hair was longer, his skin tanned. The battered denims, scuffed work boots, and grubby cotton shirt were far from the tailored suits that Chad favoured in his previous life as a top executive. To begin with, it frightened her. She had a moment of doubt when she realised that the man she loved and knew intimately, could now be a stranger. He believed he had lost her, that she was dead, and now she stood, his late wife, a few feet from him. She wanted to give him a chance to confirm she was no apparition. When he opened his arms, and she fell into them, the rightness of the world clicked back into place, and all she could do was say his name, over and over again.

Once they prised themselves apart from one another, Chad led them to sit down on the rickety stools in the stable block, the eyes of the horses on them, and Madeline gave her account of what had happened.

Chad sat in silence for nearly an hour, as Madeline described to him the pain and fear she had felt when she thought she would be exposed, and how she had worked with Dustin to fake her death. 'I couldn't stand staying on the island because I was convinced I'd lose you.' Chad shook his head and Madeline took his hand and hung on as if he were her anchor. Afraid that if she let go, she might just float away and disintegrate, billions of particles drifting off into the ether. 'The thought of not having you made me feel I couldn't go on, that I simply could not exist. I felt I had to go, to become someone else and make another life. I loved you so much, Chad. I *love* you so much. I couldn't face you telling me you no longer loved me in return. And it drove me to do the most stupid thing I've ever done. I made a huge mistake. And now I'm here to beg your forgiveness.'

At last he spoke. 'You would never have lost me. I don't know why you ever thought you would. Your past never caused me any pain. It never caused me not to love you. What caused me pain was thinking that I'd lost you before I could tell you that you were always a woman to me. Always the woman for me. You will always be the only woman for me.'

'I am so, so sorry, Chad. I wasn't honest with you. I kept my past secret. I let you marry me without admitting who I really was, and I had no right. I thought you'd be angry, that you'd never want to see me again, and I couldn't stand it. Can you ever forgive me?'

Chad stayed silent, digesting what she'd said.

'I love you, Madeline. I always have and I always will. I can forgive you for not sharing your past. But I don't know if I can forgive you for what you've done since. It's hurt me so much. I need time.'

*

For the next few days, they tiptoed around one another. Chad showed her to one of the spare rooms and said she could stay until he figured out what to do, but that he couldn't speak to her while he processed everything she'd told him. It was agony for Madeline. Every morning, she longed for him to come to her in the stable block. But every morning, he got up early and went out riding, leaving her to wander around the farm. She had no idea how long to stay, how long this would take, whether Chad would ever want her back. But she kept her despair and pain at bay by spending time in the stables, grooming the horses, riding them around the paddock at the back of the house.

Waiting to find out her fate.

Now she was in the stable block, a week after she had arrived, enjoying the last of the afternoon sun streaming in through the windows, combing the pinto's mane. The horse made appreciative snorting sounds. 'You like that, girl?' She scratched it under the chin and the pony nodded its head. Madeline laughed. 'You do! Clever girl!' She patted its flank. 'You're a real beauty, you know that?' The horse nuzzled her. Something about the presence of the animal made her feel calmer, less fraught. She understood why Chad had come here, the solace he had found with his horses. 'You've been looking after him well,' she murmured.

A shadow fell over her shoulder. She knew that shadow well. She turned to see him, aching with longing for his voice, his touch. At the same time, terrified of what he was about to say. When Chad spoke, it wasn't what she had prepared for.

'How exactly did you track me down?' Chad asked, leaning back against a wooden shelf of polished tack, his arms folded.

Madeline carried on running the comb through the pinto's mane, her hands trembling. She couldn't work out what answer would be least likely to spook him, and in the end she opted for the truth. 'I didn't. It was Tabitha Tate, helped by Dustin.' Chad looked surprised. 'Don't ask me how, the woman is a genius.'

He was quiet, his brow furrowed, thinking. Madeline cursed inwardly. She must have got it badly wrong. Of course he wouldn't want an investigative journalist to track down his whereabouts. He was a private person, and this was a massive invasion of privacy. *If he didn't hate me before*, she thought, *he must hate me now*. She had messed up once again. Just how many ways could she get this wrong? He would never take her back. She closed her eyes for a moment, leaned her forehead against the warm shoulder of the pinto, so Chad wouldn't see the silent tears streaming down her face.

'I guess I owe her one,' Chad said. Madeline gazed at him, feeling her heart leap.

'You do?'

'Yes. Because if not, I would never have got my wife back.' He waited a moment then opened his arms. 'I love you, Madeline. Despite everything you've done. I may not agree with your reasons, but I do understand them. I spent the whole week wrestling with whether I can forgive you.

My head says no, but my heart says yes. And I can't ever fight my heart.'

She ran at him, feeling him hold her tight, her body melting into his. Tears streamed down her face. 'I'm sorry,' she stuttered in between sobs.

He kissed the top of her head. 'I know,' he said. Crying too. 'I know. I love you. I love you, Madeline. And we're together again. We can face anything if we're together.'

'Do you promise?'

'I promise.'

'For better or worse?'

'Well, there's certainly been some worse.'

Madeline smiled through her tears. 'Time to think about the better, then.'

They collapsed onto the floor together, Madeline kissing his neck, his ears, the space between the frown lines on his forehead. She thought her heart would burst with happiness. She had the only man she ever truly loved. Maybe everything was going to be alright, after all.

CHAPTER 50

Tabitha

'I think I've finally got a lead on the vigilante killings,' Tabitha said to Dustin. 'I've got an anonymous email from someone who says they witnessed Mickey's death in Castillo del Amor. They've included details that the press never released – and they know that Honey was Caspar Felix's goomar.'

'You still think the Mafia is responsible for the killings?'

'It fits, doesn't it? The coded mutilation, the messages carved into flesh, the villa Mickey was killed in... Even the word 'hitlist' points to mob involvement. And it would explain the email. It's probably a Mafia whistle-blower who's too scared to go to the cops because they know the police are in the Mafia's pay.'

'What else does the email say?'

'That I have to go to the Halcyon Hotel at 3 p.m. tomorrow. He'll be there, and he'll give me the evidence I need to blow the case wide open. All I have to do is go alone.'

'I don't like this one bit. What if it's the killer? You've seen what he does to people! They're barely recognisable after he's finished with them. And what about what happened to Candy? This island is cursed. You're mad to say yes to this. Come on. You need to turn this email over to the police.'

'No way. I want my reputation back. I want my status back. I want what I had before all of this! I need this scoop, Dustin.'

'But now that Madeline's paying you for finding Chad, you never need to work again!'

'It's not about the money, Dustin,' Tabitha snapped. 'You have no idea what it's like to be cancelled. Frozen out. It's so humiliating. I want to be able to show my face again. Fuck, I want to be able to write again! I'll never get my Madeline Kane book published. Not if I don't clear my name. And I've uncovered some really exciting stuff about her past. I mean, do you even care about my career?'

There was a pause. Dustin looked hurt, and Tabitha reached a hand across the table to take his.

'I'm sorry. I know you're just looking out for me. But this is something I really have to do.'

'Something that's worth risking your life for?'

Tabitha considered. 'Yes. I know that sounds stupid, but I'd risk a lot for this. It's my whole identity, there's a lot wrapped up in journalism for me.'

Dustin sighed. 'OK. Fine. No police. But at least let me come with you. I can run surveillance from outside, be your back up if things go south. I've only just found you. I'm happier than I've ever been. I can't stand to lose you.'

Tabitha gazed over her laptop at Dustin, enjoying the way the breeze on the terrace ruffled up his hair. His brow was furrowed and he looked more handsome than ever.

Tabitha nodded.

CHAPTER 51

Jake

Jake snapped shut his mobile phone and sat down on the sand, looking out at the sea. The brightening morning light seemed to melt across it, like butter on a warm pan. Adrenaline was rushing through his body, and he wished there was someone around to high five. He'd just got off the phone to the exclusive fireworks company who only last week had created the display for Kylie Jenner's baby shower. They'd agreed to slash the initial price they quoted to Candy, because Jake had promised them Harry and Meghan were flying in from the States and the media coverage would be off the charts. It wasn't *exactly* confirmed that the duo could make it, but if they didn't, Jake could handle that afterwards.

As well as his own press contacts, he'd allowed Madeline Kane, who was taking over La Mirage – along with the island – to bring her own camera crew to the event. She wanted to livestream it around the world, and then afterwards turn it into a documentary about the island. He had agreed, but on the condition that the camera crew film his big speech from the left, which was his most flattering angle. He went through his mental ticklist: fireworks, cake, visual effects, canapés, cocktails and the all-important guestlist had been sorted by Candy weeks ago, with the bills sent straight to Jake's most gullible investor. He promised to repay them as soon as La Mirage started making money. He didn't know what that useless Candy had been complaining about. Party planning was easy if you kept your wits about you.

Jake breathed in the clean, salty air, and enjoyed the slant of sunlight that glistened off the sea. The only thing left to finalise was his costume, and his seamstress would be flown in tomorrow do the final fitting. He was going to be dressed as Louis XIV, the Sun King, and Candy had found a theatrical costumier who was making everything to Jake's measurements: white silk breeches, a pearl-studded brocade waistcoat and a midnight-blue velvet coat, embroidered with gold thread. To top it off, the costumier had designed a leather half-mask, painted and gilded, and decorated with diamond dust to give it the most beautiful shimmer. She had even sourced him a custom-made perfume – a fragrance inspired by the gardens of Versailles, with notes of rose, cedarwood and a touch of orange blossom.

So wrapped up was he in the fantasy of striding into La Mirage as the Sun King that it was a while before his ears picked up the distant hum that was coming from somewhere over the horizon. He shaded his eyes with his hand, and looked into the sky. A helicopter was coming into view, the blades echoing louder with each passing second. It was clearly headed for St Augustine's, and Jake wondered who it could be. It wasn't unheard of for celebrities to stop off at the island for a Michelin-starred lunch on the way to France, or perhaps it was one of his guests, flying in early for the launch. He felt a thrill at the thought people of walking through the grand entrance of La Mirage in just two days' time. The best thing about his brilliant costume theme was that he could tell the press all sorts of celebrities would show up, and no one would be able to contradict him because all the guests would have their faces hidden.

Jake's binoculars were slung around his neck as usual, so he trained them on the helicopter in the distance to see if he could judge the level of celebrity by the size of the chopper. His eye was caught by a logo stencilled on the side. Had the Halcyon Hotel changed their branding? The interlocked Hs stamped on the side were painted in gold rather than the hotel's usual sage green. Maybe it was at the request of someone super-famous. He wondered which of his esteemed guests it might be.

Jake took out a joint and began to smoke it, waving cheerfully up to the helicopter ahead.

CHAPTER 52

Tabitha

Tabitha strode into St Augustine's five-star Halcyon Hotel in her bright orange trouser suit and clashing pink Louboutins with a confidence she didn't feel. In her many years of reporting, she'd never met a member of the Mafia before, and she wasn't sure what to expect. Heavies? Guns? She had no idea. Christ, she wasn't even certain that the Mafia were involved at all. It could have been sent from anyone. The anonymous email had been sparse with information, simply telling her to present herself to reception, and she would be shown up to the right room. Dustin was parked outside the hotel, binoculars trained on the front entrance.

The receptionist greeted Tabitha at the front desk. She was a slender brunette in a pale pink shirt with the hotel's logo, an intertwined HH, embroidered in sage green on the pocket. Her hair was swept into a neat chignon, and she exuded calm efficiency as she gave Tabitha a key card for the Conrad Room.

'I'm afraid your friend is running late. Please let yourself into the suite, and wait there for your meeting. I'll accompany you upstairs.'

Tabitha sent a quick text to Dustin explaining the situation, and reminding him to keep an eye on the front door of the hotel. They had agreed that if things got weird, Tabitha would message him 'SOS', and he'd call the police and then come straight up. They'd also agreed that if Tabitha didn't message him every twenty minutes, Dustin would raise the alarm.

Tabitha followed the receptionist as she strode, heels clicking on the hardwood floor, into a lift wallpapered with the same 'HH' logo as her shirt. She pressed the button for the top floor, and they emerged into a long corridor lined with an empty conference suite and two bathrooms. Finally, they reached the door marked Conrad. Tabitha felt a trickle of sweat on her back. It was eerily empty up here at the top of the building. She put a hand in her bag and gripped her recorder like a comfort blanket, reminding herself that if this source had the information she thought he did, it would be the scoop of the decade. It would get her exactly what she needed back: her reputation as a cutting-edge journalist with whom everyone wanted to work.

The woman opened the door and ushered Tabitha inside. The suite was gorgeous. A small vestibule containing a wardrobe for coats and a huge vase of pink roses opened into a large sitting room with floor to ceiling windows. The bedroom boasted a beautiful four-poster bed draped in sage-green silk.

'Have a seat,' said the receptionist, gesturing at a burgundy velvet sofa. 'I'm sure your friend won't be long. I'll have coffee sent up.'

Tabitha had felt reassured by the woman's cheerful presence, but as soon as the door clicked shut behind her, the silence seemed to hum with malevolence. Tabitha suddenly realised how isolated she was. What was she thinking, agreeing to meet an anonymous stranger here? Was her career really worth risking her safety? The gnawing feeling in the pit of her stomach was getting worse. Her eyes glanced back and forth between the door and her watch. Time seemed to crawl. She'd give him five more minutes, she decided, and then she'd cut her losses and get the hell out there.

Her neck prickled as if she was being watched, and she got up suddenly and wheeled around. The door was still closed. God she was jumpy. To pass the time, she went over to the vast windows that overlooked the Cove. She could see the great hulking yacht Nemesis from the window, and an image of Candy, her lifeless form claimed by the waves, flashed through her mind. Despite the warmth in the room, she shivered.

The door next to her was ajar. She pushed it tentatively, and stepped back, as if fearful of what was inside. But of course it was just the bathroom, a huge space with slate walls and a copper freestanding bath. On a shelf was a range of Penhaligon's products, a small stack of face cloths, and a jar containing neroli and geranium bath salts – the same brand as the one she'd had at home in LA. The one that had gone missing from her apartment. A cold dread seeped through her.

She had to get out, back to the car where Dustin was waiting. He was right, it was stupid of her to come here alone. She ran the taps and splashed water on her face, drying it on the closest thing to hand: a bathrobe with the hotel's HH logo embroidered in gold on the front pocket. Something scratched at her brain, but she ignored it. She had to get out as soon as possible. But at the bathroom door, she hesitated. What if someone had crept into the bedroom while she was in there? What if they were on the other side of the door right now, with a glinting kitchen knife, waiting silently for her to come out? Her scalp prickled. She shook her head as if to shake the image away. Told herself to get a grip, stop being ridiculous. She swallowed, counted to three, and then swung open the bathroom door in one swift movement.

The suite was empty.

Tabitha let out a breath. Her imagination was in overdrive. She kept picturing Gayle Weathers, the reporter in Scream who had to run away from a masked figure who stalked her through corridors and kitchens.

She headed for the door, but just before she reached to open it, a faint noise in the corridor made her pause. A shuffling sound, as if footsteps were creeping across the parquet floor outside. She moved closer, put her ear to the door. Was she imagining it, or could she hear breathing? She tried to swallow, but her throat was completely dry. She tried to tell herself no one was there, but just as she had gathered enough courage to open the door and step into the corridor, she heard a click. Somebody had just slid a key card into the slot. Tabitha froze. The door handle moved slowly. Whoever was there was trying not to make a sound as they pushed the door open inch by careful inch.

Tabitha's mind was racing as fast as her heart. There was nowhere to run. Her only option was to move with the door, allowing it to push her back into the corner of the entrance hall, against the wall. She held her breath and tried to still the quaking in her legs as a tall figure, clad in a black latex suit, crept into the bedroom. The heavy door slammed shut. Tabitha's heart thudded in her ears. It was the killer she'd seen on the footage of Mickey's murder. How could she have been so stupid? To risk her life for the sake of a story. Hands shaking, she felt in her pocket for her phone. Would she be able to text SOS to Dustin without making a sound? She pulled it out, her fingers slippery with sweat. She could see the figure prowling around the suite, and she prayed he wouldn't turn around. He opened a wardrobe slowly and deliberately, then bent to look under the bed. Tabitha moved to the wall opposite her, only a step away, her back pressed against it. She closed her eyes briefly and prayed: please, please, please. Please let her hear the click of the bathroom door next.

Miraculously, her prayer was answered. The killer stalked into the bathroom, and Tabitha seized her chance. She reached for the handle and sprinted out of the room, the heavy door slamming behind her. She didn't care how much noise she was making as she bolted down the corridor. Her mind raced through options. The lift would be too slow. The staircases too confined. Bathrooms? Cleaning cupboards? The conference suite? She spotted a sign pointing to the lavatories and rushing towards the ladies, before swerving at the last minute into the men's. It was empty. She pushed open one of the cubicles and crouched on top of the toilet, so her attacker couldn't see her feet. She thought about locking the door but felt that would be too obvious, so she left it ajar. It swung slightly in front of her, creaking ominously in the silence. Gulping for air, she listened for any other noise, straining her whole body to hear. Nothing. Her phone was still clutched in her hand and she tapped out an SOS to Dustin on shaking fingers and hit 'send'. Her heart plummeted. No signal.

A faint noise reached her ears, and her whole body froze. It was that shuffling sound again, which now she recognised as rubber-soled shoes treading softly over parquet floor. Sweat trickled down her back as she listened to the footsteps grow nearer. After each step, there was the swishing sound of a swing door opening. It sounded like the killer was methodically pushing open every door of the women's toilets next door, hunting down his prey. It wouldn't be long before he arrived in Tabitha's bathroom. Step. Swish. Thud. Step. Swish. Thud. This time accompanied by a terrifying new sound, a raspy whisper, barely audible: 'Guilty. Guilty. Guilty.' Tabitha's palms started to sweat. She looked around desperately. She had to do something. This time, there was nowhere to run.

She crept out of the cubicle and placed herself in front of the door to the bathroom. She braced her feet on the floor and waited for the inevitable. Step. Swish. Thud. Step. Swish.

The figure framed in the doorway loomed before her, his masked face blank and terrifying. The black latex suit made him look like a creature from another universe. Inhuman, with no distinguishing features. He raised a black-gloved hand and Tabitha sensed rather than saw the glinting kitchen knife plunging down towards her. She ducked and then, using every ounce of strength she possessed, she flung her phone at the killer's masked face. It hit him high on the forehead and there was a satisfying crack, as if it had connected with bone. The knife clattered to the floor.

The masked figure lunged for Tabitha, but the split-second delay she had created was enough. The killer's grasping hand seized only a few strands of her hair as she pelted down the corridor, lungs burning, adrenaline surging through her body. Around the corner, a lift stood open as if by divine intervention. She flung herself into it and pressed the 'close doors' button, her heart thudding in her ears, almost drowning out the sound of those footsteps approaching once more, but striding this time, picking up pace. She hammered the button, and finally the doors began to close, the slice of corridor narrowing, narrowing.

The masked figure appeared in view, a fraction too late to stop the doors, but not too late to give Tabitha one final glimpse of him before the lift moved off: one hand clutching the sharpened kitchen knife, the other hand raised in a silent, mocking wave.

Panting, Tabitha hit the button for the ground floor then pressed for the third. The door opened and she darted down the corridor to a set of stairs. She clattered down them two at a time, praying she'd created enough confusion to elude her pursuer. She reached the first floor and crouched down behind a metal trolley bearing piles of white bed linen. She needed to get her bearings and find an escape route. For all she knew, the Hitlist Killer had accomplices. They could be at the front of the hotel now, waiting to grab her if she left by the main entrance. She looked around frantically and her eyes landed on an open window at the end of the corridor. She ran for it, forcing it open. It was one storey above what looked like the hotel's kitchen garden, with a greenhouse and rows of planted herbs. The earth and grass looked like a soft landing, and to the left of her window was a trellis covered in wisteria. Praying it would hold, she clambered through and swung herself onto the trellis, her heels snagging on the wood, climbing down as carefully as she could before landing awkwardly in a rosemary bush.

There was no exit from the garden to the street, but a swing door led back into the building, and Tabitha pushed through it hoping for another way out. She found herself in a white corridor just off the kitchens and there, at the other end of the corridor, was a fire escape door that looked like it led onto a side street. Her muscles were screaming at her but she forced her legs to keep moving, and ran out onto the street. When she got there, she sagged against the wall, and tears started to stream down her face. She was out. She was safe. She was alive.

A hand touched her shoulder and she screamed and jolted upright. She was about to throw a punch when she realised she was looking into the face of the person she most wanted to see in the world. She fell into Dustin's arms, sobbing. He soothed her, rubbed her shoulders, stroked her brow and tried to make out what she was saying.

'Calm down, Tabitha. Take a breath. Tell me what happened. Your SOS just came through a minute ago. I've phoned the police, and they're coming. I'm here. Shhh. I'm here.'

Tabitha could barely breathe, let alone speak. The way the tall figure in black latex had waved goodbye, mockingly, as if he knew he would see her again soon, was implanted in her brain.

'It's the Hitlist Killer,' she gasped through her sobs. 'He's here. He's on the island. He's inside! He just tried to kill me... and... he's going to try again.'

CHAPTER 53

Sheena

It was 6 p.m. and the sun bathed the upper deck of Nemesis in a warm golden glow. The water in the ink-dark swimming pool shimmered in the light, and the rays glanced off a magnum of Cristal chilling in an ice bucket. It could have been an advertisement for a high-end relaxing holiday, if it weren't for the sense of fizzing adrenaline which was palpable between the women on deck.

Farrah was pouring out two glasses of Cristal while Sheena, who was settled in the booth-style banquette, checked her lip gloss in a gold compact.

'I'm not sure why we're bothering with makeup,' Farrah said, 'when we're all going to be wearing masks.' She gestured at the masks lying ready on the table. Pink lace studded with tiny emeralds for Sheena, silver filigree with diamond dust for Farrah, gold-leaf for Amanda, white mother-of-pearl for Helen and a beautiful hand-painted papier-mâché for Catherine, with real peacock feathers fanning out from the top.

Sheena added a final slick of lipstick and smiled. 'We can't be our best unless we look and feel our best. And anyway, masks don't stay on all night.' She winked, and gave Farrah an appraising look. 'You look phenomenal by the way.'

'Thanks, so do you.' Farrah was swathed in a crystal-encrusted dress, paired with sky-high Giuseppe Zanotti heels. Sheena was a burst of colour in a sequinned Halpern jumpsuit.

'I just hope I can get on and off the tender in these shoes without any unfortunate mishaps,' Sheena said, glancing at her towering D'accori platforms. 'Nikki might have to carry me.'

Farrah gave a wicked smile. 'I suspect you'd rather enjoy that.'

Amanda appeared in a gold fifties-style halter-neck dress with a full skirt. Her blonde hair fell in soft waves. 'Is this glam enough?' she asked. 'Olivia just asked if I was a fairy!'

'You look gorgeous,' Sheena said. She handed her a glass of bubbly and raised her own glass. 'The hottest mama at the launch. Joint first with Farrah, of course.'

'I'll drink to that,' Amanda said, tilting her glass towards Farrah.

Helen emerged on deck, radiant in a white strapless Roland Mouret dress with a cut-out that showcased her toned midriff. 'Wow,' Farrah exclaimed. 'I hope your policeman's going to get an eyeful of that.'

Helen forced her mouth into a smile. She hadn't told the others that she and Matt were over. 'Sadly not,' she said. 'After Candy's post-mortem, he went back to London. I think that's it for us.'

Farrah came over to hug her. 'Oh, honey, I'm sorry,' she said, shaking her head. 'I know how much you loved him.'

'It's his loss,' added Amanda, rushing over to throw an arm around her friend.

'Don't set me off!' Helen blinked back a tear. 'This mascara's not waterproof.' She fluffed her hair in an attempt to look positive. 'Right, girls, what are we drinking?'

'Cristal,' Sheena grinned, handing her a flute. 'We're back on the real stuff now that we're celebrating.'

Amanda gave Helen's arm a squeeze. She knew her well enough to know that despite the brave face, she was devasted. She clinked glasses with her. 'At least you look incredible. Your little black book of lovers will have been missing you. They'll be thrilled to have you back in circulation.' She winked.

Helen laughed, then, catching sight of herself in the mirrored bar, tugged at the hem of her dress. 'You don't think it's a bit short?' she asked, remembering what Matt had said about her inappropriate behaviour at her age. 'Not too… young?'

'Never,' Sheena said. 'Not with a body like yours.'

Catherine was the last to appear, still in her kimono, her hair wet. Sheena frowned. 'You'll need to get a move on, we'll have to head off soon.'

'I'm not coming,' Catherine said.

Sheena raised a sceptical eyebrow. 'Aren't you feeling well?'

'I'm not in the mood for a party. I don't think I can face it. The flashbulbs, the attention. It's been so long.'

The others exchanged glances. Farrah poured a glass of Cristal and gave it to Sheena. 'Come on,' Farrah coaxed, 'you know we can't go without you. You're the star of the show!'

Catherine narrowed her eyes. 'But I'm not though, am I? I'm the co-star of some mystery woman you won't even tell me about. Haven't we been here before? Look how that turned out.'

Sensing that this was a classic Catherine diversion tactic, Sheena stepped in. 'Look, I'm not letting you get cold feet now.' She handed her the fizzing glass. 'Get that down you and remember you've got your own reasons to come tonight beyond giving the world back their favourite star. You've got Lee to come all the way to the island to beg for your forgiveness, so relax about the new casting. This is your chance to get public and private revenge on that weasel and that alone is worth turning up for, isn't it?' Catherine's eyes sparkled at the thought of Lee grovelling on his knees the way he left her grovelling on hers, and Sheena could tell she was relenting. 'Anyway, this is a big night for all of us! Not just you. Madeline Kane's flown back from Australia especially.' Sheena had hoped Madeline would be so enamoured at having her husband back she'd let them do the launch without her, but no one loved the spotlight more than Madeline Kane.

'I still can't believe you did a deal with that cow,' Farrah said bitterly. 'She's the one who got us locked up!'

Sheena gave a conciliatory smile. 'You know there's no way I can do a reboot of *Falcon Bay* without her. She owns the island! Be practical'. Farrah gritted her teeth into the best smile she could manage. Though she hated to say so, she knew Sheena was right. 'We all know that sometimes you have to bury the hatchet for the sake of the bigger picture. Let's just say Madeline and I have reached an understanding, businesswoman to businesswoman. The past is the past, and this is the future, our future! In a few hours, we'll be officially back and the whole world will know it.' She smiled from ear to ear and downed her drink in one. Her high spirit seemed to lift the mood on the deck, as the women followed her lead, downing their drinks and refilling their glasses, looking much more relaxed.

'God, I can't believe we're really doing this,' said Helen in excitement. 'I mean, just over a month ago we were in prison! And now we're about to dominate the TV industry once again. Sheena's right. Let's get this party started.'

Only Amanda didn't look as enthusiastic as the others. Her brow furrowed slightly. 'I don't want to be a downer,' she began.

'Oh God, what now?' Sheena said, rolling her eyes.

'Are we really sure we want to spend all our money on the reboot? If it all goes wrong, Madeline has the Kane Foundation to fall back on. But we'd be fucked. Now I've had a taste of luxury life, I don't want to be poor.' Amanda looked gratefully at one of the polo-shirted girls waiting until she was needed.

Sheena grinned conspiratorially. 'I wasn't going to tell you yet, but let me allay your fears. I can, as of an hour ago, confirm that Netflix outbid Hulu for the streaming rights. Madeline and I are about to sign a deal so big you'll get all the money we invest in the show back at least three times over. Don't forget that a lot changed in TV while we were in the slammer. It's all about streaming box sets now. No one wants to wait a week to find out what's happened in their favourite shows. We will be the ultimate binge watch and before you know it we'll be number one in sixty countries. So now let's all chill. We're safe, and so is our money. No more negativity!' Sheena raised her glass towards Amanda, who looked reassured. 'The train back to the top of the mountain has well and truly left the station, girls. And we're sitting in first class.'

'Jake's going to freak out when we turn up to his launch party, and turn it into our own!' Amanda laughed. Farrah too looked delighted at the prospect.

'Indeed,' Sheena said with scorn. 'Finally, it's time for that vile man to get his just desserts. Which he will, as soon as I'm on stage. It's not just the new co-star I'm keeping as a surprise. I've got a lot of things up my sleeve for tonight, and you're going to love them all. Jake won't though!'

'I don't understand why you can't just tell us now,' Helen said. 'I know you signed an NDA, but I think we're beyond keeping secrets from one another, after all we've been through together. Just tell us who it is.'

'It's a surprise! You've just got to trust me. I promise you won't be disappointed.' Sheena raised an eyebrow.

'No, come on. Who is it?' Amanda pressed.

'I'm not telling you. You just have to trust me.' She turned to Catherine. 'Answer me this, as your agent and your friend. Would I put you opposite someone who wasn't brilliant?'

Catherine shook her head.

'You'll all love her, I promise. She'll be a great sparring partner for Catherine. With *Stranger Things* being a mega hit, retro is in vogue. Think Joan Collins and Linda Evans at their height in *Dynasty*. She'll help us put the show back on top.'

Catherine was softening. 'OK. It sounds workable. So long as she doesn't steal all the column inches.'

Sheena saw Catherine's enthusiasm, and pounced. 'She couldn't if she wanted to, darling. You'll always be the star of the show. Plus every media outlet we've ever heard of is coming. I've already briefed the camera crew to put one camera on you at all times, so if you want Lee to suffer, now's your ultimate chance of global humiliation. And they know how to do live re-touches before the stream goes out.'

'Well,' said Catherine, clearly swayed by talk of her already perfect face looking flawless to the world, 'If it's for the sake of the show…'

Farrah and Helen raised their glasses to Catherine, and grinned.

'I'll help you finish getting ready.' Sheena caught hold of her and propelled Catherine away and back to her stateroom before she had a chance to object again.

PART 5

CHAPTER 54

Tabitha

'Wow,' said Tabitha, craning her neck to look up at La Mirage from the glass walkway that ran across the beach to the entrance. She kept her hand firmly entwined with Dustin's as she did so. She didn't exactly feel like going to a party, after her close escape from the Hitlist Killer yesterday, but Dustin had already promised Madeline he would help run security, and Tabitha didn't want to stay home alone without him. Besides, this was probably the safest place to be on the island right now. They'd told the police every detail they could, and a perimeter had been set up around the building to stop any unknowns from entering the site. Tabitha was determined to put aside her fears and try and focus on the reason she was here: to get the scoop she'd been hunting for ever since she was cancelled. She would do anything to get her reputation back as a kickass journalist, and she thought she might be onto something regarding Madeline's heritage. She needed to be brave.

The walkway was lit by rows of twinkling lights, illuminating the specially constructed channel beneath their feet that led to the sea and had a pump to ensure seawater surged up and down constantly, like waves. Up ahead, wolves wearing tuxedo jackets appeared to be racing up and down the façade of the building, lit by a spotlight that gradually changed colour from orange to red, making it look as if the skyscraper was on fire. The wolves were holograms, but they were so lifelike, guests were giving them a wide berth as their queue snaked towards the grand entrance. 'It's such a shame that Candy isn't here to see what she did. She really did do an amazing job.'

Dustin squeezed her hand. 'She did good,' he said. 'She'd be really happy. Do you think we'll ever find out the truth about what really happened to her?'

'I don't know,' said Tabitha. 'The post-mortem ruled it an accident. But I just can't shake the feeling that those women were involved somehow. I just wish I could figure out why.'

Dustin stroked her knuckle. 'I love that you care, but let's put it out of our minds, just for tonight. You're my date, we're out in public for once. Let's enjoy the party.'

'I wish you didn't have to do a security shift.'

'It's just a couple of hours. It'll make Madeline more comfortable having me there for her big moment. And the money's too good to turn down.'

'I'm so glad she and Chad are back together. They're really made for each other.'

'She sounded so happy on the phone. Energised, too. Excited to publicly announce her new venture on the island.'

'I thought Jake was the one making a big speech? The press briefing said he'd be on at 9 p.m. and the fireworks at 10 p.m.' But as she said it, Tabitha realised there was no way in hell Madeline was ever going to let Jake bask in his own glory in front of a crowd of hundreds, with millions watching the livestream from home. Not after what he did to her island. She tingled with excitement. If Madeline was going to hijack Jake's speech, there'd definitely be fireworks. And they'd be the kind that would make headlines tomorrow.

They'd nearly reached the front of the queue. The couple in front of them — a famous starlet Tabitha had seen on last month's cover of *Vogue* and the lead actor in a TV show about the apocalypse — strode through the velvet rope and onto the red carpet that led to the front entrance of the skyscraper, gilded to look like the golden gates of the palace of Versailles. It was their turn next. 'I'm kind of disappointed I don't have to blag my way in tonight,' Tabitha said to Dustin. 'I've crashed Heidi Klum's Halloween party before, and security for that is tighter than a Versace corset.'

Tabitha leaned over the young man standing by the rope with a clipboard, and spotted their names under the heading 'Madeline Kane Entourage'. He handed them an embossed gold card with a picture of a peacock on it, which would gain them entry to the VIP area on the roof. On the back was one rule: no removal of masks in the VIP room. Smart move, thought Tabitha. Celebrities love nothing better than being completely anonymous — after they'd shown their faces on the red carpet of course. She strode down the red carpet and struck a pose for the paparazzi. As the bulbs started popping, she grabbed Dustin's hand and pulled him in for the photo.

Dustin grinned. 'Does this make us official now?' He leaned in for a kiss.

'I guess so,' said Tabitha, kissing him back hard and enjoying the feel of his rough stubble on her face. She pulled away reluctantly. 'We'd better stop blocking the red carpet. Let's put our masks on and go in.'

If the façade of the building was impressive, the lobby was breath-taking. At its centre stood a towering fifteen-foot cake, designed to mimic the skyscraper itself, roped off like a work of art. But it was the surroundings that had made her catch her breath. Tall white pillars covered in ivy woven through with sparkling lights were dotted around the vast floor, and flames shot up the white walls, appearing to disappear into the shadows at the very top of the building. At the same time, as if by magic, water cascaded down, dropping into dark pools that had been sunk into the foundations.

'How have they done that?' she asked Dustin, in awe.

Dustin shrugged. 'It's not actually that difficult. There's a sheet of glass separating the fire and water.'

She kissed his neck, then licked the same spot with the tip of her tongue. 'You're so clever,' she said. 'And you look hot in your mask.' It was a bronze helmet, topped with a design of horses and chariots, which made Dustin look like a sexy Roman soldier. 'Play your cards right tonight and I'll let you do me Roman-style later.'

Dustin pulled her towards him, and she could feel he was already hard. 'Only if you keep this on too,' he said, running a hand up her bare leg. She was wearing her favourite Roberto Cavalli maxi dress, an electric green see-through chiffon that was split to the thigh. Black lace underwear and black Louboutins completed the look. Her own mask was dramatic too: green sequins, with a lavish plume of black feathers.

Surrounded by vines, lit by candlelight, enclosed by the cascading wall of fire and water, she felt like a river goddess.

A discreet cough made them step apart. A waiter in white silk breeches and a blue velvet jacket was tilting a silver platter towards them. 'Foie gras crostini, Madame?'

'Delicious,' said Tabitha, taking two and popping one into Dustin's mouth before he could say a word. She leaned over and whispered in his ear, 'As much as I want you to ravage me right now, I have to go and find someone. I discovered something pretty explosive while researching Madeline's past, and there's someone at this party who I'm certain can confirm it – if I catch her at the right moment.'

Dustin tried to protest, but his mouth was still full of canapé.

Tabitha lightly pinched his bottom and licked his neck again. 'You'd better start your shift in any case. Bye, darling. I'll see you on the roof terrace for Madeline's announcement.'

Before Dustin could swallow his crostini, she had blown him a kiss, disappeared around a vine-covered pillar, and melted into the crowd.

CHAPTER 55

Jake

Jake reclined on a red velvet chaise longue and took a sip from his champagne flute. He surveyed his rooftop, and felt that even the Sun King himself would be impressed.

Running around the entirety of the vast rooftop was a cloistered walkway, known as 'The Ring.' This could be accessed from anywhere on the rooftop, and it housed the four massive elevators – one at each corner of the building – as well as stairwells, storage rooms and utility cupboards, all hidden from view by discreet green baize doors. The VIP area took up the entire east wing of the rooftop and existed across two floors. Above him was an open-air mezzanine level, strictly for VVIPs only. It had a roped-off drinks area where guests could sit on white horsehair banquettes and enjoy the best view St Augustine's had to offer. Behind the drinks area, a wide set of stairs led up to the helipad, which was on a raised platform in the north-eastern corner of the building. Beneath the mezzanine, a secluded lower floor was screened off from the main bar and dancefloor by a row of potted bay trees. Half of this VIP area was open air, and half was covered by a gilded wooden roof structure, lavishly draped in silk and brocade, in a take on Marie Antoinette's opulent boudoir.

It was here, at the foot of one of the four-poster beds that had been placed around the room, that Jake Monroe was reposing. He had to admit Candy had done a fabulous job with the décor. Peacocks were weaving around the four-poster beds, and lights were twinkling in the potted trees. The VIP area was already full of masked partygoers, some in modern dress – he was sure the woman in the red sheath was wearing Valentino couture – and some in eighteenth-century French lace.

His cock stirred in his silk breeches. Two of the courtesans he had hired from a high-end escort agency to entertain his investors were fondling each other on one of the four-posters, and a third was sat on Jake's knee, straddling his thigh and watching the other girls. He closed his eyes. Thumping house music pounded in from the west wing, where David Guetta was on the decks, in front of a vast screen flashing guillotines in an ironic nod to Bastille Day.

The woman on his knee, who he remembered was called Coraline, was grinding in time to the beat, and he groaned as she reached a hand behind her to cup his balls through his tight trousers. She signalled to a passing waiter, and within two minutes a silver platter of quail eggs and pistachio-coated scallops appeared in front of him, along with a bottle of Bollinger and two fresh glasses. She turned to face him, straddling him now, and popped a quail egg in his mouth.

'So, Sun King,' she murmured, tracing a finger down his neck to the top button of his frothy collared shirt, 'which of these are your most important guests, hmm? The ones you want me to, you know, butter up?'

Jake looked around. He had promised the planning official 'a night to remember' in exchange for permitting him to dig the foundations of the west wing into sandy earth rather than rock. Sure enough, there he was, leering at the girls on the bed, stuffed into a court jester outfit that was much too tight. Reluctantly, Jake patted Coraline's bottom and sent her off to woo the official. It wouldn't do to have him blurt out any nasty truths at the party.

Besides, Jake needed to mingle. What was the point of having Naomi Campbell at your party if you didn't make her aware that you were the host? The trouble was finding out which guest she was. Every woman here seemed to be tall, statuesque, and dressed like an A-lister. While the VIP area rule about keeping masks on might have drawn the celeb crowd, it was making things difficult for him now.

He knew that Candy had invited a handful of influencers too – only those with more than 2 million followers, of course – and he wondered if he could position himself in the background of one of their shots. He assessed the women around him, enjoying the anonymity his mask gave him, using it to gaze at breasts and arses for as long as he wanted. He was pretty sure he spotted Naomi Campbell in a skintight acid green dress, perched in a dark corner near the absinthe bar – but as he swaggered towards her table, she got up and walked off. He cursed himself. He should have lowered his mask.

Jake took a crystal tumbler of absinthe and knocked it back. He wasn't too worried about gate crashers in the VIP area; the natural hierarchy of power and status would prevent the plebs from trying to access beyond the golden rope. There was just one guest he couldn't bear to see at his launch. He couldn't imagine she'd turn up, but, just in case, he had briefed the bouncers at the front entrance not to let anyone in matching Honey Hunter's description. They had been supplied with photographs, voice clips and videos of her, and they were instructed that under no circumstances should she be permitted entry. He didn't think she would want to return to the island she fled from in any case, but nevertheless, he scanned every woman that passed for the long legs, tell-tale curves and golden hair that he knew so well.

He looked at his rose-quartz pocket watch, hired as part of his costume, and saw that the time was 8 p.m. He still had forty-five minutes until he had to position himself on the moving plinth behind Guetta, ready for his big speech at 9 p.m. He grinned wolfishly. That was definitely enough time for Coraline to have her wicked way with him; the planner would have to accept another of the girls. He found Coraline writhing theatrically on one of the four-posters, the fat planning official looking on. Jake clicked his fingers at her.

'The Sun King demands your presence,' he said, and she bowed gratifyingly and got off the bed, ushering the official towards the other girls. Jake led her to The Ring, where they took an elevator down to a private area on the floor below. Jake did not need to flash his pass at the security guard outside as they walked through an unmarked door into the luxurious office that had been assigned as the green room for tonight. He laid out four lines of cocaine on the glass table. He snorted two and gestured to Coraline to help herself. He sat down on the leather sofa, and pressed a button on the remote control. The huge TV opposite sprang to life, showing a choice of the building's CCTV channels. He selected the one pointing at the two courtesans fondling each other on the bed, cropping out the fat planning official. Jake unbuttoned his silk breeches, freeing his cock which sprang up eagerly. He pushed Coraline onto her knees between his legs, grabbed her hair and watched the girls on screen as she moved up and down.

But although Coraline sucked, licked and caressed in the way that only a true expert could, Jake couldn't get fully aroused. The last time he had been in this room it had smelled of new leather, cut through with the lemony scent of cleaning polish. Now, though, there was a distinct undertone of a sensual, spice-laden fragrance, as if someone had just drenched themselves in perfume before joining the party. He was certain it was Opium, by Yves Saint Laurent. But nobody other than him or the DJ was supposed to be back here. And the only person he knew who wore YSL Opium was the woman he currently feared most in the world.

CHAPTER 56

Madeline

Madeline and Chad, anonymous in their masks, and with plenty of their own security detail, as well those employed by Jake, had had no trouble in getting beyond the golden rope into the VIP area. 'I didn't expect to be congratulating Jake,' Madeline said, raising a glass of champagne to her full lips, 'but it's a pretty special launch he's pulled off. And we own this building now. It was *very* good of him to do all that work for our sakes.'

Chad nodded and smiled, before leading Madeline to one of the four-poster beds. 'Almost makes me feel sorry for the guy, knowing what we're about to do to him.'

Madeline sat Chad down on the bed, and perched herself on his knee. 'Let's not forget what he did when he thought I was dead. He exploited my body, my death. He made me into a freak show attraction. The Great White Death Experience? Even the name is foul.'

'It was crass, I agree. But look at the tourists and money he's brought to the island. I can't help but feel he deserves his moment in the sun before he leaves St Augustine's behind for good.'

'What that snake deserves is a prison sentence. I have information that could send him there – but I'm not handing it over to the cops. No, all I'm doing is stealing his thunder with our announcement about the new show, just like he's done to others a million times. Sure, it'll be embarrassing, but he's off to Dubai tomorrow anyway.' Madeline leaned against her husband's chest. 'I'd say I'm being more than generous by holding back.'

Chad kissed the top of her head. 'And what about us? When are we going to decide what to do next?'

Madeline slid her arms around his waist and squeezed. 'If you don't mind, then after this I need to really focus on the *Falcon Bay* reboot. I want to do this thing properly. I want to bring it back to life in a new way and with a new audience. It should be great for the Kane Foundation too.'

Chad smiled, but it didn't quite reach his eyes. 'It's a good show. The best! And St Augustine's is a pretty place to live. Maybe we'll get a couple horses.'

They were quiet for a moment. Madeline could feel that behind Chad's smile was a hidden sadness. In a sudden rush, she knew exactly how their lives should look, and what would make her husband happy. She spoke before she had time to think it through. It just felt right. 'I know how you feel about Rainbow Creek,' Madeline said. 'And now I've been there for a few weeks, I can see why you love it so much.' She paused, turned to face him, and took his hands in hers. 'Let's base ourselves out there, together. We'd have to get satellite Wi-Fi, and I'd need to fly over occasionally, but once we've done that, I can run the show from there.'

He turned to her, surprised. 'You mean you'd live out there? In the middle of nowhere?'

'That is the very least I owe you,' she said. 'Your dream.'

'You are my dream,' he replied.

'Well,' said Madeline, a smile playing on her lips, 'I guess now you can have all your dreams at once. And so can I. We can have it all: each other, the show, the foundation, Rainbow Creek. After tonight, it will be just us, together forever. And I'll make sure you are my priority for the rest of my life.'

CHAPTER 57

Sheena

'Well, well, well,' Sheena said, gazing around at the flames licking up the walls of the lobby while water cascaded down. 'You have to hand it to Jake. La Mirage is pretty spectacular. And this is a great party so far. I'm certain that's the Duchess of Sussex, over there, the one in pink satin, holding an oyster. I'm not sure how he managed it.'

Helen scoffed. 'He got other people to do it, that's how,' she said. 'His only contribution is taking the credit. This should be Candy's triumph.'

The girls' guilty silence was interrupted by a silk-clad waiter bearing bottles of Cristal with toppers shaped like Marie Antoinette. They took a coupe each. 'Don't go away,' Farrah told the waiter, downing her drink and taking a second.

'I wonder where Jake is,' Sheena said, her eyes scanning the clusters of people gathered by the twinkling, ivy-draped pillars. 'Madeline said he'd planned his speech for sunset, at 9 p.m. That's in about half and hour.'

'He won't be in the lobby – the party's on the rooftop, 105 floors up. Anyway he's probably feeling up some floozy,' said Farrah. 'I swear to God, I can't wait to see his face when you and Madeline appear just minutes before his speech, and hijack his big moment. I bet he's been planning his speech for weeks.'

'I don't think we'll see his face sadly,' Helen said, reaching out for a pistachio-crusted scallop as a waiter floated past. 'Sheena said Madeline's bodyguard is going to lock him in the green room and make him watch it on CCTV.'

'We'll probably hear his screams of rage.' Amanda's face lit up with pleasure. 'After what he's done to us, this humiliation is the least he deserves.'

Sheena noticed that Catherine hadn't touched her drink. She seemed miles away. 'Come on Catherine,' she said, going to stand beside her. 'We're here for our show, remember? This is your career! Your reputation! Your big return! And you'll finally get your chance to get back at Lee for what he did to you. He's flying all the way here to beg for forgiveness, on one knee, only for you to finally give him the justice he deserves, in front of the whole world. You must be planning to get a thrill out of that.'

Catherine gave a hollow laugh. 'Maybe it's not as important as I thought it was. Anyway, I'm just not sure that getting revenge on Lee will make everything miraculously feel better.' She looked pointedly at Sheena. 'Not after what happened to Candy.'

Her voice had risen, causing Helen to look anxiously around for cameras. Sheena caught hold of Catherine's wrist. 'I know you're struggling but let's get through tonight. You look dazzling, and you're stronger than you think. This is your chance to shake off dead wood like Lee and get back to the show you love. This is going to be the mother of all comebacks. The one that gets you back to the Catherine we know you want to be.'

Catherine faced her, a look of resolve in her eye. 'You're right, Sheena.' She lifted her drink to her lips, drank down half of it. 'One for all. All for one,' she said. 'Let's get *Falcon Bay* back on the air. And you're right, that bastard Lee does deserve humiliation. I'm going to enjoy it.' Her eyes sparkled, and Sheena saw a glimpse of the old Catherine back with them again.

'Don't you have to be on the podium soon, Sheena? That looks like the way up,' Farrah said, indicating a lift with a red rope placed in front of it, manned by a security guard in a bronze half-mask topped with a horse and chariot. He looked strangely familiar, but she couldn't think why.

Amanda followed her gaze. 'Is it just me, or do we know that guy?'

Sheena stalked over, her dress tight around her legs. 'I'm Madeline Kane's business partner,' she said to the security guard in her most imperious voice, 'and we need to meet her backstage in ten minutes. Could you kindly escort us up to the VIP area? East Wing, Floor 105.'

The man grinned knowingly beneath his mask and unhooked the red rope. He ushered the women into the lift and stepped in behind them. All four walls of the lift were mirrored, and the endless reflection of her friends' sequinned dresses dazzled Sheena's eyes. The lift opened into a covered walkway which encircled the building, and they walked from there onto the enormous main rooftop, where the party was in full swing. It was a magnificent sight. Above her, the sky was dyed pink and orange by the setting sun. About fifty feet in front of her was a vast marble bar, and behind that, bodies undulated on a glass dancefloor, the DJ on a raised stage at the northern end of the rooftop. Behind the crowd was a row of potted trees strung with lights, which she assumed cordoned off the dancefloor from the secluded VIP area beyond. As the security guard in the chariot mask led them through the throng, Sheena surveyed the dancefloor, and saw that many guests wearing heavy satin costumes had torn them off to reveal slinky outfits underneath. She couldn't help staring at two women who had stripped down to neon underwear and were grinding against each other at the edge of the crowd.

The security guard beckoned them into the area behind the trees, and Sheena caught a glimpse of four-poster beds and strutting peacocks before they were led up some stairs and behind a gold rope to an open air mezzanine which ran the full length of the east side of the building. From here they had a clear view of the dancefloor, and beyond it, the huge sky with its orange sun. If they looked up to their right, craned their necks and squinted, they'd be able to catch a glimpse of VIPs arriving by chopper onto the helipad on the floor above.

'Mrs Kane says only Ms McQueen is to come backstage with me. The rest of you are to stay here.' He gestured to the white banquettes arranged on the platform around smoked-glass tables bearing bottles of champagne. 'The launch is sponsored by Bollinger, but Madeline thought you'd like some Cristal while you wait for the show to start. I'll have oysters brought over too.'

At the sound of his voice, Sheena suddenly realised exactly who this security guard reminded her of.

'Dustin? Is that you? What the…?'

The security guard raised his mask, revealing a pair of familiar blue eyes. 'It's nice to be in business again, Ms McQueen. I'm working for Madeline now. I'll be your producer again when we reboot the show.'

'He got hot,' Helen mouthed to Farrah, who bit back a smile. He really had.

'Madeline's headed backstage now, so I'd recommend you join her immediately,' Dustin said. 'I'll take you back to The Ring, and we'll make our way from there. Your surprise guest is waiting there too, along with the camera crew.'

'The Ring?'

'The cloistered walkway where we got out of the elevator. It's the only way to access the rest of the building from the rooftop.'

'What about Jake?'

'All dealt with. He won't be interrupting your speech.'

Sheena nodded and started to follow Dustin. But as she did so, Catherine's hand shot out and grabbed her wrist, wheeling her round and pointing a raised finger into the sky. 'There he is. That's Lee. I have to intercept him if my plan is going to work.'

Sheena followed Catherine's finger, caught the whir of blades as an orange helicopter came into land on the helipad. 'You'll miss the big announcement, Catherine. Can't Lee wait? Don't you want to know who your surprise co-star is going to be?'

'Not until I've dispatched this co-star first,' Catherine said bitterly. 'Trust me. This drama only goes my way if I control the staging.'

'Fine,' said Sheena, realising time was ticking and she wasn't going to win this fight. 'I'll tell the paps to come up. Can you deploy one of the camera crew there, Dustin?'

Dustin nodded, and Catherine tottered away, still clutching her coupe of champagne. As she followed Dustin down towards The Ring, Sheena reflected that Jake – or at least, Candy – had managed to pull off something pretty amazing tonight. Which made it the perfect setting to destroy Jake's reputation once and for all. She smiled to herself. Vengeance was so close she could almost taste it.

CHAPTER 58

Catherine

There were three choppers on the helipad and Catherine could see that Lee was about to alight from the one on the left. She was waiting for him at the top of the wide stairs leading up from the mezzanine, her cameraman a couple of steps down so Lee wouldn't see him.

Her years on *Falcon Bay* had given her a knack for knowing where the lighting would be most flattering, so she tilted her head so that the sun's rays would cast her in a golden, dewy glow. Her hair whipped in the wind. It was a still evening, and yet the breeze up here, 105 floors up, was strong enough to give her goose-bumps. She turned to look down at the beach. The distance was dizzying. She was stood higher than the Empire State Building. If one of her chandelier diamond earrings fell off from up here, it would probably kill someone on the beach below. The thought of it made her toes tingle, as if her feet itched to jump.

She wondered if Candy had felt like this, moments before her death. She could picture it vividly. A young woman, a red dress. A fatal plunge. Would she ever learn to live with the fact she'd been on the boat when it happened? That she might have been able to stop her?

Lee Landers stepped off the helicopter, and ran towards Catherine. He was as handsome and as sexy as ever. He lifted her in his arms, and as she landed she made sure she was facing the stairs, where the cameraman was hidden.

She controlled herself, and glanced surreptitiously in the direction of the cameraman on the stairs, hoping he'd hear his cue. 'I'm so glad you came.'

'I was always going to come! It was only ever you, Catherine. You're so gorgeous, look at you, how could I resist.'

His velvety voice stirred something deep inside her, and Catherine thought what the hell. She might as well give the viewers at home what they wanted. She slid one leg forward out of the slit of her dress, revealing a toned thigh. She wanted to make Lee believe he could have her again, and show the world what he was losing.

Lee reached out a hand, stroked it up her leg, his chocolate brown eyes boring into hers. Her skin fizzed with the memory of his body on hers. He had been the best lover she had ever had. Maybe one more time before she got her revenge wouldn't hurt? But Sheena's voice rang in her ears: *Lure him in. Let him think you want him. Then humiliate him live on air, like he did to you.*

'Oh, Lee!' she exclaimed, giving the cameraman his cue. She saw him emerge from the staircase, and creep towards them. She hoped the sound boom would be strong enough to pick up the next part.

'Tell me Lee,' she said softly in his ear. 'Tell me that you tried to trick and con me. Before you say another word, admit what you did to me. That everything was a calculated move. Admit that you lied, schemed, did whatever you needed to get my money. Tell me here and now that you're a scumbag and a liar, and then tell me why I should even consider giving you another chance, let alone marry you, after what you did. Go on – beg me.' As she spoke, she threw her scarf back off her shoulders, revealing her décolletage and her corset beneath.

Lee was so distracted by her full breasts, the scent of Chanel N°5 emanating from her cleavage, that he didn't notice the cameraman creep closer in from behind, framing the pair of them and picking up every word that passed between them. Lee ran both hands up Catherine's side, bringing a thumb up to stroke her cheek, her lips. So aroused was he that Catherine barely needed to prompt him further. The truth poured out like he'd been unplugged.

As he admitted to Catherine that yes, he was a gold-digger, a liar, that he'd schemed and conned people in the past but that now he had changed, his tone became more desperate. 'Every day without you has been torture, Catherine. I've dreamed of this reunion for months. I'll do anything – *anything* – to get you back.'

Catherine raised a finger to silence him. 'If you mean it, if you really mean that you'll do anything for my forgiveness, then turn around and face the cameras,' she said. 'The same cameras that you humiliated me on in front of millions. You tell the world what you want, and who are, and then I might be able to forgive you.'

Lee wheeled around, coming face to face with the cameraman. Two paparazzi emerged from the stairs, and a flashbulb popped in his face. Ever the professional, he cupped his hands in front of his crotch to hide his bulging erection and addressed the camera directly.

'Hello to you viewers at home. I'm Lee Landers, and I have an announcement to make. A year ago I humiliated the most important woman in my life, and I've regretted it ever since. Catherine Belle is the most glorious creature in the world, and I now throw myself at her feet and ask for mercy.' He turned back to Catherine, and fell on one knee, looking up at her, clutching one of her hands in both of his. 'Catherine, I am nothing compared to you,' he said. 'I am nothing without you. I know I've been a scumbag but please, I'm begging you to give me one more chance. Please, Catherine, forgive me.' He turned to look directly at the camera. 'Please, world, forgive me. Let me make this right.' On this last sentence, he stood up and took Catherine in his arms. She couldn't help but enjoy the feel of his strong, hard body pressed against hers. But even more than that, she savoured the knowledge that what she was about to say would destroy him, as he had tried to destroy her.

She moistened her lips and took a step back towards the soft lighting she'd spotted to her right, keeping their hands linked, and her gaze locked to his. She knew she had her best side facing the cameras, and smiled to herself when she realised that Lee was being filmed in profile, which he hated because it made his nose look big. 'Lee,' she opened, her voice as husky and golden as it had always been when they were making love. 'On the day we were to be wed, I believed that you loved me. Instead, you humiliated me in front of the whole world.' Her face flushed with shame and embarrassment, which she knew looked pretty on screen, and she paused to touch Lee's face tenderly. 'Today, I want to thank you.' She leaned closer towards him, but ensured her honeyed voice still carried to the sound boom.

'Thank me?' His face was a mix of happiness and confusion.

Catherine got closer still. 'Yes. I want to thank you for not marrying me. For not standing by me while I was wrongfully imprisoned. If you had, then by the time we filmed our scene I'd have already fallen hook, line and sinker down to whichever sewer you crawled out of to try and con your way into my life and into the limelight you so desperately crave.' Her eyes narrowed. Above them, her catlike lash extensions fluttered in the wind, making her look even more beautiful as her expression changed from soft to hard in an instant.

Panic flashed across Lee's features. As he'd always had a limited acting range, Catherine knew that her words were starting to sink in.

'Look around us, Lee. Just like that day, all the cameras are on us. We're live again, in front of the world. I tricked you and you fell for it. You're here tonight so I can give you a taste of what you did to me. Thank God. As humiliating as it was, I'm glad that I was arrested during our vows. Otherwise I'd be married to the kind of lowlife who'd no doubt have drained our joint accounts whilst I was innocently locked in prison.'

The cameras zoomed in to catch Lee's reaction. He was so stunned he could barely speak; his lips seemed to be moving but no sound was coming out. She turned slightly, to address the viewers at home, giving Lee a view of her flawless shoulder. She spoke directly to the camera and pointed dramatically towards Lee, whose eyes had gone dull, void of all bravado.

'To all of you watching at home, this is the real Lee Landers. A slimy, rotten, scumbag liar.' She turned back to Lee, one hand on her heart, the other making a sweeping gesture towards the party below them, her movement grand and dismissive. 'So, Lee, why don't you take one last look around at everything you crave, and give the audience their last look at you. Now go and crawl back to where you came from with someone who is as desperate as you are. I'm on top of the world. And you? You're at the very bottom. Which is exactly where you deserve to be.' Catherine's tone was laced with contempt.

Lee began walking away, his body sagging as his expression crumbled. He was a man defeated.

'Well,' Catherine concluded with a note of finality. 'Now we've dealt with Lee, let's get on with the show. I believe there's a very exciting announcement coming up soon.' She winked, and the cameras took it as their cue to swivel away, taking in a panorama of the highest rooftop in Europe, and the view into the night sky and across the sea to France.

Catherine knew that in the edit suite backstage, a producer would be seamlessly cutting to the next segment: a view of the raised platform on the dancefloor below them, in preparation for Sheena's big announcement. She strolled off her makeshift stage, and into a cacophony of flashbulbs and shouts. She smiled triumphantly, and her emotion was genuine. Catherine might just have given the performance of her life, and she quietly thanked Sheena in her head for making her come tonight to do this. It was exactly what she needed: closure.

CHAPTER 59

Helen

After Sheena and Catherine had left, Helen settled herself down on one of the banquettes and waited for the show to start. Her heels were killing her and, judging by the way Farrah and Amanda flopped down beside her, theirs were too.

Having taken Sheena to see Madeline, Dustin returned, and stood at the very edge of the mezzanine, keeping a close eye on the raised platform at the end of the glass dancefloor below. She sneaked a look at Dustin, standing by the gold rope. He was a lot more handsome than she remembered from their *Falcon Bay* days, especially in that sexy bronze mask that made him look like a soldier. Had he been working out? She was in desperate need of distraction from the pain of losing Matt – a younger man might be just what she needed. She stretched her arms above her head so that if he turned around, he'd have a good view of her toned midriff in her Mouret dress.

Her eye was caught by a tall woman in an acid green skin-tight dress and a matching mask. She was sashaying up the stairs, and towards their banquettes. 'Hello, ladies,' the woman said, sitting down opposite them and pushing her mask off her face. It was Tabitha Tate.

Helen narrowed her eyes. 'What do you want?' Now that the Candy case was officially closed, the last thing they needed was a reporter sniffing around.

'That was quite the take-down of Lee Landers by Catherine. I've been watching it on my phone. The @sussexroyal Instagram posted it with the hashtag Queen. #Queen! Coming from them! Where is she now?'

'She's gone to powder her nose,' Amanda lied, her tone cool. None of the women were going to tell a journalist that Catherine had most likely gone to a quiet corner to pop a few Xanax.

'Could you kindly fuck off, please?' Farrah added frostily. 'None of us want to be interviewed for your shitty little book.'

Tabitha looked scathing. 'Jeez. Calm down, ladies. I'm not here to interview you.'

'Then why are you here?' Helen was suspicious. 'I thought you were writing a book about us.'

'I'm afraid you're all extras in this one,' scoffed Tabitha. 'That is, unless you've got any secrets you aren't telling me?' She winked teasingly. 'No. My book is about Madeline Kane, and I've discovered something *very* interesting. I'd be shocked if any of you knew about it, even though your good friend Catherine plays a starring role.' She placed a finger mockingly on her chin. 'Now, why could that be, I wonder?'

Amanda let her anger get the better of her. 'For God's sake, we don't know what you mean. Either stop speaking in riddles or sod off and leave us in peace.'

'Oh, I'm not leaving this table, babe. I'm staying right here to hang out with my boyfriend. Have you met him?' She blew a kiss at Dustin, who turned and gave the girls an awkward wave.

Helen fumed. If Tabitha was writing a book about Madeline, and shagging Dustin – who was clearly working for Madeline – did that mean they'd all have to work with Tabitha on the reboot of *Falcon Bay* as well? Burying the hatchet with Madeline was bad enough – Sheena had convinced them it was worth it to save their careers and their reputation, but Helen had an awful suspicion that it might just turn into everyone's worst nightmare. And if nosy reporter Tabitha was part of it, that made things a million times worse. Yes, Helen loved *Falcon Bay*, and she'd follow Sheena to the ends of the earth, but at what cost? And now Tabitha was writing a book which somehow involved Catherine… probably yet another attempt to take her down and frame her for Madeline's non-death. Christ, what a mess.

Tabitha tilted her head and fixed Helen with a long look. 'Now, do remind me why you girls are allowed up here, in the VVIP area, given that the last time the world saw you was in a courtroom? Ah yes, if I remember rightly, you're about to go into business with Madeline Kane.' She gave a tinkling laugh. 'God, you must be *really* desperate to get back on TV if you're prepared to team up with the woman who put you in jail.'

Farrah squared her shoulders and thrust out her chin. 'We're professionals, and we're treating this as a professional relationship. Madeline Kane and Sheena McQueen are the dream team, and a *Falcon Bay* reboot is the dream show.'

'Save that line for the press release, sweetheart,' Tabitha drawled.

'Listen, you low-rent scumbag,' Helen hissed, 'we're here to do a job and that job is something we all love more than anything. If revamping *Falcon Bay* means working with Madeline, we work with Madeline. Business is business after all. As I believe you know all too well after what you did with Honey Hunter's story.'

'That book made me millions,' said Tabitha, but her arch expression was beginning to crumble, and Helen knew they'd found her weak spot.

Farrah went in for the kill. 'You're an egomaniac, Tabitha. All of your projects are about you. Isn't the journalist supposed to be absent from the story? It's clear you've always wanted to be a star. You'd be better suited to shack up with Lee Landers than poor, gullible Dustin. And, sure, you made millions from Honey's ordeal and even won that tacky little book prize, but your self-absorbed speech when they handed it to you didn't work out very well, did it? Which is no doubt why you're trying to score yourself another tawdry celebrity biography about Madeline and Catherine. Well, good luck with that. As far as I can tell, you're still cancelled.'

Amanda chipped in, her voice dripping with faux sympathy. 'A shame really, that all you can do is write the headlines for other people's misfortunes.'

'If people like you weren't so good at fucking up the golden eggs you've been given, I wouldn't get the chance to write them,' Tabitha shot back.

Helen was just about to make a bitchy response when she was cut off by a tap on her shoulder. She looked up to see that a tall man in flattering burgundy silk breeches had joined them. He was wearing a dark red mask over his eyes, and as Tabitha looked up at him quizzically, he raised it briefly to reveal kind blue eyes framed by square black eyebrows.

'Matt!' Helen couldn't believe it. 'I thought you'd gone back to London!'

Matt walked round to stand in front of Helen. Then he got down on one knee and pulled out a velvet box, causing Amanda and Farrah to gasp loudly. 'I couldn't leave you,' Matt said, pushing up his mask so that Helen could see his handsome face. 'I want to marry you, Helen! Whatever's happened in your life, that's the past. I don't care what you've done. I forgive you. I love you. And, my God, I want you.' His eyes raked her body, pausing at the cut-out midriff. 'I may be only a policeman, but if I'd been in the SAS I would have scaled this entire building just to see you in this dress.'

Helen smiled, snaked an arm around his neck, and pulled him onto the banquette for a kiss. As his tongue ran over her lips, a fire ignited in her belly, its warmth spreading down to her thighs. 'Do you really mean it, Matt?'

'Yes, Helen. I mean it. I want to marry you. If you'll have me.'

Next to them, Amanda and Farrah squealed in excitement, and even Tabitha looked caught up in the moment when Matt opened the box and produced a huge sparkling ruby.

'Oh my God, Matt! Is this—'

'Yes. It's Judy Garland's. I've been following the estate auctions online.'

Helen's heart swelled as she plucked it out of his hand and onto her finger. It fit perfectly, just as, she knew, she fit perfectly with Matt.

'Let's get out of here,' she whispered into his ear as he stood up and came in for a long slow kiss. 'Sheena gave me an all-access backstage key in case of an emergency.' She pulled a key card out of her cleavage.

Matt raised an eyebrow. 'Do you think we qualify as an emergency?'

Helen brushed the front of his breeches where there was a tell-tale bulge. 'I think this does,' she said, and led him down the stairs. As they followed the route Sheena and Catherine had taken a few minutes earlier through the dancefloor and towards The Ring, she had a brief flash of regret that she wouldn't get to see Sheena and Madeline's speech, or finally see who the new *Falcon Bay* star was. In her old casting days, she would have already known, been in on the secret. Tonight she was going to be as surprised as everybody else. And now she wouldn't find out until after the viewers back home. Still, she thought, as Matt placed his hand on her pert bum and gave it a squeeze, the man of her dreams was worth making sacrifices for.

CHAPTER 60

Amanda

Amanda watched Helen and Matt run off like two giggling teenagers, her expression soft and loving. She took Farrah's hand in hers and gave it a squeeze. 'Wasn't that the most romantic thing you've ever seen? I'm so thrilled for Helen. Oh, I just knew this was going to be one of the best nights of our lives.'

Farrah smiled at her. 'I know. It makes you believe in love again, doesn't it? Perhaps not all men are snakes like Jake and Lee.'

'Dustin's not a snake,' Tabitha added, her animosity towards the girls melted by the proposal she'd just witnessed. 'There are some good men out there, I promise.'

Amanda flashed her a smile. 'I'm glad for you. Really, I am.'

Farrah looked like she was about to make a catty comment, but grudgingly bit her lip. There seemed to be a tacit agreement that Amanda and Farrah wouldn't sully what promised to be a big night for everyone.

Amanda tuned back into her surroundings and realised

that the music, which had been gradually getting louder, was now reaching a fever pitch. She turned her attention back to the dancefloor. The guillotine visuals on the screen behind the DJ were fading out, replaced by a view of the famous Cove of *Falcon Bay*, the very beach that was over a hundred floors below them. A sense of anticipation swept through the crowd on the dancefloor. Something big was clearly about to happen. The heavy beat reached its climax, and then, all of a sudden, the music went off and the DJ disappeared from the raised stage, which now filled with blue smoke. Dry ice curled towards the crowd clustered on the glass dancefloor as two women appeared to float up through the floor and then glide through the smoke to the front of the stage.

Even Amanda, who knew what was coming, was shocked to see Sheena and Madeline side-by-side like close friends after two years of abject hostility. Stepping off the hydraulic podium, which must have come up through a trapdoor in the floor, they glittered in the light from the flattering yellow bulbs that had been strung across the roof. They made quite a pair, Sheena McQueen in her sequined jumpsuit and Madeline Kane, in a dark green floor-length sheath scattered with Swarovski crystals. Madeline was the first to speak.

'I realise you were expecting Jake Monroe to arrive on the stage and open La Mirage,' she said, her voice low and smooth in the microphone. 'But Mr Monroe is currently indisposed, and myself and my new business partner have an announcement you'll all want to hear.' She passed the microphone to Sheena.

'Is anybody here a fan of *Falcon Bay*?' Sheena asked, playfully, keeping her voice light. The crowd whooped and yelled. Someone near the front shouted: 'It should never have ended!'

Sheena nodded, smiled. 'I'm so glad you think so,' she said teasingly. 'Because myself and the legendary Mrs Kane are here to make a very special announcement. We are producing a high-budget, no-expense-spared, full reboot of the show. And it will air on a major streaming service next year.'

More whoops filled the air. Madeline Kane held up her hand for silence, and took the microphone from Sheena. 'All your favourite characters will be returning. And that includes our newest star. A fabulous actress who never got her shot at *Falcon Bay* before it wrapped. Please put your hands together, to welcome the woman the whole world has been looking for... The woman who will star in our new show... Honey Hunter!'

Amanda's jaw dropped. So that was the surprise guest Sheena was being so coy about! How on earth had Sheena and Madeline tracked her down? Even the police were having difficulties. Amanda leaned over to grab Farrah's arm excitedly. 'Everyone's been trying to get Honey since she became a recluse! This is going to be bloody massive for our show!'

Farrah settled back into her banquette, and smiled with satisfaction. 'It's not just great for the show, Amanda. It's also fucking terrible for Jake. We did it! We stood united, and we've totally ruined his big night. Where is that rat, anyway? I want to laugh in his face and tell him he's never, ever getting his moment in the sun.'

CHAPTER 61

Jake

Jake could not remember a time when he had been angrier than this. He was completely alone, stuck in the green room he'd been in with Coraline, watching helplessly on the screen in front of him as Madeline and Sheena rose up on the hydraulic podium and strutted onto the stage through clouds of dry ice.

'Fucking bitches!' Jake cursed aloud. At 8.40 p.m., exactly twenty minutes before he had been due to step out onto that stage, a security guard in a bronze mask had knocked on the door and suggested that he escort Coraline into the front row of the audience, allowing Jake some time for the final rehearsal of his big speech.

Shortly after that, another guard had come into the room and changed the TV channel so that Jake could see the stage. 'For your cue,' he had said. Why the fuck had he agreed?

In hindsight, Jake realised that if he hadn't been snorting that line of cocaine at exactly that moment, he might have noticed that something was amiss. But with his mind on his speech and the drug rushing through his brain, it wasn't until he finally turned to the huge flat screen TV to look at where he'd soon be making his entrance that he saw the dry ice had already started to curl over the stage. It wasn't supposed to do that until he was ready to enter – what the fuck was happening? It took him a good while before he noticed there were two women on what was meant to be his podium. He had to blink twice before he could believe it. Not just any women, either. Two of the women he hated most in the world. His opening moment had been well and truly hijacked.

'Fuck!' he screamed again, and threw his whisky tumbler at the mirror he had only moments earlier used to admire his reflection. He'd agreed to Madeline's lawyers' deal, and now she was fucking breaching it. This was supposed to be *his* party, *his* crowd, *his* farewell speech! It was his *legacy* for Christ's sake! The last public image of him before he moved to Dubai was meant to be Jake Monroe: the Sun King, wreathed in dry ice, at the centre of the most lavish party known to history. It was supposed to be his big exit, one that would set him up around the world, show what he'd done, allow him to leave with his head held high. He'd planned a gracious speech about his achievements on the island, and how he was now handing it back to Madeline and Chad, and stepping away from forty years of television to deliver forty years of magnificent buildings around the world. And those disgusting *bitches* had tricked him.

Judging by a logo projected on the screen behind the women which read *Falcon Bay: A New Era*, they were about to announce a reboot of the show *he'd* spent years turning into a sensation. He'd been screwed over by that witch Madeline Kane yet again, and seeing that smug hag Sheena McQueen smiling like the cat that got the cream next to her made his blood boil.

He'd already tried and failed to open the door, and now he banged it, hard, and yelled at the top of his voice. He raged as he realised he'd been locked in by the state-of-the-art electronic keypads that he himself had insisted on being installed in La Mirage. The security guards were supposed to be his employees for fucks sake! When he uncovered the turncoat who had agreed to do this for Madeline, he'd eviscerate him. Pull his guts out through his throat.

He picked up a statuette from one of the awards shelves and flung it at the door. It made a dent, but the door didn't move. He flung another, it bounced off, and shattered the glass coffee table. He shouted 'bitches!' and picked his way through the glass on the floor to bang on the door again. His hands had gone red, his voice was raw from shouting and swearing. When he paused to draw breath, he realised the sound on the flat screen had changed: he could no longer hear Madeline's low drawl over the speakers. Instead, music was playing, and the crowd was roaring somebody's name.

He turned back to the TV, and what he heard them shouting made him freeze in fear. He couldn't bear to watch. On instinct he picked up the chipped statuette from the pile of glass on the floor and smashed it, hard, into the television. The picture on screen splintered, but he could still see the stage so he punched it with his bare knuckles, wincing as a chip of glass lodged in his hand. But even that wasn't enough to prevent his worst nightmare coming true.

The HH on the helicopter he'd seen from the beach hadn't been the Halcyon Hotel logo.

It was Honey Hunter's.

Honey Hunter, who was bathed in spotlights, rising up from the hydraulic podium in the floor and striding out to meet Madeline and Sheena on the stage.

Now he was looking not only at two of the women he hated most in the world, but the one woman who had the power to destroy him completely.

He hated to admit it, but Honey looked incredible. Like a goddess that had just stepped out of a golden, shimmering sea. Under a clinging floor length gold dress that rippled like water, her skin was dewy and radiant. Her eyes were as big and blue as he remembered, and as the camera lingered on a close-up, he could see they were full of unshed tears. He wanted to kiss her. He wanted to hold her. As frightened as he was – an emotion that did not trouble him often – he still couldn't take his eyes off her. She awoke an obsession in him that he had always failed to control. Saying that out loud would get him cancelled, ripped apart, but it was Jake's truth. Guilt, fear, and blind hope surged through him. He wasn't religious but he prayed aloud that Sheena and Madeline had only flown her in for a ratings boost, and not because Honey had somehow figured out what he did to her, and was ready for revenge. He held his breath, and waited to hear what Honey was about to say.

CHAPTER 62

Tabitha

Tabitha couldn't believe her eyes when Honey Hunter emerged onto the stage, so composed and calm that it was impossible to believe she had spent the last twelve months as a total recluse, while a terrifying serial killer murdered in her name.

The audience of hundreds gasped audibly, and Tabitha imagined the millions watching around the world would feel just the same as they witnessed Honey's shock return to live TV. Tabitha didn't need to look at her phone to know that #HoneyHunter would be the number one hashtag trending on all socials. Flashbulbs dazzled the crowd as the paparazzi jostled to get a better view of one of the most famous women in the world, who had only been seen once in the last year, when she appealed to a murderer to stop killing in her name.

Tabitha fished out her recorder from her clutch bag, and pressed the button. Considering she was working for Madeline, she couldn't believe she hadn't been told in advance that Honey was the surprise guest, and she felt a brief flash of anger towards Dustin who must have known but kept it a secret from her. Surely, with his tech skills, he was the one who tracked her down? But then again, as a hardened hack, keeping something like this secret is exactly what she'd have done herself. She decided she'd forgive Dustin – after giving him a deliciously sadistic bollocking, of course.

She dragged her mind back from what was spiralling into a full-blown fantasy of Dustin's grovelling apology, accompanied by some penitential toe-sucking, to focus on what was happening on the stage. She needed to hear whatever Honey was about to say so that afterwards she could go backstage, show that she'd really listened, and then apologise to her face-to-face. Of course, she'd find a way to get an exclusive story out of it, too. She could see the headline now: Honey Hunter Overcomes Tragic Past to Star in *Falcon Bay* Reboot!

When Honey began to speak, it became clear that what she was about to say was a hundred times more sensational than even Tabitha could ever have imagined.

'Hello, La Mirage,' Honey murmured into the microphone. 'Hello, world.' Her voice was soft, like melted butter. The crowd stopped roaring, and started to listen.

'Have you missed me?' she said, with a tone that Tabitha found curiously ominous.

Sheena and Madeline had stepped back to either side, so Honey was front and centre. The crowd's applause was deafening, but Honey's reaction didn't appear to be one of gratitude or pleasure at the adoration; her eyes turned steely, her shoulders stiffened, and she leaned towards the microphone.

'Well, I haven't missed you,' she said, her voice no longer soft and velvety, but suddenly hard and full of rage. The crowd fell into a tense silence as she continued.

'But I'm here again for you to gawk over, so you've all got what you wanted now, haven't you?' she hissed, gesturing at her body, clad in a tight gold dress which showed off every curve and sparkled in the lights. Tabitha could tell from Madeline's clenched jaw and Sheena's flickering eyes that they weren't expecting this, that Honey was going rogue from whatever speech they'd carefully rehearsed together. Tabitha had a horrible feeling that something very bad was going to happen, though she didn't know what.

Honey glanced across the packed room, and a cruel smirk crossed her lips. 'These two women think my arrival tonight is to announce their "feminist" reboot of their crappy TV show, *Falcon Bay*. The one I was supposed to appear in three years ago, when they lured me away from the safety and sanity I'd finally found during my years away from all the showbiz bullshit. They probably think I am about to thank them for making me a star again.'

Sheena's mouth dropped open, and Madeline's eyes widened.

Honey laughed mirthlessly and glared at them both. 'You needed me *because* I am a star. I won a fucking Oscar, and that's what makes you a real star, not some dying-on-its-arse soap that is way past its expiration date. But do you know the price of stardom? It's worse than being a captured animal. You two might not be male, but you are no better than the Harvey Weinsteins and the hundreds of other evil beings in the world of showbusiness. And I am one of the poor fools who are your pieces of meat, ripe for trafficking to anyone who wants a bite out of our flesh. Do you know how many paedophiles abused me when I was a young Disney princess? More than I can count, or would even want to try.'

Tabitha saw Sheena wince at these words, presumably blocking out the terrible memories of when she herself had been raped as a teen actress. Sheena was open about it being one of the reasons she'd reinvented herself as an agent: to ensure the power was always in her hands. It looked like Sheena was about to say something, but then Madeline moved suddenly, fleeing the stage, running as fast as her six-inch Manolos would allow her. She didn't get very far. A beefy security guard dressed in black with a gold armband stepped smartly in front of her, and frogmarched her to the side of the stage. It looked as if she was shouting Chad's name at the top of her voice. Sheena's gaze followed Madeline as she ran, and yet she stayed, standing tall and firm, only her eyes betraying that she, too, was scanning for an escape route.

'Look,' Honey snarled, gesturing to Madeline's attempted exit. 'If even the rats are fleeing the building, it shows we have sunk to a whole new level of rot and decay. Sorry, Madeline. No one is leaving here tonight.'

Tabitha's heart plummeted to her feet, but she made sure her recorder was still picking up sound. Whatever happened tonight was going to be explosive. She glanced over at Amanda and Farrah, who were sat open-mouthed listening to Honey's tirade, and sensed that they felt it too.

'You see,' Honey laughed maniacally, 'these women believed I was going to team up with them again and just… forget!' She spat the word. 'Forget what happened to me last time I was on this island.' She pointed a perfectly manicured sharp nail toward a still restrained Madeline, and for the first time since she'd known her, Tabitha saw genuine fear flicker across Madeline's face.

'Many people broke me. Many people created the damaged goods that stand before you tonight.' Honey's tone dropped for a moment. 'I should never have been here in the first place, and I wouldn't have been, if my vile publisher Mickey Taylor hadn't lured me back into this nightmare world that I'd already tried to escape. Naively, as damaged people tend to, I believed his lies. Three years ago, I believed I'd be safe here in St. Augustine's. None of the people who are supposed to protect us care for anything except the money they can make from us.'

She paused, clearly savouring the audience hanging on her every word. The atmosphere was so thick with tension you could slice it with a knife. Tabitha caught sight of a cameraman in a *Falcon Bay* shirt run around the crowd to get a better angle on the stage. He, like Tabitha, had realised that despite the palpable fear in the room, the event unfolding before them was television dynamite.

Honey scanned the crowd. She spoke softly into the mic. 'Which camera am I on?' Her voice was quiet, dangerous, and it chilled Tabitha to the bone. Most of the camera operators seemed to be in shock, but the ambitious young guy in the *Falcon Bay* jacket raised his hand nervously, and gestured to his camera, where a red light was blinking. 'Zoom in,' Honey said, and when he did, she spoke directly down the barrel of the lens. 'Hello all of you at home. Thank you for watching. I can't right these wrongs without you.' She blew a kiss at the camera.

'Fucking hell,' Tabitha said under her breath, and wondered what on earth was coming next.

Honey pointed at the screen behind her. 'Before I continue with my speech, I'd like to show you a little film.' She clapped her hands. 'Action, please!'

The screens that had been showing the *Falcon Bay: A New Era* logo blinked into life. Gruesome images appeared on the screens, and Tabitha's eyes widened. She recognised the pictures: they were the crime scene photos of the murders committed by the Hitlist Killer. Tabitha kept her cool but on the dancefloor pandemonium erupted. The sanitised, blurred images that had been released to the press were nothing compared to these graphic photos of a carnage no one outside of a courtroom would usually see. Guests gasped, covering their eyes with their hands as each mutilated corpse filled the giant screen. The chilling soundtrack of the victims begging for their lives boomed out of the speakers, adding to the horror.

Tabitha's eyes returned to Honey, who had a satisfied look on her deranged yet beautiful face. For a fleeting moment, Tabitha was reminded of Tiffany, the killer girlfriend from the Chucky films. The surreal tableau in front of her seemed ripped from a horror movie, yet the terror was all too real.

Amidst the chaos, as some guests fled the room, retching or clutching their stomachs, Honey looked like she was enjoying herself. 'Too much for you, is it?' she cackled with derision. 'I thought everyone loved horror movies?' She laughed again. 'Well, I do! I'll say one thing for Hollywood: their studio costume vaults are a treasure trove.' She pointed at her slender arms. 'A bit of padding here, a fake bicep there,' she boasted, 'and it's amazing what a latex suit can do to flatten the chest.' Honey seemed to be speaking directly to Tabitha as the pieces started falling into place. The tall figure in latex. The glinting knife. The gold HH on the bathrobe when the hotel's logo had been green. She couldn't believe she had been so stupid.

Honey was still talking. 'It wasn't just any latex suit: one of the spares from when Michelle Pfeiffer played Catwoman in *Batman*. I auditioned for that, you know,' she flashed a twisted smile, 'but apparently, I wasn't hot enough.' She laughed. 'Mind you, I got to wear it in the end, and I doubt even Michelle Pfeiffer – who I love, by the way – would have shown such commitment in this role. I did wonder if the costume would give it away, but I suppose it was rather dark in those videos. Not one single internet nerd figured out it was clearly a woman's suit.'

Tabitha's stomach lurched. She had to escape. She looked around feverishly, but the only two exits from the mezzanine were now blocked by three black-clad men with gold arm-bands: presumably Honey's security team.

'Oh yes, I see you are all beginning to get it,' Honey continued, with another deranged chuckle. 'There was no Hitlist Killer. I soon realised after what happened to me at the hands of the evil people who run this show, followed by the grabbing hands of my twisted kidnapper, that the only person who would get justice for me… was me.' She paused for effect. 'Of course, I needed a little help. I needed someone to film me, someone to provide a venue, someone to bike the footage over to the thickest journalist in the world – take a bow, Tabitha Tate! – and of course, a few men to make sure you keep watching.' She gestured at the bodyguards with the gold armbands dotted around the room. 'It's ironic that the Mafia are depicted as the bad guys when they've been the only good guys in my life. They protect me. Once a goomar, always a goomar.'

Tabitha closed her eyes. Despite her foolishness, she had been right about something: Honey really had been the sidepiece of a Mafia boss, and Dustin was right that the Mafia had been involved in the killings. If only she had listened to Dustin! They could have gone to the police and probably had Honey arrested by now, if only she hadn't been so fixated on getting her stupid story.

The crowd was transfixed, staring at Honey with open mouths. Honey's rage seemed to be building. 'The monsters you saw on that screen exploited, abused or degraded me in one way or another. That's why I cut bits off them: a cock for a pervert. A tongue for a liar. I wanted them to be abused, destroyed. Like they did to me.' She tilted her head and narrowed her catlike eyes. 'But there were two people who escaped their fate. Oh, don't worry. They will die tonight. Let me show you one of them.' The rotating crime scene photographs were replaced by a still of what looked like CCTV footage. 'But before I press play, let's talk a little bit about complicity. Because nothing happens in a vacuum. For evil to flourish, other people need to let it happen.' She shot a venomous look towards Madeline, who had now given up struggling against the brawny arms of the bodyguard, then turned back to the crowd. 'Let me show you what it means to be the star of a show run by Madeline Kane.'

She pressed play, and the audience fell silent as a new scene began to play out.

CHAPTER 63

Amanda

Amanda's mind was racing. She couldn't believe that Honey was a killer. She looked so delicate she could barely hold the microphone, let alone wield a knife. Like Tabitha, she'd been looking desperately around for an escape route, but had concluded it was impossible; three guards had placed themselves at the wide steps leading up to the helipad, and three more were barring the stairs leading down from the VIP mezzanine. Even if she managed to pass through them, she'd never get into The Ring, which she could see from here now had a guard standing in each of the archways.

But from the moment Honey pressed play, Amanda's thoughts were focused only on the film. She was so puzzled by what she saw, she stood up and went to the front of the mezzanine to get a closer look. It was a full colour image of Honey, asleep on a bed. She recognised the bed: it was in one of the Cove's most luxurious villas, usually given to A-list stars of *Falcon Bay*. It was so intimate that she wanted to look away – she could see Honey's chest rising and falling – but something kept her glued to the footage. It seemed to be some kind of CCTV, and the timestamp was dated 2 a.m., two and a half years ago. Amanda remembered that evening – it was the night before Honey left the set of *Falcon Bay*, never to be seen again.

In the stillness of the footage, a curtain fluttered in a night-time breeze. The room was dark, but moonlight was coming in from a window, and Amanda could make out Honey, sleeping on her back in a white silky negligee, one arm flung out across the pillow. She seemed dead to the world.

On screen, a door opened. A male figure entered the room, and carefully closed all the shutters, plunging the room into darkness. Then he switched on a light by the bed, and stood there, back towards the camera, admiring her sleeping form. He leaned forward and pulled the straps of her nightgown down over her shoulders to reveal her creamy breasts. He cupped them reverently in his hands, and ran his hands over the rest of her body. She stirred lightly, and he paused, as if frightened she might wake up. He picked up a bottle of pills by her bedside table, crushed one into a powder, and rubbed it on her gums. He paused again, waiting for her to become still, watching her all the time. Then he turned around to take off his trousers and drop them on the floor. Only now did the camera pick up his face.

It was her ex-husband. Jake Monroe.

Behind her, Tabitha gasped aloud, and so did Farrah.

Amanda swayed. She thought she was going to faint.

Farrah came up beside her and touched her arm. She looked like she was about to be sick. 'I knew he was a bastard,' Farrah whispered, 'but this? He's the father of our children for God's sake!'

Amanda allowed Farrah to lead her back to the banquette to sit down, and placed her head between her knees. She took two deep breaths. She had known Jake was sleeping with Honey before she fled, everybody had, but why would he do something like this to her when she was unconscious? He deserved to be locked up, and after tonight, he would. So too, surely, would Honey. After confessing to being the Hitlist Killer, there was only one place she was going, and that was the secure mental health wing of a high-security prison.

On stage, Honey's mouth tightened as the footage continued to play out. On the screen, Jake flipped her over onto her front, pushed her legs apart roughly and lay on top of her. He reached out a hand and switched off the lamp, plunging the scene into total darkness.

Nobody spoke.

'There you have it,' said Honey, her eyes like stones, her voice gaining an edge as sharp as the knife she'd used to gut her predators. 'The man who was supposed to be my producer was also my rapist. And this woman,' she swung a gold-painted fingernail towards Madeline, 'waited until she needed something from me before showing me the footage. After she quite literally stepped into my shoes and stole my part on *Falcon Bay*.'

Madeline had been standing stock still at the edge of the stage, a frozen expression on her face, but at this she came alive, lurching forward out of the bodyguard's grip to tear the microphone out of Honey's hands. 'That's not true,' she said emphatically into the mic. 'Yes, I had CCTV everywhere when it was my island, but I never checked the footage at the time. As soon as my right-hand man Dustin came across this, I had him track you down and send it to you.'

'Liar!' Honey screamed in return, tearing the microphone back from Madeline, and shoving her in the chest so she thudded into the chest of the bodyguard. 'You only told me you had it because you wanted me to do your dirty work of blackmailing Jake! Well, I didn't do that. I want to kill him instead. If I succeed tonight, you'll be as guilty as me!'

The audience's murmuring had reached a loud buzz, and the atmosphere had completely changed. As Amanda peered around, a new movement up on stage caught her eye. Something – or someone – was crawling out of the trapdoor that housed the hydraulic podium. There was a gasp from the audience as a bloody hand appeared on the stage, followed by the ragged, torn sleeve of what had once been a velvet jacket. Audience members pointed, and some started to approach the stage, but were held back by Honey's guards. In the chaos, a male figure emerged. His silk breeches were torn, both hands were bloody, and he was limping on one side. It was Jake Monroe, and he seemed wild with fear and rage as he snatched the microphone from Madeline and addressed the crowd. His voice was hoarse, as if his throat was raw from shouting.

'It's a fake video!' His voice was pleading. 'You know about her stunts, it's not real, it's CGI, you have to believe me!'

Somewhere in the crowd, a voice shouted 'Rapist!'

'You can't believe her,' he croaked into the mic. 'This bitch locked me in the green room so she could spread her lies.'

'Get off,' booed a voice from the crowd.

'No! Not until you believe me! It's a set-up,' he was shouting over the crowd, who were hissing and booing. 'I had to break through the ceiling and crawl through the air ducts to get up here.' He held up his ragged arms as evidence. Sweat was pouring down his face and his hands were shaking. 'Please! You have to believe me—'

'That's enough.' Honey's voice was like ice. She clicked her fingers, and one of her men dragged him over to watch from the side of the stage with Sheena and Madeline.

There was a pregnant pause.

'We still love you Honey!' came a lone cry from the crowd.

The golden talon pointed towards the voice. 'You *love* me? Don't make me sick. All of you, one way or another, have enjoyed my downfall. I bet every one of you has devoured that disgusting book detailing what that deranged surgeon did to me. Now, where is that rotten reporter?'

Amanda's heart was in her mouth as Honey scoured the VIP mezzanine until her eyes came to rest on the woman sitting next to her.

'Tabitha Tate,' Honey whispered, and a chill ran down Amanda's spine. 'The next person on my kill list after Jake Monroe. You were lucky that night in the hotel. You won't be so lucky tonight. In fact, none of you will.'

'What does she mean?' Amanda whispered to Farrah, but Farrah shook her head, just as puzzled.

The crowd looked confused, too, as Honey turned to the man holding Jake. 'Thank you. Bring me my bag. Then you and your crew need to leave. You've done what you came for.'

As soon as the bodyguards had left the rooftop, leaving the exits unguarded, the crowd started to surge. People swarmed towards The Ring, bashing the buttons for the four elevators, and running down the stairwells as fast as they could.

Sheena clattered up the stairs to the mezzanine and folded Farrah and Amanda into a hug. 'I don't know what the fuck is going on but we need to get out of here. Where are Helen and Catherine?'

Amanda spoke quickly. 'We haven't seen Catherine since she went up to the helipad to meet Lee, and Helen's with Matt in a suite – oh Sheena, they're engaged! It was wonderful—'

'There's no time for this,' interrupted Farrah. 'We have to leave. Now!' But the crowd was so thick downstairs, they could barely move.

'There's no way we'll get out until later,' said Sheena, assessing the number of people below, all trying to barge past each other. 'I'm going to try and get Honey off the stage. I'm good at talking crazed actresses down from a ledge.'

'No!' Amanda caught her arm, but Sheena was too strong. She wriggled away from her, ran down the stairs, and wove back through the throng towards Honey.

'Stay where you are!' Honey was spitting with fury now into the mic, completely caught up in her tirade. 'Whether you're here in front of me or watching online, you've violated me for years. Remember what Marilyn Monroe said to Joan Collins back in the fifties? "Beware of the wolves, honey." It's fitting that we have these holograms all over the walls tonight – because in all these years, nothing has changed – until tonight. This whole industry is rotten, especially this cesspit of an island. And tonight it's literally going to crumble. Who'd bribe officials to get permission to build a skyscraper half on rock, half on sand? A corrupt prick, that's who. But it's not just Jake Monroe who's corrupt. You're all rotten. All of you! Tabitha Tate – you're a bloodsucking bitch. Sheena

388

McQueen – you're a manipulative hag. Madeline Kane – you turned me into a killer.' She drew a breath and turned to speak directly to the cameras again. 'And as for you at home. Why are you all so obsessed with celebrity downfalls? You're horrific. This whole entertainment world needs cleansing. If I can do one thing before my sad journey in showbiz is done, it will be to leave with a bang – taking all you corrupt pieces of shit with me. The only people who ever cared for me were Caspar Felix and his loyal protectors. Thanks to them, this building is ready to blow. Nobody is leaving here alive except for them.'

Amanda gasped as Honey pulled a black control panel from the clutch bag the guard had given her, and brandished it high above her head. It looked like a bigger version of the remote control Dan had used to set off fireworks from the beach on Olivia's birthday. Amanda had the bizarre thought that Honey was going to set off the fireworks display that had been so touted in advance of the La Mirage party.

Amanda barely had time to formulate the thought before the high-pitched sound of a rocket pierced the air, and a burst of green and red sparks exploded above Honey's head. Despite the panic in the crowd, people looked up, pointed. Three brilliant streaks of silver shot into the air, and cascaded into a shower of electric blue and royal purple.

But Honey herself did not look up – and Amanda noticed that she had not yet pressed a button on the device in her hand.

It couldn't be her who was setting off the fireworks. Besides, the expression on her face was not one of celebration. She looked crazed, enraged. She looked like a suicide bomber.

Amanda's mouth went dry. She looked at Farrah and saw her own fear and desperation reflected in her eyes. She took Farrah's hand and managed to croak out the words, 'I think she's going to blow up the building.'

On stage, Honey gripped the detonator firmly, and glared out at the audience while more fireworks exploded above her head, each one more extravagant than the last, filling the air with the smoky scent of gunpowder. She spoke into the microphone, and this time there was a conclusive tone to her voice. 'I hope you enjoy these fireworks, too. See you all in hell.' Her finger pressed down on one of the red buttons.

A huge explosion rocked the building, knocking Amanda into the glass wall of the mezzanine, her ears ringing with a sound like a clanging bell. She looked down and saw that in one corner of the open rooftop, a vast chunk of floor had fallen away. In its place, there was only a black, gaping hole. Underneath her feet, the floor creaked and the whole building swayed. Below her, people were screaming and running for the exits, a stampede of bare feet and stiletto heels. She caught sight of Tabitha and Dustin making their way down the stairs from the mezzanine to the dancefloor, but where were Farrah and Sheena? Farrah had been right next to her, and Sheena had been downstairs, trying to reach Honey. Christ, how close had she been to the explosion? She raced down the stairs and searched desperately through the heaving crowd, calling out her friends' names in a voice that was increasingly hoarse and choking with dust and debris. The ringing sound in her ears had been replaced with piercing screams.

Then Amanda looked around her. Only one corner of the building had gone down, and Honey was still standing on the stage, glowing in her bright gold dress, brighter even than the fireworks still exploding above her head. She was radiant in her anger, an avenging angel sent from heaven to bring fire and brimstone down on the world. Desperate hope surged through Amanda's chest – if Honey was still standing, perhaps the rest of them would make it out alive? But then she saw it. Honey's key pad had two buttons. Only one had already been pressed down. Now, with an expression of pure, delicious satisfaction suffusing her beautiful face, Honey put her thumb on the second. There was a moment of silence, then a hideous grinding sound. Before Amanda could even call out, the entire western half of the building had sheared away, disappearing with an apocalyptic cloud of dust into a vast crater that revealed the famous sea view behind them. The marble-topped bar, the raised stage with its hydraulic podium, half of the helipad and half of the glass dancefloor were suddenly gone. And so, too, was the bright gold figure of Honey Hunter.

CHAPTER 64

Sheena

One minute, Sheena was on the edge of the dancefloor trying to get to Honey and the next minute she was scrabbling about on the floor. The shockwave from the explosion had sent her tumbling onto the ground, and before she had time to think, she had pushed herself up into a crouch and sprinted away from the crowd, towards the secluded VIP area under the mezzanine. A fierce pain tore through her right ankle as soon as she started moving, and she collapsed on the floor against a velvet chaise longue, breathing heavily. She must have landed on her ankle when she fell. She bent over to take off her cripplingly high heels, but the clasp was too slippery for her hand to get any purchase. She barely had time to understand that her foot was slick with blood before a grinding roar assaulted her ears and the air filled with choking dust and smoke, followed by the sound of what seemed to be a hundred fire alarms going off at once.

Crouching with one arm covering her face and head, the other braced against the chaise longue, Sheena's whole body was shaking uncontrollably. What the fuck had just happened? As the smoke began to clear, she caught glimpses of the horror and destruction Honey had left in her wake. The potted bay trees that had screened off the VIP area from the dancefloor were in splinters. Instead of the stage where Honey had been standing, there was empty air. In place of the marble bar, there was a cloud of thick grey dust. Peering through it, Sheena could make out bodies strewn across what remained of the glass dancefloor. Her eyes watered and she raised them to the sky. It was an ominous shade of orange that made her heart thud in her throat. She felt as if she was in a seventies' disaster movie like *The Towering Inferno*, but without any hope of rescue. She could hear the wail of sirens in the distance, and the thud of helicopters somewhere in the sky. She'd never get down to the bottom of the skyscraper — making it back up to the mezzanine, and then to the helipad, was her only hope. A jagged tear ran across the roof terrace just fifty feet or so from where Sheena was crouched against the wall. It was as if a giant JCB had bitten off half the building, leaving the other side of it swaying, but still standing. She recalled Honey's accusation in her speech about Jake's illegal foundations, dug half in sand, half in rock. Another tremor shook the building and she tensed against the chaise longue, watching in horror as the remains of the glass dancefloor twenty feet away from her began to bubble and crack. The building gave an agonising groan, like an iceberg breaking, and a huge chunk of glass fell away and spiralled down into the night.

The ringing in her ears was so loud that she barely heard the roar of the flames. She felt the heat before she saw it: fire licking up around the jagged edge of what had once been the stage, feeding on everything in its path. A deafening crash sounded to her left. A flaming rafter had broken loose, falling onto a four-poster bed and engulfing it in fire. The flames snapped out at her like a ferocious animal, their heat scalding her skin. She backed away, screaming as her broken ankle sent jolts of pain up her leg.

She knew she had to get out. Hordes of people were stampeding for The Ring, clawing their way past each other to get to the stairwells. Sheena didn't rate her chances in the crush, and anyway, she'd rather die up here than go down into the bowels of a building that could eat her alive at any moment. There was still a ringing in her ears that she couldn't tune out. But she knew she had to focus. Where were her friends? Amanda and Farrah had been on the VVIP mezzanine with her, which as far as she could tell hadn't yet gone down. But were they still safe? And what about Helen and Catherine? She took a deep breath to try and calm her panic, spluttering and coughing as she drew acrid smoke into her lungs. She spotted an abandoned Hermès scarf on the floor and limped over to pick it up. Placing it in front of her mouth to filter out the smoke, she tried to regulate her breath while she formulated a plan.

She had to get back up to the mezzanine and then up to the helipad. She'd seen three choppers up there earlier, and she prayed to God that there was at least one still there. If God was listening, perhaps Catherine would be up there too. Her foot was agony, and she dropped to a crawl. She moved gingerly along the floor, dodging tongues of flame and falling sparks, aware that the makeshift wooden roof structure, covered in highly flammable satin drapes, could give way at any moment. Her hands and knees started to blister but she forced herself to keep moving until she saw them: the stairs to the mezzanine were intact. She got to her feet and hobbled up them, finding herself standing back among the banquettes, in an area that the fire had mercifully not yet reached. She called out for Amanda and Farrah, scanning for them as she picked her way through the debris. Sheena limped towards the stairs up to the helipad, praying that they too had escaped the worst of the blasts.

As she approached the stairs to the helipad, she began to shudder. A vast chunk of the staircase must have collapsed when the western half of the building sheared away. The sight in front of her was terrifying. What had once been a broad landing leading to the stairs had been reduced to a ten foot wide strip of floor. The staircase that rose up from it, which had once run half the width of the buiding, was now no more than six feet wide. Its left-hand edge was a jagged mass of splintered planks, that fell suddenly away into deep black nothingness. Reaching the staircase felt like walking the plank, and Sheena knew that climbing up the staircase, with that 382-metre drop on her left, would take every ounce of courage she had. But she also knew that her life depended on her making it up to the top of these stairs. Heart pounding, she placed her good foot, still in its silver D'accori platform, on the first stair, testing its weight. It creaked ominously, but held fast. Wincing, she brought the other foot to the second step, clutching onto the banister with her right hand so tightly her knuckles had gone white. As she mounted the third step, she caught a new smell on the breeze. The scent of orange blossom and cedarwood, and an undertone of something musky: fear. She heard a crunching sound, and wheeled around just in time to see a ragged figure, his face covered in soot and his hands bloody and blistered, step on a discarded champagne glass and stumble almost as gingerly as she had, across the remaining strip of floor towards the steps. It was Jake.

'You rapist bastard!' Sheena's voice had gone gravelly; her throat felt like sandpaper.

Their gaze locked, and Sheena saw a flare of realisation in Jake's eyes. There was only one route to escape to the helipad, and Sheena was blocking it.

Even streaked with sweat, blood and dust, Jake managed to inject a sneer into his voice. 'Fuck you, I'm getting out of here. Let me through!' He barrelled forward, one arm out in front of him to shove Sheena to the side to get past.

But Sheena was too quick for him. She grabbed the lace ruffles at Jake's throat, her other hand braced on the banister, holding Jake firm on the stairs, his back to the sheer drop. Their eyes burned with mutual hate. 'No chance,' Sheena said, pulling his face close to hers, enjoying the flicker of fear in Jake's pupils as he realised what she was about to do. She could barely feel the pain in her ankle as they tussled.

'Let go of me you fucking bitch,' he spluttered, clawing feebly at her hands, trying to release their grip on his shirt.

'My pleasure,' she murmured. And, with a hard kick of her bad foot, Sheena McQueen pushed Jake Monroe off the staircase, and into the empty blackness of what had once been the west wing of La Mirage.

Jake's scream was swallowed up by the night as he fell. Sheena stared after him, a glazed look on her face, then blinked twice and turned to grip the handrail again. As she made her agonising way up the stairs, she prayed that Catherine was still up there, and that Farrah, Amanda and Helen had found their own routes out. But even as she prayed, the tears fell. Because, deep in her heart, she understood that finding all her friends safe was far too much to hope for.

CHAPTER 65

Helen

One moment she and Matt had been half naked, ripping each other's clothes off on the huge luxurious emperor bed in the 102nd floor suite, and the next, an explosion had ripped through the room, tearing it in half, leaving them looking out into the night sky like dolls in a dolls' house. It didn't feel real.

'We're not going to make it out of this, are we?' Helen spluttered, her eyes stinging both from the smoke and from holding back tears.

Matt looked at her, his face drawn and pale. He didn't answer immediately, but his silence was enough.

'Let's try to get to the stairs,' he said, gripping Helen's hand tightly as they moved out of the suite and through the choking smoke into the corridor. They pushed through a door and found a staircase where the air was a little clearer. Helen kicked off her heels and they sped down it, still holding hands, praying that the staircase would lead them outside. But halfway down the building, around what must have been the

50th floor, Matt stopped so abruptly that Helen crashed into him. He turned around and cradled her in his arms. 'I think our journey ends here, my love.' Helen looked behind him. The stairway was blocked by a huge pile of debris – she could see chunks of ceiling and sparking cables among the rubble. That explained why the air was cleaner here: the rubble was blocking the fire from making its way up the stairwell.

'Maybe we can go back up, try one of the doors?' Helen was sobbing now, and she knew how desperate she sounded. 'There must be a way out!' She took Matt's hand and yanked him back up the stairs, back to a plain white door with a metal plate bearing the floor number 52. Wisps of smoke were curling around the edge of the door and Helen hesitated before grabbing the metal door handle and wrenching the door open. She screamed at the pain, her hand forming blisters immediately, but she knew this was their only shot and pulled them both inside before the door closed.

They were standing in a wide corridor, flames licking all around them, smoke filling the air. Helen looked around desperately, finally spotting an exit sign which looked like it led to another staircase. She pointed towards it with her good hand, and together they stumbled, hunched over, down the corridor. Helen's eyes were swimming, her vision blurring, she could barely breathe. Was that still the exit sign, glowing faintly through the smoke? Matt had his arm around her waist, she was leaning on him now, stumbling towards their escape.

Suddenly, a loud cracking sound echoed through the corridor. The ceiling above them was giving way, slowly disintegrating under the ferocious heat. Debris began to fall around them. Helen and Matt looked at each other, knowing they were out of options. Matt took off his jacket, wrapping it around Helen to shield her from the heat, and leading her to a corner which the flames had not yet engulfed. He pulled her close and kissed her. Helen kissed him back, tenderly but passionately, infusing everything she wanted to say into that one kiss.

'Close your eyes, Helen,' Matt whispered, pulling her closer against his chest.

She closed her eyes, feeling completely defeated, but inexplicably calm. Matt's arms tightened around her, and she sank against him.

'Let's exchange our vows, Helen,' said Matt, clutching her more tightly.

Helen couldn't speak, she was in too much pain.

'Say them inside your head,' Matt told her. He always knew what she needed.

They stood there, embracing each other as if they could somehow protect one another from the inevitable. As the ceiling collapsed, time seemed to slow. Helen let Matt's words ring in her head, an incantation. 'I take you, Helen, to be my wife. For ever. Eternally.'

Helen's last thought was how lucky she had been to find true love in her life.

And then, the world went dark.

CHAPTER 66

Tabitha

On the beach under the burning tower, the horror of what had just happened hit Tabitha like a runaway train. Adrenaline was still pulsing through her veins. Her throat ached from the smoke. Her eyes stung. She blinked and tried to look up, shielding her eyes from the dazzling orange glow of the all-consuming flames. In her mind, she replayed her final moments in the building. She remembered Honey, the flash of her gold dress as she disappeared into the smoke and flames, like a fallen angel snatched down to hell.

She remembered how her final despairing cry had echoed in Tabitha's ears as she scrambled for the exit. But it had all happened so fast, she could barely remember how she had escaped. She remembered her fear as she swept the crowd for Dustin. She remembered the screams all around her, the chaos as hundreds of people stampeded for one of the four staircases at each corner of the skyscraper. She had crawled through the wreckage, dodging six-inch heels, her knees stained with sticky blood that had pooled on the rooftop's floor.

Then her hand had touched a stiff, cold body lying on the ground. It was a man, and his neck was lying at a terrifyingly unnatural angle. 'Oh, God,' she uttered, wondering whether she could help him. As she went to move her ear towards his mouth, she realised who it was: Lee Landers. And he was dead.

She had nearly lost it then – her breathing coming in shallow gasps and her vision blurring. But just in time, Dustin appeared through the crowd. Good, kind, weird, lovable Dustin. He was screaming something at her, but she could barely make it out. Her ears were still ringing.

He grabbed her under one armpit and wrenched her up, pushing her forwards towards The Ring. Flames were beginning to lick their way towards their feet, but not too fast to outrun. His strong grip urged her on, and she thought he was leading her to the crumbling steps up to the helipad, but no, he turned right, under a vine-strewn pergola that was beginning to spit in the heat, then left down a long corridor until finally, gasping for breath, he stopped in front of what looked like a plain white wall. From left and right smoke was curling through the corridor towards them, and Tabitha could hear a distant crackle of flames getting closer. 'What are you doing? Are you mad? We're trapped here!' Tabitha's voice sounded strangled – or was that just the effect of her ringing ears? She was trying to keep her fear under control but she could feel a tightness welling up in her chest.

'Panic room,' Dustin said shortly, in between gasps of breath. 'Jake had it installed because of the Hitlist Killer. It's got a private lift and its own back-up generator. And he left his all-access key card in the Green Room.'

Tabitha looked more closely at the plain white wall, and saw a thin line of grey. It must be a carefully hidden door. Relief washed through her like a wave, and she thanked God for Jake's paranoia. But the smoke in the corridor was already starting to swirl around her ankles, and the roar of the fire was now close enough to pierce the ringing in her ears. 'Hurry!' Tabitha yelled at Dustin, who was swiping his key card over the line again and again. 'We're running out of time!'

'The key card's melting!' Dustin sounded frantic. 'I'm trying to get the magnetic strip to connect!' Finally, there was a beep, and the door swung inwards. They slipped inside, closing it behind them just in time to shut out the devouring flames. Inside the cool, sound-proofed room, the silence was eerie. But they weren't safe yet. Tabitha could feel the building groaning and twisting around them. They had to get out before the whole skyscraper collapsed.

Dustin pulled her over to a corner of the room where another door was set in the wall. This must be Jake's private elevator. An escape pod. Dustin started mashing his key card against it desperately, but nothing was happening. Despite the chill in the room, sweat was pouring down his face. 'It's fucked,' he said despairingly, looking at Tabitha with terror in his eyes.

'No,' said Tabitha, gathering a strength she didn't know she had. 'We're not going to die up here! Think for a minute. There's no way in hell Jake wouldn't have a backup escape route. What if he got locked in here without the key card?'

'You beautiful genius!' Dustin's grin took over his whole face. 'You're right, there'll be a code somewhere too – look, the mechanism's right here!' He pointed to a discreet key pad recessed into the wall. 'If the brand is Duolex or FailSafe, I know the override code. I'll try them both.'

Tabitha stood stock still and squeezed her eyes shut. She could feel the panic rising again, but she counted her breaths in her head. She had got to eight when she heard the best sound she had ever heard in her life. The 'ping' of an evacuation lift arriving, and opening its doors to welcome them.

As they stumbled through the sound-proof door into the evacuation lift, a wall of noise hit them like a truck. They were standing in a thin cylinder, so close to the air they could almost touch it. Flames crackled against the night sky. Steel beams groaned, twisting under the load of the shattered skyscraper. Then, with a jerk, the lift kicked into life. Forty seconds later, they were on the beach, looking up at what was left standing of the burning wreck of La Mirage, breathing heavily as they understood what they had just escaped from.

Despite the horror, Tabitha felt a surge of love for Dustin. She wanted to hold him. To kiss him right there. His face was smeared with ash, and his eyes were bloodshot, but she wanted to peel off his sweat-soaked shirt, to tangle her hands in his dishevelled hair and yell to the world, 'I love him!' But a terrible tearing sound pulled her attention back up to the sky. The skyscraper stood like a tree that had been struck by lightning. Half of the building had been torn away and bits of rubble were now strewn across the beach. What remained was now visibly swaying. As she watched, a chunk of building gave way, crashing in a shower of sparks down onto the floor below.

Dustin was craning his neck to look up too. 'Tabitha! We need to run before the rest of it comes down!'

She took a few steps back, but couldn't tear her gaze from the burning building. A sudden movement caught her eye. A figure, stumbling out of a top floor window and plunging into the dark. Their clothing burned as they fell, streaking through the night like a meteor. Tabitha could see that others were trying to save themselves by climbing out along the jagged steel girders left behind by the explosion. She saw them silhouetted against the blaze, the sound of their cries drowned out by the roaring of the fire, the wailing of sirens and the beating of helicopter blades overhead. There were still hundreds of people up there, trapped by the blaze on the rooftop and the suites below, trapped in their own private hell. She desperately wanted to help them, but she knew there was nothing she could do. She pushed the horror to the back of her mind and forced herself to switch off her pure human emotion. There would be time for her feelings later. For now, she had work to do.

Dragging Dustin by the hand out of the orbit of falling debris, she looked around and spotted just what she needed. There, parked on the grassy area above the bay, was a broadcast van from one of the international news teams. She beckoned Dustin to follow her, and he looked at her in disbelief.

'It's what I do,' she said helplessly, taking his hand and striding across the beach. Her Louboutins sank into the sand – how was she still wearing these after everything that had happened? – and she kicked them off. A technician was standing by the broadcast van, staring up at the tower with his mouth open in disbelief. He didn't see Tabitha coming towards him. 'Hey!' she shouted. 'Hey you! Follow me. We have work to do.'

He looked at her blankly, still dazed. 'Our reporter was inside. She... She was at the party. I'm just here for outside shots.'

She slapped him round the face. 'Snap out of it. Not anymore. Get your camera. Connect it to broadcast on my Facebook live.' She handed him her phone with the code. 'Let's go.'

As if on autopilot, the technician did as she asked, and Tabitha saw her own ash-streaked face reflected back at her in the lens as she grabbed a microphone, plugged it into her phone, and turned to face the camera. The red light was blinking.

'This is Tabitha Tate, reporting live. I'm here in St Augustine's, the filming location for *Falcon Bay, a soap opera which is now off air.* Many of you will have seen tonight's awful events unfolding live online. Not only are hundreds feared dead after an explosion, but there are still people trapped in the building who face a desperate struggle to escape. I, and others, have witnessed harrowing scenes that I can barely describe.' Tabitha swallowed, trying to keep the emotion from overwhelming her voice. 'What I do know is that people are jumping from the building to avoid being consumed by the flames. Police, ambulance, fire engines – please. Anyone who can get here to help. Please send as much help as you can. We need to help them.' She paused to wipe away a tear, and the cameraman took his chance to train the camera on the inferno, where flames reached upwards, angrily grasping at the sky. The roaring sound of collapsing concrete still filled the air, and the metallic scent of burning steel hung over everything. Tabitha could see tiny figures high up on the helipad – on the one part of the skyscraper that had been built into rocky foundations and was still miraculously standing. But she didn't know if a helicopter could even reach them, so thick was the smoke and so high were the flames. The technician lingered on the building for a few more beats, before turning back to Tabitha.

She squared her shoulders, raised her microphone and spoke directly into the camera again. 'To anyone watching with loved ones trapped inside, our thoughts are with you. Stay strong. Help is on the way.'

CHAPTER 67

Madeline

Flames licked the edges of the collapsing building, smoke rose in suffocating plumes, and the distant sound of sirens was all but drowned out by the cacophony of devastation below. Madeline had been searching frantically for Chad – he wasn't in the hordes of people cramming into the four remaining stairwells, nor, thank God, in the dead bodies strewn around what remained of the rooftop. Madeline was praying she had made the right decision, to go the opposite way from the rest of the crowd, first up to the mezzanine and from there up the treacherous splintered staircase that led to the helipad – the only place she believed she'd have a hope of escape.

When she burst onto the platform, eyes wide with terror, her heart practically exploded with joy. Chad was standing at the far corner of the helipad, streaked with soot but otherwise unharmed, having what looked like an urgent discussion with a helicopter pilot. She ran towards him, shouting, but the police helicopters hovering above her, their rotors churning the hot, dense air, made it impossible for him to hear her. He turned as she approached and she threw her arms around him gratefully. His body felt tense; she prayed it was due to the danger they were in and not because Honey had broadcast something so shameful about her. Her fears were allayed as Chad pulled her away from the fire rising behind her, and kissed her passionately on the lips. His voice was as hoarse as hers when he spoke. 'I've been searching for you everywhere. Thank God you came up here. This is the last helicopter left. The pilot says he'll take us if we get on right now.'

There was an almighty crack from the far side of the roof and a large chunk of floor fell away in a great cloud of rock and dust.

'Get in now!' the pilot shouted. 'The roof is crumbling – we have to go!'

As her stiletto made contact with the steps of the chopper, Madeline could feel the searing heat from the fire behind them singing her clothes.

Suddenly a sharp cry pierced the air behind them. 'Wait!'

Madeline turned towards the sound. Sheena, Catherine, and Amanda – their faces smeared with soot, hair dishevelled, eyes red from smoke and tears – were frantically patting down Farrah. Her dress had caught a spark, and one sleeve now hung off her, tattered and black. Chad pushed Madeline up the steps onto the helicopter and ran towards the women to help. Once the spark was out he started pulling the women towards the chopper. 'Come on!' Chad shouted, his Southern drawl almost drowned out by the noise of the whirring blades. 'You all need to get onto that chopper right now! It's our only way out!'

'But what about Helen?' Amanda was weeping, tears running down her face. 'I can't find her!'

'Matt will have got her out,' said Farrah. 'Chad's right – we have to go!' She took Sheena's arm, and she and Amanda helped her hobble towards the chopper. Madeline saw through the window that her ankle was bloody and swollen.

But as the three women approached, with Catherine following behind, Madeline realised something. There were six people, but only five seats in the chopper. Helicopters were notoriously sensitive to weight; if they were too heavy, they would all go down. One person would have to stay behind. She opened the door and yelled out at Chad. 'Get in right now! You can't afford to wait for them!' Her voice was even raspier than usual with all the smoke in her lungs. She could see that Sheena had realised it, too. She had paused at the base of the ladder and was looking frantically around, performing a head count. Six people. Five seats.

'There aren't enough for all of us,' Amanda said, her voice high with panic.

'I'm not paid enough to die on the job!' The pilot's voice boomed out through speakers attached to his headset microphone. 'I can't take any extra weight. It's five or none!'

Farrah started to wail. 'My son! I have to see him! Let me on there! Amanda, you can't leave Olivia. Sheena, Catherine – come on!' She pushed past Chad and pulled Amanda onto the chopper, then ran back to help Sheena clamber in.

Sheena turned, one foot on the step, realising Catherine was still behind her, standing next to Chad. 'Catherine, get in! Move!' But Catherine was still standing out on the roof, as if she was frozen to the floor.

The ground beneath them rumbled ominously, sending a shockwave through the floor which threw Chad off his feet. Madeline screamed at him to get in, but before he could pick himself up off the floor and get on the ladder, Farrah yanked Sheena up the steps and got in behind her.

One seat left, and two of them still on the roof.

'You get on, Catherine,' Chad urged, his strong-jawed face resolute. 'I'll stay.'

Madeline's heart pounded in her throat. 'No!' she yelled through the door, reaching for him with her hand, 'I've just found you again! I'm not leaving without you! Get these bitches off! We were here first.'

Catherine, who had been standing apart, observing the scene with a distant gaze, suddenly stepped forward and pushed Chad up the steps and into the last seat. Sheena looked out in horror, and reached through the open door for Catherine, but before she could speak, Catherine came to the window and locked eyes with Madeline.

'Madeline,' Catherine said, swallowing hard.

'What? You want to get on? Too late!' Madeline tried to close the door but Catherine's grip was strong.

'Somebody close the door,' yelled the pilot. 'We have to fucking go!'

Catherine climbed up one more step, and reached inside to take Madeline's hand in her own. Madeline instinctively recoiled, this was a woman she'd hated all her life. But she'd made Chad get on the chopper. The least she could do was allow her some final words. Catherine's eyes were brimming. 'I was told something tonight. Something that has changed everything. Madeline, I wanted to talk to you about it, but there's no time. I owe you so much more than I can ever make up for. Go! I want you to live.'

'What are you talking about?' Madeline was totally confused. 'What do you owe me? This building is about to collapse and take us with it! Close the door! We have to fucking go!'

Catherine said hesitantly, 'Madeline... I'm your mother.'

A stunned silence fell upon the group, pierced only by the distant sirens from below.

'What the fuck?' Farrah was staring at Catherine, open-mouthed.

Madeline's stomach dropped. Was this a ruse? A way of forcing Chad off the helicopter, so Catherine could take his place? If so, it was nasty.

'What convenient timing' she snapped. 'Now get off the ladder and shut the fucking door or I'll push you off myself.'

But Sheena had gone white. 'Is it true?' she whispered to Catherine, leaning out towards her through the open door.

'You know it is, Sheena,' said Catherine, tears running down her face. 'You've always known when I'm telling the truth.'

Madeline looked directly into Catherine's eyes, searching for any sign of deception. But all she saw was a raw, painful truth.

The pilot pulled a lever, and the instrument panel lit up. 'I'm leaving now whether the door's open or closed! Get that fucking woman off the ladder!'

But for Madeline, time was standing still. 'How? When?' she stuttered.

'I had to give you up when you were just a baby. They took you away when you were six months old. I've regretted it every day. But I never… I never had any idea it was you until tonight. Tabitha Tate had the proof. She told me tonight. It's going in her book – if she gets out of here alive. She was looking for you, Madeline. She wanted to tell you after she'd checked the dates with me. I've done nothing for you your whole life. I don't deserve to live. Make Falcon Bay be my legacy. I pray one day, you'll find it in your heart to know I really, really loved you. I'll always love you. You'll always have a mother.' Flames flickered around her legs and she batted them away. The pilot increased the throttle and the rotor blades picked up speed. It wouldn't be long before they were airborne.

'Head for the boat!' Farrah yelled. 'It's right there – get to Nemesis.'

Madeline was torn. She was desperate to escape, but was what Catherine said really true? The blades were cutting through the air with urgency now. She could feel the chopper about to lift off the ground.

Catherine tried to shut the door but Sheena forced it to stay open. 'Don't go, Catherine! You can't!'

'Sheena,' Catherine said softly, her eyes flicking briefly away from Madeline, 'I love you. You're the best agent and best friend there ever was. But Madeline's my daughter. Save her, and save yourselves. Now leave!' Catherine stepped down off the ladder, gave a violent push, and the door closed with a snap.

The building trembled violently beneath them, and Madeline saw the needle on the instrument panel move from orange to green as they finally rose off the shaking ground.

Sheena screamed as another huge crack ripped through the floor where Catherine was standing. Catherine stumbled, fell, scrabbled onto her knees and looked up at them as the helicopter pulled away from the hungry flames. Even with her dress torn and bloodied, her hair blowing wildly and her face streaked with tears, she still looked stunningly beautiful.

Madeline, still in shock, couldn't look away. Suddenly a strange, blurred vision appeared in her mind. A woman, with sad eyes, leaning down over a cot. Was it her imagination? Or was it a memory? Could Catherine, the woman she'd loathed ever since she got her thrown off her first ever television job, really have been her birth mother? Her mind raced with questions, with doubts, yet something in her gut told her it was true. She could feel tears gathering in her throat, and her eyes started to fill. Chad pulled her close as the chopper rose up through the smoke and Catherine blurred out of vision. The other women were sobbing and comforting each other, but no sound came from Madeline's lips. For once she was out of words.

As the chopper soared away from the building and out over the sea, a gut-wrenching roar seemed to split the air. Madeline pressed her face against the window once more, and looked back to the hell they had just escaped. The last section of rooftop had given way, finally succumbing to the inferno below. Amanda, Farrah and Sheena clutched each other's hands and shed silent tears as Madeline twisted around in her seat, her eyes desperately scanning the gaping maw of the building for the mother she'd wanted to find all her life.

She wasn't there.

CHAPTER 68

Madeline

The moonlight glinted off the dark purple sea that stretched out to the horizon. On the deck of Nemesis, Madeline stood looking out at the sky cast in a sickly orange glow from the burning tower behind them. She wished she hadn't told Chad she needed time alone, to process everything that had happened. Her mind was spinning, and she needed her level-headed husband to help her make sense of it all.

Below deck, Sheena was glued to the live coverage of the inferno on TV, trying to pick Helen out in the crowd. She'd been certain that if Tabitha got out, Helen had too, convinced that she hadn't got in touch because the phone lines were jammed. Madeline hadn't the heart to tell her there was a more logical, and more likely, explanation for her silence. Amanda and Farrah were watching over their children in the nursery, smoothing locks of hair away from their foreheads while they slept. When the helicopter had landed, Lauren had raced out of the cabin and up to the helipad on deck, both children clutched in her arms. Farrah had hugged Max so tightly Madeline thought she would squash him flat. 'I thought you might never see me again,' she kept whispering, as she covered her son in kisses, 'I thought I might lose you. I had to come back for you.'

Amanda, meanwhile, seemed to have no words. But as she scooped Olivia up into her arms and let her nuzzle into her neck, she gave her a look of love so pure and whole that Madeline felt a sharp stab of jealousy. She had never known a mother's love. And now she had come close to it and lost it again, all in one day. It was all too late. Much too late.

She rubbed her arms to warm them up. After the heat of the fire, she thought she'd never want to be hot again, but the night air was freezing out on the water, and she hadn't thought to borrow a coat when Sheena had suggested she change into something from her wardrobe.

In the solitude of the shower, she had scrubbed and scrubbed, until the water had washed away the blood and the soot and the ash, and her hands had stopped shaking from the shock. But she wasn't able to wash away the day's revelations. Catherine, her nemesis for all these years, a woman she had hated with all her heart, was her mother. In the steam of the shower these words had swirled around her head, bringing her more questions than comfort. She'd come up on deck to get some perspective, take some air. But her mind was still filled with everything that had happened before the helicopter took off. Catherine's last words, her beautiful face. The pilot's desperate shouts as they pulled away.

She heard footsteps behind her, approaching the rail. Chad came towards her, his face full of concern, and draped a thick Barbour over her bare shoulders. 'I know this isn't your usual style, but it was all the crew could spare.' Madeline smiled gratefully. She clearly hadn't been thinking straight when she'd chosen a flimsy sleeveless dress from Sheena's clothes rail. Chad gently took her chin in his hand and turned her face to his. 'Madeline, my darling.' He paused, as if what he was about to say was difficult. 'I know you said you wanted time on your own. But I have to ask you something. What Honey said, about you covering up footage of Jake's rape. Is it true?'

Madeline looked back out to sea, blinking so that the horizon blurred into the sky behind her tears. Chad's words hung heavy in the air. She knew his love for her was strong, but she also knew his values as a Southern Baptist boy were stronger still. He would never forgive her if he knew the truth. 'Why do you have to ask? Don't you trust me?' She was stalling.

Chad put his hand on top of hers so they held the rail together. He sighed. 'When I thought you were dead, I had nothing. I was casting about for a purpose. I teamed up with Jake, I gave him shares in our island. I can forgive you for abandoning me... but I can't forgive you for allowing me to align myself with that... that rapist.' He spat over the edge of the boat, as if the very word offended him.

Madeline delivered her reply with a performance worthy of a standing ovation. She turned to face him, and allowed the coat to slip off her shoulder, revealing the top of one delicate arm. 'Chad, I swear to you, I had no idea Jake was doing this until after I came back from France. As soon as I saw the footage, I had Dustin track down Honey and send it to her anonymously. I thought it should be her choice to decide what to do. To call the police, or to seek revenge. I promise you. My hands are clean.'

'So there's no truth in Honey's claim that you saw it at the time, but you only sent it to her when you wanted to take revenge on Jake for stealing the island?'

Madeline looked him straight in the eye, and blinked back a tear. She dropped her voice to just above a whisper. 'There's no truth in that at all. I do feel guilty, though. Honey was clearly disturbed, and I should have checked the CCTV to see what was going on. After all, back then it was my show. My island. But I wanted to give everyone their privacy. And I promise you, I showed Honey as soon as Dustin accidentally came across the footage.'

Chad reached out and tucked a lock of raven hair behind one of Madeline's perfect ears, then dipped his head to kiss her red-painted mouth. 'I'm so relieved,' he said, when he pulled away. 'I'm sorry for asking and I hope you understand why I had to. I love you, Madeline.'

'And I love you, Chad,' she sighed, and relief flooded through her body. He'd definitely believed her.

'I'm sorry to break into your thinking time,' he continued. 'I know you have a lot to process. I'll go down to our cabin, wait for you in there. When you're ready, let's talk to the women about chartering the boat away from this madness.' He gestured into the orange-tinged sky, thick with the sound of helicopter blades and distant sirens. 'Let's sail to France, get away from this nightmare island. There's nothing we can do for those poor souls now.'

As Chad disappeared below deck, Madeline heard a slow clapping sound.

'Bravo. Spoken like the true actress you are.' It was Sheena, not downstairs watching TV as she had thought, but emerging from behind a mast, where she must have been waiting in the shadows all this time. Like Madeline, she had showered, put on a full face of make-up and changed into fresh clothes – she was dressed like a haute-couture pirate, in a pair of Galliano leather boots worn over a midnight-blue trouser suit. She was limping slightly and clinging to the mast to stay upright, but otherwise she looked ready for battle. Behind her in the distance, the remains of the tower continued to belch smoke and flame into the air. All of a sudden, Madeline realised she didn't have the energy to fight. 'What do you want, Sheena? The reboot's over, dead in the water. What else could you possibly want from me?'

Sheena tapped a fingernail to her lip, as if she was thinking. 'Now let me see. What do I want? Well, it's simple, really. I want everything we planned to do. I want us to update *Falcon Bay*, reboot it for the modern age, make a ton of money from the streaming platforms. And I want to rebuild all our reputations – which Honey has shattered along with that twisted wreck over there.'

Madeline turned away from Sheena to look out to the horizon again. She couldn't bear to watch the horrific carnage unfolding on the beach. 'You'll never change, will you?' She trained her eyes on the sea, and a shoal of tuna glided past the boat with barely a splash. 'Your best friend is somewhere over there, dead, and you're here, talking business. I thought I was a tough bitch, but you're something else.'

Sheena's voice cracked as she spoke. 'That's something for us to process another day,' she said. Then she gathered herself, and said bitterly, 'I may have lost my friend, but you lost your mother. You must be grieving too.'

'I lost someone I hated,' spat Madeline, wheeling around to face Sheena, ignoring the tiny splinter of sadness that pierced her heart. 'It's not the same.'

'Come on,' Sheena said scornfully. 'Admit it. We're a pair of bitches. We're perfect business partners.'

'What – business partners who keep trying to double-cross each other? I can't think of anything worse.'

'I can't think of anything better.' Sheena leaned back against the mast and winced in pain, her ankle clearly agonising, even strapped into those leather boots. 'We're both business-minded. We love revenge. And we know each other's secrets.'

'Ha,' Madeline laughed mirthlessly. 'I don't have any secrets. Not since you blackmailed me into revealing the truth about the body I was born into.'

'Oh really, Madeline? Are you telling me that scene I just witnessed between you and Chad wasn't an Oscar-worthy performance? I know you'd seen the tape of Honey and Jake before you sent it to her. Don't you remember? When we first discussed the *Falcon Bay* reboot you told me you discovered "a little something" three years ago that would guarantee Honey would join the cast.'

'You can't prove it,' Madeline sniped.

'I don't have to,' Sheena retorted. 'I just have to convince your beloved Chad that you lied. And that won't be hard. So, unless you want me to go down and tell him right now, you'll agree to the reboot – along with a 51 percent controlling share for me.'

Madeline raised an eyebrow. 'Fine,' she said lightly. 'You win, Sheena. We'll let the dust settle because we don't want to look insensitive. Then we'll get the reboot off the ground.'

Sheena nodded, satisfied, and turned to make her way slowly back below deck. Madeline was impressed, despite herself. Her broken ankle must be agonising, even strapped up in those leather boots. She waited for Sheena to get halfway across the deck before she opened her mouth. 'Not so fast.'

Sheena turned her head and spoke archly. 'Have I left something out? We can negotiate the finer points in my cabin if you desire.'

'No, Sheena. You've left nothing out.' Madeline was toying with her now. 'But I have.' She watched confusion spread across Sheena's face. 'Didn't you ever wonder why I kept that footage of Jake and Honey from all those years ago, even after I faked my death? Honey's right. I needed dirt on Jake. And I didn't tell her until it benefited me to see him destroyed. Well, I like to gather dirt on all my enemies.' Madeline paused, and saw a flash of fear in Sheena's eyes. 'I had Helen Gold followed, you know. On that warm midsummer morning, when she visited her mother's grave.' Sheena's face had gone very pale. 'It's so curious, don't you think,' Madeline continued, 'the strange things people choose to leave behind at the grave of a loved one?'

The air between them crackled.

Sheena, finding nothing on deck to hold on to, was gritting her teeth in pain. 'What do you want, Madeline?'

Madeline tapped a fingernail against her lip, in a mocking echo of Sheena's earlier gesture. 'Now let me see,' she said.

'Oh yes. I want you to know your place. I'll do a deal with you. We'll make the best fucking show the world has ever seen. But you should know that I'll hold on to that USB for ever. And if you ever betray me, if you *ever* double-cross me, I'll tell the world that you and your cronies shoved Ross Owen off a cliff, and covered it up.'

Sheena nodded, tight-lipped.

'And our partnership will be on forty-nine percent, not fifty-one.'

'Fine.' Sheena was still very pale, but the ghost of a smile hovered around her lips.

'Now,' said Madeline. 'If we're going to be partners, we can't have any more secrets. Agreed?'

'Yes.' Sheena's voice was barely more than a whisper.

'Say it!' Madeline's hair whipped in the wind.

'No more secrets.' Sheena looked like she might be about to faint from the pain, but she spoke firmly this time, and tossed her head defiantly.

Madeline left the railing and took two steps towards Sheena. The women were face-to-face now, an arm's length apart. 'Then there's one last thing I need to ask you. Just so we know exactly where we are. Exactly *who* we are.' There was a beat of silence, and the air pulsed between the women. Madeline could tell that Sheena knew what she was about to say. 'Did you do it, Sheena? Did you kill Candy?'

Sheena's gaze didn't waver. 'Yes.' She paused. 'I did it.'

Their eyes locked, acknowledging the monsters within them both.

Madeline broke the silence. 'We're both as bad as each other then,' she said, quietly.

'What do you mean?' Sheena sounded wary.

Madeline forced herself to look Sheena in the eye. 'I said, we're as bad as each other. I tried to kill Catherine, I wanted her to die in the shark tank. I planned to bring her in with me. As you know, I fell into the safety tank. If she hadn't withdrawn her hand when I put out my own I would have pulled her into the real tank. She would have died.'

Sheena put a hand to her mouth, made a strangled noise that might have been a sob.

Madeline waited a moment, then spoke. 'Now that everything's out in the open, let's make a pact. We know each other's secrets now, all of them. We both have enough to take each other down. Whether we like it or not, we're bonded. We have to swear not to tell anyone. Not Chad. Not the other women. No one. It's just us now Sheena.'

Sheena wiped her eyes and dragged her gaze to meet Madeline's. 'We should do it Calvin's way,' she said. 'Pinkie promise.'

Madeline had a sudden flash of memory. Her and Sheena, in their very first jobs as teenage actors. She had been in the wrong body back then, with the wrong name, Calvin. But the one good thing in her life had been Sheena McQueen. They had been close friends. Friends who made pinkie promises to each other. Madeline blinked away a tear, and nodded. She offered her arm to Sheena, and helped her hobble over to the yacht's railing, where they could look out over the placid sea with its peaceful moon, so incongruous with the hellfire burning behind them. They wrapped their little fingers around each other, and shook their entwined hands up and down solemnly, sealing their pact.

As they disentangled, Sheena put a hand on Madeline's arm. 'When you come to terms with what has happened, if you ever want to ask me anything about Catherine, you can. And please believe me, I genuinely didn't know she was your mother. I don't think she did either.'

As if by tacit agreement, they turned around and leaned their backs against the railing, so they were now staring out together towards the apocalyptic scene on the burning beach. Sirens were still blaring, and fire and smoke still rose from the twisted wreckage of La Mirage. Dark figures darted here and there, helping fetch and carry buckets. Occasionally two people would emerge from the rubble carrying a stretcher.

Sheena sighed in despair. 'All those people,' she said softly, and Madeline knew she was thinking of Catherine.

A sudden grinding sound made Madeline startle, and she felt Sheena stiffen beside her. But it was just the anchor retracting into its hatch. The yacht's engine began to purr, and then roar, and before long the prow had swung to the south, and the boat was slicing smoothly through the sea.

'Chad told the crew to head for France,' said Madeline, watching the flaming building retreat into the distance, and feeling only blissful relief that they were leaving it behind.

'Good idea,' said Sheena, fixing her eyes ahead, purposefully not turning to look back at the carnage. 'I don't suppose you know anywhere peaceful, where we can all lay low, regroup, start afresh?'

Madeline smiled. 'Do you know what Sheena, I think perhaps I do.'

Epilogue

It was around nine hours since Honey Hunter had brought death and destruction raining down on St Augustine's, and the sun was just beginning to paint the sky with pale pink streaks. On the land below, the shattered skeleton of what was briefly the world's tallest skyscraper lay like a vanquished colossus, while the few final survivors of the blast, dazed and disoriented, emerged from the rubble.

The Cove hummed with action. Journalists, TV crews, paramedics, firefighters, police, do-gooders and rubber-neckers had been swarming over the beach for hours, held back from the still-smoking remains of La Mirage by hastily erected crime scene tape. Reporter Tabitha Tate, who had now been streaming to her Facebook Live for seven hours straight, had just finished interviewing a survivor who managed to climb down one of the lift shafts just after the second explosion tore the west side of the building away. Tabitha looked wiped out, ready to drop, and any observer would have noticed her handsome, slightly nerdy boyfriend standing just out of shot, clearly desperate to take her home.

What that same observer would not have noticed was a lone figure, skulking in the shadows on the opposite side of the cove, just beyond the craggy cliffs which separated the sandy beach from the grassy scrubland that led into the forest.

Because this lone figure did not want to be noticed. From his vantage point, he could hear the cries of the wounded, could smell the acrid tang of smoke and dust which would surely linger over the island for days. But he himself was ready to turn his back on it all, and disappear. He touched a bruise at his neck which had already gone purple. It was far from the worst injury he had received tonight, but it was the one that made him angriest. He drew a ragged breath, allowing a cocktail of relief and fury to wash through his battered body. He mentally gave thanks to the architect who had designed the padded air vent he had fallen into when he was shoved off the tower's topmost staircase. The vent zigzagged down the outside edge of the building. It provided a serpentine maze that had become his lifeline, complete with a narrow ladder, presumably there for repairs, which guided him down and away from the flames. And with each step down, he had vowed retribution. Honey. Madeline. Sheena. These three women and their cadre of conspirators had ruined his reputation as completely as a stiletto heel on a parquet floor. Their scheming faces burned behind his eyes, and with each throbbing pulse of pain coming from his blistered hands and twisted foot, his resolve hardened. Each step down was a silent declaration of war. The machinations of those vengeful women had thrown him into the abyss, but like a phoenix, he was ready to rise from the ashes of their treachery.

Jake Monroe was alive, and with that simple fact, the scales of power had just tipped. The world thought him dead, a casualty of the La Mirage catastrophe, but in his survival lay the element of surprise. They would not see him coming. There would be no rest, no respite, until he had reclaimed what was his. And as the sun began to rise over the pale blue sea, he disappeared into the forest, where a woodland path would take him to a jetty and a small motorboat which lay waiting just for him. Jake Monroe smiled. For he knew that in this world of power, glamour, ambition and fame, it was not the winners who should be feared. It was the ones who have nothing left to lose.

About the Author

MELANIE BLAKE is the internationally bestselling author behind the sensational trilogy that began with *Ruthless Women*, the *Sunday Times* #4 bestseller that sold 250,000 copies in its first month, and its bestselling sequel, *Guilty Women*. She's also a successful playwright, having adapted her first novel *The Thunder Girls* into a play which broke box-office records for a new work – a credit she still holds to this day. Melanie's books have been translated into nine languages, and captivated more than a million readers worldwide.

Melanie's stories are exhilarating rollercoaster rides packed with all the glitz, glamour, passion, and intrigue of the blockbuster novels of the eighties, yet reflective of the world we live in today. When Melanie was asked to write a foreword to a new edition of Jackie Collins by her publisher, it was a dream come true as Jackie's bold and fierce characters have always inspired her. Then the *Daily Mirror* dubbed Melanie 'Jackie Collins for a new generation,' and the journey that started with devouring Jackie's steamy novels as a teenager was complete.

Despite the amount of coverage she gets in the media, Melanie's success belongs to her fans, who've stayed with her throughout her journey and often interact with her on social media. She loves providing them with escapism, fun, and glamour and now, to thank them for their support, she's formed her own company, Piranha Publishing, to produce the most beautiful, covetable hardback possible. So if you're holding this limited, signed, red-edged edition in your hands, know that this was made just for you.

Melanie loves hearing from her readers, and you can follow her on X and Instagram, @MelanieBlakeUK or visit her website melanieblakeonline.com.

Acknowledgements

First and foremost, a giant heartfelt thanks to YOU my readers - without your continued belief in me and passion for my rollercoaster reads, you wouldn't even be holding this book because I would never have got this far. Your decision to embrace my first book, *Ruthless Women*, and propel it to the top of the charts worldwide, ignited a whole trilogy and led me on a journey I only ever dreamed of. The thought that you are now have made it to *Vengeful Women*, the final book and my personal favourite of the trilogy, fills my heart with joy – I sincerely hope you loved every minute of finding out what happened to our leading ladies on *Falcon Bay* as much as I loved creating it. If you make this one as big a hit as the others there may well be a *Ruthless Men* waiting in the wings … but only you can determine if that ever makes it to print – so spread the word far and wide and let's keep going…!

It takes a team to get a book out into the world, so let's get the red carpet rolled out for the fabulous actresses whose faith in me made this whole literary adventure possible. You opened up the glittering gates to 'soap land' and gave me the insight and inspiration to write this trilogy. Over two decades later, and I'm still blessed to call you my friends for life, especially Claire King and Beverley Callard – true warriors who inspired me beyond anyone I can ever describe.

To my fierce media team Tiger Team Creative, who help my novels reach their audiences – Rina, Divia and Ilona, you ladies put the sizzle in sisterhood.

To my real-life co-stars Amanda Beckman and Danielle McEwen who keep my life on track. Thank you for always being your fabulous selves.

Huge thanks to my beloved friends Caroline & Pam, Claire & Reece, Nick Jones and Jon McEwan. Your friendship and loyalty mean more than words can say.

Special thanks, as always, to my editors extraordinaires, Laura Palmer and Maria Malone, who helped me overcome my dyslexia by embracing my style and encouraging me to pour every ounce of 'Melanie' onto each page.

A rousing cheer for Gary Jones for believing in me when no one else did by making me a national newspaper columnist, to Nicola Jeal for her support through *The Times*, and to Caroline Waterston who helped me live my dream by being the first to put me on a magazine cover. I couldn't have got this far without you Caroline, and I am eternally grateful. The irrepressible Dermot McNamara for always being the fuel whenever my tanks run low, to Nicky Johnston for always capturing my imagination on the outside the way I feel inside, and to Daniel Cocklin and Ant Donovan at Donovan Graphics for turning my ideas into reality.

My dream of being an author didn't come true till I was forty, which proves it is never too late to do what you love. My advice is to work hard, never give up, and don't listen to the haters who tell you 'no'. Believe in yourself, and go for what lights you up – and your ride on life's rollercoaster will be truly spectacular.

With all my love, Melanie Blake xxx